WRECKED LOVE

HOLLOWS GARAGE
BOOK 2

KATE CREW

Cover Designer: Books and Moods at booksandmoods.com

Trigger Warnings: Sexual content (Consensual), Panic attacks, Acts and references to domestic violence, illegal activities, References to car wrecks, Violence, & Explicit Language.

For those with scars, physical or unseen, this book is dedicated to your resilience and strength.
Beauty thrives amidst the marks of a life lived fully.

ASH'S PLAYLIST

King of My Heart / Taylor Swift *

Willow / Taylor Swift

Grave / Nessa Barrett

Midnight Rain / Taylor Swift

Mad Woman / Taylor Swift

A Little Messed Up / June

Dirty Thoughts / Chloe Adams

Goddess / Xana

Killing Boys / Halsey

Read the Room / ELIO

Mastermind / Taylor Swift

Black Widow / In This Moment

Cowboy Like Me / Taylor Swift

Villian / Bella Poarch

FOX'S PLAYLIST

Reckless / Jaxson Gamble
Bad Guys / Billie Ellish
The Fighter / In this Moment
Bonfire / Phix *
Sick of me too / Lonr.
Nervous / NOT A TOY
Tailspin / For You
Horns / Bryce Fox
Anti - Hero / Taylor Swift
Something to Lose / June
When you say my name / Chandler Leighton
I follow / LOI
Labyrinth / Taylor Swift
Vicious - Bohnes

ONE
ASH

THE LAST TIME I was out at this club, dancing to the beat under these pulsing lights, it was to celebrate a win. To celebrate being rich, popular, and a top racer in my events that week. It was to celebrate how perfect my life had been at that moment.

Or at least how perfect I thought it was.

Now I was here only to force myself out of my apartment after weeks on end spent locked up alone inside. It was my choice, of course. Ever since the accident, I didn't want to be anywhere but home.

I grabbed another water, eyeing the guy who seemed to think he had a shot with me tonight.

He had that 'I'm going to get lucky' glint in his eye, and I almost felt bad at how sure he seemed of it. The moment he started talking about his band and how awesome he was, I knew it was game over.

Not that there was much hope in the first place.

I wasn't into musicians, and definitely didn't have any interest in guys that only talked about themselves.

I downed my water, and made my way back to the dance

floor to let myself get lost in the music, trying to have some fun, but not even five minutes later, my chest tightened, and I knew what was coming.

It had been eight months since my accident, and I still couldn't push myself to one hundred percent. Most days I couldn't make it to sixty percent. Even if my body didn't protest, I could feel the panic attack building in my chest, and I knew I'd reached my limit.

I don't know why I thought this would be fun.

Another guy stepped in front of me as I walked off the dance floor, grinding against me like I'd invited him. I pushed him back, the tightening getting worse, pulling at the muscles in my arm now.

The panic was going to take me if I didn't get out of the crowd.

I should have stayed home. I used to love this, but now I only wanted movies and the safety of my bed.

I finally made it to the table, falling back and taking a breath. I hated that even in the strobing lights and ear-splitting music, the world around me felt dull. I wasn't interested in being here any longer and somehow that felt like the last tie to my old life breaking. It wasn't a freeing feeling like I would have hoped for.

It was a death.

I knew now that I could never be that same person again, but it left me wondering who I was now.

I used to love coming here, dancing away the stress, and having fun with my friends. I was trying to hold on to the pieces of my past that I loved, but none of it gave me the same feeling.

Aside from the panic attacks, I seemed to feel nothing at all anymore. The realization was more upsetting than I could have imagined.

It made me worried about what would happen when I tried to

race again. The nagging fear that the thing I always loved would never bring me joy again.

I wanted my life back.

"What's up?" Celina asked, sitting next to me as I took deep breaths. "Not taking one of those cute ones home?"

"Nope. One talked about himself, one asked to kiss me, and the other just grabbed my ass and went 'Hell Yeah!' which is really not a turn on," I said, taking short, shallow breaths. I focused every part of my mind on breathing and talking to her, trying to make the panic subside before it took over. It had happened so many times since the wreck that I knew if I caught it early I would be able to stop it, but I only had seconds to try to gain any control over my body before I spiraled.

"What's wrong with the kisser?"

"He literally walked up and asked out of nowhere. Maybe flirt for a second before asking to kiss someone? I don't know, give it some sort of effort."

"Sounds like you're being picky."

"Sounds like it because I am. I'm sick of fuck boys."

"That's new," she said with a giggle. I did always like the confident, upbeat attitude of the everyday fuck boy, but it was one more thing that had lost its appeal now.

"Well, lucky for you, you won't have to go home alone tonight," Aubrey said.

"I *want* to go home alone tonight."

I had barely been out of my apartment in weeks, aside from my two college courses and the grocery store.

I hardly counted myself in college, but I was taking my business courses as seriously as possible, knowing I would need every bit of help I could get in my life.

I needed to start getting out into the world again, but pushing to get ready had felt like dragging myself out of mud. The thought of taking someone home now sounded like hell. The thought of the small talk alone made me want to run away.

I came out tonight for a break from hiding myself away, not to hook up with a random guy. I hadn't even thought about guys in months, and I was careful tonight to be inconspicuous, from leaving my car at the apartment to telling my friends not to let anyone else know I was coming out with them.

It was all to stay away from David, which, these days, meant staying away from my dad. I had to sneak around more now, while living in my own apartment, than when I wanted to sneak out in high school and get drunk at a friend's house.

"Why's that?" I finally asked, pulling myself back to reality. "Wait, what did you say? What do you mean, I'm lucky?"

Celina giggled, the five cocktails having gone to her head now.

"Because David is on his way and can't wait to see you."

It was like cold water being dumped over my head. "You invited David?"

"Yeah, he goes on and on talking about you and, you know, I just got so sick of it. I finally told him to come hang out."

I was already digging for my purse and getting up. "Great, you guys have fun. The one thing I told you was not to invite him and that's exactly what you do? No wonder I haven't been out with you guys."

"Wow Ash, calm down. He's just coming out for a drink."

"No. No, he's coming out because he wants to corner me and apparently you guys do not care. Have fun with David. I'll see you two around."

They both giggled as I turned.

"Always so dramatic, Ash. Fine, go home and just call us when you're sober so we can hang out again."

Laughter erupted, but I was already walking to the front doors. I was completely sober, and any belief I had about them and our friendship disintegrated. They didn't care about me or my safety, they cared about drinking, partying, and me paying for it all. They knew David had been getting worse and didn't seem to care that I wanted to stay away from him.

I stepped out, needing to find where I could wait and call an Uber, when a tall, gorgeous guy leaning against his car in the parking lot caught my eye. He looked up, and for the first time that night, my heart gave a small jump. Why couldn't he have been in the club tonight? He gave a smirk before looking back at his phone.

I was so distracted thinking of him that I didn't hear someone come up behind me, grabbing for the purse that was slung across my chest.

"Give it to me now!" he yelled, but I was already trying to pull it over my head to hand it over. He kept yanking it harder, pulling me backwards.

"Let me go and I will!" I yelled, stomping at his feet as I pulled at the strap.

He held on tight, not giving me an inch of room to pull it off.

"Here, take it. I don't care, just take it." I yelled again, but the strap was caught on my dress now.

His hands suddenly grabbed at me harder and I screamed.

"Get off!" I kicked, trying to break free and run, but he held on. I pulled back my elbow and jabbed it back into him. It only connected with his chest, and it was enough that I could break free.

I turned and ran, the darkness stealing my breath as I realized he was still after me.

TWO
FOX

Earlier that Day

Scout ran into my apartment, launching herself over the back of the couch next to me.

"Are you ready to go?"

"Just about. Are you?" I asked, looking over her clothes.

"Yeah, what's wrong?"

"Nothing. I thought you and Quinn would be all dressed up."

She shrugged. "I'm not really in the mood."

"And why not?"

"Nothing you want to know about," she said, the frown deepening as she sunk further into the couch.

"Hey," I said, knocking against her arm as I pulled my shoes on. "What's that supposed to mean? I'm always worried about you and your problems."

"This one is about a guy, and I'm pretty sure you've said that you definitely don't want to hear about that."

"No. I said I only want to hear about it if you are prepared for me to kill them in the event they upset you."

"Isn't that a little extreme?"

"For other people? Maybe. For you? Not at all. You're one of the happiest people I know. If you're upset, someone really fucked up and they deserve what's coming to them. Now come on, tell me."

"You really are a gossip."

"No, someone just needs to keep everyone's drama straight in this place. Come on, tell me."

"Well, what I thought was a date the other night was apparently not. According to everyone, and I mean everyone at school, we are just friends. I was put in the friend zone, Fox."

"Oh," I said with a wince. "That's not fun."

"No, not at all. And it's nothing you can help me with."

"And why not?"

"Have you ever been put in the friend zone?"

I thought back, struggling to find an example. "Maybe."

"Exactly. You're the playboy from every girl's dreams. This is one you can't sympathize with."

"Just because I'm not put in the friend zone all the time doesn't mean a damn thing. I don't get close enough to even risk the friend zone. You're just braver than me."

She rolled her eyes, but couldn't help the smile spreading across her face.

"See, that looks better. Come on."

"Fine, but going on dates isn't brave."

I wrapped an arm around her while I grabbed my keys and wallet, pulling her to the door with me.

"Yes, it is. Why do you think I don't do it? Trusting someone like that?" I faked a shiver. "I'd rather fight a bear."

"You're never going to get a girlfriend with that attitude."

I laughed. "Are you saying that girls don't like to hear that you would rather fight a bear than date them? Damn, I wish you would have told me sooner. I was wondering why that pickup line wasn't working."

"Fox," she said. "What's your plan, then? Wind up old and alone?"

"Alone? Am I ever alone? I have you. I have all five of you who never leave. How would I be alone?"

"You know what I mean."

"I'm fine, Scout. I promise." I pulled her in, kissing her head before heading down to the cars.

Quinn, Ransom, and Jax were waiting around their cars.

"Where's Kye?"

"Already waiting in the car. We didn't realize we would be waiting for you to prim and prep yourself for an hour," Jax said.

"You're just jealous that you couldn't look this good, even if you did spend an hour getting ready."

He pushed me, making me fall towards Quinn. Her arms came out, stopping me from falling completely against her.

"Well, hello beautiful," I said, picking her up and spinning her away from Ransom.

"Hi, Fox," she said sweetly. "Are you trying to start a fight before the night even begins?"

"Always."

Ransom was already pushing me out of the way.

"Fuck, Fox. She's already mine. Find your own," he said, sweeping Quinn away.

"I just like messing with you. You know that."

"Yeah, and it works every damn time," Jax said, laughing.

Quinn rolled her eyes and pointed to the car. "Alright, enough. All of you into the cars and let's go before we miss our reservation."

"Wow, reservations. We're fancy now," Jax said, sliding into his car.

Ransom and Quinn got into his and Scout jumped into hers. She would always ride with me before, but since she got her new car, it was hard to pry her out of it. Not that I blamed her.

We built her a nice car, and she deserved to drive it everywhere.

Without another word, everyone pulled out and headed to the downtown part of our city. We lived on the side that was more spread out, giving us room to drive the cars out onto emptier roads when we wanted, and head to the fancier side when we wanted to go out.

In seconds, I was forgetting about the day, every worry melting away as I drove.

I meant what I said to Scout. If my life was only filled with the crew, I would be happy.

BY THE TIME I made it halfway, my mood was ruined.

My car was acting up.

The engine kept jumping when it shouldn't be, setting my teeth on edge the entire way here.

I should have just ridden with one of the crew. It would have been easier than trying to navigate these small roads while worrying about the car. I had already guessed there was something wrong with it, but wasn't expecting it to be this annoying.

People littered the sidewalks, walking in and out of bars and restaurants, and for the first time in my life, I was getting claustrophobic. These outings were Quinn's idea. Her plan to make us more cultured and presentable was going to a new restaurant every once in a while. I had never minded. It was a nice change of pace from takeout at the garage, but all I could think about now was going back and figuring out what was wrong with my car.

I cursed as I looked around, realizing I was basically lost now with no idea what direction I was even supposed to go. I was about to call Quinn when a scream rang out.

The girl I'd been checking out just seconds ago was now running in my direction, away from a man who seemed to be yelling at her.

"Get away from me," she screamed. "I already gave you everything!"

Her high-heeled boots were hitting the ground hard as she ran. I couldn't figure out how the hell she could do that without her ankle rolling, but she was doing it and moving fast. The guy kept pace behind her as she yelled again.

Her wild eyes met mine down the sidewalk.

"Help. Please help," she yelled as she got closer. The guy was catching up to her, so I took a step forward, letting her go by until I realized she thought I wasn't going to help, already angling to turn the corner.

I snaked an arm around her waist, pulling her back and shoving her into my car. She fell inside and I slammed the door, turning back to the guy still running towards us.

"Hands off my girlfriend," he yelled. His eyes were glazed over in a drug induced state, a purse clenched in his hands.

"Actually," I said, knowing damn well that I loved to play the hero. "That's my girlfriend. Give back the purse and get the fuck out of here."

His eyes darted around, seemingly assessing his options.

I knew I looked intimidating enough. At six foot five and muscled, the guy would at least have to think twice about doing anything more.

"I need the girl. Please," he yelled, trying to push around me as I grabbed the bag.

"Oh, well, since you said please."

The guy tried to step around me.

"It was sarcasm. You don't get the girl. Now go on. It's done."

"No. No, I need her."

The windows of my car were tinted, obscuring everything inside, and even this close I couldn't see inside. He yelled again, my attention swinging back to him just in time to see him jump forward.

I wasn't ready, wasn't expecting the sudden attack.

His arm swung up, and then arched down. I didn't see the glint of the metal until it was too late. I raised my arm to block it, but the metal already reached my face. The blade slid through the skin, slicing through my eyebrow and cheek before hitting my lips. It was like being burned. The blinding pain was so hot and deep that I couldn't even make a sound.

I let out a string of curse words, pulling a leg up and kicking the guy away. Seconds went by before I could hear his footsteps running away and the car door open.

I tried to make sense of the world around me to shut the door again.

She needed to stay in the car.

I could feel the warm trickle of blood down my face as I leaned back against the fender, trying to focus my eyes on anything. I just needed something to stop the sudden spinning.

"No. Oh no. Can you hear me?" Her voice filled the air as her hands grabbed both sides of my neck.

"Can you hear me? Can you see anything?"

"No." It was the only word I could find. I shut my eyes, trying to open them again, but there was nothing but blood now.

Her arms wrapped around me, pulling me upright and towards the car.

"No, I can't see. I can't drive."

"Just get in. We have to get you to the hospital." I heard the door click open, and I tried to shift my focus to it, but another door clicked shut.

Pain ricocheted through my head as the driver's door opened and closed.

"I'm so sorry. We need a hospital." I could barely keep up with what was happening. The engine roared to life, and the car lurched forward, honking as tires screeched. I struggled for a coherent thought, the world becoming a fog as the pain took over. It was a blinding, hateful pain. The kind I would give anything to end.

All I could see was long hair and dark clothes sitting in the driver's seat of my car. "Well you're not Quinn or Scout," I said, not knowing who else would have the nerve to drive my car with hair like that, but Quinn wasn't good enough to navigate these streets this fast and neither of the girls were blonde.

She yelled out something, but I couldn't hear. My head rolled back, and I went with it. The pain making the world go dark.

THREE
ASH

My heart was beating out of my chest and my hands shook as I put the car in gear and veered into traffic. Luckily, I was already familiar with this type of car. The Supra one of my favorites that I had driven before, but the small road was packed with people and I barely made it ten feet before having to stop again.

"Move!" I screamed, as I leaned on the horn.

The guy was passed out, his head back against the headrest. I could see how bad his face was cut now. Blood dripped down to his chest, and I wanted to push something against it to stop the bleeding, but there was nothing I could reach while not crashing the car.

Traffic slowed again, and I put down the window.

"Get the hell out of the way. Move!" A parking spot opened up, and I used it to cut the corner, cutting off three cars, but not caring. Cars lined the road and drove so slow I could have walked faster. I weaved through them, trying not to use the side-walk, but still jumping the tire up onto it to get around another car. My elbow almost stuck to the horn as I shifted.

He groaned, and I reached over, deciding to use his own shirt, pulling it up and pushing it against his face. "Hold that there."

Abs flashed, and I quickly looked back at the road. "I'm sorry. I'm going. We'll get you to the hospital."

His hand smacked at the console as he tried to lean forward. "Ransom."

"I'm not kidnapping you?" I said, not knowing why he would think there's a ransom. "You were attacked."

"No." His bloodied fingers reached for a radio that was mounted under the dash near me, but I smacked his hand away, trying to grab it as a voice came over the radio.

"Who the fuck is driving Fox's car?"

Blood coated my hands as I pulled at it again, finally breaking it free from the holder. I tried to hit the button, my fingers sliding off.

"Dammit," I yelled, trying again as another voice came.

"That's definitely not Fox."

My fingers finally gripped. "Ransom?" I said the word, not knowing if they would understand.

"Yes? That's me."

"Your friend, he was — Get the fuck out of my way!" I screamed as the car in front of me slammed to a stop. I leaned out the window, screaming at them again. "Your friend was cut. I need to get him to the hospital now."

Quiet filled the car. "How bad?"

"Bad. I think it's pretty bad."

"Find somewhere to stop. I'll get him there."

"No, I'm not wasting time to stop. I'm going now."

"I can get him there faster," he said. His words were calm, but mine weren't.

"I can get him there plenty fast and stopping will waste time, but he's asking for you."

Another guy's voice came over the radio.

"I just passed her and from what I see, I think she can get him there fast enough." I looked down, the car hitting ninety as I got on the highway, ready to push it faster.

It was Ransom's voice now. "Jax, get Quinn and Scout. Call Kye. Try to keep Scout calm. Meet us there."

"Got it."

His voice came back. "Fuck, you are fast. I'm coming up behind you."

I looked back, a sleek black car moving through traffic. It moved next to me and then pushed in front, revving and honking as cars moved over, giving us space to move faster.

"Are you okay?"

"I'm fine, but there's just so much blood. I can't stop it and drive." The car jumped, something was off, but I pushed it again, not daring to hesitate. I would give him my car if I blew it up, considering the guy saved my life and was now bleeding out.

"Just get to the hospital. Fox will hold on."

I listened, gripping my fingers tighter around the steering wheel to control the shaking. "Fox?"

"His name."

Another groan came from next to me and I reached over, grabbing his hand with my bloody one. "We're almost there, Fox. Your friends are coming. I'm so sorry." The words came out like a sob. How had this night gotten even worse?

He groaned something, but I couldn't make out the words.

"Okay, please hold on," I said again, not knowing if it was for my sake or his.

I pulled off the highway, following Ransom's car as he continued to make a path for me. The driving wasn't hard for me, the motions coming from muscle memory, the clutch and shifting like a second nature, but I had never driven under this type of stress. Not only that, but it had been months since I really drove like this at all. It felt good and terrible all at the same time.

The hospital came into view and I raced to the front doors, throwing the car to a stop and jumping out, running around to the other side, cursing that I was still wearing heels.

What a fucking night to wear stiletto boots.

The other car came to a stop, and a guy got out, his dark hair and clothes matching the car, tattoos snaking over his arms and even one peeking out on his neck. He wasn't the type of guy I was ever hanging around, but his eyes were full of tenderness as he looked from me to Fox, who I was trying to drag out of the seat.

"What the fuck happened?" he asked, grabbing onto him and pulling him from the car.

"A guy was trying to attack me and he stopped him. We didn't know the guy had a knife until it was too late." I was breathless, trying to help him with Fox. His big body seemed to collapse over and over as he kept trying to regain control.

"Playing the hero again, Fox?" he asked, the words so light compared to the situation.

"He *was* the hero." I demanded, wanting to stick up for him.

"He always is," he said, but his words weren't mean. Nurses came over as we pulled him inside, grabbing for Fox as Ransom told them what happened.

I couldn't move for a moment, blood covering my hands and now my dress, too. Another car revved behind me and I turned.

Two girls and a guy ran inside, going right past me to Ransom. "What happened?"

"Where is he?" the smaller red-headed girl demanded. Ransom pulled them both into a hug. "They took him back. He took a knife to the face. I'm assuming a lot of stitches, but he'll live." He nodded in my direction. "She said he was trying to save her."

"He was. I mean, he did. Somebody grabbed my purse, but then came after me. I — I didn't want any of it back, but he kept coming at me. He, Fox I mean, he put me in his car and tried to stop the guy."

"Always the golden hero, isn't he?" the other guy, who I assumed was Jax, said. He walked in with a blonde guy and they all circled around. The red-headed girl elbowed him. "What? It's going to get him killed at this rate," Jax said.

"Don't even," she warned, "you all like to play heroes."

"Sorry, I'm Quinn," the brown-haired girl said, coming to pull me into a hug, not seeming to mind that I was covered in her friend's blood. "This is Scout, Ransom, Kye, and Jax." She pointed to each one, and I smiled back.

"No, *I'm* sorry. I didn't want him to get hurt. I didn't think the guy would do anything like that. I thought Fox would scare him off. I ran, and he grabbed me to throw me in his car, and before I knew it, his face was cut." I was running on, my words falling over each other as I held back a sob.

"It's ok," Quinn said. "It's all right and not your fault," she said. "We know Fox well enough. He wasn't going to sit back and watch something like that happen without trying to intervene."

"Yeah. Yeah, of course," I said, trying to get the panic in my head to clear. "I'm really thankful he was there because I can only think what that guy was going to do to me. Can you tell him thank you? Tell him he saved my life?"

"You can stay and tell him yourself if you want. We will all be hanging out here anyway, and don't mind one more."

I gave a tight smile, not wanting to sit with these people who obviously cared about this guy and have them stare at me all night, blaming me. My stomach churned at the thought of then having to face him when he woke up.

“No, I should go. I really shouldn’t stay. Just tell him I’m so sorry and thank him. He just, he saved me.”

Quinn nodded with sad eyes and I knew that was the look I was going to get all night if I stayed.

I turned, not wanting to look at their stares anymore.

I made it out of the main doors and moved into a dark corner of the parking lot, waiting for a car to come get me, thankful that I still had my purse and phone.

And that was all thanks to Fox, too.

My night had started bad, with my friends inviting David out when they knew I didn’t want to be around him. I guess I couldn’t really call them my friends now. They were people that pretended to be my friends. I knew they would be pissed at me now anyway. They had expected me to pay, racking their tab up until they couldn’t afford it, and would now have the nerve to be mad at me for leaving.

Then getting mugged and chased. Then, seeing Fox, his handsome face hardening as he pushed me into the car and slammed the door to stand and protect me. He didn’t even know me, but was willing to put himself in danger for me.

Now he was in there with all his friends and it made me wonder who would show up for me if I was the one in the hospital. My dad maybe, if someone knew to call him. I doubted anyone else would. David would come, just to take control of the situation and trap me when I was stuck in a bed with no other option.

My body sagged, exhaustion setting in. The car came around and I got in, looking back at the hospital as we left.

I hoped that Fox was going to be ok.

But I was too much of a coward to stay and check.

FOUR
FOX

I WOKE up with a deep headache, but I couldn't feel much of my face, the skin numb and half of it bandaged.

I looked up with my one uncovered eye, realizing I was in the hospital. Unfortunately for me, it hadn't all been a dream.

I groaned, and a chorus of my name filled the room.

Quinn and Scout already had their arms around me, asking me so many questions I couldn't keep up. The groggy hangover from whatever drugs they gave me making it hard to think.

"Let him breathe," Jax said, and they pulled back, searching my face.

Quinn touched the unbandaged side. "Sorry. We've been so worried. How are you?"

"Fine. But I can't feel my face."

"They have you pretty drugged up," Scout said. "But they said you can eat as soon as you want." Her face lit up like that was the best news ever, and my stomach growled in agreement.

"Perfect. Can you go get me something, then?" I asked, trying to smile, but my lips didn't seem to work.

"One of everything," she said, leaning down to kiss my

cheek before nearly running from the room, grabbing Kye as she went, and Jax not far behind, never passing up an opportunity to eat.

"How long have I been here?"

"Since last night," Ransom said.

"Only Scout could have that much energy after staying in a hospital all night."

"I don't know how she does it without an ounce of coffee," Quinn said, moving to lean against Ransom.

"What's going on with my face?"

"The knife sliced it good. They stitched it up and said it was a clean enough cut that it should heal pretty nicely, but..." Quinn's words died out and she looked at Ransom.

"You're going to have a wicked fucking scar across you face forever. Unless you try plastic surgery. They won't know how bad it will look or how much it could be improved until it heals more."

"So, I'm mangled for life?"

I liked my face, and now I was being told it would never look the same. Thoughts of monsters and zombies flashed in my mind. I was going to look like one now.

"Mangled? No. Scarred? Yes," Quinn said. "But like Ransom said, we won't know how bad and you can't mess with the bandages yet. Then you have to leave the stitches alone for a while."

"Fuck. Are you kidding me?" I groaned.

"Do you remember everything?" Quinn asked, and I nodded.

"Pretty much everything, up until getting in the car. I remember the girl running towards me, the guy on her heels and trying to stop him. She screamed, and the knife sliced." I made a motion, but remembering the feeling made my stomach churn.

"But you don't know who she was?" Quinn asked.

"No, I was trying to find you guys to figure out where to

park, and she came running. She drove me here?" I asked, remembering her talking to me, telling me she was getting me to the hospital and after I realized I didn't know her, asking her why she was driving my fucking car so fast. "Is my car okay?"

"Not a scratch," Quinn said.

"Yeah, whoever she was, she could fucking drive," Ransom said with appreciation. "It took me a minute to catch up to her after I realized it was your car, but not you driving. She stayed right there with me the entire ride here and I wasn't going slow."

"You knew it wasn't me?"

"She hooked a right turn that was deadly. You could never," he said with a smile. "I reached out on the radio and she answered. I was worried your car was being stolen for a minute before she asked me to come with her. That you needed help."

"Okay, then who is she?" I asked, needing a name for her face.

They both looked at each other and looked back at me. Quinn was who spoke up.

"We don't know."

"She drove me here, and then what? Ran away?"

"Close. She stayed while they brought you back and then left." Ransom said, "She was hot, though. Like beauty queen hot."

Quinn's mouth fell open as she hit him on the arm. "You can't say that."

He leaned down, murmuring something to her before she turned to me, rolling her eyes. "He's not lying, though. Completely gorgeous."

"And somehow knows how to drive as good as any one of us. I won't say better until I see it again," he mumbled, resigning himself to a nearby chair.

"So I basically save her life, and apparently fuck my face up permanently, and she can't even stay to say thank you?" I don't know why it outraged me so much, but it did, filling my chest with an irritation I couldn't place. I didn't actually expect anything from her, but who doesn't even say thank you?

"She was really upset. She ran out of here once they brought you back. She did want me to let you know that she said thank you."

I waved my hand over my face. "And what, couldn't even stay a few hours to say it to my face? Glad she was too busy to even wait around to say *anything* to me. I can't even know the fucking name of the person I did this for?"

The haunting dream I had all night of her running towards me was burned into my brain. Now she couldn't be bothered to say thanks? Can't look at my face, which was going to be scarred forever. An anger settled into me. "Who does that?"

"She was scared, Fox. Everything that happened and then all of us ran in, demanding to know what was going on. You know we can be a scary group," she said, but I stopped her.

"Enough Quinn, get out. I want to be alone." I didn't know if it was the painkillers or just the pain, but my mind was going. Something breaking inside me, making every word they said like shards of glass under my skin.

Ransom jumped up, and I knew he was coming to her defense.

"You say one fucking word and we're going to have an even bigger problem, Ransom." He looked from me to Quinn, the pain on her face clear, but I didn't care. Couldn't care.

They would get over it.

I'm the one who could never be the same again.

Quinn stopped at the door. "I told her your name. I told her about the garage too. She might come around."

I didn't look at her. I realized this girl telling me thank you wouldn't change my face.

My life was ruined whether I ever saw her again or not.

FIVE
FOX

3 Weeks Later

Every morning seemed harder.

I rolled over, covering my face with a pillow to hide from the world a little longer.

Every day was just another one to get through, even when I didn't want to.

I could get up and go through the motions, but it was harder to care about what was happening around me when my face was bruised, marred and, honestly, disgusting.

The constant pain wasn't helping either, even if it had dulled.

A knock came from the front door, but I ignored it, preferring to keep my face hidden under the pillow.

"Fox?" Jax yelled into the apartment, stomping around looking for me before sticking his head into the bedroom.

"Fox. Get up."

"Go away. It's Saturday. I don't have to work."

He ripped the pillow away from me and stalked over to the curtains, pulling them open. "Doesn't matter. Still stuck with us today. Remember? Car show and then the cookout."

I sat up, staring at him. “Car show?”

“Scout’s birthday? She asked us all to go to that car show with all the drifting and racers. Personally, I think she’s looking for a new boyfriend, but who am I to judge? Come on.”

“Shit.” I ran a hand through my hair, ready to rip it out. “I forgot.”

“Yeah, no shit. Get up. We’re going soon.”

“Can you guys go without me this time?”

He reached into the closet, throwing a shirt and a pair of pants at me. “And piss off Scout? Nope. Get ready.”

“Jax, my face looks worse than Freddy Kruger. Just leave me to sit here. Alone. In the dark.”

“That’s pathetic even for you, Freddy Kruger. Stop pouting. You took a knife to the face. You, of all people, can turn that around somehow to make women throw themselves at you. And you will. Starting at the car show.”

“Even the words sound ridiculous. You want me to pick a girl up, looking like this, at a car show? A place that is so notorious for hot women to begin with?”

“That’s the plan. Listen, I get this sucks. Not that I get it first-hand, but I can tell how bad it sucks. You can’t just sit here stewing in your misery.”

“And what? You were voted to be the leader on getting me out today?”

“Lucky for you, I volunteered. You’re welcome for that because Quinn and Scout are chomping at the bit to get in here and drag you out by the ear.”

I groaned, grabbing for the clothes. “I’m sick of all of you.”

“Yeah, I fucking bet. Sometimes I’m sick of myself, but I’m stuck with me, and you’re stuck with us. Suck it up, Buttercup.”

“You’re an ass.”

“You’re one to talk. Five minutes and I’m sending in the

hounds," he yelled, walking back out and slamming the door behind him.

I knew damn well the hounds meant every single one of them barging in here and making this even harder. The downside of having a group of people who cared about you meant not getting to sit and wallow when you wanted. I thought I deserved some amount of pity, but apparently three weeks was enough time for them. They had been trying to get me to go out for the last two weeks now that the doctor said that it's fine. Most of the stitches were out, but the entire thing was still nasty, the jagged cuts and bruising making my entire face look distorted.

I got up, looking at my face in the mirror again.

I could barely stand to look at myself. It was like a wreck that no one would be able to look away from. I knew going out was going to mean hundreds of stares, but how was I supposed to adjust to this being my new normal now? No one gave you a pamphlet on how to handle the mental damage, just the physical.

By the time I shut the apartment door behind me, the entire crew was waiting at the landing to the garage, and I was in an even worse mood.

"Lucky," Quinn said. "You had about two minutes before we agreed to come in to get you."

"I heard." I walked past her into the garage to my car. "Can we get this over with?"

They jumped into cars, not saying another word until Scout slid into my passenger seat.

"What are you doing? Why aren't you driving your car?"

She shrugged. "Figured you wanted the company. I ride with you most of the time, anyway."

"Yeah, well, not today. Go drive your car."

"I don't have the keys on me."

"Scout," I warned.

"Fox," she said, settling in and clipping her seatbelt on. "Are you going, or do I need to drive you? This is for my birthday. Should you really say no to me?"

I groaned, but started the car anyway. It was still having issues, but I didn't really care lately. She wasn't getting out now, and I was too burnt out to fight her, or any of them, on this. I could go, watch them have fun for a few hours, and then get back here. Then I would be left alone until Monday at least. I only hoped that no one would give me shit for a few hours of standing off to the side.

What was I thinking? Of course, they were going to give me shit.

"Can you guys just back off?" I asked, realizing she hadn't said anything else, but I'm sure it was all there, waiting and ready to come out.

"Back off what? Getting you out of your cave?"

"Yes."

"No," she said. "You moping around isn't going to help you feel better. It's one time in weeks."

"And what? Now you are all experts at what will make me feel better? I didn't realize any of you had gone through this."

I could hear her groan and I didn't even have to look at her to know how dramatically she was rolling her eyes.

"No, none of us have, but that doesn't mean we haven't seen you completely change. You are mopey, angry, unhappy. We only want you to feel better. To be back to the Fox we know and love."

I gripped the steering wheel tighter as I pulled into the parking lot.

"Yeah, well, sorry to disappoint you all. I think that guy is gone, and I don't see how he is coming back. I'm not the same person now." I slammed the car in park. "If that means you guys don't want to be around me, then so fucking be it, but either decide that now or let it go. I can't make myself be anything other than this."

I waved a hand over my face.

If I was going to look like a monster now, I sure as hell shouldn't be judged for acting like one.

I didn't look over. I hated fighting with Scout. I loved everyone on the crew, but she had always been my shadow. No matter what was happening, she always worked to keep up and be right there next to me. Losing any of them would feel like ripping out a part of myself. Hell, we just went through the adjustment of losing someone, but losing Scout would be the worst kind of pain.

She got out and walked quietly next to me, but it didn't stop my endless feeling of dread. I was quiet as we walked in, letting the rest of them lead us to a ring where the cars were lined up.

As the crew gathered around to watch, I let myself get absorbed in the cars in front of us. For a moment, I forgot about my face, and got lost in the roar of engines and blur of cars, until a kid walked past, his eyes wide as he looked at me.

"Mom," he said, grabbing her arm. "It's Frankenstein."

The mother quickly shushed him, pulling him out of view and earshot to hear what she had to say. I knew kids were kids and quite honestly, I didn't blame him for the comparison, but it still stung.

I retreated farther back, turning and coming face-to-face with Rachel, the girl I had been almost seeing before the accident.

If the punches wanted to stop coming, I would take it anytime now.

"Fox?" she asked, looking up at my face, inspecting every inch.

I could see the moment it registered. That she knew exactly who I was, and I could see the horror flash over her face. She tried to hide it at least, but there was no way to get rid of it completely when you were still looking at it.

"Yeah," I said.

"Oh, wow. I mean, I wondered why you hadn't called, but I figured…" Her words died out. "What happened? Are you okay?"

At least I could be honest about that part. "Knife fight."

She took a small step back.

"Oh. Wow. Um, well. I have a boyfriend now." The words came out so fast that I didn't believe them, but didn't particularly care either.

"Don't worry. I wasn't planning on calling." I waved a hand at my face. "Obviously."

"Wow," she said again. Now it was starting to get on my nerves.

"Yeah, I get it. You can go. I won't be chasing after you or anything."

"Right, sorry. It was just a shock. Sorry. I'll uh, see you around."

"Doubt it," I mumbled as I turned.

"Shouldn't you be leaving me alone now?" I asked Jax as he stepped up next to me.

"Was that Rachel? Weren't you seeing her last month?"

"Yes."

"Right, and I'm guessing, based on your ecstatic look, that it didn't go well."

"Good guess."

"Come on, don't even worry about it. You barely liked her."

"That's not the point.," I growled, pulling out my keys. "I'll see you guys at the garage."

I was already walking away when he yelled. "You better be there, Fox. You know what happens if you're not."

I rolled my eyes, holding back from flipping him off only because there were still kids around.

I knew what would happen. They wouldn't leave me alone.

They never left me alone.

I could beg them to leave me be and they would break the door down to bother me. I could move to the Alaskan wilderness and they would show up on snowmobiles, ready to drag me back.

I knew that I should be happy to have people that care about me, but there was nothing left in me to care, much less to be happy about, right now.

I wanted to be left to throw my own pity party, and figure out what life was going to be for me.

I needed them out of my space and head, and there was only one place I could get that. So I took off, getting in the car and driving until the sun was about to set and it was time to get to the cookout.

SIX
ASH

THREE WEEKS HAD GONE by since that awful night, and all I had been doing was pacing my apartment over and over.

Fox was on my mind every second of the day, wondering if he was okay, wondering if he was healing.

Wondering if I should go to apologize and thank him myself.

It took the full three weeks, but I had finally gained the courage to do it, planning to go by their garage and tell him in person.

After an hour long pep talk while I got dressed, I was ready. I didn't want to show up empty-handed, so I dug for an extra turbo that I had. I knew it would fit his car, and I figured a nice gift might help my case of him not hating me for what happened.

Quinn had told me they all worked at a garage, slipping me the name before I left in case I wanted to come by. At the time, I couldn't understand how she thought that was a good idea, but I was glad now. I couldn't imagine not knowing anything about him, not knowing how to find him. Even if they did all hate me, I couldn't just sit around and not tell him thank you. I had tried for weeks, and the guilt of it was nagging at me so much I was hardly sleeping.

I grabbed my keys and headed out, realizing halfway out the door that if I showed up in my car, they would know way too much about me. My car screamed money, especially to people who knew what they were looking at.

The garage wasn't far, but I didn't want to walk all that way.

I groaned and called another cab. I liked driving, preferred the control and freedom, so taking a cab around felt too restrictive, but so was everyone finding out who I was. If I even was that person anymore.

The turbo was heavy and awkward enough that I had to put it in a backpack just to not look ridiculous.

The cab moved down the streets, my heart hammering harder the closer we got. The thought of walking into a group of people who may very well hate me was both a horrible and familiar feeling.

Their garage came into view, the faded black paint of the name on the wall sounding familiar.

I clicked my phone on and searched. Hollows Garage was a fairly newer shop that was putting out very fast cars. I finally realized that I remembered their name because I had seen their cars in action. A guy had brought one to my dad's track, the entire team impressed by its power right out of the gate.

The gift almost felt stupid now, but it wasn't exactly something he could get himself, so I pushed forward.

The car came to a stop, and I got out, pulling the bag with me as I tried to calm myself down. My hands were shaking as I stepped into the open garage door and saw no one inside.

I knew it was Saturday, but I figured they would at least be here until five. Then I heard voices and laughter coming through the back door.

I looked around the corner. Great, I was interrupting a party now. I had never been nervous at parties or events, having grown up around hundreds of them, but knowing Fox was on the other side of this wall was making me lose my nerve.

Quinn's voice echoed in the garage. "Come on, Fox. Dance with me. You always do."

"No," he said.

"Please," she said again, and I peered out. His back was to me and she was trying to get him to stand as the music played in the background.

"Knock it off, Quinn. Dance with your boyfriend and leave me alone. I'm here and that's it. I agreed to come sit here, nothing else."

Ransom came and snaked an arm around her. "We got the bear out of the cave. Can you please stop provoking him?" he asked.

My eyes flew to Fox. Had he been hiding away? Was the pain that bad?

I stepped into the doorway and Quinn's face lit up. "You're here!"

Everyone looked at me and I gave a tight smile, setting the backpack down by the door. All eyes turning to me except Fox's.

"Hey," I said, giving a small, unsure wave to everyone.

"I can't believe you came. Fox," Quinn said, kicking his leg. "She's here."

He didn't turn, didn't even attempt to look at me as his back stayed straight.

I was the girl who ruined his life. Did I really think showing up here to say thanks would help? The entire thing sounded ridiculous now.

Panic tore through me like I've never felt. I needed to go.

"I shouldn't have come. Sorry." I turned on my heel and walked back out, forgetting the backpack, but not caring.

"Wait!" Quinn yelled. "Wait!"

I debated on what to do before I stopped and turned to her.

"Not just fast in the car, huh?" she said with a deep breath. "I've been hoping you would remember us and stop by. Please don't go."

"Why?" My nerves were calming down as I realized at least one of them didn't hate me.

"Two reasons. One, I've been dying to know who you are. What's your name?"

"Ash."

"Just Ash?"

"I just go by Ash."

"Ok, no problem. Second, I wanted Fox to meet you. Actually meet you, you know, under better circumstances."

"Based on him not even looking at me, I don't think he agrees. I can take a hint when someone doesn't want me around."

"He doesn't even want us around, and he loves us. He's been having some trouble healing and handling it. I think — I mean, I'm trying not to get involved," she said, shaking her head. "Actually, no, I am, but I think seeing you could help."

"And if it doesn't?"

She bit her lip. "I will get you out of here faster than you can blink. I might not be a great driver, but I can keep these boys away from you long enough to get out of here."

I couldn't help but smile, her words coming so genuine and light. "Fine, but I'm holding you to that."

She nodded. "Come on. One thing though."

"Yeah?"

"Fox's face. It really did get some damage, and he's not doing well with it. He's always been so good-looking and I think the sudden change is hard on him, so maybe just make sure you can keep your face…normal when you see him."

I thought back to his face as I ran towards him. It felt like good-looking was an understatement.

"I think you flinching away when you're the…" Her words died out as a look of horror crossed her face. I knew what she was about to say, when I was the reason it was like that.

I gave a tight smile. "I'm not going to turn away in disgust or anything, if that's what you're worried about. I know he has that because of me. I've been trying to find a way to thank him, not make it worse."

She sighed in relief. "Ok good. Come on."

Quinn pulled me back into the yard again. The area was set up for a cookout, with tables and a small fire pit to sit around.

"Everyone, this is Ash. Ash, this is everyone." She went through their names again and the girl, Scout, came over, her voice dropping low.

"Come to help tame the bear?"

"Scout!" Quinn scolded, but both smiled. "He doesn't seem to like that nickname."

He still hadn't turned to me, but everyone had dispersed, leaving him at the edge of the party alone now. Quinn nodded, encouraging me over.

I took a deep breath. I couldn't hide away now. My only choice was to face this bear. I walked around his chair, moving to the seat right in front of him. I looked him over as I sat, hiding my sharp intake of breath.

Good-looking was still an understatement.

The cut on his face was bad, the skin pulled together where it had been stitched, the area bruised and more of it fading with yellowed spots. There were still stitches above his eyebrow, but they looked like they should come out soon. The knife had sliced from above his eyebrow down his cheek to his lip, somehow missing his eye, thankfully.

Even with the red and bruised skin, and with the cut, his sharp jaw, blue eyes, and perfect lips still showed through. For a moment, I couldn't believe this was the man who I had helped scar for life.

His eyes were trained on me, looking me over, judging every inch of me, and I didn't blame him.

Was I even worthy of being saved for the sake of his life being so messed up now? For him to be in so much pain? I thought about my life lately, and could believe that I was worth it.

I kept my eyes and breath steady, used to being judged like this, people looking me over and making their assumptions. He didn't know much about me, but I knew he was still coming up with his decisions. I just couldn't tell what they were.

I knew the one I had come to, and it was making my heart race.

"Hey," I said. "Sorry for crashing your party."

"It's not my party. I was forced to be here," he said, obviously still grumpy.

I shrugged, thinking of every party I had been dragged to. "Been there. Don't like your friends?"

"Not today." His tone and gaze weren't giving anything away, and it was already starting to annoy me.

"Sorry I haven't come by sooner. I didn't know what to say, or if you would even want to see me."

"And you decided you had something to say?" The words were edged with annoyance, making me want to push back.

"Actually, yes. I wanted to say thank you. I don't know what would have happened if you weren't there that night. I had already given him everything, and he was still coming after me." A shiver ran through me at the thought. "So thank you."

He didn't say anything for a moment. "You're welcome."

He wasn't going to give me a damn thing. Even though I knew I didn't deserve any more from him. I thought I would get something more than indifference, but that might be better than the possible alternatives.

There was nothing else to say, it seemed.

I did my part in saying thank you, and I would never have to see him again once I gave him the gift and left.

Maybe then the guilt wouldn't be so overwhelming.

"Don't move," I said as I got up, my legs brushing against his, the light touch making me uneasy.

Even with an angry, red cut down his face, Fox was too good looking for my nerves. The quiet indifference setting me more on edge.

I walked past the group and leaned in the doorway to grab the bag, and headed back to Fox before sitting on the table in front of him, crossing my legs and pulling the bag into my lap.

"I brought you something." I knew all his friends were listening to our entire conversation, pretending that they weren't, but none of them were great actors.

"It's not much, but I don't know what to get for someone who saved my life."

"I don't need anything," he said. "I don't need your pity, or a thank you gift." There was still no anger, no tone to indicate anything but annoyance.

"Well, actually, I think you might need this," I said, wrestling with the zipper on the backpack that was sticking and making this whole thing even more embarrassing.

"Oh please," he said, with an eye roll. "I don't need another damn thing of flowers, or get well soon teddy bear."

"Hey!" Scout and Quinn said in unison, proving that they were all listening in and must have given him both.

Finally, the zipper broke loose, and I reached in, pulling out the only gift that felt right to give him.

"Well, that's no fucking teddy bear," Jax said, walking over to look at the brand new turbo in my hands.

"What the fuck?" Fox asked as I slid closer, handing it over to him. He took it from me, which made me sigh in relief, hoping that meant it was an okay enough gift.

I ignored the jolt that went up my arm when his hands touched mine.

"You bought him a new turbo?" Scout said, pure admiration in her voice.

I could feel my cheeks warm and I tried to ignore that, too.

He looked over the bright red turbo, a color I had picked out for my cars, and then he flipped it over, seeing the word Holt stamped into it.

"How did you get this?"

"What do you mean?"

"It's a Holt turbo. They don't just sell these at the store."

"Shit," Ransom said. "That would be amazing on your car."

He wasn't wrong, but Fox's words hit me. I had grown so used to them around that I forgot my dad had them produced only for his cars, and his team's cars, which made it next to impossible to explain how I had one.

"I just — Um, well, I bought a car, and it was sitting in the backseat," I said with a shrug. I tried to look casual, but I didn't think it was working.

"And you just thought you should give it to me?"

"Well, your car seemed to be having a few issues the other night. I thought this could help. If the turbo is the problem, now you have a new one, and if it's not, at least you have a new one to install."

"How did you know that?" he asked, his tone low. His lips pulled into a tight frown, which seemed to make him wince from the cut. Could he really be mad that this is what I brought him?

"Know what?"

"That my car was having trouble. That it could be my turbo?"

"Are you a mechanic?" Scout asked, her voice almost shaking in excitement.

"No, not really a mechanic. Not the way you guys are. I just like cars. I didn't realize you guys were that Hollows garage. You're becoming pretty well known for the work you do."

Fox nodded. "Yeah, and how do you know that? It seems like you know a lot for someone who just likes cars."

"Damn Fox, back off a bit. The woman just gave you the best possible get well gift in the world," Jax said.

I hid my smile. I was liking Jax more and more.

"It doesn't matter how I know that. Just that I do. If the gift is a problem, I can take it back."

"That's not the problem," Fox said.

"Then just say thank you and move on," I spat.

His lips twitched like he wanted to smile, but fought it, keeping them pursed tight. "Fine. Thanks."

I nodded, not knowing if there was anything else to say

"Is that all, then?" he asked, his tone cool.

"That was it," I said, rolling my eyes and grabbing up my bag. I didn't expect much when I walked in, but that went worse than I imagined.

"Thanks again, and nice to see you all," I said, stomping out through the garage.

Quinn ran after me, yelling my name as she went.

"Wait, Ash," she said, catching up. "Please, wait."

"Quinn, you guys are great, but I really should go."

"No, I get it, but I hope you can understand that Fox has been a little rough lately. The rest of us do want you here. Would you please stay and eat with us?"

"Quinn, that's nice of you to offer, but I really don't —"

"We can sit you on the other side of the yard from Fox. Please? He won't be able to bite from there and we would like to get to know you."

I looked over her shoulder into the back yard. I couldn't see any of them, but I could hear the happy chatter and Jax still going on about the turbo. They really did seem nice, and I knew how pathetic it was that I hadn't actually been around people in months.

I'd become a hermit in my apartment. The one night I did try to go out, I almost killed Fox, and that really dampened my enthusiasm about going out again.

"Fine. Just for a few minutes, then."

"Perfect! Come on. Oh, and just in case you run out again, what's your number? I'll text you, so you have mine."

I rattled it off and waited as my phone pinged.

"Perfect. Now, let's go have some fun."

She dragged me back, pulling me to a bench next to Jax.

"Hey, Ash. You stayed!" he said, patting the spot next to him. "Couldn't get enough of us?"

"I don't know that I actually had a choice."

"Of course not. Better watch out. Quinn and Scout are little vipers when they have their mind made up."

I smiled, watching them talk with Fox. "It looks like they are going for him now."

"Oh, they are. They want him to play nice with you."

"Why? Wouldn't it be easier if I just left, and he didn't have to see me? I feel like it will be a bad reminder."

He shrugged. "Maybe, but they want Fox to snap out of it. They want the normal Fox back. They mean well, but I think they are pushing a bit too hard today."

"Can you tell them to back off a bit?"

He rolled his eyes. "Trust me, they won't listen. Ransom

tried to tell Quinn, but it didn't seem to sink in. They are just worried and I don't think they really see that he might need to take it step by step."

"Is there anything I can do that will help and not make it worse? I feel horrible about it."

"Great that you say that because Kye and I were just talking." I looked over, Kye hearing his name and turning to us with a grin.

"We have an idea," Kye said.

"Why do I feel like any idea from you two is going to be a very bad idea?"

Jax's smile brightened. "Because it usually is, but this time I think I'm spot on." He turned back to the group, throwing an arm behind me and leaning back. "Hey guys, I just had an idea."

"We had an idea," Kye corrected.

Everyone stopped and turned to us. Fox's eyes landed on me, and the irritation in them made me lean back next to Jax.

"With Fox out of driving for a while, we all know that we've been looking for a driver to step in for us at the Legends races," Jax said and looked over at me. "It's coming up in a few weeks, and unless we find another driver, we're out. And I think we've found one."

My eyebrows jumped, but I kept my eyes on Jax, not daring to look at Fox again.

I forgot the ripple effect that an injury like that causes. It wasn't just his life I messed up, it was all of theirs.

"You want me to race with you?" I asked, trying to not let my mouth fall open. "How do you know I even want to? Or can?"

"First of all, you're partly the reason we are down a driver, so you owe us. Second, we all saw you drive. I know damn well you can figure out how to get down a straight road. We can help teach you enough to do it."

"That was different," I said, looking over in time to see Fox look away from all of us. "I was under pressure."

"Pretty sure we can give you enough pressure on race night if it means you drive like that," Kye said. "It's actually a genius idea. The Legends race is a big deal for us, and we were all pretty upset at having to drop out."

"Legends race? I didn't realize you guys were entered into that," I said before realizing what my words implied.

"So you know it then," Fox stated. "Are you already on a team to race?"

"No. Nothing like that," I said. "I've just heard about it. It's a big deal for a lot of people, and pretty well known." I wasn't going to add that I was supposed to be on the Holt racing team, but after the wreck and leaving, I didn't know if I would ever race with them again.

"Is it settled, then? Ash is going to stand in as a driver for Fox until he's good to race?"

"What, no," I said. "You guys barely know me. I could be a serial killer. I could be a terrible driver. I could be a horrible person. You can't just add me to your team just like that."

They looked around at each other.

"What you do in your free time is your business," Jax said with a laugh. "Just as long as you race with everything you got."

"And I'd risk the serial killer thing if it meant having a chance at winning. We worked for years just to get entered. Now we finally have our chance and will have to back out unless we find someone," Kye said.

I looked at Fox, the guy who seemed to be growing more irritated at my presence every second I was there. "And you?"

His eyes trained on me and my stomach flipped. "Do whatever they think is best."

"You have to care," I said. "I can't just take your spot."

"Come to the track on Thursday," Jax said. "You can show him, and all of us, that you can do it."

"I like your vote of confidence, but I don't currently have a car to race. The car I do have is in pieces and I don't know if it would work, anyway."

"Can it be put back together?" Kye asked.

"Yes, but I can't do it overnight."

"Then we will help. We can all make sure it's done," Jax said.

My mouth hung open

"This seems ridiculous. Do all of you really think it's a good idea?"

"Honestly, I do," Ransom said. "Jax is right. It seems like you have some ability to drive, and we have been looking for someone to help us out since they told Fox he wouldn't be cleared to do it."

"So, it's settled then?" Jax asked again.

I knew Fox didn't want me to agree. I could imagine that he wanted them to choose anyone else to help, and based on this entire conversation, he would rather me turn it down.

His eyes were heavy as he watched me. All of them seemed to be waiting for my answer, but I didn't know which one to give. Part of me liked the thought of racing with a team again, the other part of me thought that taking Fox's place had to be wrong on countless levels.

Fox's lip seemed to curl now, the frown turning into a snarl, and I knew his answer.

Which meant I knew mine.

"No, not settled," I said, getting up and grabbing my bag again. "I think I need to think this over. I don't know that it's a great idea."

I caught Fox's eye once more before he turned away, his hardened stare finally aimed at something other than me.

Saying no would be the right choice, the only choice, when the alternative was spending more time in Fox's company. I didn't know how much of that glare I could actually take before guilt ate me alive.

With that, I left, not saying another word as I walked away and didn't look back.

SEVEN
FOX

I HAD to give the crew credit.

They waited an entire day before barging into my apartment and demanding that I apologize to Ash and get her to join our team.

One whole day.

"Come on, Fox," Kye said. "You know we need her help."

"And that means we need *your* help," Jax said.

Ransom flopped back on the couch, grabbing Quinn. "So that means you have to go beg Ash to race with us," he said.

"You want me to be the one to go beg the girl to race with us, when she's the reason I can't race in the first place? Do you not see the problem with that?"

"Your attitude is the only reason she hasn't already agreed to it."

"There's no way in hell you know that's the reason. Maybe she just didn't like you guys."

Scout's mouth dropped. "Rude."

"Come on, Fox, we need your help."

I looked around, all five of them staring at me with hopeful eyes. They wanted me to be the old me, the one that would swoop in and fix everything.

As bad as I wanted to be that person, it felt like a ghost of myself. Someone I knew, but hadn't talked to in a very long time.

They knew all the right words to try to pull that guy back, though.

"We need you, Fox," Scout said. "We need her, too. Please. This would be my first year racing at the Legends race. I really don't want to have to give it up." Her face fell.

As much as Scout knew how to push my buttons, she knew how to break me, too. I would never do anything to let her down. At least nothing as big as this.

"Fine," I growled, leaning my head back. "I will go talk to her. Once. If she doesn't want to race with us after that, that's it. I won't be trying again."

"Fine. I'll take it," she said.

I didn't want to see her. More than that, I didn't want her to see me. The guilt and pity in her eyes about how I looked was enough to make me never want to face her again.

Now I was agreeing to beg her to join our racing team when we didn't even know if she could race. It seemed like the worst idea possible, but it's what they all wanted, and somehow I would do anything for these people.

"Where am I supposed to find her? We know nothing about her other than her first name. Also, is that not concerning to anyone else after what happened to us before? Shouldn't we find out more about her before we just let her in?"

"We're not letting her in anything other than racing with us. It's not like she's working with us or living here. I don't see that there's a problem with not knowing much about her yet. She obviously cared enough to get you to the hospital. She was nice enough to show up here and apologize in person, and overall, she seems nice. I don't think having her meet up with us to race and practice is the same as having her join our group," Jax said.

"Whatever. It's your choice, not mine. But again, how am I supposed to talk to her when we don't even know who she is?"

"She said she's going to work out," Quinn said, not looking up from her phone. "I just texted her, and she told me where she's going. You can show up there."

"Now I'm stalking the girl?"

"No. It's not stalking. She just told me what she's doing. You're just showing up and politely begging her to help us."

"Right, that's what every girl loves. A guy showing up where she works out, looking like this, to beg her to hang out with his friends."

I think every single one of them rolled their eyes.

"Stop the dramatics," Kye said. "Just suck it up and talk to the girl."

"I can give you a few tips if you're nervous," Jax said, wiggling his eyebrows.

"Alright, everyone out. I'm doing this one favor, and then everyone is going to leave me alone about my attitude for at least three days."

Groans and agreements filled the room, and thirty minutes later, I was standing in front of the gym that Quinn directed me to.

It wasn't the run-down gym in town, either. It was the fancy two-story one on the outskirts, and it was packed with Jaguars, Aston Martins, Rolls Royce, and every other expensive car you could think of filled the parking lot.

Great, not only was I having to talk to her, but it looked like I was going to have to pay a good amount of money just to be let inside.

I drew the line at waiting in the parking lot for her to come out.

I walked in, the woman at the front desk blatantly staring as I asked to come in for the day. It was obvious she wasn't thrilled with how I looked, but lucky for me, she still had to let me in, regardless.

The place was huge, and it took me a full twenty minutes of wandering around until I finally found her tucked away in the corner of the weight lifting room.

Guys filled each bench, glancing up at me as I walked by.

I tried to keep any shred of confidence I could, but my scowl deepened. What else could I do when my pain was on display for everyone to judge? All anyone would see when they look at me would be weakness and ruin.

Ash did a double take, glancing up and away so fast I barely saw it until her head whipped back to me.

"Fox? What are you doing here?" She was obviously as pleased to see me there as I was to actually be there.

She was wearing a cropped hoodie and tight workout outfit that was making me feel nervous to even speak. Why did she have to be so beautiful on top of everything? Every perfect curve of her face and lips was not helping me find my words any faster.

I prayed to anyone that would listen that I wouldn't seriously have to take up Jax and Kye's offer to help me talk to women one day. At this rate, though, it was bound to happen.

"I was told to come find you and figure out if you were racing for us."

"Oh. That."

"Yeah," I said, sitting back at one of the benches. "Pretty extravagant for a gym, don't you think? I don't see the need for an over-the-top fancy gym just to workout."

I glanced over as she rolled her eyes. "For your information, I work out here because it's safe for me to do so. Cameras, security systems, staff on site. I can work out without having to be on guard the entire time."

"I guess that does make up for the cost of this place." I really did sound like I'd never spoken to a woman in my entire life. "Does that mean it's still giving you problems? I mean, is what happened still bothering you?" I asked.

"You mean the getting mugged and attacked thing? No. Honestly, I thought it would bother me more, but it doesn't really. Worse things happened that night and they weren't to me. You kind of took the worst of it for me."

I looked away, hating that it was even brought up. "Why the top of line security, then?"

She laughed. "Aside from being a woman who wants to workout alone at any time of the day without being harassed? I have some people in my life that I don't want to bother me. It's nice being here and knowing I won't run into them."

"Oh, that's not the response I was expecting. You're being honest, though? You have no problems from what happened?" I asked again, finding some comfort in the fact that I at least succeeded at one thing that night.

"Honestly, no. I mean, things like that happen in cities all the time and I was lucky to not be hurt. I might keep a can of pepper spray on me more often, but really, thanks to you, I'm okay."

"Well good. Anyway," I said, leaning back and grabbing the bar and lifting over and over. I hadn't worked out in weeks now, but there wasn't much weight on it. "Are you going to race with us or not?"

She put a hand on her hip, watching me. "Why were you voted the spokesperson for this? I would have thought Jax was taking that spot."

I forced my tongue to the roof of my mouth, biting back every comment that was on my mind. So she wanted Jax here, then? Glad I got slashed for Jax to find a girlfriend, finally.

"I was voted as the spokesperson because apparently I'm the reason you haven't agreed yet."

"Well, I'm not going to lie and say that wasn't partially true, but that wasn't the only reason."

I put the bar back and sat up. "Well, they need you to do this, and I need them to leave me alone, so aside from me, what's stopping you?"

"My car, for one. I told you, it's in pieces, and second, while I might have raced before, it's been a while. Why does it matter so much to you?"

"Because it isn't fair for Scout. This is her first year being old enough to race in this and it's my fault she can't now. Not only that, but the entire crew has worked day and night getting ready for this. If there's a way I can stop them from having to pull out, I'm going to do it. I can get your car ready and you can race with them. You barely have to win as long as they do their part, which they will."

She grinned. "Like I'm going to agree to race and then not win."

My eyebrows shot up. "So it would be accurate to say you're competitive, then?"

"Some have said I'm a little *too* competitive."

It wasn't a surprise. She seemed ready to challenge everything I said, and when she wasn't saying it out loud, her lips were pursing like she wanted to. "Have you decided if you're going to do this?"

"Not yet."

"Then I bet that I can outlast you on the bench. If I win, you race, no questions asked. If I lose, then I'll leave you alone with no obligation."

"You would risk leaving it up to me?"

I nodded, knowing I wasn't risking anything. If she agreed, the crew would be happy. If she didn't, I did my part and the crew would leave me alone.

And anyway, I was competitive, too. There was no way I was going to lose.

I wanted my three days of peace and quiet.

EIGHT
ASH

Fox was here.

He was standing in the gym. My gym. Asking me to agree to race with them.

Actually, betting me to race with them.

The competitive part of me was already agreeing, never being able to turn down a challenge.

“While I do like the sound of that, it doesn’t matter when I don’t have a car. I told you, I need to practice.”

“We have plenty of cars to practice with, and we are literally a mechanic shop. We can get your car fixed. You have a lot of excuses, though. Are you worried about me winning?”

“Not at all.”

“Then I will add a clause that says if I win and you have to race with us, then you will have a car to do so.”

“Fine, the weights have to be fair to our body size.” I didn’t hide my obvious stare at his arms. There was no way I could actually out lift him if we compared weights.

“Of course,” he said, as he put weights on the bar and laid down. We decided it was whoever could do the most reps within one minute wins. That's how I ended up sitting on the bench opposite him, staring at every arm muscle that seemed to be working hard to push that bar up over and over.

I lost count of his reps, apparently too busy trying not to stare at flexing biceps and forearms.

The alarm on my phone went off and he put the weights back, sitting up with a grin.

"Alright, think you can beat that now?"

"I know I can beat that."

The problem was, I didn't actually know what number I needed to beat to win now.

He sat back, stretching his legs out and crossing his arms. The cut across his face really did make him look more intimidating, which I didn't need right now. There was something unnerving about someone so hot watching you do something so not hot.

I laid back, the phone buzzing to start.

The good thing about my competitive side was that I could usually turn it on without a thought. In seconds, I was lost in my own head, thinking of all the reasons I shouldn't race, and all the reasons I should.

I didn't know how long it had been, but my arms started to burn, each rep moving slower and slower.

Sweat beaded on my brow until I didn't know if I could physically do another one. There was no way I was beating him, but I wasn't giving up until my arms gave out.

The bar came down, and I took a deep breath, trying to decide if I could do another.

Fox leaned forward.

"Again," he whispered.

"What?"

"Do it again."

"I'm trying. I don't think—"

"Again, Ash. Now," he growled, the command sending shockwaves to my core.

I pushed up again, my arms shaking.

"One more time," he said.

Anger burned through me that he thought he could boss me around, but my body still listened. At least it wasn't looking like I was going to lose now.

The buzzer went off, and I took a breath. The bar stuck on my chest.

"Could you possibly help?"

Fox laughed, getting up and grabbing it with one hand to put it away.

"Good to know you take competitions seriously."

"I'm sorry. Was that supposed to be a test?"

"I wanted to see how competitive you are. Can't be out racing with someone who doesn't want to win. And finding out how well you listen was just a bonus."

I tried to ignore what that meant. "I'm assuming that means you won and I have to race."

There was a beat of silence as he watched me.

"No. You won, and you get to decide if you want to race or not."

"You're lying. There is no way I just won."

He shrugged. "Weren't you keeping count?"

"No. I…got distracted and lost count."

"Then you're going to have to believe that you won, but I need an answer now. The vipers won't be happy if I come back without an answer."

"Do the girls know that you all call them the vipers?"

"I actually meant the entire crew, but yes. They know I call them vipers, and I believe they are flattered," he said with a smirk.

I watched him as I thought it over. I did want to race again.

The thought was a surprise even to me after months on end of shot nerves since my wreck.

A familiar phantom pain shot through my chest and I looked at Fox's face, wondering if he was feeling that pain for real right now.

"If you guys will help get my car going, and understand that I need to ease into racing, then I will do it."

"Seriously?"

"Seriously. I was already on the fence about it, but it's obvious that you care about your friends, and I can admire that enough. Like I said, my car gets fixed, your team wins, and maybe I can make up for the fact that the only reason you can't race is because you saved my life."

"I think saving your life could be a stretch."

"I think based on the cut on your face, you saved my life."

"I don't need you to help the crew just because you pity me."

"Don't you? You're here asking me to do this and I'm agreeing. Now you're mad about why I'm doing it? Make up your mind."

"Fine," he growled. "Whatever reason you need, as long as you do it."

"I'll do it."

"Great," he said, getting up and grabbing his phone. "I'll tell one of them to swing by and look at your car. Decide what we need to get it going."

"You work fast."

"The big race isn't far off. And practice races are Thursday. We can get you down the street once or twice and see if you can even get down a straight road."

I knew the shock on my face was clear, but he wouldn't know why that shock was there. If only he knew who he was talking to. Not that I was going to tell him now. I could only imagine the response I would get if I came clean now.

And based on the panic attacks I got every time I even thought about racing, there was a big chance that I *wouldn't* be able to get down a straight road.

"We will see if I can. And Fox?"

"What?"

"Don't tell me what to do again."

He rolled his eyes. "No promises. I have to see if you can even race first."

"If I can race? You have the nerve to say that when you're the one here asking me to help you and your team?"

"I'm sorry? Do you suddenly have your own champion race team that you haven't mentioned?"

He crossed his arms, leaning back with a smug smile.

"No," I said, the reminder a sting.

I once had my own champion race team. I was basically a leader on that team, and now it was gone.

"Exactly. My team is down a racer because I had to save your ass, so I suggest you see this as a favor, not me begging. And yeah, if you can't race, you can count on me telling you what to do because you're going to have to learn and learn fast."

"I don't need you to teach me anything."

He looked me over. "Right. We will see about that."

I crossed my arms, scowling and already debating on going ahead and coming clean with who I was when his phone rang.

He didn't hesitate, clicking the call and pressing it to his ear.

"What, Scout?"

He was silent, listening, but his eyes stayed on me.

"Why don't you have your car?" he asked her.

She must have gone off on him because he shook his head.

"I was doing what you told me to and politely asking Ash to race with you guys."

He gave a forced laugh and handed the phone over.

"Don't forget that you already agreed."

"Hello?"

"Ash! You're going to do it? You're going to race with us?"

"Yes, I was just telling Fox that I agree, as long as he isn't an ass."

"You didn't actually use those specific words," Fox said, the deep, lazy tone doing something to me that I wasn't expecting. I looked up, not wanting to meet his eye.

"I can almost guarantee that he's going to be an ass, at least for a while," Scout said. "But he really is a big softie. I promise this is going to be so much fun."

I smiled. It was hard not to believe her.

"Alright, give me the phone because I know damn well she's talking about me," Fox said. I handed it over, yelling my goodbye.

"I'll be there shortly," he said into the phone before ending the call.

"Expect us to come around at some point to check out the car. I'm sure Quinn will text you. Or Jax," he growled. "I'll talk to you later."

He got up, heading out of the room before I could get another word in.

I felt like I had made a good decision racing with them, but I couldn't ignore the weight that settled deep in my stomach.

I knew how to race.

I'd been doing it all my life.

The problem was that I haven't been able to do it in months, and I was quickly worrying that I would never be able to again.

NINE
ASH

I STOOD IN MY KITCHEN, staring into the fridge. It was frighteningly bare and I really couldn't think of anything I could make out of peanut butter and ketchup. Part of me hated living alone. I liked noise, I liked the chaos of everyone around. I liked not trying to figure out how to cook something halfway decent for one. We always had people coming and going at home and I hadn't realized how used to it I became until getting here.

My phone rang as I fought myself about what type of food I wanted to order.

Quinn's name flashed across the screen and I was glad I had remembered to actually save the number. It had been two days since I told Fox I would race and I hadn't heard a word from any of them. I had secretly hoped that meant they weren't going to follow through on it and I would get to hide away alone here in my apartment, but it didn't seem like that was going to be an option now.

"Hello?"

"Hey, Ash. Are you home? We wanted to stop by and take a look at your car."

"We?"

"We."

"Who is we, Quinn?"

"Listen, we're a package deal. You take one, you take us all."

"Which one am I supposedly taking?"

"Me, I guess," she said with a laugh.

They moved fast, and I was actually surprised they were coming at all. "Come over. I'll be in my little garage. You won't miss the car."

It didn't take more than fifteen minutes before a line of street cars pulled in. All four of them lined up, somehow in sync with each other as they parked.

"Well, damn," Jax said as he got out. "You said you had a car sitting around. You didn't mention it's exactly what you need for racing."

"It's in pieces. How is it exactly what I need?"

The engine was still torn apart, and I didn't think it actually had brakes anymore after someone took out the lines and failed to replace them. The car had sat in my dad's garage for months with the promise that his best mechanic was going to replace basically everything on it. It was supposed to come to me stronger and safer than ever, but I found out too late that my dad and David never actually wanted it fixed. They had plans for me to never race again after my wreck.

Maybe it was out of love, out of care for me after seeing me in such bad shape, but it only made me feel weaker. The pain of having the people who were supposed to support you telling you that they didn't believe you could handle it anymore was enough to break me.

"I see that," Jax said, looking it over. "Fox mentioned that you have raced a time or two. Is this the car you used?"

"No, not this one. I thought I would get it running again, but really haven't had the care to."

"What happened to it?"

"My dad had it for years and then he got bored with it, I guess. He didn't want it anymore, and I was happy for the project."

I looked at it again. It was still in great shape. It was going to be the car I raced with after I wrecked mine, but I never got far enough on the project to even drive it down the road.

"Really, Ash?" Kye asked, pulling open the driver's door and sliding inside. "An RX7? Fox is going to fall over when he sees this. And it looks like you're off to a great start. You have great parts on it."

"Yeah, my dad loved to drop money on his cars, so I was able to get a lot of nicer ones."

"And I assume he has a garage?"

"Yeah, that's where this was for months until I brought it here. I thought they were fixing it, but I never saw what was completed."

"Why bring it here? I'm guessing he has tools if he has all these parts," Jax asked.

"I had a falling out with him. We don't talk much right now, so bringing it with me was the only option to keep it."

"Ahh," Ransom said. "Do you have other family then?"

"None that I talk to."

"Good thing you have us to come barge in and fix your car now. Let's look it over and see what we need," Jax said.

They all nodded and got to work, checking under the hood and under the car. I liked working on cars and knew enough to do a good amount of repairs, but every time I thought about finishing this car, I was only filled with exhaustion. It wasn't the car I wrecked, but it was the same model, and the dread that still came over me at the thought of my wreck didn't help my motivation.

Now, with a team of people here ready to help, I was actually starting to feel a spark of excitement again.

That died out the moment Jax rolled out from underneath with a grimace.

"I hate to be the one to tell you," Jax said, "but you need a whole new engine."

"What? Why? It's torn apart, but it should be usable."

Kye rolled out too, the small lift I had gave just enough room to see under the car. "I don't know who told you this was a good engine, and I don't know the last time you looked under here, but there's a big hole in the side of it."

"There's no way. I saw the engine myself before it was set in it. It was fine."

Jax grimaced. "Sorry, Ash. With that hole, there's nothing we can do except put a new one in it."

"No, there's just no way. I looked it over myself."

"When?"

"Months ago now. It was still at my dad's shop."

Kye walked over, showing me a picture of the side of the engine he took, the giant hole obvious.

"I would guess that someone else has touched it since then, because this would be deliberate. There's no way a non-running engine is going to blow up randomly and the pieces are inside the engine, meaning it was hit from the outside.

"So someone did it on purpose?" My voice was a squeak, but I knew I shouldn't be shocked. No one wanted me to race again, but I didn't think David or my dad would stoop this low.

"I would say yes. Do you know who would do this?"

"I have a few guesses, but it's not important now, is it?"

I sat back on my stool in the corner, not knowing why my eyes were filling with tears. It felt like the last straw with the car. Everything I did to fight to go back to racing and the moment I got behind the wheel, I had a panic attack. I still fought, though.

I fought to have the car repaired, the body shop taking months to fix this one, and then fighting my dad and David to repair the mechanics of it. I already knew they didn't want to help me, but to find out now the engine has been junk the entire time and I missed it? They hadn't even tried.

Which meant they had been lying to my face for months. None of them would have missed this by accident.

Fox's car pulled in and parked next to the others. I didn't know why he was here now, but I didn't want him to see me like this.

"Fine, the car's junk, then. I don't know what you guys expect of me. I can't race with you."

Fox walked in, catching the last part of my sentence.

"Why aren't you racing now? And is this the car you were going to race? This is nice. Like really fucking nice," he said, walking around it.

"Not so much when I was just informed the engine is trash."

Fox looked up, looking at each of his friends, who all nodded.

"Big hole in it. Not getting that fixed," Jax said.

"And that's why you're upset?" Fox asked.

"Yeah. I mean, among other things that have happened with this car, this feels like the last straw."

I stared off, not able to look at Fox any longer. I still couldn't believe this was the man who saved my life and ended up in the hospital because of me. The one who was permanently scarred because he wanted to make sure I was safe that night. I couldn't believe I had agreed to race with them, like that would make up for what he did for me.

"Listen," I said. "Maybe racing with you all isn't going to work out. I might be able to find someone else to help out if you give me some time." I knew plenty of people that raced. One of them had to be open to racing with a team they didn't know.

Silence stretched on and I didn't get up. I knew they would be upset, but this was for the better. I would never get my car ready in time and even if I did, it was obviously painful for Fox to have me around. It seemed like the nicest thing I could do was back out and leave them alone.

"No. We'll bring it to the garage," Fox said, coming to my side. "We can find an engine for it and still get it ready in time."

"No, really, it's fine. That's too much."

"You said you would do this," Fox said, his voice dropping low next to me. "Are you sticking to your word or are you backing out?"

I finally looked up, meeting his eyes. He looked so close to snapping, the cut a constant reminder that I owed him.

"No. I'm not backing out."

"I said if you agreed, we would make sure your car was ready, and I stick to my word. We will bring your car to the shop at some point and you will still be practicing with one of ours."

"Okay."

My words were quiet, but my mind was screaming. I had been fighting so long by myself to get back to racing, now others were fighting me to get back into it. The sudden change made me more uncomfortable than having them help me with the car.

"Perfect," Quinn said, jumping up. "It sounds like it's time for a break, then. How about we go get something to eat?"

A round of yeses before she turned to me.

"Want to come?"

"I can't," I lied. "I have plans."

"Alright, then. Do you want to come hang out tomorrow? We can go out or something."

"Maybe, I'll text you."

She smiled bigger and threw an arm around Ransom. "Great!"

Fox turned, not waiting for an answer as he stalked back to his car.

Jax shook his head. "Seriously, Ash. It's not a problem. We can have this done in no time."

We both watched Fox getting in the car and slamming the door.

"I just don't know if this is a good idea. It's obvious he doesn't want me around, and I don't blame him. I don't know if I would want to be around the person who did that to me."

"You didn't do that to him. He played the hero a little too hard. I doubt he even regrets it."

I knew first hand that a person needed time after an injury, but I didn't know what I needed to give him time for. I would race with them and then be gone. I wasn't here to join their team forever, and I wasn't trying to beg Fox to be friends.

I would keep my distance, win their race, and move on with my life.

TEN
ASH

I WORKED on homework throughout the day. I was only taking two classes this semester, but was determined to ace them both. I wanted to prove to both me and my father that I could accomplish this and one day run his business, even if all he thought about now was David running it with me.

My stomach churned as evening came, but I still headed to the garage, ready to hang out with Quinn. She had convinced me to go out tonight and even if it was just out to eat with her, it felt like a big deal.

I walked into the darkened office, surprised when I didn't see anyone in there. I was supposed to meet Quinn there at 6 and it was already 6:15. I knew I was a little late, but I couldn't imagine she would leave without me. I stepped out into the garage, where one of the doors was open.

Fox was leaned over a car, his back to me, shirtless. I froze, watching as his back muscles flexed and strained to turn a wrench. I could see two small random tattoos on his back and the sweat that beaded between his shoulders. It was a strangely hot day, and I had cursed that this morning, but was suddenly grateful for it now.

He groaned as he pulled again, filling the garage with the noise, my stomach flipping at the sound. My shoes were quiet on the garage floor as I walked over to him.

"Hey Fox," I said.

The wrench slipped as he jumped. "Dammit," he groaned, grabbing his hand.

It was a common enough occurrence in my life for tools to slip and fingers to crunch that I reached out on instinct, grabbing his wrist and pulling him to the sink.

He let out a round of curses. "What are you doing? Let me go."

I stuck his hand under the water, making sure there were no deep cuts or blood. My heart raced, not believing that I could really be unlucky to scar him again.

"I'm fine, Ash. I just hit it," he said. "Just leave it, I'm okay." His tone was sharp, but he didn't pull his hand away.

"You might have broken your finger."

"I didn't."

"Then let me look at it."

He was quiet, letting me inspect his fingers as I tried not to focus on how big his hands were.

I turned it over and over again, biting my lip at the worry of him breaking a finger because of me.

"You're right. I don't think it's broken."

"Like I said. Now are you done or do you need to kiss it too?"

I was already moving, pulling his fingers to my lips and pressing a kiss to the sore spot, looking up at him as I did. His eyes darkened as he watched me.

"If you like to listen so well, why don't you tell me what you are doing here?"

I dropped his hand and stepped back. He was a beast of man and the menacing tone didn't help.

"I came to see Quinn."

"She's not here."

I rolled my eyes. "Thanks. I figured that out myself. Do you know where she is?"

"No, I don't keep tabs on her."

I finally took him in. He did have a few tattoos scattered on his chest and stomach, but one caught my eye.

"A black widow?"

He looked down at his own tattoo. It was a small one on his chest. "Yeah, what about it?"

"Why did you choose that?"

"I don't know." He shrugged. "I went with Ransom while he was getting a tattoo and decided to get one. This was the first one that got my attention."

"Hmm."

"Why?"

"Just an interesting choice."

A car pulled in and a door slammed, both of us turning away from each other. "There's Quinn. Now you two can leave."

I was about to snap back at him, but Quinn stomped in. Her face was a mix of anger, and holding back tears.

"Sorry I'm late. Ransom was being an ass."

Fox's face broke into a smile and he laughed, "So does that mean you're finally coming to your senses and choosing me?"

"Yep, let's go," she laughed, still almost crying.

He pulled her in, wrapping an arm around her shoulders like he hadn't just been snarling at me. It was night and day, Jekyll and Hyde. Almost run me out of the garage, and then turn and be sweet to her.

"I recall something about the Bahamas?"

"I just got into a fight with my boyfriend about moving in

together. I think running away with you to another country might be moving a little fast."

He didn't hide his scowl. "You don't want to move in with him?"

"I do but I don't."

He waited, calm and not pushing.

"I'm just worried it will change. That he'll get sick of me there. Then what?"

"Sick of you? He's obsessed with you."

"Yes, now," she said. "But what happens after a few months and he can't stand me around all the time?"

I couldn't say anything, having nothing more to go off of than David, who I couldn't stand after three months of dating, and even then I kept dating him out of guilt.

Fox took a deep breath. "I have something to tell you then that you're really not going to like hearing."

"Fox," she growled, and I held my breath, wondering what ball he was going to drop on her right now of all times.

"You've been living with Ransom for basically the last several months." His lips pursed, and he gave an apologetic smile.

"No, I live upstairs."

He shook his head. "How many times have you slept there in all the months since moving in?"

She shrugged. "A few."

"A few times in the past seven months? Yeah, sounds like you're living there."

"I just don't know how to let it go." She sniffed. "What if he does get sick of me and doesn't want me living there? Where do I go then?"

"Back upstairs." Fox said, "That apartment is for you and Scout. No one is going to take it away or not let you go back to it. You know none of us would do that even if you and Ransom did break up. I don't think that's happening, though. I'm pretty sure he would rather die."

She took a deep breath, and he kissed her on the head.

My mouth had dropped open. Not even knowing what to say or how to take this. Fox was nice, actually nice, to everyone but me, apparently.

I couldn't figure out what to think.

"I guess you're right. I just get so panicked. I know he wouldn't do anything to hurt me, but it's still hard to have my heart out there like this."

"I can imagine." Fox said, his voice still soft.

"I should go back and talk to him."

"Probably before the house is wrecked," Fox said with an easy smile.

"I'm sorry, Ash. I didn't mean to make you come down here for all this. We don't fight all that much, but when we do, I'm just a mess."

"It's ok. Really, go talk with him. We can hang out on a different night."

"Scout and I have these girls' nights. We have one planned this week. Do you want to come with us for that?"

"Absolutely." I said.

"Did you drive here?" she asked, turning to look outside. "I didn't see a car."

"No, just got a cab. It's all right. I can get back, just go."

"Fox, can you take her home? I feel bad. You spent all that money to get here. You shouldn't spend more to get home."

"It's fine. Don't worry about the money. I can walk home."

"No, Fox will take you. Right?"

A scowl came across his face. "Just go home, Quinn."

She nodded, pulling him into a hug and then me, saying thanks to us both before leaving. I stood still until she was down the road and then took off walking, not needing to spend another second around whatever asshole version of Fox I was going to get next.

"Ash, wait," he said, grabbing his keys and running after me. He had to stop and shut the garage door, so I was already on the sidewalk by the time he yelled again.

His car started, and I picked up the pace.

I heard him pull beside me as I walked. "Ash, get in," he yelled.

"I don't need to. I'm walking." I said, trying not to let the hesitation come through in my tone. The drive was only fifteen minutes, but walking meant an hour or more. Plus, I would have to weave through the college campus, which meant creepy guys lurking around as it got dark.

"No, you're not. Get in."

"Don't act like you have any authority to tell me what to do."

He sped up and pulled the car over, getting out and stomping over to me.

He was still shirtless, the sun fading on him as he stalked closer. I looked over his chest, my eyes lingering at the small black widow tattoo. Somehow, this golden boy looked like the devil in disguise. His blonde hair, bright blue eyes, and sharp jaw trying to trick us all into thinking he was an angel. Now all his anger and focus was turned on me and I couldn't believe the thrill that ran through me.

"Get in the car or I'm dragging you in."

"I'll fight back."

In a flash, he was behind me, pinning my hands hard against my back.

"I never doubted that."

"Fox." I gasped, heat pooling between my legs. "Let me go."

"No, you're not walking that far home alone. It's almost dark. We both know what happened last time you tried to do that."

He pushed me forward, still holding my hands behind me. “You’re hurting me.”

“No, I’m not. You just want me to loosen my grip so you can slip out.”

He held my wrists as we reached the car and I tried to pull away again. “How are you going to get me in the car without me running?”

He yanked me back into him, his mouth at my ear now. The sudden jolt against him made me hotter. “If you run, I am just going to catch you over and over again. I won’t be responsible for anything happening to you walking home alone.”

He pushed me forward, pinning me between him and the car. A quiet moan escaped me as I lost all control and pushed back harder against him. I knew I was supposed to be hating this, but I was only getting hotter the tighter he pushed against me.

“Wait, are you enjoying this?”

Embarrassment flushed across my face, and I was glad he couldn’t see it. “Well, you are pushing certain parts against me.”

With a quiet laugh, he took hold of both my wrists and wrapped his other hand around my throat. His fingers closed on my neck, each one flexing with a small amount of pressure.

Waves of heat and ecstasy washed over me from the powerful touch.

He pushed up against me more, every hard plane of his body against mine now.

“I like –” My words cut off as I took a breath, trying to find any shred of self control.

He laughed harder now, his body shaking mine.

“What, baby? You like my hands on you when you don’t have to see me? When you don’t have to look at my face and see what the fuck was done to it?” he growled. He tightened his grip higher on my neck, making it impossible for me to turn my head.

“That’s not fair to say when you won’t let me see you.”

"Get in the car," he growled in my ear, letting me go entirely, and I stood there frozen. I couldn't believe I had just let him grab me like that, and I was shocked at how much I liked it, not thinking twice about letting it continue. I ducked under his arm, starting back home.

And when he yelled out my name, I ignored him.

He could follow me or leave. I told myself I didn't care, but as his car quietly drove behind me the entire way, all I felt was relief.

ELEVEN
FOX

My phone started ringing, waking me from my deep sleep and making me curse. I'd barely been able to fall asleep, thoughts of a blonde hellion keeping me wide awake most of the night.

I don't know why she had to make that noise when I touched her, and I did not want to think anymore about how much I enjoyed it.

I still connected the call, a nagging worry that something could be wrong not letting me ignore it.

"Why are you calling me so early? I will literally be at the garage with you guys in like two hours."

"There is a rock through our window," Ransom said.

"What?"

"Someone threw a fucking rock through the garage window," he said again, slower this time.

"Just one?"

"Oh sorry, was that not enough for you? They chose the biggest window in the office and spray painted one of the cars that was outside."

"Damn. I can call to get the window fixed today. We'll send the car out to the paint shop."

"Yeah. Okay."

"Any ideas who it was yet?" I asked, already getting up and getting dressed.

"Not yet. Might know more in the next hour or so."

"Alright, I'll get up and head down there."

I clicked off and got ready, heading out before twenty minutes had gone by.

I knew Ransom was on edge after everything that happened to us last year, but things had been quiet for months. I doubt this had anything to do with that.

That thought was gone just as quick when I saw the car pull out behind me.

It was a brand new Nissan GT-R with a custom paint job, making it almost iridescent in the sun.

It trailed behind me, not staying close enough to cause a scene, but it was the dumbest choice of car to use if you were trying to keep a low profile.

Normally, I would choose not to lead them right to where I was headed, but based on the fact they knew where we lived, I already guessed they knew about the garage.

I called Ransom back.

"Hey, there's someone following me there. Do you want to grab a few photos?"

I told him about the car and slowed as I got closer. The car must have noticed the change because it suddenly turned, veering fast down a side street.

Ransom and Jax were out in front of the garage, waiting as I pulled in.

"They took off right before I got here."

"Who was it?"

"Don't know. Someone in a nice GT-R. No one that we know, though."

"Could it be someone from another race team? With a car like that, they would have to have money."

"Could be. Anything about who threw the rock?"

"Not much. Blacked out car with some detailing we couldn't make out. Looked nice but we couldn't decide what kind of car it was. Too far from the cameras."

"Fuck, I hate that this is happening," Ransom said.

"Then don't worry about it. You guys have enough to focus on with the races, and I can handle this. I told you I would help more, and I meant it."

"What are you going to do?"

"Go out and ask about the car, both of them now. At least if we narrow that down, we might get an answer."

Kye stopped as he walked up, eyes wide as he looked over at the window.

"What the hell happened?"

"Someone's pissed at us again. Know anything about it?"

"Nope," Kye said. He turned and headed to the car he was working on. I could see Ransom and Jax were thinking the same thing I was. Kye knew something he wasn't telling us.

"While I know Kye wouldn't be up to anything behind our backs to hurt us, we all know he's still getting himself into trouble. This could be something to do with him."

"And following you?" Jax asked.

"I don't know about that one unless he really pissed off the wrong person. I'm going down to the parts shop. I'll ask about the cars," I said.

"We'll clean up here," Ransom said. "And maybe keep a closer eye on Kye."

I headed out, making it to the parts store with a list of things

I needed to grab. By the time I made it inside, I had an extra fifteen texts from Ransom, Kye, and Jax adding to that list.

I sat making my order when a mess of blonde hair caught my eye.

"Ash?"

Her eyes widened as she looked around, seemingly looking for an escape.

"Don't let me stop you. You can run right out of here."

"I wasn't trying to run."

"Right. Everyone stands in the middle of the room like a deer in headlights looking for an exit."

"I was just surprised to see you here."

"At a parts store? One that my friends recommended to you?"

"I guess that would be the first place to find you," she huffed. "Well, I'm done anyway. I just came to get a few things Jax told me to buy."

She was at the counter checking out, and I groaned when I saw Liam walk in. I turned, hiding my face and hoping he would just leave me alone.

"Fox?"

"Liam."

"Haven't seen you around in a while. Someone said you got in an accident."

I didn't turn around. "Yep."

I caught Ash from the corner of my eye, turning and running right into Liam.

"Oh, sorry, beautiful. Didn't know you were going to whip around like that," he said, holding her arms as she steadied herself.

I didn't miss the small step back she made, or the jumping eyebrows. "Sorry."

She tried to step around him, but he moved with her, acting like it was an accident.

"I'm Liam, by the way."

"Ash," she said with a tight smile.

Honestly, I hated Liam.

We were never friends, but at some point we became enemies, and I knew he was going to be pleased to see my face shredded.

He ignored me, more interested in Ash.

"You come around here a lot? I don't think I've seen you here before," he said.

I finally turned back towards the counter, sick of Liam's lazy ass flirting that I could only hope was unwelcome. I didn't care if she was going to help the crew or not. If she started dating Liam, she was out.

"She hasn't until recently. She's racing with us for the Legends race now, though, so she needed a few things."

Liam stepped back after one look at my face.

"Oh, shit. What the fuck?" he said.

They set my parts on the counter and I grabbed them.

"He's an asshole, Ash. I suggest staying away from him," I said.

Liam laughed. "You're one to talk. If she's hanging around you lately, my face would be welcome company."

"Funny that we both know your face is only welcome because mine was ripped apart. See you later, Ash." I wasn't going to listen to any more of it. Liam was too much to deal with on a good day.

I realized as soon as I got in that I forgot to ask about the car that followed me.

I debated going back, but that idea was gone as I watched Ash walk out with Liam. My fingers tightened on the steering wheel. I wasn't getting back out now.

I did warn her.

If she wanted to mess with Liam, that was her problem.

It would give me a great reason to kick her off the team. A reason that the crew would agree with. Liam was known by everyone as a liar and a rat. He would turn his back on a 'friend' in a heartbeat if it meant he was given what he wanted. Most of the racers we knew didn't like him, so it seemed like he was floating around town now, trying to find his next group of victims to leech off of.

She stood talking to him and I tried not to care.

I guess it would be a win for me either way.

Either she runs off with Liam and I never have to see her again, or the crew gets their fair chance at racing and then I still never have to see her again.

I would be free from her soon either way.

TWELVE
ASH

I DIDN'T WANT to go to the races. I wanted to stay home, wrapped up in my fuzzy blanket with takeout. It made it worse that Fox didn't actually want me there, even if the rest of the crew seemed excited about it. It definitely added one more reason for me to stay in my house. Quinn seemed to have a different idea and demanded that I be ready and outside by eight.

I was learning fast that she was hard to say no to. They all were, and I knew they would also be asking me to race tonight.

My chest tightened, the old injury feeling fresh every time I thought about getting behind the wheel again.

I had to find a way to get over it, though.

Quinn pulled up, and I jumped in.

"We're swinging by the garage to get with everyone else," she said as we made our way over. She told me more about the crew as we went over, and I wasn't surprised when she spent extra time telling me about Fox and how great he always was.

I could see the garage now. The old brick building looking more welcoming than ever and I thought it could be the people that were starting to grow on me more than the building. Five cars were lined up at the edge of the parking lot, and each one started to pull out when they saw us round the corner.

"You don't ride with Ransom?"

"Sometimes, but sometimes I just like trying to race him there. The man never loses, and it's infuriating. Plus, I thought it would be fun to go with you."

She moved through the gears, trying to catch up to him. She was shifting at the right time, but slow. Every time she gained on Ransom, he would move out ahead. We came to a stop at a stoplight.

"You need to beat him off the line this time. I think it's the only way you'll come close to beating him," I said.

"I know, but I don't know how yet," she said. "It's really annoying."

"I know how." I smiled over at her, and her smile grew.

"Tell me what to do."

I walked her through it before the light changed. "Hold the steering wheel tight, though."

Quinn listened, and the car jumped forward as she raced Ransom down the street, the small change giving her a better head start.

She raced the entire way there, and I coached her, watching as she kept better speed with him now. Jax and Fox flanked her as we went down the highway, with Kye and Scout behind us.

"This is a pretty awesome crew you have."

She smiled. "Yeah, they are amazing. I haven't even been around for a full year and it feels like I've been with them my entire life."

"I'm jealous," I said, meaning it. I'd never had that. Even when I was little, I never had a true best friend. I thought it was David for a while, but everything changed after we started dating. Then, any friend I tried to find had already known that my family was rich and wanted to latch onto that.

"Don't be," she said, knocking my hand. "You're a part of it now, too. Pretty sure if you join the team to race, you have to be a part of the crew."

I gave a small smile, knowing it wasn't true. They didn't even know who I was, but I appreciated the sentiment.

We pulled into the races, each of them lining up in perfect unison next to each other. You could tell they were comfortable with each other's driving, probably coming here every week to hang out.

Countless other cars lined the street where they would race, everyone here to have fun, practice, and make money betting on races.

I tampered back more jealousy and got out.

"Shit," Jax said. "That was you driving, Quinn?"

Ransom had come over, picking her up. "That was amazing. You've gotten a lot better."

She smacked his arm. "No thanks to you. What, are you worried I might beat you? Ash helped me with all that."

"Sorry," I said, raising my hands. "I'm dedicated to helping any girlfriend kick their boyfriend's ass in a race," I joked, and he smiled back at me before turning to Quinn.

"No complaints from me. You can kick my ass in racing every single day and I'll come back begging for more."

"You two are so cute, it's sick." I said, turning away to Kye, who was looking at me with narrowed eyes.

"What's up, Kye?" I said.

He was quiet a lot of the time I had been around him, but it didn't seem to be for any other reason than he was listening and observing the world around him, ready to jump in when needed.

"You know you are supposed to be on our team. Are you ever going to tell us how you know how to drive so well?" Kye said, the statement blunt but not rude. Fox's eyes narrowed now too, but I didn't think it was for the same reason that Kye's had.

"Or if you even know how to drive at all," Fox added.

"Pretty sure you do know that I can drive, and do you really think I have an RX-7 and don't know how to drive at all?"

"Who knows? We know nothing about you. Maybe you were right. The night of you driving me to the hospital was a fluke, and you can't drive at all."

"Wow, you're in quite the mood tonight."

"Well, I don't want to be here, so let's get this over with." He leaned back on his car, scowling at everyone.

"That makes two of us," I mumbled.

Jax stepped towards me, nudging my arm.

"What do you say, Ash, want to race me and prove him wrong? We can sweeten the deal, and if I win, you take me out to dinner."

"That doesn't sound like it benefits me at all. What would I win?"

"If you win, I'll buy the next part for your car."

I laughed. "Part of my choice. You are not buying me a spark plug and calling it fair."

"Deal."

I was agreeing to the race before I could even think that I wasn't ready. I had always been ready to race, agreeing felt like second nature, but now panic and the reality of actually doing it was already setting in. I needed to get out of this.

Now.

"Well, while I would love to, I don't have a car to race," I said.

Fox reached into his pocket, pulling out his keys and handing them to me.

"Here, my car is all fixed now. Someone gave me a turbo that seemed to fix some issues. Let's see what you got."

I stared at the keys. Of course, he was going to step in and 'help' the exact moment I didn't want him to. He wanted to make sure I could drive, and he did say he would do whatever was needed to make that happen.

"No, I can't race your car."

"You can and will. I don't mind."

My hands started shaking, the keys rattling until I snapped my palm closed around them. He must have taken that as a yes, because he stood up.

"Go get ready, Jax. I'll get her set up."

He walked over to the car and beckoned me over.

I could only follow, my limbs feeling like a zombie as I went over and slid behind the steering wheel.

My hands still shook, and I gripped it harder, trying to focus on my breathing now, the shorts breaths doing nothing to calm me down.

Fox crouched down next to me, going over some of the buttons until he looked over.

"Ash, what's wrong?"

"Nothing. I just haven't raced in a while."

"Yeah, I don't think that's why you look like you're about to throw up. What's going on?" He pulled at my hands, trying to get me to loosen my grip. "Ash, take a deep breath. What's wrong?"

"I can't do this," I said, my breathing getting more shallow. "I can't."

I finally looked over at him, meeting his eyes as tears threatened mine. All I could think about was the wreck, the pain, the feeling that I would never get out. Each feeling nagged at my brain, telling me it was going to happen again the minute I tried to race.

He finally got my fingers uncurled and held onto them.

"Deep breaths, Baby. Just take a breath."

I struggled to pull in another, the overwhelming dread taking over making tears blur my vision.

"The last time I raced, I wrecked." My words were shaky, but I had to tell him. "It was bad. My car was pretty much totaled," I said, forcing each word out.

"Shit. Why didn't you tell me? Were you hurt?" His eyes scanned my body, but with the hoodie on, he would never see anything that happened to me.

"Yes. It took me a few months to fully recover, but the thought of doing this again." I took another deep breath. "I'm sorry. I don't think I can."

He stood up, his lip curling as he grabbed his hat, bending it in his hands before pulling it on again. "Of course you can't fucking do this. If any one of us would have known you were in a wreck, we wouldn't have asked you to do any of this in the first place. That could take months to be ready. And then, on top of that, it could take months to get you to a place to actually be winning."

"I am sorry. I really thought I could handle it."

"Right, like you didn't know you were having panic attacks just getting behind the wheel." He paced now, anger rolling off of him like electricity. "You lied and now we are right back at square one."

"You don't have to be such an ass. I tried, okay. I was going to try."

"I'm not trying to be an ass. I'm trying to figure out how the hell I'm supposed to tell everyone that they have to drop out because of you. Again."

I pulled at the harness that was over me, but not clipped yet.

"You know what? I'm leaving. Since it's all my fault that you can't race and I keep letting everyone down, then don't bother me again."

He grabbed for my hand, pulling me back to him.

"No, you are not running off. You agreed to race, even though you knew damn well this was happening, and now you are going to help me figure out how to fix it. You wasted a week of time that we could have been looking for someone else to help us. Why?"

"Because I wanted to try. I thought I could do it."

"Do you still want to try?"

"With you? No, I —"

"I don't care if you don't like me. Do you think I like you? Because of you, I look like a fucking monster. I don't care if we aren't friends. I need them in this race and that means I need to find someone to take my place. So I'm going to ask you again. Do you still want to try?"

He was still holding me, his grip getting harder as I tried to step back.

"Yes, but it's not that easy. I can't just get in, and magically be able to do it again."

"No, but you can get back in the car. You can take the first step."

"What? Did you not listen to me? I can't," I was almost yelling now, the sound of the races drowning me out.

He pulled me forward, dragging me back to the car, but it wasn't to the driver's seat.

"What are you doing? Where are you taking me?"

"We've all had wrecks before. If you would have told me, told any of us, we wouldn't have assumed you were going to be racing already. Every single one of us would have helped ease you into it. So, for now, the first thing you're going to do is go down the track again, but as the passenger."

"With you driving?"

"I can't formally race at the Legends race because of their rules, but this isn't a sanctioned race. I can see perfectly fine to drive."

I let him maneuver me into the passenger seat, too stunned to fight back as he sat me inside and pulled the harness over me.

I did want to race again, but I didn't think it would be as easy to fix as taking a ride down the track with him.

He flashed a bright smile. "Ready to trust me with your life again?"

THIRTEEN
FOX

"No, no, no, no. Maybe I'm not ready for that. Fox —"

I shut the door, leaving her to work it out herself.

She could get out if she really wanted to. I wouldn't force her, but I knew the first time back after a wreck was the hardest.

"Hey!" I yelled to Ransom, who was hanging all over Quinn. "Hey!" I yelled again, finally snapping his attention away from her. "I'm driving."

Eyebrows jumped and some furrowed, but no one yelled back.

By the time I slid in next to Ash, she was buckled into her harness. For some reason, that soothed part of me. At least she wasn't absolutely terrified of me if she was trusting me to drive.

"You're ready then?"

"Yes," she said, her fingers tight around the harness. "Other than my dad, I've never ridden with anyone else while racing."

"Worried?"

"Worried about racing down a road as fast as possible with a guy that may want to permanently disfigure me as payback for doing it to him? No, not at all."

"You think I would want you to be in pain to make myself feel better?"

I would be the first to admit that having to help the girl who was the reason your face was fucked takes your place with your own friends really did suck, but I wouldn't stoop that low. "I would never need, or want, an eye for an eye. Or in this case, a face for a face."

"I don't know. You hate me for what happened to you. I can't say I would blame you if you did."

"And yet you still stayed in the car." I pulled forward, angling through the heavy crowd, headlights and spotlights lighting the way, bringing me to the starting line. I was thankful my eyes weren't damaged because even with one bad eye, it would be hard to navigate these streets.

"I need to be ready to race," she said.

"Deep breaths. It will be fine, and I am not going to hurt you."

I pulled up near the starting line, waiting for Jax to get there, letting the car leave us in a rumbling quiet.

She looked over at me, eyes wide in surprise, and I followed her gaze, expecting to see Jax, but a pair of boobs filled the window instead.

I put the window down. "Can I help you?"

"Fox? You know you can always help me. I heard you got into a bit of an accident." She leaned down onto the window more, her boobs even further in my face. "I was curious how bad it was."

Somehow, things with this fucking cut only got worse. Now I was going to have this girl going off about how disgusting I was, right in front of Ash.

"Just curious?" I asked.

Fuck, this was going to be so embarrassing.

"Yeah, you know I'm sure you're still plenty fuckable though, babe," she said, laying a hand on my forearm.

I turned to her, letting her see the extent of the cut and trying to look as confident as I could.

Her eyes went wide, and she leaned back, forgetting to pull her hand away.

"Oh, wow. What happened?"

I went to answer, but Ash beat me to it.

She must have undone her harness, because she was suddenly leaning over me and placing a hand dangerously close to my cock. The moment I thought it was bad, it got worse.

Her face came close to mine as she looked up at the girl.

"He got in a fight for me," she said, her tone so sweet I barely recognized it.

She locked onto my gaze when our eyes met, unfazed by the cut on my face. "He doesn't like other guys touching what's his, you know?" Her eyes looked down at the girl's hand still on my arm. "I don't like it either."

The girl pulled her hand back. "Oh wow, I didn't realize—"

"Realize that he was still fuckable? Great, now you do know. I'm pretty sure we have to get ready for the race."

Ash didn't move off the top of me, and hell if she didn't adjust her hand a little higher on my thigh. If she moved any more, she was going to find out this vicious, sweet way she was defending me was actually turning me on.

This was the closest I have been to having sex in months, and there was no way I was going to be able to control the growing problem if she didn't move.

I couldn't even care that she was lying. The cut, and the pain, made me very much unfuckable, but when one of the hottest women you've ever met was touching, and defending you, was to care if she was lying or not.

"Ash," I warned.

"Have a good night," she said, hitting the button for the window. She moved back to her seat, pulling the harness back down and not saying a word.

"What the hell was that?" I asked, shocked at her coming to my defense so quick.

"Oh, come on, don't tell me you're mad at me in this situation. She was being an asshole. I just made her realize it. Who comes up to someone's car to check if they still want to fuck them? I can't believe that's who you were sleeping with."

I could only laugh as she continued to surprise me. "Is it any of your business who I was sleeping with?"

"No, but maybe choose people who aren't that shallow."

Jax's car revved up next to us.

"Time to go."

"Great. So excited," she said, annoyed.

Even if I didn't like her all that much, I still felt bad. Coming back after a wreck is the hardest thing to do.

I reached across, grabbing her hand and setting it on my right forearm.

"Just hold on. We'll be okay."

She nodded and took me seriously about holding on. Nails bit into my skin even though we still hadn't moved.

I knew as soon as I did it that I shouldn't have put her hand there. My cock was still thinking about her leaning over and touching me. Now it wasn't listening to my demands to focus on racing.

The guy brought us to the line, and I got the car ready, Ash's fingers digging in harder as I shifted the car.

"Deep breaths. You got this. I've got you."

"Fox," she whispered. The sound comforting something in me that I didn't know needed comfort.

We were seconds from taking off. Even though it wasn't a high stakes race, I knew it was high stakes for her. There was no need to worry about winning against Jax. I was only worried about getting her ready to race with the crew.

That's why we were here. That's why I was here. It was to get my crew in their competition and help them to win.

I would repeat that as many times as needed until my brain figured out that it was the truth.

The guy's arms went up, and I took off. Hitting through the gears until I was giving all that I was willing to with her in the car with me.

There was no reason to break my car on a practice run, anyway.

I made it down the track in seconds, but Jax still won.

Ash's pointed nails had to be drawing blood at this point with how hard she was digging into my skin.

"Are you okay?" I asked, as I turned the car slowly back down the track. She looked to her hand still on me and pulled it away. Her lip curled as though I suddenly disgusted her.

"I'm fine."

"Sounds like it. Tell me the truth, Ash."

"Yes, I'm ok. I'm glad I did that but you can imagine how embarrassing it is to not be able to do this."

"It's not embarrassing, it's normal. Coming back after a wreck is never easy. Do you know how many people never do?"

"Right now, I would like to be one of those people. I could be curled up on my couch watching a movie."

"What movie?" I asked as I pulled in, trying to distract her.

"What movie would I want to watch?" she asked, surprised that I asked.

"Yes. Which movie?"

Her brows furrowed when I looked over. "A comfort one. The Proposal, Pride and Prejudice. Oh, 10 things I hate about you."

"Hmm, interesting choices."

"Why? Because they are romance movies?"

"No. I've only seen one of them, and I liked it."

She pulled the harness off and turned in her seat, a smile spreading across her face. "Which one?"

"You made it down the track," I said, changing the subject. I tried to be tolerable. I was trying, but I couldn't pretend we were friends. And I thought admitting that The Proposal was one of my favorite movies would put us way too close to friends.

The fact that I was already wanting her hand back on me was already too much.

"Try to ride with someone else tonight and see if it helps. We will go out driving soon."

I jumped out, stalking off into the crowd. I needed a breath away from her. I needed to remind myself that we were not, and never could be, friends.

FOURTEEN
ASH

I WATCHED FOX DISAPPEAR, and I didn't blame him. I wanted to disappear too. So I did the next best thing and threw the hood of my sweater up, heading in the opposite direction of him, and hoping I didn't run into anyone who might recognize me.

When I finally slowed, I realized I made it almost the entire way around the track. I needed to slow down, so I started looking over the cars, not really paying attention to them as I tried to calm down.

"Like the car that much?"

A guy had come up next to me, his blonde hair and green eyes sharp in the dim lights.

"What? Oh, yeah. It's great." I said, and it was. The hood was up and I could see it was clearly well built.

"I'm glad you like my car. You're Ash, right? I met you at the parts store."

"Oh, yeah, I was wondering where I knew you from."

"That was me. You know, I don't see anyone in the car with Fox racing usually. Why the change?"

"He was showing me a few things." I looked over to Fox,

who was leaning against his car, watching the races, not even remembering I existed.

"I could show you a few things too, if learning is your interest."

Wow, I really walked myself into that one.

"No, thanks. Not interested in learning anything else."

The next race ended and I could hear laughing coming from Fox's direction. I looked up to see a few girls circled around him, and I knew it was the source of the laughter.

Was everyone out to see how fuckable Fox was tonight?

And should that really be bothering me?

I stalked over, forgetting about Liam, who jogged up next to me.

"Where are you going?"

"I have to talk to Fox."

I stepped into the little circle they had created with Fox, looking over each one of the girls. One of them was the same girl that had come over to the car earlier.

Liam came up behind us, putting himself between Fox and me, immediately making me uncomfortable.

"What's going on?" I asked, looking around at each of them.

"Just talking with Fox," one of the girls said.

I looked at Fox and his eyebrows jumped, his lips a thin line now. He looked as uncomfortable as I felt, and I didn't think I wanted to know what they were saying to him.

"Hey, Fox," Liam said. "What have you been up to? Ash, here told me you were teaching her some things about racing."

"Something like that," he replied dryly.

"How nice of you," he said, his smile growing. "Looks like being the local freak show is going to be your only chance to hang out with the girls now, huh? That cut is really going to make it harder to steal all the girls now, Fox."

"Never tried to steal any girls," Fox said. "I can't help that they would come to me."

The cocky statement making me smile, the small flicker of Fox coming out just when he needed him too.

The disgust on Liam's face deepened. I thought I could see it the other day, but it was obvious he didn't like Fox. "I'm not sure what girls you're going to pull now that you look like that."

A shiver of disgust ran through me. Liam sure seemed to like me, though.

He placed a hand on my lower back, slipping it down an inch like he was about to grab my ass.

I gave a sweet smile to Fox and then turned it to Liam.

"Does that mean you would offer to take me home tonight, Liam?"

He cocked an eyebrow. "Why? You don't want to ride with beasty here anymore?"

"That depends. Do you really want to go home with you?" I asked as sweet as I could.

If he was skeptical before, he wasn't now. "Yes. I think that would be best for all of us. And then you don't have to suffer through another night with him."

I gave him my fake smile that got me through plenty of situations when I needed to look sweet and innocent.

Fox's face was stone, and I couldn't tell if he thought I was serious or not.

"Well, too fucking bad. You couldn't even pay me to go home with you. Who says such nasty things to someone? And then thought you would get laid for it?"

I pushed him away and slid next to Fox. Now that I was close enough, I could hear the quiet laughing that rumbled his chest.

I took that as an invitation, moving closer as Liam's face turned more and more red.

"What a fucking bitch," Liam said, his eyes trained on me as he stepped forward.

Fox stepped forward, blocking any path Liam had to me.

"Don't even fucking think about it, Liam. Just fucking go. She doesn't want to go home with you. It was a joke."

"And you want me to believe she wants to go with you? Yeah, fucking right, Fox. Get over yourself. She just feels bad for you, and it's fucking pathetic."

I peeked around Fox, sliding my hands around his stomach.

"You're the one I feel bad for, Liam. That you think you could be so nasty to someone and still be attractive? I would think it's no wonder why any woman would choose Fox over you."

Liam's face drained of color before he exploded, jumping at Fox with fists raised. Fox pushed him back enough to make him stumble, his fists never even connecting.

Like they knew something was happening. The crew was suddenly surrounding us.

Luckily, I was no longer holding onto Fox and the only question Scout had as she sidled up next to me was, "Who's winning?"

"Fox, I think. Although, from the looks of them, Liam really didn't stand a chance to begin with."

Jax and Ransom grabbed onto Liam, pulling him farther away from Fox as Kye said something to Liam, making him turn and stalk off without another word.

"Wow, you guys are efficient," I said, the entire fight over within minutes of starting without a punch even being landed. "I'm impressed."

"These guys have gotten older now and don't want to fight as badly. A couple of years ago, there was no stopping their fist fights. It's almost like they've grown up or something," Scout said.

"Or something?" Fox asked. "Maybe it's because we have grown up and fighting doesn't sound as fun when you are in your twenties with a shoulder that already wants to fall apart."

"Fox was a big fighter," Scout said. "I still think you made money off those fights."

"And I will never tell you if that's true or not because you do not need to know," he said with a smile as he pulled her under his arm and into his side.

His eyes found mine, and I was just about to ask him more when a body came at me, picking me up with a yell of my name.

"ASH!" I scrambled, looking down to see my friend Ollie.

"Ollie?" I yelled, wrapping myself around him.

His face was full of happiness as he planted a kiss on my cheek.

"Where have you been, babe? I haven't seen you in so long!"

"Around here. School," I said, my words stopping as I followed Ollie's gaze.

He was looking right past me to Fox and Scout, who seemed to be staring at us. Actually, the entire crew was staring now.

"Well, hello handsome. Who is that looking at us? Oh my god, did you get a new boyfriend! He's hot. A bit dangerous." He wiggled his eyebrows. "That might be a good thing. Don't eat this one alive like the rest of 'em."

"No, he's not, and what do you mean, the rest of them?" I laughed.

Fox pushed away from the group still gathered around him.

"Going to introduce us to your friend? He seems to know you pretty well."

"Pretty well? She hasn't even told you about me? Wow, Ash, we've been friends for years. I'm Ollie. My boyfriend is around here somewhere, but he likes cars as much as she does."

"His boyfriend is a good racer and would race with me sometimes. We used to hang out a lot."

"Glad to hear that someone knows all about Ash because I'm realizing pretty fast how little she has told us."

"Oh." Ollie's face fell. "I see there's some trouble in paradise."

"Fox, now's not the time," I said. "Go back to your friends if you're going to be rude."

"Maybe it is."

"Okay, but can we talk about this tomorrow? This really isn't the place, and I don't need everyone in the world knowing my business."

"Why? What are you involved in that you can't tell us?"

The crew walked over, staying back, but not far enough that they couldn't hear every word.

I didn't need the entire crew to find out this way, and I knew Ollie could spill everything about me without even knowing I was keeping it a secret. I grabbed Ollie. "Come on. Let's go."

Fox's words made me pause. "You're going to have to stop lying to us at some point. Why not now?"

"I'll talk to you guys later." I said. My body felt undone, everything about the night leaving me strung out.

I pushed into the crowd, holding onto Ollie like an anchor as he brought me over to his boyfriend's car and whispered something to him. In minutes, I was loaded up on a quiet drive home.

FIFTEEN
ASH

THE THING that sucks more than lying to people you actually like is knowing that if you came clean, everything could change. It's not like my secret was necessarily a bad one, but it was a big one and I didn't know what to expect when I did tell them.

Deep down, I knew I owed Fox the truth, but fear was holding me back when it was clear to see that he hated me. Maybe I was making it a bigger deal than it needed to be, but having friends that just liked me for me was a feeling that I wasn't expecting to find when I agreed to help them race.

The moment everyone knew could mean the beginning of the end, and I hated to admit how much I liked this new beginning. I wasn't sitting alone in my apartment anymore. I wasn't grieving every single thing about my old life. I felt like the fog over me was clearing, and I even made a small amount of progress going back to racing.

It was a small step, but one that was putting me on a high. I felt like myself, or at least the self I wanted to be again.

With Fox, I was able to go down the track and not have a full panic attack.

The months of grief and healing took its toll until one day I lost myself completely, and I didn't know how badly I needed to go out and find her again until this morning.

I needed to be that girl again, but better.

Fox had his friends pushing him to heal and move forward, but I didn't think any of them understood as much as I could. If I didn't owe him before for saving my life, I owed him for what he did last night. He pushed me just far enough out of my comfort zone to see what I could have again, all while still keeping me safe.

I still didn't know how to help Fox, but I thought of something that could. It was why I found myself loaded up in one of the cars from our track along with two coffees and two donuts, heading to his apartment unannounced. I had texted Quinn to see if she would help me out and she rapid fired texts to me with where his apartment was, where I could park, and how he would be home all day.

I parked and made my way upstairs, trying to keep my heart from racing and hands from spilling coffee as I knocked and cracked the door open.

"Fox?" I yelled, walking into his kitchen area.

I spun at the sound of footsteps, nearly dropping the coffee and donuts at the sight.

"Yes?" he asked, scowling at my surprise visit.

"Oh, sorry," I said, looking anywhere else in the room other than his very uncovered body. "I figured you would be in bed or something."

"In bed? It's after twelve already. And why would that make barging in here better? Trying to bring me lunch in bed or just annoy me before anyone else gets the chance today?"

"Both? Although, I wasn't going to literally bring you lunch in bed. Just use it to coax you *out* of bed. I've been told you have plenty of days that you don't even leave your room."

"Well, step one is done then, and you have successfully annoyed me, so good job. Your work here is done. Now leave."

I finally looked back at him, crossing my arms as I tried to gain some sort of composure.

There he was, every bit of him on display, casually leaning against the counter, holding a cup in his hand, and wearing nothing but a towel hanging teasingly low on his hips. My eyes involuntarily traced the V-shape at his waist, and for a moment, I silently pleaded with the universe to let that towel slip.

"You are naked."

"I am not, and I wasn't aware people were just going to barge into my apartment."

"I brought coffee and food. Everyone said you weren't busy today."

"That really doesn't explain why you just let yourself in. What if I *had* been naked?"

"Then my curiosity would be satisfied right now."

"Well, you can keep being curious." He hadn't moved, but I could see a small twitch of his lips. "What are you doing here?"

I was lost in thought, staring down the length of him. I hated to admit how much I wanted to touch him. Abs like that were meant to be touched. I couldn't actually think of another reason to have them other than to let me run my hands over them and follow the lines down under the towel.

"Hmm?" I finally looked up, meeting his eye, and trying not to glance back down again. I would have been embarrassed if I weren't so invested in trying to figure out how big his dick was based on the towel outline.

Before I could let my eyes wander downward once more, he took a step closer, his hand gently tilting my chin up to meet his gaze. "Would you like to see what's under the towel?" he asked softly.

"I can't say that I would mind. Again, I'm curious."

"How about this?" he asked, walking around the corner and sitting down. "You come get on your knees and beg. Then, I drop the towel."

He flashed his cocky smile, taking a sip from his cup, and a surge of frustration made me want to wipe that winning smirk right off his face.

But I wasn't going to. No, today was different. I came here with a purpose, and that purpose was to offer my assistance, not to engage in a battle of egos.

Today, I was determined to be kind and helpful.

"Not a chance."

"Then you're not seeing anything, so keep your eyes up here and tell me why you're in my apartment."

I handed him the coffee, taking his cup out of his hand and setting it down next to him. "This one's better."

"This one is a bribe."

"That's true, but a delicious one."

"Maybe," he said, taking a sip. "Tell me what you want."

"To go out for the day."

He stared, still sipping the coffee, and I tried not to let my eyes slip lower again.

I failed.

My eyes jumped back to his, and I swore. I definitely saw an outline that time.

"Can you please get dressed?"

"Again, this is my apartment. I could be naked if I wanted."

"Alright, go ahead then," I said. It was my turn to sip my coffee and stare.

I won this time as he got up.

"Hellion," he mumbled. "I am going to get dressed only because it seems like I'm not getting you out of my apartment until you tell me what you want, and that doesn't seem to be happening until you stop trying to decide how big my dick is. This does not mean I'm playing into whatever scheme you have. We aren't going out for the day."

"Or how small," I said to his back as he headed into his room.

"Excuse me?" he said, stopping at the door.

"Or how small your dick is," I said louder with a shrug. "I'm just saying."

"Do you go around wondering about these things often?" he asked, leaning against the doorway with a smile.

Each move was killing me.

I could honestly say I've never cared about a man's body the way I was suddenly caring about his, but there was no way I was going to tell him that.

It's like every little inch of ground I gained, he found a way to call me out on it.

With a laugh, he turned and made his way into the bedroom.

"Jerk," I muttered, sitting to eat and drink my coffee.

By the time I was halfway through my donut, he walked back out.

"You know I heard that, right? Not making a convincing argument to want to hang out with you all day if you're already calling me names."

"There's no argument. I already have the day planned. We already have tickets to a game, and I rented a car."

"Why would you rent a car? We have cars. Plural," he said, seeming to mind a little bit less that I was there now that he had something to eat.

"Because we are going out to have a fun day and you're going to like it, so I got a fun car."

"What game are we supposedly going to?" he asked, biting

into the last of his donut. I made a mental note that one was definitely not enough.

"We can go grab something to eat and then we're going to a baseball game."

"Why?"

"To have fun?"

"You think I'm going to believe that you are doing all this just to have fun? I'm going to ask again. Why are we going out?"

I crossed my arms, figuring this wouldn't be a time to lie.

"Listen, you helped me a lot with the racing stuff already, and the saving me stuff. I want to help you now."

"Help me how?" he asked, cocking an eyebrow.

"By going out and having a good day, and getting over this idea that you should hide yourself away up here or be so upset every time you do have to go out," I said, trying to keep my tone nice. I have been told I have a bitchy tone, and knew now wasn't the time to let that out.

"And you think one day will fix all of that?"

"No, of course not. Just like me riding with you once during a race isn't fixing me, but it's a start."

"I guess I'm not understanding how going to a game and out to eat is going to help."

"By getting you out and seeing that people either don't care what you look like or do still think you're hot."

"So your plan is to take me out, give me a pity party of some sort, and then try to get me laid?"

My stomach rolled. "I'm not out trying to get you laid. Maybe just a phone number if you really need it."

"No, thanks. I don't need any more phone numbers. The women that have my number now either run at the site of me, or barge into my apartment and force me on dates. It's a lot to keep up with either way," he said with a deep laugh.

"I am not forcing you on a date. It's just going out with a friend."

"Friends? Not really. And anyway, my friends do not walk in here and look at my dick like that."

"Fox!"

"Ash."

"Can we just go?"

"What's in it for me?"

"I'm helping you feel better."

"Yeah, right? What is actually in it for me?"

I leaned back, already knowing this was coming.

"Aside from taking you out for a day and paying for everything while letting you drive the car I have? How about I be a barrier for you."

"A barrier? What are you going to be, my bodyguard or something?" he asked, crossing his arms. I was losing him more than getting him interested.

"For when you want to sit up here and feel bad for yourself. I can help you get the crew to give you space if you want."

"How?"

I shrugged. "I don't know. I'll tell them we are out practicing. They think you are gone for the day, but really you just get peace and quiet."

"And you're doing all of this because you feel bad for me?"

"No, I'm doing it because you have helped me and deserve some help back. And what's the harm anyway? We go out and if you don't have fun then you come back here and keep doing what you have been doing."

"What car did you rent?"

"You have to agree before you get to know."

"Fine. We have to stop for another coffee, though. This is delicious."

"Wow, look at that. Already feeling good enough to make demands."

"It does help the ego to have a girl come around begging to hang out with me," he said, pulling on a hat and heading to the door.

I jumped up, following after him. "I wasn't begging."

"Bribing, begging, same thing."

"I don't beg."

"We'll see. Where are the keys?"

"What have I done?" I mumbled, pulling out the keys. We made it to the garage before I could hand them over.

As soon as I did, he stopped, making me run into his back.

"What are these?"

"Keys, Fox. It's how you drive the car."

"Smartass," he said. "What the hell kind of car did you get?"

"Come on." I reached for his arm as my smile grew. "Come on. Come see."

I pulled him outside to the Jeep. It was the fastest one I could come up with that wasn't too over the top. I still needed the idea that I rented it to be somewhat believable.

"A Jeep?"

"The fastest one I could find."

"A track hawk? Hell, yes," he said, jumping into the driver's seat and starting it up.

I jumped into the passenger seat and was surprised to see Fox smiling. The genuine happiness on his face was a little shocking after days of scowling.

"Worth spending the day with me?"

"Maybe. I'll let you know after the second coffee," he said, but he was still smiling. The ease that had come over him made me even more relaxed.

We made it to the same diner where I grabbed the coffee and sat down to eat.

Even as we sat there, I still felt at ease, Fox being friendly enough and surprising me at how much we had in common.

It made me quickly realize the flaw in my plan.

When Fox dropped the attitude and didn't worry about the cut, he was charming as hell, and I couldn't help but love every minute of it.

SIXTEEN
FOX

BY THE TIME we made it to the game, I felt better.

Unfortunately, Ash was catching on that her plan was working, and I was having a hard time hiding it.

She wasn't pressuring me to have a good time. She was just making me go out. She hadn't even asked if I was enjoying myself, and really, I couldn't imagine she actually cared all that much. It seems like she just felt responsible to try to help me.

I thought she would be pissed at me after I was a dick to her at the races, but if she was still, she hadn't brought it up.

"Fox? Are you listening?" she asked. "Do you want another drink?"

I finally looked back over at her. She had dressed up for the game in shorts and someone's jersey. Honestly, I didn't know any of the players. I barely watched anything other than racing, and even that was rare anymore. I was too busy at the garage, and since the cut, I hadn't wanted to watch anything related to racing when I knew I wasn't going to be able to race with the crew.

It didn't matter if I knew whose jersey it was or not. She

looked amazing. I expected to feel more self-conscious, but her laid-back attitude was working, and my mind was wandering away from the cut. Far enough away that I was realizing how hard I would have been chasing her if it wasn't for the scar. And that was bringing a whole new awareness to us sitting so close.

"Yes, please," I finally said, shifting in my seat and hoping she hadn't seen how much I was looking at her.

"Wow, a please? This really is working. I'll be right back."

She headed down, and I watched as some of the players looked over, watching her walk down the stairs, and I could only roll my eyes.

I couldn't blame them, but the nerve of someone to openly stare like that at a girl he didn't even know. Like there wasn't a doubt in his mind that he could get her.

It hit me then that I had been the same way. Could I really have looked like that before? The cocky grin, the open stare, the blatantly large ego that let everyone know what I was doing and why.

I should have gone with her.

She was trying to be nice and I could try to do the same.

As I debated what to do next, I figured that helping her would at least get it off my mind. She had already passed the players by the time I made it down the steps, but the same one who had been staring at her before stopped her. I couldn't hear his words yet, but his smile let me know that it was all flirting. It was the smile I would have had on my face if I met her in any other way.

Even that night, before the cut happened, I saw her walk out and had already been debating talking to her but was so caught up in the car and being lost that she had disappeared behind the corner before I had a chance. And seconds later, she had been running right back at me.

I made it down the steps and tried not to flinch at the thought of the knife again. I needed to get over thinking about the pain. It was the worst part, and sent me into a spiral each time. I thought of her in those damn heeled boots instead, wondering if she still had them.

"Really?" Ash said, smiling back at him as I walked up.

It was fine. She could stay down here and flirt. I just wanted my drink.

"Oh yeah, do you want to come down and see it?" The guy offered.

"Hey," I said, interrupting and trying to suppress the curl of my lip. The guy looked over at me, his eyes widening just enough to notice.

"Whoa dude," he said.

"I know. I just came to carry the drinks," I said, looking at Ash, who smirked.

"Of course. Thanks so much."

I rolled my eyes and grabbed them from her, standing frozen for a second.

"That's it." I turned, gritting my teeth at my own awkwardness. One cut and my entire life goes out the window. I couldn't even carry on a normal conversation anymore. I wanted to bang my head against a wall. I always knew what to say, social outings didn't give me anxiety before and now all I could think about was what to say to not sound ridiculous, how to react to people's obvious stares, or even what I was supposed to do with my hands. I was always comfortable in the world and now each time I went out felt like the first time in my life.

Just like now, the entire time I couldn't think about anything other than I was marred, and he wasn't. It stopped all ability to continue a conversation.

She *should* stay down there with him.

A hand snaked around my bicep, latching on as I walked back up to our seats.

It was Ash, holding on and smiling at nothing.

"What are you doing? You can stay down there. I'm fine."

"No, thanks. I just stopped to be nice. I'm glad you came down."

She stumbled, holding tighter on my arm as I went up another set of steps. I stopped, letting her get her footing before starting again.

"Slow down, Bigfoot. My legs aren't that long," she said.

I would beg to differ, but ignored the thoughts of her long legs.

"Not my fault, Bambi. You're walking like you've never done it before."

She huffed, but kept quiet as we sat back down.

I regretted the short walk back as soon as her hand left my arm. Every second she was touching and talking to me kept making me forget everything else. I didn't know how all the bad thoughts could come crashing back to me one second, and then disappear like a distant memory when she touched me.

"How in the world do you have a group of friends that love you so much when you are so impossible sometimes?" she asked.

I smirked. "They luckily met me when I was nice and charming, not a jerk, as you called me. Now they just feel obligated to stay around me."

She rolled her eyes. "They obviously think you have redeemable traits. I'm still waiting to see them, though." Her smile grew, and she knocked against my arm.

I turned back to the game with a laugh, but I didn't know what to say. I hoped those things were still in me, but if they were, it was buried underneath my own pity and anxiety.

A few minutes later, she leaned back into me. The smell of coconut and vanilla hit me, and I had to resist the urge to move closer.

"See any girls you want to talk to?" she asked, a startling reminder that we were not on a date.

"Why? Ready to play wingman? Maybe I can find a girl and we can go on a double-date. Your boyfriend down there will be so excited," I said. It was a joke. I didn't want to deal with dating in any capacity. I couldn't imagine the questions and looks that would come with trying to hit on anyone.

She looked down and didn't seem surprised when the player winked at her.

"Fine, if that's what you want. What girl did you want to talk to?"

I looked at her as she scanned the crowd. I didn't know if I should be in awe of her for being so nice to me when I've been so terrible, even to the point of finding me a date, or annoyed that she really thought I would come with her and leave with another girl.

"Haven't seen one yet."

"Want to walk around and look?"

I drug my hand over my face. "No. What do you think is going to happen? We walk around, I point to a girl, and you force her to hang out with me too?"

"No. Something more like we walk around. You see a girl you want to talk to and then you walk up and flirt with her. Something I've heard that you have done plenty of times, and can do again."

"What's that supposed to mean?"

She laughed. "Don't act innocent. Quinn and Scout have informed me that you're a player and a flirt. Now come on, let's go." She grabbed my arm to stand up, but I held her in place.

I would do a lot of things to keep her off my back, but this wouldn't be one of them.

"Not a chance. Maybe I *was* a flirt or a player or whatever you want to call it before, but not now."

The day was quickly going downhill.

"Then how are we supposed to make you feel better?"

I couldn't hear her, though. The words were drowned out as I saw both of our faces come across the jumbotron. It was my face I couldn't look away from, though.

There was nothing like hating how you look and then having it blown up on a big screen in front of thousands of people. Even on a good day, being put on a kiss camera next to a girl that didn't want to kiss you was my own personal horror story.

I wanted to stand, but my legs went numb. Ash grabbed my arm and said my name, but I could barely hear over my racing heartbeat and the crowd's constant chanting.

"Stop. I'm leaving. Now."

Her hands wrapped around my face and she turned my head.

In seconds, her lips were on mine and I could hear the crowd's tone change, but I was lost to what they were saying.

I was frozen. Ash's lips moved against mine and her tongue swiped against my lips. Like muscle memory, I finally made a move, kissing her back and exploring her mouth with my tongue.

I didn't know if it was the fact that I hadn't kissed anyone in months, or that it was so unexpected, but fuck if it wasn't the best kiss of my life.

It had to stop.

"Ash, that's enough. Pretty sure your point was made."

"No, I don't think it was yet."

She tried to pull me back in, but I held her in place.

"No, it's done. All of this is done."

"It's not done if you don't stop it."

"I'm stopping it. I need to get out of here."

Her face fell, and she turned, looking forward for a second before standing up. "Okay, let's go."

"Okay," I said. I didn't want her to be mad, but I wasn't

going to be able to take anymore. Everyone in the stadium would be looking at me now.

She didn't race ahead of me. She didn't shy away when our arms bumped. She just held her head up and walked out. We made it down to the bottom of the steps and the guy from earlier tried to get her attention. I don't know if she didn't see or didn't care, but she walked right past, strutting out of the stadium like she owned the place. There was something in the way that she moved that left me stunned. I basically just humiliated her in front of everyone, but she wasn't letting anyone see that it bothered her.

Maybe it really didn't.

By the time we made it to the car, I was even more of a mess.

We got in and she slammed the door.

"How did you think kissing me was going to help the situation?" I finally said.

"I don't know. I couldn't let you sit there spiraling into whatever place you were headed. How did it make it worse? Was it that terrible?"

"No, I just don't know how any of this was a good idea."

"I was trying to be nice. Why are you freaking out about this? It's not like I'm going to be pining after you and chasing you around like a puppy dog. I was just trying to help."

"That isn't what I was concerned about," I said through gritted teeth.

"Then what?"

"I don't know what to do!" I finally yelled. "It's like two fucking people in my head. There's the person I was that would have kissed you in a fucking heartbeat without a thought, and then there's me now that doesn't even know what to do when you kiss me. It's like two people constantly fighting and I know what I should be doing, or could be doing, but it's not working. My brain can't just shut up and do it and my body won't move without my brain. All the time. Every fucking day has become a fight." I was basically yelling, losing all control as my heart raced. I felt suffocated. The car was too small without enough air.

"Deep breaths, Fox," she said, the words calm and sweet. The same stupid words I told her.

I gave a tight laugh, the painful sound making me feel more pathetic.

"It's like that when I race," she said quietly. "It's like my body knows what to do, but my brain won't let it. It starts rolling through every second of the wreck and just paralyzes me. I know I can race, I know how, my body knows how, but each time I just can't do it."

"To me, that makes sense with racing, but I can't make it make sense for just living my life."

"Maybe that's because you know steps to take for fixing it with racing, but not with life?" she asked, seemingly tiptoeing around my feelings based on the flinch of her face.

"Sorry about the outburst."

"Have you thought about the fact that you could be having panic attacks?"

"I feel like I would know if that was happening."

"You would be surprised. I didn't know that's what was wrong with me until I had a few of them. I wasn't trying to make anything worse with the kiss. I truly thought it might help distract you."

I didn't hate the kiss. I hated that it happened because she pitied me, not that it happened, but I didn't think there was any use saying it out loud. She would swear up and down that she didn't pity me to be nice and then pretend everything was fine.

My hands flexed on the steering wheel as I took another deep breath.

"Thanks for at least going out for a while. I don't get out

much lately and I was actually enjoying myself before all that," she said.

"Up until you had to try to make out with me," I said, trying to smile, but I didn't have it in me. It didn't seem to faze her, though.

"No, I enjoyed that too. Although, if there's a next time, I expect a bit more enthusiasm and participation. You know, sitting there doing nothing for seconds on end isn't the best technique," she was smirking now, trying to lighten the mood, and I appreciated her not fixating on my confession.

"Well, I wasn't expecting you to try shoving your tongue down my throat. Really caught me off guard." I relaxed in the seat, feeling better knowing there weren't thousands of eyes on me.

"I did not!"

"You did too," I said.

"I was trying to be nice. You looked like you were in hell."

"Baby, you're so nice to me, it's making me sick. Don't think you have to kiss me just to be *nice*. That's not how this works. I don't take pity in the form of physical favors."

"That's not what that was."

"Why are you lying? Again. Stop acting like you did anything back there except feel bad for me and try to make it better."

"Is that so horrible?"

"Yes, it is. I would rather live the rest of my life never being touched again, or to be the laughingstock of an entire stadium, then have someone do it because they feel sorry for me."

She didn't say anything for a while as I headed back to the apartment.

"You act like it's so terrible. Like no one can stand to look at you. That's not true."

"Isn't it? Do you know what people have said to me? How

they react? I have to see it over and over and over. That damn flinch that everyone does when they look at me. They think my face is disgusting, then they feel sorry for me. Even you did it when you met me. Do you understand what that's like? I can't go anywhere and just live my fucking life."

"What does it matter what they think? Why wouldn't you just ignore them? Aside from the attitude, you obviously have a good personality somewhere in there if your friends love you so much. Why do you think the only thing you bring to the table is your face?"

I forced out a laugh. "Isn't that easy for someone beautiful to say? That's what you say to people you don't find attractive. And as for ignoring them, you try to ignore someone flinching as they talk to you."

"Beauty is in the eye of the beholder," she said.

"Great, break out cliche quotes. That does help."

"I'm just saying that people who care about you don't care if there is a cut on your face. I'm sure some people even find it more attractive knowing how you got it. It's an obvious sign of your strength."

"Easier said than done," I said, turning onto my street.

"But you can do it. You can keep getting better, and healing, and soon you'll feel like it's not even there."

I parked the car on the street outside my building, letting the car idle in front. She made it sound so easy, like I could just forget that it was there. And just like everyone else, she wanted me better.

She wanted me to be different.

That realization ruined every part of the day that I had enjoyed.

"You have a lot of fucking nerve telling me how to live my life like this when it's your fault. If I had never met you, I would be fine. I would be racing, I would still be good-looking, hell I probably wouldn't have had to live the last two months of my life in constant pain. Saving you wrecked my life, so don't you fucking dare act like you have any room to judge me or how I'm handling it. I thought you were taking me out to try to have a nice time, but it's just like the rest of them. You want me back to who I was. *That's* who you wanted to be with today. Not me. Him. Sorry to disappoint. Don't fucking do that again."

I got out, slamming the door behind me and only seconds went by until hers opened and slam shut.

"Fox, wait! You're right, I shouldn't have gone that far. That's not what I meant. I wasn't —"

"I don't want to hear it. Thanks for the day. The car was fucking great," I said, cutting her off and walking inside. I wasn't going to sit around and listen to more. She was going to tell me anything I wanted to hear. Apparently, that's what she had been doing all day.

I knew the guilt would be a lot from her side, but it didn't mean I had to wait around and hear her pretty lies.

I only needed her to help the crew. I didn't need her to be my friend.

Now I just needed to remember that, and forget about that fucking kiss.

Fuck my life that I was hot for the girl who made me completely un-fuckable.

SEVENTEEN
ASH

I SPENT the rest of the night, and into the day, thinking about Fox and that damn kiss.

The second I touched him, I had know that it was a bad idea.

The thought of kissing him caused a heat to rush through me, and I tried to shut it down.

I think it was clear why he didn't like me. A little too clear, honestly, but I knew I couldn't blame him. I would hate me too if the roles were reversed.

At the end of the day, he wanted to help his team win, and then for me to leave. I was the reason his life was ruined, and he didn't want me around.

I don't know what I was thinking. At first, I did just feel bad, but the more I was around Fox, the more I wanted to keep being around him.

But I needed to put an end to it, needed to just work on my racing and finish all of this. I didn't need a group of friends who I was lying to or to like a guy that couldn't like me. I was supposed to be working on my courses, healing, and finding a way to talk to my dad and fix this mess with David.

I was surprised to realize that I didn't miss everything from my old life, but I still didn't know what life I did want now.

Any identity I had in my life before was gone and I didn't know what pieces I was supposed to pick up and take with me, or where I was going.

I flopped back over my couch, the weight of my own thoughts dragging me down. I wanted to curl up and watch a movie, but a knock at the door made me freeze.

I wasn't expecting anyone to come to my apartment. It had become my own little hidden sanctuary and aside from the crew and Ollie, no one knew I was here.

Would Quinn or Scout come? Maybe it was one of the guys to pick up my car.

Or maybe it was my lucky day, and it was Fox here to beg for forgiveness.

I pulled open the door and fear shot through me. I moved to shut it quickly, but his hand reached up to stop it.

"David." I pushed the door back until it was almost closed, leaving only an inch or two to talk to him. My phone was still sitting on the couch and the moment I let the door go, he was going to let himself in.

My heart pounded, thudding so loud in my ears that it made me feel dizzy and lightheaded.

"Hey Ash." His voice was quiet, sad even, but I knew now it was fake.

"What are you doing here?"

"I came to see how you are doing."

"No, you didn't. What do you want?"

"Of course I did. You haven't been home in months. I just finally tracked you down a few weeks ago and then you ran from me. Luckily, Celina felt so bad for me. She told me where you lived yesterday."

It was a lie. Ollie was the only person who knew David, and knew where I was now, and he wouldn't have told him.

"No, she didn't. She doesn't even know where I live. I don't know how you found out, but you need to leave," I said, moving to shut the door.

His hand came up to stop it. I tried to push it back, but he was stronger, holding it firm.

"*Fine*, I followed you home from the gym. I knew you would have to go there at some point. I'm sorry, I just needed to find a way to talk to you and you won't respond to me."

My skin pricked, knowing whatever was happening wasn't good, and definitely wasn't about to get better. My chest tightened, cutting off my breathing more.

"Come on, Ash. This is ridiculous. You need to come talk to us. I miss you. Your dad misses you. We want to move on and work on the business. We just need you there now."

"Really? For what? To stand by your side and act like the perfect little girlfriend while you go out fucking other girls and tell me you're not? Or to give you my cars, trophies, and life so that you don't have to feel like your girlfriend is better at something than you?"

"It was like one time with another girl and I said I'm sorry. I was drunk. As for the cars and trophies, I have my own."

"Barely. You used my wreck as a reason for you to take *my* place at *my* races that I had lined up. Why would I ever come back to that? As for the other girls, it was sure as hell not one time. I have proof of at least three separate occasions. That's the least of my concerns now, though."

Not that I cared anymore, but I wasn't dumb enough to delete the evidence.

"It was just one time, and it was only because of the after party. You know how it gets after a race. I get all hopped up and need somewhere to go. I love you, though. You're the only one I care about. We can move past this if you just give it a chance. Things were not that bad. You were still hurt from the wreck and I think now that time has passed, you would see that it can all be fixed."

My lip curled, disgusted that I ever liked this man. It was only a by-product of being told your entire life that you two were meant for each other, that you're destined to be together only because your parents were best friends. And I fell for it. I fell for the belief that he was perfect for me, when in reality he only wanted to quiet me. He wanted me weak and incapable, hating every moment that I spoke up or fought back. He hated that I raced and was better at it. Every day I spent with him made me lose more and more of my mind until I couldn't figure out what was real or not.

"We did give it a chance and then you tried to wreck my career. I can move past a lot of things, but that isn't one of them."

"Are you really one to talk to me like this, Ashton? I saw that fucking guy drop you off the other day, or should I say, saw him grabbing at you and following you home. I almost called the sheriff."

"What are you talking about?"

"I saw it. He followed you back here. His stupid fucking car. What's his name?"

"You're stalking me?" I asked, my voice going higher.

I had come to expect a lot of shitty things from David, and had gone out of my way to not let him know where I was, but it was surprising to hear how close he had been watching me, invading my life when I didn't even know it.

I had never felt that level of invasiveness in my life, and it was making my skin crawl.

"That's none of your business. We haven't been together in months. Where I go, and who I go with, isn't your business."

"We didn't break up, Ash. You said you needed to get away for a while. What am I supposed to think that means?"

I laughed. "If you thought we were still together, then why have you been sleeping around?"

"I haven't been sleeping around."

"So you haven't slept with anyone else since we broke up?"

"I mean, I didn't say that. I did get lonely, but that was only because you left me."

I didn't hide my gag. "You're pathetic and I know the game you're playing. Poor David. Like you're the victim in all of this? You know what? It doesn't matter either way. I don't want you here. Leave. Now. I know what happens next and I'm not going to stand in my apartment and be told I'm the one losing my mind."

"No, I need to know why you won't talk to me. You haven't responded to any of my texts."

"I blocked your number."

I cut David off and barely talked to my dad. His idea of a conversation was wondering why I wasn't talking to David, not apparently caring that he was trying to ruin my life and my grip on sanity.

He had even managed to get my dad on board about not letting me go back to racing. Although my dad said 'not yet', he would never clarify when I would be allowed to try again. Now, I was just supposed to rise above that and forgive him, the perfect girlfriend, one day the perfect wife. I'm sure the comments on me needing to stop driving fast cars and leave that to the men would have come in full force if I stayed. They had already been on track for that conversation, their subtle hints not so subtle any more.

"Those girls didn't mean anything," he said.

"I saw multiple girls driving your car around. I know exactly what that means." He was so possessive of his cars. I hadn't noticed at first, only getting to touch his cars after we had sex. It was like some disgusting prize that I didn't know about.

I knew exactly what a girl driving his car meant, and I had taken notice of it happening, even if I didn't care.

He made me feel like I'd lost my mind and there were so many times I thought I had. Convincing me that he didn't say things, or didn't mean it how I took it, even deny things I had complete proof of. It was to the point that I questioned my own sanity because of his words.

"David, you need to leave."

"I had to come by and ask you a question."

"No, just go."

"What, you don't even care what I have to say?"

"Why would I?"

"Because you're supposed to love me," he said.

Something churned and if I wasn't uncomfortable already, I was now. The feelings shifted as he gripped the door harder. "Go away, David. This is going too far. You don't actually need anything and you need to leave."

He ignored me, though. "No, I can't. I need you. What have you told your dad about me? Why is he suddenly so adamant that you need to come back before we move forward with the business? He's not even letting me race, Ash. What did you tell him?" His voice shook in anger and I knew we were passing the point of this ending with any decent outcome.

"Did you come over here just to threaten me about talking to my own dad?"

"No. No. Sorry, I really did come to see how you are doing. I've just missed you. I've missed you so fucking bad." His hand snaked in, reaching to grab me.

I shrieked, slamming his arm in the door. He slammed back, the door swinging open full force and knocking into the side of my face, my jaw exploding in pain.

I stumbled back, as the world realigned. "Shit, Ash, I'm so sorry. Why didn't you move? Why did you hit my arm? It was just a reaction. Shit," he was inside the apartment now, pulling me back up and putting his hands all over me. "Why were you in the way? Let me get you ice."

A gutted laugh bubbled up from inside me. "In the way of you pushing the door into my face? We've been here, haven't we?" I held my face, and screamed, "Get out. Just get out or I'm calling the cops." I was already scrambling for my phone as he ran out the door, not looking back.

The next twenty minutes were a string of curse words as I put ice on my face. Luckily, it wasn't bad. Some redness and a bruise was all that would be left, but it still hurt like hell. How Fox had made it through getting his face cut up was beyond me.

It was no wonder why he was always being an ass. I couldn't even think straight as the pain thrummed through me.

I had moved out, moved away, cut off contact from David, but my dad hadn't. My friends hadn't. No one else had noticed how far he was spiraling out of control. Part of me even wondered what was really happening that was making him desperate enough to start stalking me. I was surprised that my dad wasn't having him take over my spot in the races, but it did make sense with how bad he was at it.

I glanced around. My apartment feeling different than it did before. I knew I didn't want to be here tonight.

I grabbed my keys and phone, locking the door behind me.

I didn't know where I would go at first. Most days like this, I just drove around, but I didn't feel like being alone now.

I pulled off into a parking lot, taking a deep breath. I knew exactly where I wanted to go.

I texted Quinn.

Are you busy tonight?

Movie night at Fox's. Want to come?

I groaned. Of course it was there.

No. Don't want to crash your party.

The phone started ringing, Quinn's name flashing.

"Please come," she said. "It will be fun. There's no such thing as crashing a movie night that you are invited to."

"I don't know. At Fox's? I think I'll skip this one."

"No, come on. Isn't there some rule for bonding before you race together? Shouldn't you all get together and hang out?"

"No," I said with a laugh. "No rules for that."

"Give me the phone," Scout said. "What are you doing tonight that's so important that you can't hang out with us?"

I looked into the mirror, the bag of ice still pressed to my face. "Nothing, I just don't think I need to hang around more than necessary."

"Not true. And quite honestly, I was going to invite you to girls' night next week, but if you're only interested in us because of racing, then I guess —"

"Scout, you know that's not the only reason. I like hanging out with you guys. I just know that I'm not welcome tonight."

"No, no, I understand," she said, feigning sadness. "I didn't take you for one to run away from a challenge, and we all know Fox is a challenge right now, but if you don't like us, that's fine." The dramatic sigh at the end really added to her theatrics.

"Scout!" I yelled, laughing now. "You know that's not true."

"No, it's fine. Sit at home alone instead of in the company of funny, exciting people."

"It's not like I want to sit here alone tonight, I just —"

"Great! Then come over. I'll keep the beast at bay and you

can enjoy your night. See you soon!" The words came out, and she hung up, not giving me a chance for a rebuttal.

Fox wasn't lying when he called them vipers. They knew what they wanted and got it, and I respected them even more for it.

I did like hanging out with them. And aside from Fox, they did all seem to like me enough to have me around. After the game, I didn't know if he would even want to look at me, but I could always leave if he was obviously upset.

I got ready, holding the ice as I went. It was the first time in so long that I might have friends that weren't just hanging out with me for my last name. People that thought my dad having money, and then me, that I should provide everything, every single time. I did feel bad keeping my secret from them, but it made everything easier. I could be myself, and in return, they would be themselves. There were no expectations other than me racing with them.

Which, honestly, was enough of an expectation with my current problem with racing.

My body flamed at the embarrassment of telling Fox that I wasn't ready yet. Then the way he stormed off. I knew he was worried I wasn't going to follow through, that I wasn't going to be able to race once it came down to it.

I pulled off my hoodie and looked at the scar across my chest. I was stronger than this. I was stronger than my wreck. And technically, I had already raced again. I just hadn't been the driver.

My eyes jumped to my face. The angry patch red and angry where the door had hit, but I hoped I could hide it enough. I had grabbed my makeup bag, doing what I could to cover it, along with leaving my hair down, but it was hard to miss right now. Luckily, it didn't hurt too bad now other than a dull throb.

It shouldn't look too bad until tomorrow, so I thought that would keep it hidden from everyone.

I pulled up to the curb around the corner from Fox's, now torn between not wanting him to know what kind of car I had and hoping that my car was still there when I got back. It wasn't a bad neighborhood, but it didn't take much for someone wanting to steal a car like mine. I grabbed my bag and took a deep breath, stepping in front of Fox's door.

I knocked, praying to anyone that would listen for him not to kick me out immediately.

EIGHTEEN
ASH

I OPENED the door and stepped into Fox's apartment after yells of 'come in' came from the other side. As I shut the door behind me, my eyes caught sight of the couch, every inch of it seemingly covered by someone.

"Wow, you almost need a bigger couch."

Fox just shook his head. "At the rate we're going, we are going to need a bigger building."

"Let's just start with the couch. We just finished this place," Ransom said.

"Come on, Ash. Sit down. Kye is trying to get the movie going," Quinn said.

I walked over, seeing that the only open seat was next to Fox. Quinn solidified my assumption that she did this on purpose when she wouldn't meet my eye.

Fox was laid out on the end of the couch, the section just big enough to fit him, in black shorts and no shirt. The man really didn't like wearing a shirt. Then again, with abs like that, I didn't blame him. His hair was still damp from a shower and he looked so relaxed that I wondered if he might give this dislike for me a break for the night. After the other day, I didn't know if that would be possible, but he did look calm even though I was here now.

I settled back onto the couch, listening as everyone started to talk and joke, giving Kye shit for not being able to load whatever movie they had chosen.

"What the fuck?" Fox said, and I looked over at him, surprised to see his eyes on me.

I let out a deep breath. So much for putting it aside for a night. I should have known the attitude was coming.

"What? Don't tell me you still want to fight about the other day," I said.

"No. What the fuck happened to your face?" he asked, the words quiet and angry.

My hand went up, covering the still sore spot. "Wow, thanks. Way to be nice." I kept my hand over it, knowing it wouldn't hide it, but hoping he would change the subject. "It's nothing. Don't worry about it."

"You and that fucking word. I'm not trying to be nice." He was already standing up, grabbing my arm. "Get up," he said. "Go. In the hallway. Now."

"You can't order me around," I said as he pulled me with him.

"Right now I can. Go or I'm going to take you there myself."

I turned back to the crew, each one of them with raised eyebrows as they watched him drag me out.

"Wow, thanks for the help!" I yelled before he slammed the door behind us.

He turned, jaw tight, as he looked me over. "What the fuck happened, Ash?"

"I had an accident with a door."

His face darkened, the scar giving a deadly look to him.

"I'm not joking around. Tell me what happened. It looks like someone hit you."

I wrung my hands together. I knew I should tell him. At least it was telling someone that David had found out where I was living. Especially now that he seemed to be watching my every move and that included seeing Fox drop me off the other day. But I just wasn't ready to tell him, or the group, everything about who I was, not yet.

"A guy I used to know."

"A boyfriend?"

"Something like that," I said, not wanting to tell him how wrapped up in my life David truly was. "I don't know how, but he apparently found out where I lived and decided to stop by my apartment. I think I took care of it, though."

"Right. Because a guy going to the length of hunting you down just walks away when you ask nicely."

"I can only hope."

He shook his head and the quiet way he stared off made me worry about what he was going to do next. He looked in pain and I wondered if I was giving him a headache or if it was just the pain of his cut.

He stepped forward, wrapping his arms around me until I was surrounded by him. He was warm and smelled so good, the deep scent of his soap making me take a breath.

It wasn't what I was expecting, and all I could do was freeze.

"Fuck. Have you told anyone about this?"

"I've tried. No one I told has really believed me. He's kind of known as a good boy. He can do no wrong to the people I have talked to," I said. I suddenly wished I could tell Fox everything, but I knew it would be too much.

"Well, I believe you. You can always call me if you need help."

I nodded into his chest.

"And if you are too busy hating me at the moment?"

"Still call me. I'll pick up. And if you hate me at the moment, then call any one of us. Any of us will be ready to come and help if you need it."

I smiled into him, the gentleness of his touch such a contrast to his almost threatening tone.

"Hey, Fox?"

"Yes."

"Does this mean we're friends?"

He stepped back, dropping his arms and leaving me chilled at the sudden loss of heat.

"No. It means that I didn't get a nasty scar across my face just so someone else could hurt you."

"Oh. Well, that makes sense, I guess. Not friends."

He huffed. "I just meant that we don't have to be friends for me to be there if you need help."

Tears welled in my eyes for the first time that night and I took a deep breath, trying to stop them. Somehow he was always so close to being sweet but never quite there and after the day I had, I just didn't want any debate with him now.

"Wait. Don't cry. That makes it a lot harder to be annoyed with you for the baseball game stunt. Come on," he said. "Fine. We can be friends tonight. What would make you feel better? Are you hungry?"

I nodded, realizing I hadn't eaten all day. "I would love a burger. And a coffee."

"Burger and coffee?"

I gave a strangled laugh. "That sounds great."

He shook his head. "Alright, burgers it is. Let's go."

"What? No, the movie's about to start."

"Do you care about a movie from five years ago that you have probably already seen, or do you care about food?"

"Food."

"That's what I thought." He gave a tight smile and headed back inside. "We're going to grab something to eat. Do you guys want any?"

A resounding yes echoed through the room as he grabbed his keys and wallet.

"I figured. We'll be back."

He walked out, not saying a word, as he led me down to the garage and to his car.

"Aren't you forgetting something?"

He stopped, looking around. "No?"

"A shirt?" I asked.

"Oh. I have one in the car I can throw on."

"How do you just forget a shirt?"

"It's basically summer. Consider it a gift. My abs are a hell of a lot better to look at right now than my face."

With that, he slid inside, slamming the door behind him. I took a deep breath before following, keeping my eyes forward as I pulled on a seatbelt. "There is nothing wrong with your face."

"Except for the giant cut running through it."

"I stand by what I said." I didn't know how he thought it was that bad, but I wasn't going to go down that road again right now.

"Why are you doing this?"

"Doing what?"

"Taking me out for food because I had a bad night."

"Because I'm a sucker when a girl's upset. Obviously," he said with a flash of his charming smile. "And anyway, I thought we called a truce for the night?"

"A truce is one thing. Being nice and making me feel better after a shitty day is another."

He shrugged. "Maybe I'm just hungry."

"Maybe you just like hanging out with me," I said, a smile growing on my face.

"Or I'm just hungry," he growled again.

"Fine, fine, keep telling yourself that," I said.

He called in our order and headed to the diner.

"Are we just going to sit here in silence?"

"You can put music on if you need."

"Yes, I do need." I connected my phone and picked the first song on the list.

I sang along, dancing in the seat, and losing every thought in my mind. It unknotted every muscle in my shoulders, letting the weight of the night fall off.

Fox pulled into the parking lot and turned it down.

"I'm running in. Enjoy your angry girl music." He smiled, and leaned over the console. For a split second I thought he was leaning in to kiss me, but he only shook his head and turned it back up.

"Fox!" I yelled, grabbing from the pile of clothes in the back. "We are all in awe of your abs, but pretty sure you have to put a shirt on." I threw it out the window to him as he looked down, laughing.

If this was Fox without the defenses and anger, I could definitely be his friend. Something about knowing this was who he was with all of his friends, but so cold and defensive to me, brought that weight back.

I still remembered seeing him before the accident. The moment I walked out of the club and saw him against his car. If we had met any other way, would we be different from how we were now? Or would he still not like things about me? With him, it was too hard to tell.

The next song played, and I let myself tune everything else out but the words. There was no point in trying to think about the what-if's with Fox. We were friends for a night, not for life.

A shadow came across my window and I turned to see a guy standing next to the car. Actually, three guys.

"Yes?"

"Hey. What's someone so pretty doing waiting in the car?"

I snorted. "You say that like it's a bad thing."

"Well, someone so pretty should be shown off, right? What kind of guy is leaving you in his car?"

"The polite kind that is going in to pick up our order. Are you implying he should have waited in the car and I went in to get the food? Would that have made him more of a gentleman?"

"No, I'm implying that he should have brought you inside."

"Because I'm a doll that needs to be shown off? Maybe the other boys will be jealous and want me to?"

I could see Fox walking out, the scowl back on his face, but it wasn't the same one he gave me.

"Pretty sure he doesn't need the ego boost like you would."

The guy looked over as Fox headed straight for us.

"Are you sure about that?" the guy asked.

"Better run, boys. He doesn't look pleased that you are here."

"Whoa, dude," one of the friends in back said. "What happened to him?"

Fox got in, setting the bags in the back.

"What's going on?"

"Nothing. Just go."

I looked over at the three of them, giving a sweet smile and wiggling my fingers to wave goodbye. "Small tip," I said as Fox backed out. "Women like being a passenger princess. Bye guys."

"Did you know them?"

"No, they just wanted to hit on me, and somehow thought me waiting in the car was rude to me. Just guys trying to be impressive and failing."

"Ahh, that explains the passenger princess."

"Hey, I love getting to drive, but enjoying my time listening to music and getting my order brought to me isn't a problem, either."

"Noted. I assume you aren't easily impressed by men?"

"No, not really."

"I guess I should have assumed that."

He veered back towards town, but took a turn that I didn't recognize.

"Where are you going?"

"Just a quick stop. Not far. I wanted to show you something."

It wasn't far before he turned down a road that looked deserted.

My brows furrowed. "You wanted to show me something down a dark, deserted road? Are you showing me how I get murdered?"

"No," he said with a quiet laugh. "And it's not deserted."

"I mean, I see the houses, but it looks deserted. And I have a feeling no one is going to care if they do hear me screaming."

"No, I don't think they would. But I do think that every couple of homes still has someone there. I just know they aren't the type to worry about screams or anything."

"And, if not to murder me, why are you showing me this?"

He slowed the car, rumbling until we were barely moving down the deserted road.

He pointed to two houses. "That was Ransom's house, and mine right next to it."

The two homes he pointed at looked like no one had lived there in years, and even before then, I wondered if anyone should have been. Not only that, they were tiny. I think the living room at my dad's house was bigger.

"Oh, wow." It was all I could say as he crept farther down the street. It was eerie. The quiet cracked street lit up by front porches and one street light that didn't seem to want to stay on completely.

"That was Jax's home." He pointed to another house that

looked like the rest. Run down and some place I probably wouldn't have gone even on a dare.

These were the kinds of places I wouldn't, and have never, visited, but they had all lived there at one point.

"Wow, I'm sorry. How did you possibly grow up here?"

There was a house with lights on that looked a little more lived in than the others.

"That's Scout's. She still has to go there sometimes, but we keep her up in the apartment with Quinn most days, luckily. And then Kye's house is two houses down. As far as I know, his parents are still living there, but he doesn't visit at all, really."

"And you all grew up here?"

"Yeah, it's how we became so close to begin with. I think us being together was the only reason we got out."

"I don't even know what to say other than wow for the thousandth time. I couldn't imagine growing up here. It's so run down. Is it dangerous?"

"It used to be more, but it's hard to be dangerous when there aren't many people. I'm sure people still mess with shit, though. I think kids make a game of going into some of the homes."

"Why did you bring me here?"

"I get that you like us all enough and I know you feel guilty or weird about the not being ready to race stuff, but don't. Whatever you feel, whatever I feel, is put aside for the crew. We don't have to be best friends or whatever you were trying to do, and we definitely don't need to go to any more games of any sort. I don't need you to fix me or make up for what happened to my face. I just want to forget about that and help the crew win. We've worked hard to get where we are, and this race could help solidify our name even more. I wanted you to see what we had to crawl out from and see how important things like this race are to them. To us. It helps the business and gives us one more step towards never coming back to this." He waved his hand around, making me look back at each dilapidated house as my heart tightened. "I know that racing after a wreck can be hard, but I thought if you really understood what we were fighting against, you might have one more reason to try. If you've raced competitively, you know that money and trophies and glory are great, but sometimes a reason outside ourselves helps. If you try, and still don't feel like you can race, then we can throw your round somehow, but I'm just asking that you try to race again. I understand that's a lot to ask for, but if they are going to enter, they deserve to win."

I nodded. "That's actually really sweet of you. That you care like that. And of course I will try to do it again. I wouldn't agree to race if I wasn't going to give it all. I just didn't realize actually doing it again was going to be so difficult."

"If you're still in, then we will all help. Like I said, if we had known about the wreck, no one would have expected you to just go race. We can ease into it."

"Then ok. I'm still in and I will do what I can to make sure they don't lose. And thank you for understanding and not just telling me to give up."

"That will never be the solution to a wreck. And good. Then, if you're ready, we will go out this weekend and practice. Just the crew this time," he said.

I nodded in agreement, but I was still skeptical of my own abilities.

"So that's the only reason you brought me here?"

"That, and I wanted to see your reaction."

"Why?"

"You obviously want to keep who you are a secret, and this at least gave me a piece of the puzzle."

"How so?"

"I saw your nose turn up when we turned onto the street. It's obvious you're from a nicer neighborhood."

"Wow, good catch on being a jerk again. You were almost being kind there for a second."

He smiled over at me, grabbing my chin as I tried to look away. It was gentle enough not to hurt the sore spot, but still forced my face to him.

"I didn't mean it in a rude way. I'm just trying to figure out who you are. We could skip the investigation if you just tell me."

"Why does it matter?"

"Because as soon as you get close to the crew, I want to know who you are. We've had bad people around that tried to hurt them. I don't think any of us will let it happen again."

"I'm not here to hurt anyone. And you're the only one who seems to have any concern."

"I don't think you are. But maybe I'm the only one who sees that you really are a little hellion and your cute act of innocence is fooling them." He let me go and looked back to the road. "We should get back before everything is cold."

"Right. And because spending time with me is like a personal torture session for you," I said with a laugh, regretting the words immediately. We were having a nice time, and I brought up the worst possible thing between us. It was him touching me that was throwing me off. I liked it. Every time he did, I only wanted more. I hadn't been able to stop thinking about him grabbing me, holding me, and even the kiss at the baseball game. It was seconds of my life, but those seconds made my toes curl every time I thought about it.

"That's it exactly. How did you know?" he asked with a sarcastic tone, obviously unhappy again.

"You know how you think everyone flinches when they see you? You flinch every time you see me. I can only imagine touching me has to be physically painful for you. I'm surprised you even took me out tonight."

"Like I said, a sucker when a girl is upset. I would have given you anything, even if it is causing me physical pain."

My mouth dropped open. "I was only kidding, but I'm starting to think you really are in pain when you're near me!"

His chest rumbled with a deep laugh before reaching over and wrapping his hand in my hair. My eyes went wide, my head going back as he pulled my hair. It was gentle enough that it didn't hurt, but was very effective at not letting me move.

"What are you doing?" I yelled into the quiet car.

"Did you not feel how physically painful it was for me when I had you against the car? Or when you decided to basically crawl into my lap at the races? Or maybe when you had to throw yourself at me at the game?"

A shiver of pleasure came over me. "I did not! None of that is completely the truth. Maybe you're just mad because I had control of those situations, and you didn't."

"Baby, we both know who has the control here, and we both know who you want to have control, so don't play with me."

I closed my eyes, clenching my thighs together. I knew I was already so wet, and I was mad that he wasn't wrong. I loved the feel of his strong hands grabbing me, and he seemed happy to keep doing it.

I held back my moan as pleasure rippled through me.

"Exactly," he said, not letting me go. "Does it hurt yet? Does it feel like you're going to die if I don't soothe that ache?"

If I ever thought I could orgasm without my pussy even being touched, it was right now.

He pulled back hard once before letting me go, untangling my hair from his fingers.

"How wet are you now? Going to start moaning for me again?"

I let out a frustrated growl. "Fox, I —"

He cut off my words. "We're here."

He threw me a wicked smile, the shadows in the car lighting up half his face in a golden hue.

The cut really should have made him look worse, but hell, if it didn't make him look even better than before.

He got out, grabbing the bag and leaving me in the silence.

And he had the nerve to call me hellion?

That he just knew how bad he turned me on just to run away.

He thought it was over, but I wasn't done yet.

NINETEEN
FOX

SHE RAN up the stairs behind me, and I couldn't help but smile. I was already looking forward to hearing every little thing she had to say about what had just happened.

She had been right. Every time she seemed to take control of what was happening and while I was in admiration at her unwavering need to get what she wanted, I was back in control, and I knew how bad that was going to get under her skin.

"Fox, you cannot just do that and walk away."

"Yes, I can."

"No, you can't," she huffed as we made it to the door of my apartment.

"Watch me."

I went inside, leaving her in the hallway. There was something so pleasing knowing that she was wet because of me and wouldn't be able to do anything about it. She would have to sit here all night looking at my face, knowing she was the reason it looked like this and knowing she wanted to get off on it.

Fuck, my ego hadn't been stroked this good in months.

The crew grabbed for the food and she finally came inside, a sweet smile on her face.

“Hey, Fox. Can I use your room for a second?” She held up her phone. “I’ll just be a minute.”

I cocked an eyebrow. “Yeah, that’s fine.”

“Great, thanks.”

She went in, shutting the door behind her. No one else seemed to think anything strange was going on, which was a relief, but now I was on edge.

There was nothing good about that smile, the sweet way she looked at me, letting me know I was somehow in trouble.

What could she possibly be doing?

I mentally ran through everything I had in there and wondered what she could be snooping through.

I was about to go barge in when the door finally opened. She smiled at me again as she walked out, slipping her phone into her pocket.

Nothing looked different about her, and that made me worry even more.

She leaned over the back of the couch behind me. Her lips were so close to my ear I could feel her breath and fought the urge to lean back into her more.

“I hope you don’t mind,” she whispered. “I had to soothe that ache all by myself and needed somewhere private. Your bed is super comfortable, by the way.”

The words took so long to register.

She couldn’t mean that she just went and got herself off on my bed.

By the time it really hit me, she had already walked around to the other end of the couch, finding just enough room between Jax and the armrest.

She had been getting herself off in the other room, all while I was sitting here acting like I was winning this game?

Fuck.

I should have barged in. It's my room, anyway. Could she have even been mad if I caught her? I leaned my head back at the thought that I could have walked in and saw that.

She sat whispering something to Jax before playing on her phone.

My phone pinged, and I mindlessly grabbed it, lost in thought at images of Ash in my bed touching herself. I didn't know if that was an image I would ever be able to forget.

I didn't have the number saved, and looked at her, and her smile only confirmed my suspicion that it was from her.

I hit open and froze.

It was a picture.

A picture of her in the mirror on my bed, in my shirt and on her knees. The shirt pulled down to cover everything but her legs. It didn't matter. Even covered I could barely hold myself together. Her wild hair, the small smile, the body that made me want to kick everyone out and take her back into the room.

I didn't move, couldn't move, and was thankful that the room was dark other than the light from the TV. I reached behind me, pulling one of the blankets off the back and laying it over my groin, hoping it would hide the current problem I was having now.

I finally looked up, and she noticed, giving me a smile and winking.

I had been sitting here pleased with myself for winning the battle when she was off winning the entire fucking war.

I tried focusing on the movie, but the only thing I could think about was her in my room.

I could only think of one thing to text back.

Hellion.

And she was. This was just another piece of proof that she came into my life to ruin it and was doing a damn good job because this was going to be the only thing I could think of for days, if not weeks.

She knew damn well what she had done, and sitting next to Jax was icing on the cake for her little plan. Because every moment that she leaned into him with a laugh or they whispered some little joke made me want to kick him out, even if he wasn't the one doing anything.

I didn't look at her again. She wasn't going to get any more satisfaction in knowing she won this time.

Twenty minutes after she ate, she was already drifting off, her eyes fluttering, fighting to stay open. I looked around. Scout was passed out next to Kye, Jax fighting it with Ash curled up next to him, and Ransom and Quinn wide awake.

Ransom got up, pulling Quinn with him as they woke up Kye and Scout.

"Scout, go upstairs," she whispered. "Are you staying or going, Kye?"

"Going," he said with a yawn. "Have to." Jax was already standing, walking like a zombie to the door, with Scout and Kye trailing after him.

I didn't know where Kye could have to go this late, but I wasn't going to question him now.

"Do you want me to wake her up?" Quinn asked.

"No, I'll get it," I said.

"Did she tell you what happened?"

"A bit. Might be a problem again, might not."

"Does she know we're all here for her?"

"I told her."

She nodded. "Does this mean you are going to be fine with her coming around and racing with everyone?"

"Why does everyone think I have such a problem with it when I am the one who had to go ask her to?"

"Aside from the little mean looks you have when she's around, I don't know. I've wondered that myself."

I rolled my eyes. "It's fine. We've reached an understanding."

"You're not some hideous beast that needs to be locked away, Fox."

"Easy to say when you're not the one dealing with it."

"You're right. We just miss you and hate seeing you hurt. Hurt in any way. Just like you are here for all of us, we're here for you, too. No matter what it is."

I had come to know Quinn well enough that I knew she was about to start crying, and I knew the chain reaction that was going to cause if she did.

"I know," I said softly. "I'm fine. I'll see you guys tomorrow."

Ransom wrapped an arm around her to head to the door and I waited until it closed before getting up. I don't know why, but I wanted to be the one to check with her, preferring to wait until everyone left.

"Ash."

She shifted, stretching out more, but not getting up.

"Do you need to leave?"

"Leave now?" she asked.

"You don't have to. It's pretty late."

"Don't want to be alone. I'll stay."

I grabbed another one of the blankets that Quinn and Scout had laid all over the damn place and threw it over her before heading back to the other side of the couch.

She could stay. And if she didn't want to be alone, I wouldn't leave her out here by herself, but I was going to stay far, far away from her.

ASH BOLTED UP IN A PANIC, ripping me from a deep sleep.

"Oh no," she said.

"What? What's wrong?"

Bright light streamed in and I realized she was staring over at me. Her face was a mix of disgust and confusion. Was she really that disgusted from sleeping in the same room as me? It's not like she wasn't happy to stay last night.

Then again, it was a shock even for me to look in the mirror each morning.

"Good morning," she said finally, giving a small smile.

"Morning."

"What time is it?"

"Close to 8."

"Oh wow, I'm guessing you need to get to work. I should —"

"Go? Yeah, you should," I said, getting up and heading to the kitchen. "Do you not work?" I knew I was sounding like an asshole, but I needed her gone. I needed to not feel like we spent the night together, and I needed to not like the company as much as I did.

"No, not right now," she said. "But I still need to get going."

"That's fine. I don't really know what to do with a girl here when I'm not trying to get her into bed with me. We both know that's not happening here," I said.

It was supposed to be a sting, and it seemed to work based on the curl of her lip.

"Wow, so glad you cleared that up," she said, her face twisting with disgust and anger. "Glad I came over here to feel better. Really helped," she mumbled, grabbing her shoes and trying to leave.

I felt bad the second I saw her face fall. I was being an asshole when just hours ago she was crying.

"Wait, do you need a ride home?" I asked, trying to maybe not be such an asshole.

"From you?" She looked at me over. "Fuck no."

The door slammed, and she was gone.

TWENTY
ASH

TWO DAYS LATER QUINN CALLED, reminding me that it was girls' night, and that I had already agreed to go.

A night out with them sounded perfect, just enough of a distraction that I didn't have to sit around here thinking about everything, including Fox.

At least going out with Quinn and Scout meant a night of laughing and, unlike old friends, not being used for every penny they could get their hands on.

They knocked at six on the dot and I pulled it open, giving them a pose in my outfit as I did.

My eyebrows shot up as I looked them over. "Do we not dress up for girls' night?"

Their mouths dropped at my outfit. I picked out a black jumpsuit, the fabric stretchy and forgiving. The back was cut open, two small pieces of fabric crossed at the back, and the front covered everything I wasn't ready to show in the front. I paired it with a set of heeled boots and simple hair and makeup.

"You look amazing," Scout said.

"Yeah, we don't normally dress up like that, but only because neither of us is too great at it."

"Well then, you're both in luck. I've got the clothes and the knowledge to make you feel like a queen in your clothes. A powerful queen that can crush boys that want to be mean."

"I take it you and Fox are no longer friends?" Quinn asked, coming inside and dropping her bag.

"No, he was an ass. *Again.* And I'm sick of it."

"We all are," Scout said. "He's been impossible lately. He thinks the scar is the worst thing in the world. He wants to hide away like he's some beast. It doesn't matter what we tell him, and I think that's why he's being so rude to you. He was such a player before and now he thinks he is disfigured or something."

"I just assume he blames me for it. Why like the girl that ruined your life? I know we've been okay, but I think he's hung around me more for all your guy's sake than his own," I said.

They both shrugged. "I guess it's possible, but I don't think either of us were thinking that. I think he doesn't know what to do around you because he thinks he's ugly now."

I shook my head. "No more boy talk. Let's get you two ready."

I brought them into my room, passing out different outfits and shoes, until they both looked amazing.

"There, now we look like we could join Charlie's Angels."

Quinn looked down, she was in a small black long-sleeved mini dress with my thigh-high boots and Scout was in a small red cami, the loose fabric light, and a criss-crossed string holding the deep V of the front together along with some black jeans and black heels.

"We look good," Quinn said, and Scout gave out a loud whoop that was a familiar sound at the races.

I shook my head. "Can take the girl out of the race pit but not the race pit out of the girl, huh Scout?"

She smiled, her face growing red but never letting her smile falter.

"It's a compliment, Scout. You look amazing and ready to kick ass."

"No, I know. I just wish I could feel this confident all the time. It's weird being into cars and races. Guys tend to be overly gross about it or think of you as one of the guys. I don't know why I can't find a happy middle of who I am."

"I've been there. Just keep chasing the things you love and it will come to you. You obviously are confident in what you can do, now you just have to own it. And compliments, keep those guys of yours making compliments to boost that ego." I added, laughing.

They laughed as we loaded into the car and headed out. After shopping and making sure they bought clothes to dress up for next time, we stopped to eat and talk. I couldn't remember if I had ever sat and talked so honestly or laughed so much with two girls my age.

Part of me hated that I wasn't coming clean with the truth of who I was, and the other part was too happy to care.

Quinn's phone chimed, and she smiled as she read it.

"Ransom said that they are out racing if we want to swing by to watch."

"Are they out for a guy's night like us?" I asked.

"Yes, but they always love having us around. We could go to every guy's night if we wanted to. Scout and I always have fun with just us though, so we go on our own here and there."

"They just love us so much they can't stay away," Scout said with a smile. "I was with them for everything growing up. I did always decline when they went out for girls, though. It's nice having a break from them more often with Quinn and now you, of course."

"I don't blame you," I said, ignoring the sting of jealousy.

“So was that a yes or no to going? I’m fine either way,” Quinn said.

“Sure. I’m good with watching them race if that’s what you two want to do. It sounds fun, honestly,” I said, suddenly missing how many nights I would spend at the race track.

“A yes from me,” Scout said.

Quinn smiled as she texted him back. “Well, let’s go watch some hot guys race cars then.”

We headed out to the car and Quinn pulled up the map with the location Ransom sent her. They weren’t far. We were already close to the edge of town and they seemed to be set up another ten minutes away. The town was sprawling with a downtown and the college campus but quickly turned to winding mountain roads to one side and more flat empty hill country to the other. It was easy to find open roads that no one would bother you on when you went that way.

We turned, and the darkness stretched endlessly. We didn’t pass another car as Quinn read out directions.

“This is creepy,” Scout said. “They usually race closer to town on nights like this. I wonder what brought them out this far.”

“Ransom said they have bigger bets tonight, so they probably just don’t want to be interrupted.”

The entire road was dark aside from headlights pointing in every direction. It took a few minutes to find them, but finally we pulled up next to Ransom’s car and hopped out.

“Wow,” Jax said. “A bit overdressed for a night of racing, aren’t you?”

I looked down over my outfit. It was definitely a lot for a race night.

“Shut it, Jax. They look great.” I jumped at Fox’s voice. He was on the other side of his car, the darkness covering him from my view.

"Hey, I never said they didn't," Jax said.

My eyes adjusted more and I could see Fox's eyes were glued on me, looking over every part of my outfit. His face gave nothing away, though.

He nodded his head, beckoning me closer.

"Yes?"

"Do you need me to apologize for the other morning? Because I shouldn't have acted like that."

"Those are almost sweet words, but I didn't hear *I'm sorry*."

He didn't say anything, taking a deep breath and looking me over.

"Are you going to come any closer or are you too scared of monsters in the night?"

I rolled my eyes. "I don't see any monsters out here."

"The dark is helping them hide. You look great."

"Really?"

"Of course."

I could barely see his face, the headlights aimed away from us, leaving me only able to see the outline of him.

"And the I'm sorry part?" I asked.

"I'm sorry for acting like that. I just got in my own head and apparently that turns me into a giant asshole."

I took a breath. "Fine, apology partially accepted."

"Partially? Damn, okay. That's fair. Are you here to watch us race?" he asked.

"Wait. You're racing too?"

"Yeah. I've lined up a few races tonight."

"I know you raced the other day, but I was in the car trying not to freak out, so I don't know if it counts as me watching you race. I'm surprised you are tonight."

"I have to get back at it at some point, so I'll take whatever races I can. And I'm glad you're here," he said, stepping closer.

"If there's one thing I still have, it's that girls go crazy for me when I race."

I didn't hide my laugh, catching his smirk as headlights passed over us. "Oh, that's the plan, then? Hide away in the car and race for the girls?"

"Something like that. It's not fully fleshed out yet, like what I would do when I actually have to face them, but I think it's a great place to start," he said with a small laugh.

"So, that's what you're wanting, then? For girls to fall all over you?"

He stepped closer again, not touching me, but close enough that we could if either one of us reached out.

"No, I guess not. Although, there is one person I would like to show that I am actually good at something. Something other than acting up and being an ass."

"I would argue that you're good at many things. Racing, fixing cars, defending people, flirting apparently, cheering people up. I won't argue about the acting up and being an ass part."

He only laughed more. The charming, happy Fox was out in full force tonight and it was hard to look away from.

"Isn't how good at racing I am still up for debate?" he asked.

"True. You better get out there and win."

He finally moved, throwing an arm around my shoulder and leading me closer to his car. "If you only knew that I never lose."

I pursed my lips. "I beg to differ. What if you come up against another person that also doesn't lose?"

He stopped, looking down at me. "I missed everything you said after the word beg."

"I think you heard me."

"Then maybe the right answer is to tease them until they *beg* to lose."

"Wow, if an ego could explode, yours might tonight. Would that actually count as you winning?" I asked.

"I don't see how you on your knees begging would make me the loser? But maybe this time I should surrender and let you win. Just this one time."

"Funny. I've been winning this entire time. How would that be new?"

He smiled, reaching up to run a lock of my hair through his fingers. "Such a hellion."

He seemed so light, so happy that it only made me happier. "What is happening? Did you hit your head?"

"What can I say? I'm in a good mood tonight. It's dark, we're racing, I'm partially forgiven, there's not much to complain about right now."

"Well, I'm glad to hear that. And as for watching you race, I'll try to not faint in ecstasy when you win."

"Good, that would be embarrassing. And not the first time it's happened to me," he said matter-of-factly.

My mouth fell open. "You're lying."

He laughed harder. "I am. Even I wasn't that good-looking. Although, now that I think about it, I'm a little annoyed women were fainting for me. I guess the scar will help cross that off my list, won't it? Faint from shock and fear."

"You really are something else, Fox." I shouldn't care to even think about it, but the moments when Fox was himself, when he shed off the anxiety and self-consciousness, he was amazing.

He looked down, flashing a bright smile.

"I'm going to race now," he said, not moving his arm off of me.

"Alright, go kick that person's ass."

"Oh, I am. And I fully expect to come back here and have you swooning over my greatness."

I could only laugh as Quinn and Scout walked over, all of us watching as he pulled up to the starting line to get ready for his race.

"Well, it looks like Fox is back for the night," Quinn said.

"Let's hope for good," Scout added.

"Don't get ahead of yourself," Quinn said. "Tonight is good for now. At least we know he's still in there somewhere."

"Are you telling me he's normally like that all the time?"

"Pretty much. Always joking, laughing, flirting. He's impossible to deal with when you're sad. His answer to everything is giving you anything you could possibly want or trying to go after whoever made you upset. It's almost infuriating."

"And neither of you ever had feelings for him?"

Both of them scrunched their noses.

"He's an older brother to me, nothing more."

"And basically the same for me. Fox was always there for me, like an older brother. I've been a little too busy being in love with Ransom to think any different. Why, Ash? Falling for all that charm."

"Among other things," I mumbled, looking back to the street where Fox was lining up.

My giddiness was short lived when I looked up, horrified as one of David's cars pulled up next to Fox. "No. That's who he's racing?"

"Looks like it," Scout said. "Is something wrong?"

"Yeah. I mean, maybe."

"What? What happened?" Quinn asked, looking around like we were about to get jumped.

"Nothing. I think I know who's racing Fox. It might just be a fluke," I said, already knowing it wasn't. I could see the Holt racing sticker on the fender of his car. The one showing everyone that Holt racing sponsored him and his races. He stuck them on everything, never passing up a chance to tell the world how important he was, or at least how important he thought he was.

"Oh, is that a bad thing?" Scout asked.

"I'm not sure yet."

There was nothing else to do but watch. They each did a burnout and lined back up, waiting until the flagger gave a signal before they took off.

If I had any suspicion that it wasn't David behind the wheel, I didn't now. He took off at a snail's pace compared to Fox, who was a quarter of the way down the road before David was even off the line.

"Typical," I mumbled, my nails biting into my thighs as I watched. David was never a racer. It was a life and career he tried to force himself into that would never fit.

It was only seconds that went by, Fox's car gliding down the track with an ease that many people would kill to be able to do. He didn't bounce around, the car didn't veer off at all. It was easy for him after years of work perfecting it. Every single one of the crew seemed to work their ass off to be better racers. They weren't expecting a thing handed to them and never thought twice about working for it. It filled me with a pride that I didn't know if I deserved to have. Did I have a place in his life to be proud of him? Or was I only here to admire from the sidelines?

David couldn't imagine anything *not* being handed to him. He was the type that thought money bought happiness, or in this case, could buy him being a skilled driver.

Fox crossed the finish line with David's car seconds behind him, and in this type of race, seconds might as well be hours.

There was no question if Fox won or not, and my body continued to thrum with pride that he beat him. Not that it should matter, but every part of me wanted him to kick David's ass, knowing that would hurt him more than any punch would.

As their cars turned to drive back to us, anger crashed into me. David was following me and it seemed like he could be following the crew now, too. I couldn't imagine he wound up here on purpose.

Their cars slowed as Fox pulled in next to us.

Scout jumped onto him as he got out, and Quinn hugged him.

"You did it! You're back!" Scout yelled. He smiled and grabbed onto her. She was so short that him picking her up to stand up straight had her over a foot off the ground.

"I don't know about that, but racing felt great," he said, squeezing her once before setting her back down. His eyes met mine in the halo of headlights.

"Well, damn, you didn't swoon."

"No, but I have to say, it was close. I stumbled there for a second."

He leaned back against his car, but my mind was stuck on David. I didn't want them in any trouble, and I knew David would cause it. I couldn't believe he ended up here tonight, or racing Fox, by chance.

"I'll be right back. I have to do something quick."

Fox's eyebrows furrowed, and I could feel his eyes on me as I stalked away. I didn't want to stop and tell him what was happening, though. I knew he would want to get involved, and I didn't want to ruin his cheerful attitude over something that I could take care of. There were a hundred people around us and I knew David wouldn't dare to do anything to me in public.

For my own sake and the crews, I needed to get David out of my life. If I didn't confront him now and try to put a stop to this, I worried that it would never stop until he dragged me back home.

By the time I made it to his car, I was ready to do anything, anything, to get him to leave me alone.

TWENTY-ONE
FOX

I HAD BEEN KIDDING about the fainting, but the running off was a bit of a low blow. With how good I felt tonight, I was almost expecting Ash to be more at ease around me, not less. I thought she was at first, some glimmer of hope there, that maybe there was something between us that she might want, but now she ran off like she finally did see a monster.

Quinn and Scout looked at each other with worry before looking at me. Without a word, I knew what they wanted.

"Yeah, yeah, I'll go see what she's doing," I said, jogging away to catch up to her.

She was moving fast, winding around the mess of cars, but I couldn't figure out where she was headed.

Finally, she reached a car, pulled open the driver's side door and leaned down. I couldn't see who it was, but I did know it was the same car I had just raced down the road.

I stopped, shock and anger rolling through me that she would honestly run right to my opponent.

Then something like disappointment washed over me as my

heart raced faster. The scar pricked, the feeling of a thousand needles running over my face, an all too familiar feeling now.

What the hell was her problem? Was it that bad that my opponents were still a better option than me?

I couldn't make out her expressions from here, but I wasn't going to wait to find out what she was doing.

Someone stepped in front of me, blocking my path to her, which only pissed me off further.

"Move," I said, trying to step around, but an arm came out to stop me.

"Hey Fox. Surprised to see you here."

"Why?" I looked down at Liam, annoyed that he looked as pissed as I felt.

It wasn't uncommon while racing for people to get pissed about things, but I still didn't know what his problem was, but it seemed like I might find out now.

"Since you're not racing with your team, I just assumed you would hide away a little longer."

"I wasn't hiding away from racing. It's pretty hard to race when half of your face is shredded."

"Right, right."

He had such a way of getting under my skin that I already felt ready to punch him the second he opened his mouth. It was a constant battle of his trying to get the upper hand in the conversation, even when it wasn't needed. I didn't care if it wasn't logical. I was already ready for a fight, and he was just adding fuel to the fire.

"Fuck off, Liam. Whatever you're trying to go off about, I'm not in the fucking mood." I looked up to see Ash's face, anger and surprise as clear on hers as it was on mine.

"You know what, Fox–" Liam started, but I pushed him back, cutting him off as I forced my way around him, heading to Ash.

"What are you doing?" I asked as she walked towards me. "Why the hell did you just run off?"

She didn't answer, the silence making every thought I had about what just happened even worse. "Why did you go talk to him?" I yelled now, trailing after her.

"I don't want to talk about it. I just want to leave," Ash said.

"Why? What just happened?"

"Nothing. I just want to leave. I need to find Quinn and Scout."

She tried to step around me, but every part of me thrummed with anger.

"No, I'll take you home. Go, get in the car."

"You can't. You have more races."

"Not anymore. Just go."

She was near tears now. I couldn't figure out why I was so pissed that she ran from me to go to him. Whoever he was, he obviously upset her.

She made it to the car and dropped into the passenger seat. I got in too, maneuvering us out of the mess of people and cars.

"Are you going to tell me what the fuck all that was? Did you get rejected or something?"

"No." The simple words, the silence. Each second was pushing me farther to the edge.

"Why?"

"Because it's none of your business. Just take me home."

"Fine," I nearly yelled, turning onto the main road and hitting the gas. "I'll get you there as fast as I can."

I pushed the car faster, trying to ignore her ignoring me, but I couldn't take it any longer.

"Why won't you tell me what just happened? You just blew me off to go talk to that guy. Why?"

"Can you please go faster? I would like out of this fucking car. I should have ridden back with Quinn and Scout."

"Faster?" I was already way past speeding, but she didn't seem to care, which was a surprise after how she reacted when we raced.

I listened, though, pushing the car fast enough that the world blurred past. I finally swung around the last corner, the back of the car breaking loose to swing.

She still wasn't even looking at me, and every moment was leaving me more unhinged. The anger and rage building was so unlike me that I didn't even know what to do with it. Weeks of not doing anything but sitting around in my own pity was leaving me so built up with every emotion that I couldn't hold it back.

"You know, I was having a great night until you pulled that shit," I said.

"Me? You're trying to blame me? Your ego is not my problem, Fox. Get over yourself. Since you need to know every second of my business. That was David. I was going to find out if he was following you. Or following me. I wanted to know why the hell he was there when I know he doesn't go to those things."

I pulled into our garage at the apartments and turned the car off before turning to face her. She wasn't waiting around, though. She was already out of the car, so I pushed my door open.

"Wait. *That* was David?"

"You're an ass, Fox," she yelled. "I meant take me to my home!"

She ran out in front of me and headed upstairs faster than I could even get out of the car.

She raced up, reaching the next landing that led to Quinn and Scout's apartment. "Maybe give someone five minutes before you assume they are running from you," she yelled as she slammed the door.

I could only head into my own apartment, getting ready for

bed, lost on what I should do next. I shouldn't have been mad at her. I should have gone with her. I would have if Liam wouldn't have stood in my way. I got into bed, trying to think of anything else, but once again, sleep didn't come easy because every time I laid down, I could only think of her. The way she smiled, the way she always called me out on my attitude, and worst of all, the things she did in this bed.

TWENTY-TWO
ASH

I SLAMMED the door behind me, hoping that Fox heard it loud and clear.

I didn't need his interrogation. Especially after confronting David.

When I had pulled open David's car door, he didn't even look surprised, giving me a relaxed smile. He hadn't given me much to go on, but it seemed clear enough that he knew the crew would be there tonight and that he had 'stopped by' on purpose.

I just didn't know what the purpose was other than to bother me.

Then he had the nerve to ask me to come watch him race. He even called it his team. Which I guess it was now if my dad handed it over finally, but that didn't stop the protective anger that flared when he said it. Between those words and him stalking me and the crew, I was ready to hit him.

The worst part was that he almost got to me.

He was telling me all the right things to make me question myself. It was like second nature to him. Come into my life, say the right things, tell me I'm losing my mind and that he will help fix it. He said that even though I deserted them, the team did need me, and that he could help me come back.

I did miss my life in so many ways. There were bad parts, of course, but I missed mornings with my dad and going out for a drive with him. I missed practicing with my team and how funny they were. I had carved out a small life that I liked now, but it didn't mean I didn't miss my old one.

And David used that against me.

I could never win when he was too busy manipulating my own thoughts. I would never be strong enough to deal with him and I was starting to realize that meant I was never getting my life back in any way.

I texted Quinn, asking for clothes to wear tonight, and she let me know where to find them. After I changed, I could only sit and stare at the wall.

The longer I sat, the more thoughts of Fox consumed me.

He always seemed to be there when I needed him. I had tried day after day to be there for him and the first night that he seemed at ease and happy, I pushed him away.

I ran to David after the race instead of him.

I knew that feeling after a race, even small ones, where you wanted to celebrate with your people. I would have been pissed if the tables were turned.

And there was no way he would have known that the only reason I ran over there was to make sure David wouldn't do anything to them.

I looked at the door.

I didn't want to sit here spiraling, and it wasn't like I couldn't apologize to him now.

AFTER TEN MINUTES pacing in the hallway, I pushed open the door to his apartment. The entire place was dark and quiet, but I knew he hadn't left.

I shuffled in, trying not to hit anything as I made my way to the bedroom, wondering what the hell I had been thinking when I thought this was a good idea.

By the time I made it to the bedroom door, I was more unsure than ever.

"Fox," I whispered into the dark room.

There was nothing for a moment.

"Yes." His voice echoed in the darkness. "Just wanted to yell at me more, or is there a problem?"

He had been awake the entire time, which gave me some relief that I wasn't creeping into someone's room while they were sleeping. Not that him being awake made it much less creepy of me.

"Yes, there is. I can't see where you are," I hissed.

He gave a quiet laugh. "That's because I usually sleep in the dark."

"You're not sleeping."

"Someone broke into my apartment."

"You don't seem too concerned," I said, trying to follow his voice and walk towards the bed.

"I think I'm safe from this specific hellion. What do you need?"

I held back the words. I needed an apology, an orgasm, and to tell him the truth, but I didn't think I was going to get any of that tonight.

"I needed to come talk to you about tonight. I would also prefer to see you when I talk, so I need to know where you're at."

"You came all this way to find me. I would hate to ruin the fun."

I gave a frustrated growl. I had made it to the edge of the bed but waited, my eyes finally adjusting to the little bit of light that streamed in.

"Ash, what are you doing here? Shouldn't you be upstairs? Asleep."

"Yes, but I had a problem."

"Which was?"

"I felt bad."

"About?"

"Everything. Not telling you the truth, making you feel bad that I ran off, and I almost feel bad about teasing you the other day."

"Glad you invited yourself to join me in here so that you felt better," he said, the tone not a friendly one. "What if I hadn't been alone?"

I gave a strangled laugh. "I know you weren't working that fast. We just got back."

"I don't know," he said. "I've worked that fast in the past."

I sat down on the bed, feeling him next to me, but didn't touch him.

"You're trying to get me to leave?"

"Yes."

"Then stop being an ass and say it. Tell me you would rather I leave so that another girl can come over."

I was met with silence, so I pushed again. "Come on, Fox. Say it, and I'll leave before you can even pick up your phone."

More silence.

"I'm waiting."

"You're sorry for teasing me the other day?"

Of course, that's the part he would hone in on. "I was really hoping we could gloss over that, but yes. In my defense, though, you started it with the hair pulling."

He gave a quiet laugh. "You should be sorry. It's all I've thought about every time I lay in this bed."

"Glad to know you didn't hate it completely, then."

"Hate it? Of course I fucking hate it. You bother me all damn day, and then you get to haunt my dreams now, too? I hate every second of it."

"So, I'm guessing that's a big no to touching you."

"Is that what you came here to do?" he asked, with what sounded like genuine shock in his tone. "I assumed you were here to rip me to shreds."

There was a beat of silence until I finally answered. "I came here alone, in the middle of the night, Fox. Do you not take hints well?"

"And you thought what? I would be begging for your attention?"

I stood up. "How could you say that? I —"

He cut me off, grabbing my wrist and flipping me onto the bed, knocking air out of my lungs.

"I'd say sorry, but I'm worried that word might not make a difference anymore. The attitude is becoming second nature," he said, a hand caressing my arm once before pulling away.

"It's a very annoying go-to defense."

"Apparently," he whispered. "You always surprise me."

"With what?" I stared up at the ceiling, taking in the comfortable bed and deep scent of Fox.

"That somehow you don't run from me forever. Even when I do act like a beast." He moved his fingers along my arm again. "You should have told me what happened. I would have gone with you."

"And caused a bigger fight? No. I was only trying to find out what he was doing and it didn't work." I closed my eyes. "Can we not talk about him?"

"Of course." His hand moved to my neck now, his fingers running up the delicate skin, through my hair before going back down. I hadn't had someone touching me so gentle in what felt like years and I could only stay still to enjoy it.

"Show me," he said quietly.

"Show you what?"

He leaned down to my ear. "Show me what you did when you were alone in here."

My face turned hot. I hadn't been lying about what I did. I had thought it would be funny to tell him the truth, and I was right, it had been hilarious.

"Why would I do that?" I said with a smile.

"Because I want to watch."

"And if I don't do it?"

"Then, I would run out of here if I were you because you're going to be in trouble if you stay and don't listen."

My mouth fell open. "If you think for one second I'm going to run—"

My words were cut off as he dragged me onto my stomach and over the top of his legs.

"That's all I need to know then."

His hand came down, smacking against my ass with a snap.

"Fox!"

"Screaming my name is better, but it doesn't get you out of trouble."

My body didn't seem to care if we were in trouble or not because I could feel myself pushing my ass higher for him.

His hand came down again, the sting of him spanking me followed by a tingling warmth.

Wetness flooded between my legs as he did it one more time. He rubbed at the same place he had just spanked, soothing the tender skin.

"Fox," I said again, the sound of my own desperation a surprise to me.

He laughed behind me, hooking a hand under my hip and flipping me over onto my back again next to him.

"Now, let's see what you did. It is my bed that you violated. I think I have a right to know."

I knew I had every chance to get up and walk out, but I still didn't move.

It was an easy decision. I moved my hand, dipping under my shorts.

"No," he said. "Shorts off. I know damn well you weren't wearing them in that picture."

I hooked my thumbs under the waistband, pulling them down and off.

"You didn't even wear underwear to come down here? You are a tease," he said, the quiet laugh reassuring me more.

"Sometimes," I said with a smile as I moved my hand back down.

The light was behind him, leaving only an outline and hiding his face in the dark.

"And you like it, don't you? You liked teasing me knowing I was turned on and couldn't think of anything other than dragging you into this room," he said.

"Yes, watching you pull that blanket over you was the highlight of my week."

"Hellion."

I dipped my fingers into myself, surprised at how wet I already was. Each command was sending a thrill through me and I was already excited for the next.

My legs fell open as I moved over my clit, rubbing the sensitive area without a care that he was watching.

I never liked being on display during sex. Even being on top felt exposing, but somehow laying here, legs open and showing Fox my most intimate moments still wasn't uncomfortable.

"Are you wet?"

I slid my fingers down. "Can't you find out for yourself?"

"No," he growled. "Tell me."

I groaned, wishing he would. "Yes. I am."

"Keep going."

I moved my fingers in slow circles, the pressure already building.

"Fox, I need you."

"No." Each word was final, there was no questioning what he wanted or what he wanted me to do. "Slide your fingers in."

"I want yours," I said, trying to match his commanding tone and failing.

"And I want you on your knees with your perfect mouth around my cock, but we'll have to settle for this."

His words shot another thrill through me, even surprising myself at how much I wanted that too.

"Please, Fox. I need you."

"Slide your fingers in, Baby. Fuck yourself for me."

If I could have any coherent thought, I might worry how easily my body listened to him, but it felt too good to fight it now. My fingers moved, pushing them deeper. The feeling was so familiar, but I had never had an audience before. I felt so hot as he watched me, his eyes watching every movement of my fingers.

I was both powerful and helpless as my orgasm built inside me.

"Fox, please," I begged, needing him.

"What, Baby? Are you thinking of my fingers or my cock? Which one are you begging for?"

"Both." I breathed as I moved faster, the edge coming as he whispered to me.

I pulled my hand away, reaching for his and dragging it to my pussy.

"Don't you want to feel how wet I am for you?"

He let out a growl when he finally touched me, hesitating for only a second before finally plunging his fingers deep into me where he stilled again.

"Move," he said, his voice quiet. I moved until I was moaning, the pleasure building.

"Look at you, taking control, riding my hand so hard. Come for me, soak my fingers," he whispered as I rode his hand. I bit back a scream as my body fell apart. He slammed into me once more, the pleasure coming and ending too fast.

He pulled his fingers out, pulling them into his mouth, "So good. I love the way you ride my hand like that. I can't wait to watch you ride my cock." he said.

"I'm ready now."

He laughed. "Oh I already see that, but it's not happening."

"Why not?"

"Because we both know that it's easy to say in the moment but think how much more you would hate me if we did that, then we wake up and I'm still an asshole to you." He was still caressing me, his calluses fingers moving up and down my side.

"Please, I want more."

"Fuck. Don't say please like that. You can do whatever you want now, but I'm not touching you anymore tonight. That was already too much."

I gave a small whimper. "That doesn't seem fair."

"Did you come down here to play a fair game?"

I huffed, staring up at the black ceiling. "No."

"Then I won't be touching you. You can hide me in the dark and not blame the beast in the morning."

"Fox," I said, not knowing what to say to that. I didn't realize he thought I would want to hide him, that I might not want to see his face. If anything, I would prefer it right now.

He hadn't moved, but I did, straddling him, and catching him off guard. I splayed my hands over his stomach, running over every inch of his hard chest and arms.

"You don't have a shirt on."

"Quite observant," he said. "Just so there is no surprise. I don't have pants on either. Only boxers. I didn't realize I was going to have company."

I tried to hide the groan as I rolled my hips once. I could feel how hard he was under me, and was struggling to think of any reason we shouldn't do this. "Really? I thought you were about to call some girl until I interrupted you."

I could feel him give a laugh, but didn't hear it. "Would I need pants for that? Not like any of them would come running. Then again, one did break into my apartment and seems to be fine with me in the dark."

"You think you need the dark to hide away in? Turn on the lights. I'm suddenly scared."

"Ash, I don't know what the goal of this mission you're on is. I was trying to be a gentleman and tell you about there not being pants."

I moved against him again until he reached out, grabbing my hips hard to hold me still.

"Oh thank you, such a gentleman." I laughed harder. "Despite the fact that a girl is on top of you, and you just watched her get off, you're trying to have a pity party for yourself. I don't want you to be a gentleman because none of the thoughts I am having are anything ladylike."

He groaned. "Didn't you get what you came for? You need to finish so I can keep my self control."

I gave a small laugh, pleasure at the thought that he wanted this as much as I did. I leaned down, pressing my lips to the base of his neck. His arms flexed as he tucked his hands behind his head, trying to prove how much he wasn't going to touch me anymore.

"I don't want your self control," I whispered.

"Without my self control, I'm just a beast that you'll be mad touched you."

"That's really what you think?" I had stilled on top of him, the words confirming what he had been leading me to believe.

"That's what I know."

"That's not what's happening, Fox."

"Stop," he growled. "If you came in here thinking we were going to talk something out, then you can leave now. You can make me whatever dirty fucking secret you're hoping for, but I'm not sitting here to talk about it and I'm not touching you so you can feel like you paid me back. Like fucking me out of pity and guilt will make everything that happened go away and make me, and you, all better."

I didn't know what to say. I did feel guilty, everyday I felt guilty that he had that scar and pain because of me, but that wasn't why I was there with him.

I wasn't there for pity or guilt. I was there because I had been thinking of him every moment and needed him. I was there because no one else had made me feel so much.

"So I'm supposed to get off and leave? No more talking?"

"Isn't that what you wanted?"

"No, not entirely," I said.

"Then what did you want?"

"Right now?"

"Yes."

I rolled off of him and onto my side before finding his face and pulling it to mine.

He froze as our lips met, but like the first time, I didn't let it stop me. Finally he broke, wrapping an arm around my back and dragging me tight against him and moving his lips against mine. I could feel the spot where his lip had been cut and hoped it didn't hurt anymore. He licked along my lips, opening them, and then moving his tongue against mine.

I gasped, realizing he was giving me something, hoping he would give me more, but he froze, pulling his head back against the pillow and breaking the kiss.

"You should go," he said.

"No, Fox," I said as I pushed up. "You kissed me back. I was surprised. It wasn't a bad gasp."

"Go to bed. Whatever you came down here for is done."

"Fox, I really —"

"Get out, Ash. The night is done. This is over."

Anger flooded me at his dismissal.

"Seriously? I crawl into your bed and then you still kick me out. You are the worst," I said with an angry growl.

It wasn't anger though, it was all embarrassment.

I grabbed my shorts and stomped out of the bedroom, making it to the living room before I heard him.

He was leaning against the doorway to the bedroom. The lights from the street throwing shadows and warm light over his body.

"I know," he said. "I tried to warn you, but you only have yourself to be mad at. Technically, you controlled everything that happened in here."

I wanted to scream. I knew he was right and I had no right to feel this way. He let me call the shots and I could have walked away at any moment, but I didn't feel like I had control of anything right now. I wanted him to somehow see this wasn't because of guilt or pity for him. I thought this would help prove it but somehow he still turned it against himself.

"I really can't stand you sometimes, Fox."

"I really can't stand myself sometimes," he said, the words

echoing as I slammed the door behind me before stomping upstairs and trying to get comfortable on the couch.

I laid back, trying to catch my breath, wondering how I could want someone so bad while being so annoyed at them, too. Every part of me was at war with myself and I didn't know who the players were, or who was going to win.

TWENTY-THREE
ASH

I HAD SLEPT SO bad last night that my eyes were already open when Quinn came out.

"Sorry, did I wake you up?"

"I don't think I was ever actually asleep."

Scout shuffled out. "I slept great. Ugh, I love the bed here. I'm so glad I don't have to go back and forth from my dad's house anymore," she said, walking out of the other bedroom and jumping onto the couch.

"How often did you have to be at your dad's house?" I asked.

"Recently it was a few times a week, but being eighteen now, I'm here permanently. Once my dad lets me back in to get the rest of my things, that is."

"Sorry. My dad's a pain in the ass, but nothing like that," I said, regretting it immediately. How could I even compare the two? I saw where Scout had to go. My dad was an ass sometimes, but he was a good guy. He gave me everything I ever wanted, even if the one thing I cared about getting, he didn't seem to think I could handle.

"Anyway," I said, trying to change the subject quickly after seeing her face. "What are we up to today?"

Quinn was looking at her phone, sipping the coffee she had made for us. "According to the group chat that is currently blowing up, we are going out racing. Including you, Ash."

"Why including me?"

"It seems like the guys have decided today is the day that you do practice runs. I don't think they can wait any longer to get you ready. The excitement for this race was already high, and now they can't even contain themselves."

My stomach turned to knots. "What? No."

"Yep. Even Fox is on board."

"He shouldn't be. Not after he was such an ass last night."

"Ohhh," Scout said. "Last night. Was this before we got home or after?"

I knew the moment my face warmed that there was no hiding that something else had happened.

"Alright, Ash. Tell us. *Please*," Quinn said, throwing a pillow at me. "Did you and Fox get together?"

"No. No, it's not what you're thinking. Not really."

They waited, not saying a word.

"Ok, something happened, but not what you are thinking, and before you ask, no, he still doesn't like me and we are holding on by a thread just trying to be friends. Maybe even more so now."

Quinn pursed her lips. "I'm sorry to tell you this, but I don't think you two are friends."

"Oh, don't worry. I wasn't under the impression we were for real. I'm only sticking around until after the races are done."

"No, that's not what I meant. I mean that I know Fox as a friend, and I'm sure the cut plays a role in his change towards you, but I also think we can all agree that you are not *only* a friend to him."

"Maybe, but I'm also not getting any ideas that we could be more than friends. I don't even know if I would want that."

I wasn't going to add that they all may never want to speak to me again when they find out how big of a secret I was keeping from them. I didn't take any of them for people who were okay with lying. There was no way that they weren't going to ask more questions if they did ever see me race, and I still hadn't found out if David or my dad were going to add their team to the list for the Legends race.

Everything felt too messy.

"If I have to try to get behind the wheel today, I am going to need something to eat. Something that won't be terrible to throw up when my nerves get the best of me."

Scout scrunched her face. "Don't even joke about that. I cannot stand puking."

Quinn started laughing. "One night Kye came back drunk and threw up outside in front of Scout. A few times. It was so bad she started throwing up," Quinn said. "I spent the whole night taking care of both of them because Scout thought she could still hear him puking from here."

I fake gagged and Scout jumped up.

"Don't you dare do that again!"

"What are you going to do about it, *shrimp*?"

Her mouth fell open, and she jumped over the couch onto me, trying to grab my head, but I was laughing too hard. The door opened as some of the guys walked in.

Jax wrapped his arms around Scout's waist, pulling her up and off of me.

"Whoa, whoa, whoa, ladies. No cat fights."

"Oh, please," Scout said, a smile on her face. "Like you guys don't get into little fights all the time."

"And I've told you. We've all told you. Don't do the things we do."

Scout rolled her eyes and leaned back onto the couch.

"What's up?" Quinn asked, as Ransom fell back next to her.

"What do you mean? Did you not see your texts?"

"Yes, but that was five minutes ago. Are you all seriously ready to go race already?"

"Do you really think any of us are ever going to drag our feet when we get to go race?" Fox said, walking through the open door.

I looked him over before jerking my eyes away. How could he look so good in just a t-shirt, shorts, and a backwards hat?

And at what point did I go from *get this guy away from me* to *please rip off all of my clothes*?

Worst of all. How could I stop thinking about getting off on him when we were in a room full of people?

I didn't dare look over at him again, but could feel him looking at me.

"So, are you guys ready yet?" Jax asked.

I looked down, all of us still in pajamas. Luckily, Quinn had some more clothes that I could borrow and not have to waste time running home.

"Give us ten minutes," Quinn said.

I didn't want to wait around any longer. I knew Fox was still watching me, so I ran to the bathroom to change.

I looked into the mirror and leaned forward until my head was against the cool glass. I couldn't believe I snuck into his room. I can't believe I literally got off in front of him. On him.

Not that I really hated any part of it.

But the embarrassment was at an all time high.

By the time I changed and walked back out, I expected them all gone from the apartment, but the guys all still sat around talking about where we were going.

I internally groaned, grabbing my purse and sitting at the kitchen counter with my back to them.

Quinn and Scout walked out seconds later, everyone jumping up and filing out.

Jax threw an arm around me as we walked down.

"Ride with me?" he asked.

I gave him a questioning look, but he only smiled. "Yeah, sure."

We got in, everyone driving their own car other than Quinn and I.

"Do you guys have somewhere you race at?" I asked after we got in.

"We found an older road years ago that we go practice on."

"I have a feeling you didn't ask me to ride with you because you wanted company."

"No, not exactly, but you do make great company." He smiled over, the happy grin genuine. Even though Jax was always up to something, his presence did seem to have a calming effect on me.

"Well, I'm glad one of you guys thinks so."

"Listen, Ransom is too obsessed with Quinn to realize there is anyone else around. Kye is too busy out making trouble, and Fox doesn't want to realize how great of company you are yet."

"Wow, I'm so glad I have you then," I said, patting his arm.

"Don't you forget it. I'm a dream of a best friend."

"What do you mean, that Fox doesn't know I'm great company yet?"

"I mean that unfortunately for me, you already want Fox, and he's too wrapped up in his pity party that he doesn't see it."

My mouth dropped open. "Excuse me?"

He flashed a bright smile. "You heard me."

"So, you asked me to ride with you to what? Tell me that Fox doesn't like me? And that you do?"

"First off, no, I don't have any feelings like that for you.

You're great and I will flirt with you endlessly, but I'm more than happy to only be friends."

"Ouch, Jax. Really breaking my heart here."

"Oh really, let's make out then, as soon as we get there, right in front of everyone, and then see how you're feeling," he said, wiggling his eyebrows with a smile. "And you can't say that you didn't just think of how Fox would react to that."

"You suck."

"Only because I'm right."

"You said first off. What is the second thing?"

"The actual reason I asked you to ride with me was for a favor. Another one, actually, considering I wrapped you into the first one without running it by you first."

"You ask a lot of favors for a man who isn't giving anything in return."

His mouth dropped open. "Are you insinuating that you *do* want to make out in front of everyone?"

"I'm simply making a point," I said with a laugh. "Are you going to tell me what you want?"

"I want you to push Fox more."

My eyebrows shot up. "Of all the things I was thinking you were going to say, it wasn't that." I couldn't hide my shock.

"I want to ask you to keep pushing at Fox. I don't know how you're doing it, and quite honestly, don't want to know, but it's working."

"It's…working? What does that mean?"

"However you are pushing Fox, it's making him…Fox again. Even this morning, he wasn't bitching and moaning about having to get out of his apartment. He was actually excited. I have spent almost two damn months trying to pull him out of there every time we wanted to go out. And even when he did go out, he was grumbling and snapping at every one of us. Even Scout wasn't safe from his outbursts, and we all know she's his favorite. And now, he's cool with all of it. Going to the races, going out with us for the night when you girls went out, now today. He doesn't complain, he even seems excited."

"And you think that's somehow my fault?"

"I know it's your fault. We all tried and maybe time has helped, but you've obviously sped it up. I just want to ask you to keep pushing him. Please. I know not racing with us is going to hit him hard, but I think you doing whatever it is you're doing is helping him come back. I also saw the scowl you gave him this morning, and I'm worried that you might give up."

I couldn't hide my laugh. The only thing I was doing to Fox at this point was sexually teasing him, and I'm pretty sure that's all he was doing back. Jax was pretty much telling me his friend needed to get laid so he could relax.

"Well, you aren't completely wrong. I've been trying to think of ways to avoid him more, but wasn't coming up with many options with all this racing stuff. As much as I would like to help, I don't think there's much more I can do. I don't think whatever is going on with him has to do with me. Maybe he's finally healing and feeling better. All that pain would make anyone grumpy."

"*Maybe*, but I think it's obvious that you like Fox and I would bet my car that you're the driving force for him finally coming back around because he didn't want anything to do with any of us. Even when we would ask him to go out racing, he wasn't interested. Now today he was the first one ready to go? So maybe a coincidence, but maybe not. I didn't think it would hurt to ask for your help. Again."

I rolled my eyes. "I think you've been watching one too many romance movies with the girls."

We pulled up next to the others on an empty road.

"But," I said. "I can try to keep being nice."

"Thank you. Now, let's get you racing." He jumped out, and I followed, my chest already tightening at the sight of the open street.

I didn't know how I was going to do it all.

Race and help them win.

Help Fox and try to undo the damage that was done because of me.

Decide if I should keep hiding who I was while realizing how much I liked them all.

I already didn't want to leave their group, but I would have to.

There was no good way to tell people that you had been lying to them the entire time, and still think that they would forgive you.

TWENTY-FOUR
ASH

FOX'S EYES were on me the moment I got out, but this time, I smiled.

Maybe Jax was right. Pushing Fox might be helping and with or without Jax's favor, I didn't know if I was done yet with Fox.

I wanted to do what no one had done for me. I knew firsthand that never-ending feeling of drowning in your own emotions and misery. It was too overwhelming for anyone to handle on their own.

Scout and Quinn walked over, eyebrows raised.

"What's going on?" Quinn asked, moving next to me to watch as the guys talked over who raced first.

"Nothing, why?"

"Oh, I don't know, because you and Fox have something going on, but then you ride here with Jax. I'm just trying to keep up."

"Jax had a few questions for me. Apparently, everyone does."

"I think things are getting…interesting," Scout said. "That, and we are all pretty nosey in each other's business."

"Alright, Ash. You're up," Fox interrupted.

"What? No. Shouldn't someone else go first?"

"No. You're racing me. Don't worry. We're going to put a speed limit on your race. Meaning you're basically only driving down the road next to me."

"Come on, Ash," Jax said, walking over. "You can do this."

Jax reached for my hand and pulled me towards Fox's car. "Just drive. Don't go fast."

I looked to Fox, who was watching Jax's arm wrap around my waist now as he led me over to the cars.

"We agreed that you'll take Fox's car today since the rest of us will be practicing."

I looked over my shoulder, Fox stalking behind us.

"Fine, but I don't know if I'm ready."

"You are ready to drive down a road. You don't have to race me. Just drive with me next as fast as you're comfortable," Fox said.

I nodded. Jax finally let me go and headed back to grab something as Fox lingered behind me.

"So how much do you know about driving a car like this?" he asked as I opened the door and slid into the driver's seat.

"Aside from the panic? I know what to do."

"Are you sure?"

I rolled my eyes. "Yes, I know how to make the car go down the road fast. Knowing how isn't the issue."

"If you need anything, stop. I'll be there."

Panic gripped me, making my heart race and hands sweat. "Maybe my dad was right. Maybe David was right. I can't do this. They told me I couldn't, and they were right."

"That prick told you that you wouldn't be able to race again? Has he seen himself race? He has no business telling anyone not to."

"They knew," I said, the panic attack taking over. "They knew I wouldn't be able to do it."

He crouched down next to me. "Ash, stop. Look at me. Do not listen to him. One wreck won't stop you. I have never seen you actually race and I have no doubt you could beat me right now. You can absolutely do this. Don't let one wreck take this away if you love it."

I took a deep, steadying breath. "What if, when I finally do race again, I suck?"

"Well, how good were you before?"

"Good. Very good."

"I'm so glad this hasn't taken away your confidence in that," he said with a grin. "There is no point in worrying about how good you would be now. All you have to do is start again. I promise that as soon as you start again, we will make you great. We can get you into racing history if you want, but for today, I only need you to drive down the road next to me."

He was holding my hand now, squeezing it once before moving them to the harness, checking that it was tight.

"Okay. It's like driving down the road. And you'll be there," I said with another deep breath.

"I'll be right there the entire way," he said, kissing my head as he stood up.

"Sorry," he said quickly. "I don't know why I did that."

He shut the door fast, heading to Jax's car to get in and line up.

Something clicked into place, every piece Fox had given me put together. It's not like I didn't know before. I guess I knew the entire time, but that thoughtless kiss, the soothing encouragement, the way he had checked that my harness was on tight before he stood.

Fox might actually care about me.

In the ten years I knew David and the few that we dated, he

never stopped to check my harness, he never asked if I was okay after a scare at the track, he never encouraged me like Fox did, and when I cried he would freeze up and scroll his phone until I walked away, not take me out for food and coffee to cheer me up.

If Fox really thought I could do this, why wouldn't I think that? I knew he could go out and handle the people who said mean things to him. I knew he was stronger than those people and I was stronger than David and his dumb words. And even though he never saw me race, he seemed to believe I could.

Fox's voice came over the radio, pulling me from my own earth shattering revelation. "You ready?"

I closed my eyes and leaned my head back. I've raced and won a hundred times. Out of all those races, I've only wrecked a handful of times and only one was bad.

My dad always told me to put any fear aside and get down the track like it's a race for your life. Every moment I was learning how to race was met with him pushing me harder, pushing me to go faster, and not give in to my fear.

I felt like this was a race for my life. A life that I could have again.

This entire crew seemed to believe in me enough to have me join their team. They did it because they believed I could race. Fox believed I could do this and even joked that I could win.

Someone who had never watched me race thought I could do this without question.

"Fox, I want to race.," I said into the radio.

"We are racing."

"No. I mean, really race. If it's you I'm racing, I want to do this."

"Is that only because you want to kick my ass?"

I laughed into the radio. "Yes, that's it exactly."

"Are you a hundred percent sure?"

I took a deep breath, pushing away images of my wreck and replacing them with images of when I won. The look on Fox's face, how excited the crew would be, how free I could feel again.

"Yes. A hundred percent sure."

"I'm about to get my ass handed to me by a girl, aren't I?"

I laughed. "Yes, yes you are."

"I can take it. Give me all you got, hellion." He went quiet for a minute. "And I mean it, Ash. It doesn't matter who wins, give it as much as you can."

I looked over at him, only able to make out the shape of him. "Alright, but be careful what you wish for." I put the radio back down, smiling so hard that I almost missed Scout's signal.

We moved up to the imaginary line she made, and I realized at the last second that no one else knew we were actually going to race.

It shot more joy through me at the thought of them seeing me race for the first time, too.

I couldn't remember the last time I felt like this before a race. Even before the wreck, David had started to ruin race nights for me, but now all I could feel was a giddy happiness at the first real chance to do something I love again.

Scout's arms went down, and I took off, hitting through the gears and letting muscle memory control each movement. I couldn't think past the finish line. I couldn't think of anything but winning against Fox.

My heart hammered in my chest, but it wasn't with fear. It was like months and layers of panic were stripping off of me with each second.

Until the happiness faded and was replaced with panic. The car moving too fast for me to think of anything but crashing.

I shifted and hit the gas harder, moving ahead of Fox and reaching the agreed upon finish line before he did, but the panic attack had already started. My heart beat was so out of control I could barely catch my breath.

I pulled the car to a stop, ripping at the harness that was now a straight jacket. I knew I didn't wreck, but I needed out. I needed to know I could actually get out. The night of the wreck I was trapped and with every second that passed now, I could feel it all over again. A panicked cry escaped as my fingers fumbled at the harness clips. They weren't working, though, none of them staying strong enough to actually click myself out of it.

The door flew open and Fox reached in.

"I need out. Get me out," I said, not even recognizing the sound of my own panicked voice.

"Shh, take one really deep breath, baby. I'm here, I'm getting you out."

I listened, realizing he was lifting the harness off.

"Good, now hold on to me," Fox said. I grabbed onto his arms, my fingers sinking into him as he pulled me out.

His arms came around me as my feet found the ground. "You're fine. You did it. You raced, and you won."

I breathed hard with my head against his chest, not moving from the safety of his arms.

"How did you know to come over here?"

"Just a guess. Are you okay? Your team of cheerleaders is almost here."

"What?"

He turned us, the crew coming to a stop as everyone jumped off of Ransom's car and broke out into different levels of cheering.

"You did it!" Scout yelled, pumping her arms up and throwing them around Fox and me both.

"You did it, and you sure as hell know what you're doing," Jax said. They all circled around, as excited as I hoped they would be. I understood why Fox wanted to give this to them and knowing that I made it a little more possible was an amazing feeling.

I laughed into Fox's chest.

I suddenly hated not telling them the truth about me. What if I told them now, and they were mad at me for keeping it a secret?

The worst part was, based on how involved they were in the racing world, they probably already knew who I was, but didn't know my face. I tried to keep some level of privacy, and while my picture came up on an internet search, I wasn't one to sit in the spotlight.

I realized I was still clutching onto Fox, and pried myself away, not liking the feelings it was bringing up.

How could I think that someone could feel something for me, or that I meant something to them, when I wasn't even being honest about my full name?

"Well?" Kye asked, interrupting my internal freakout. "You think you can do it again?"

"I think so. The racing part wasn't the problem. The not being able to get out after was."

"I'll stay down here," Fox said. "Someone else can race you, and I'll help again if you have any issues."

I looked over at him, the sun casting a golden warmth onto him. He really was handsome, and apparently sweet, and caring, and really good at turning me on.

Damn.

Apparently, Jax was right. I did like Fox.

"Thanks," I said quietly.

"Alright then, my turn to race you," Jax said. The rest of them jumped into, and onto, Ransom's car and I followed Jax around to his.

"Hey, can I talk to you real quick?"

His face lit up. "Problem? Scared to race me?"

"Not at all," I said, rolling my eyes. "I want to know how you knew I had…those types of feelings for Fox?"

"Ahh. One, it's really not that hard to see from the outside. I mean, we both know you are not treating me and him the same, or Ransom, or Kye even. Second, I'm a romantic at heart. I can tell."

"And Fox?"

"Harder to tell with his attitude and shit, but I'd say yes. We could always test that out, though, really push his buttons."

"How?" I asked.

If it was possible, Jax's smile grew.

"How about we have a good day today and then I'll pick you, and your car, up tomorrow?"

"What would that matter?"

"Trust me. We'll talk later. For now, let's race and I'll try not to piss Fox off at all today."

I looked over. Fox wasn't looking at us. He was staring down the road, his arms crossed and hat turned back the right way, hiding his face.

"Fine. Tomorrow."

I walked back over to Fox's car as Jax drove off.

"You're still fine with me driving this?"

He gave a grunt laugh. "If anything, I'm more okay with you driving it now than before. I would say based on how well you kicked my ass, you might be more trustworthy to drive it than me. Maybe you can even beat Jax."

"Could beat him?"

He smirked. "Maybe. Anything is possible, I guess."

I bit the inside of my cheek. "You're trying to challenge me, aren't you?"

"No, not at all."

"Fox," I said.

"Go on, hellion. Let's see if you can do that again or if this is beginner's luck."

Beginner? What an ass. I was more professionally trained than him.

I slammed the door shut, heading back down the track and lining up.

With the outline of Fox at the other end, the weight that had held on before was gone.

Even if I wrecked, he would be there to get me out of the car. If I win or lose, I knew he was going to be right there again to help me.

To save me.

I turned up the music and let myself drown out everything else for a second.

Jax was already lined up, and Scout waved again.

I took off, the world falling away as the music blared and the car roared.

I didn't pay attention to where Ransom or his car was at, only looked to the end of the track, to Fox.

Like every race in my life, it felt like it was over before I could blink.

Fox was at the door as soon as I stopped, pulling off the harness and grabbing onto me. I was out of the car in seconds, pulled up against his hard chest.

I didn't even have time to worry about my wreck or my panic before I was in his arms as he looked down at me.

"Wow, you're already a pro at that," I said, fighting the strong urge to kiss him.

"Are you okay?"

"I'm good. Currently, doing very okay."

"Alright. Good. Fuck, you did even better that time," he said, still holding me tight against him.

"So I won?"

"Oh, you won. You kicked his ass. Are you going to tell us who you are or how you know how to race like that?"

"I wasn't going to today."

"I'm getting more and more impatient."

"About what?" I asked innocently.

His chest rumbled with a growl as he pushed me tighter against him.

"Don't play games, Ash. We both know who wins each time."

"Based on these races, I would say it's me."

He leaned down to my ear. "Based on how much you came on my fingers last night, I would say it's me."

"Mmm, no. Based on who had the orgasm, I still think I was the clear winner for that, too. I'd offer to race again and give you another chance to beat me at that, but I'm guessing we already know the outcome."

I looked around him to Ransom, who was idling back down the track.

Fox grabbed my chin, forcing my attention back on him.

"We're racing again."

"Let me guess, you want your car back because it's faster."

"You can still take mine. I'll use Ransom's. Just as fast."

"Fine. Let's go."

He finally let me go and moved to the passenger side, but didn't get in yet.

I followed his eyes down the track, all four cars speeding down the road towards us.

"What are they doing?" I asked, watching them come into view more.

Fox swore as the red and blue lights came into view behind them.

"Get in. Go," he said.

I slid inside, turning the car on and looking over at him. He wasn't getting in, but fought with the door.

"Unlock the door," he yelled.

I hit at the buttons on my door, the window rolling down but not unlocking anything. Fox leaned in.

"Hit the button! Unlock the door."

"I'm trying. It's not working!" I yelled back, hitting the button again.

"Ash!"

"Fox!"

Scout's car flew past, followed by Kye, Jax and then Ransom, who honked as he went.

I smacked the button more, but still nothing happened.

"Oh fuck. Just go," he said before shoving his body through the window.

Fox was not a small man by any means, and watching him crawl through the window was the funniest thing I had ever seen.

"Drive! Now!"

TWENTY-FIVE
FOX

FINALLY, she took off, moving through the gears as we raced to catch up with everyone else.

But she was still laughing.

"You think this is so funny?" I said, getting myself up into the seat. "I'm starting to wonder if you did it on purpose."

"I did not. Your button isn't working."

"Right. Sure. Turn here."

"But they are going that way?"

"And I'm sure they are going to be splitting up any second now that we are behind them. Turn, Ash," I said, as she finally yanked the steering wheel. "Fuck, good thing you can drive in a straight line because you're not as good with the actual street."

"Well, I'm not used to having to navigate running from the police. Why are they after us?"

My eyebrows furrowed. "What do you mean? Street racing is illegal. We got caught. Now we have to not actually get caught, so pick up the pace."

Her hands gripped the steering wheel harder.

"This isn't as easy as it looks."

"Yes, it is, and you better figure it out because I would like to keep my car," I was almost yelling, but now that I knew how fast she was, I needed her to move faster.

"Don't yell at me, that isn't helping!"

Rain started to drizzle, the drops coating the windshield.

"Shit."

As if on cue, the rain came down harder as soon as we turned down a winding road.

"It's raining too hard. I can barely see the road."

I looked back. I couldn't tell if anyone was still behind us. The curves were too sharp, but we couldn't crawl at this pace and find out. "Pull over here. I'll drive."

I pointed down a small gravel side road. It would at least be deep enough to pull down and be out of the way while we switched spots.

"No. Won't that slow us down?"

"More than your turtle crawl down the road? No. Pull in."

"But I —"

"Pull in!" I finally yelled. I felt like she was constantly pushing me to my limit. Every part of me was an endless, confusing mess of her. "You've already ruined my face. Can you not get my car taken, too?"

She ripped the steering wheel to the left, kicking gravel as she flew onto the side road.

"Maybe if you drove like that down the road, we wouldn't be having this problem."

She screamed, her mouth closed. "Do you ever stop bringing that up? If you really blame me so much for your face, then maybe you shouldn't beg me to race with you. Maybe you should have left me alone!"

"Maybe you shouldn't give me shit for feeling bad about myself because of my face when you've been sitting at home, alone, feeling bad for yourself for months because of your own wreck. At least you don't have a walking stamp on your face about it. And what part is not to blame you for?" I yelled back.

She slammed the car in park.

"You're an ass."

"I've heard that before."

We both got out, walking around the car to switch.

"If you've heard it that many times, maybe take a hint!" she yelled over the rain.

We made it around the front when she stepped into me, knocking my arm with a smirk as she went around.

"Are you serious?" I laughed, grabbing her arm and spinning her around. "When I call you a hellion, I absolutely mean it."

"You know what, Fox? I hate that you bled for me. I hate that you're scarred," she gave a strangled laugh. "I hate you for being the hero."

"Well, you're in luck then, because I no longer want to be the hero. Saving your life meant wrecking mine. So I'm ready to be the villain. I look like a beast. Why not act like one, too?"

"You couldn't be even if you tried," she said.

My hand tightened on her arm and she tried to rip it away. I wasn't ready to let her go yet, though.

She was wrong. I could be the beast.

I hooked an arm under her ass and one behind her head, laying her back onto the hood and coming down over her.

"What are you doing?" she yelled.

"Whatever I want."

My lips crashed into hers. The need settled so deep in me that there was no chance to get out of this without kissing her.

Her lips were warm and, in seconds, confident. She pushed forward, and I didn't hesitate, moving my tongue against her lips and exploring her mouth.

Rain pelted onto my back, but I covered her enough that it didn't get to her.

I didn't know what I was doing, just that I couldn't stand not to touch her anymore.

Based on the way her hips were pushing up into me, I didn't think she minded.

"Fox," she murmured. I didn't know how the sound of my name could make me harder than I was, but it did.

I pulled back, but her hands wound around my neck, bringing me back down for more.

The feel of her warm body and the cold rain against my back was a torturous contrast, leaving me wanting to wrap her around me.

"You can't be a beast *and* a villain. You have to pick one. The beast was never the villain," she said, trying to catch her breath.

"What?"

"You said you were a beast and wanted to be the villain now. Joke's on you. The beast was always the hero of the story."

"*That's* what you're thinking about right now? The accuracy of my statements," I mumbled, finding her lips again. "Hellion. Always trying to win."

The rain changed direction until it was sideways, soaking her now.

"Come on, wrap your legs around me."

I pulled her up, loving the feel of her body clinging against me. I didn't care if she wanted to be right or win. I would let her win every game we played and argument we had if this was the end result. I angled us inside the passenger seat, shutting the door and sealing us in. The only sound was the rain still coming down hard.

We sat in silence, trying to catch our breath, until she reached for my hand, bringing it under her shirt and dragging it up her body.

"Pretty sure I can find those myself if you need me to," I

said, not surprised at the boldness. She always seemed to know what she wanted and was definitely not afraid to ask for it.

"That's not where we're going," she said as my fingers grazed her breast. I stopped, squeezing at her nipple with my thumb and forefinger, making her shudder once.

"Are you sure? It seems like a good place to go."

"A little higher."

She squeezed my hand, pulling it up above her breast to her chest. Finally, she stopped, my fingers settling on raised skin.

I knew that feeling well now.

I ran my fingers further towards her arm, not finding the end of the scar.

"You were hurt?" I asked, realizing that I had never seen her chest. She never wore anything that showed it.

"The wreck. Something broke off and cut across my chest."

I reached the end and went back, my fingers following along the scar that seemed to run from her arm to the top of her opposite breast.

She leaned back, letting me keep running my fingers back and forth.

"That is high. It could have cut your neck."

"No, it was still far enough off from killing me, luckily."

"Why didn't you tell me?" I finally asked.

"If you could hide yours, wouldn't you?"

"Probably, but don't you think that telling me would be a little different?"

"Yes, that's why I am now. Telling you about it now is hard enough. Other than me, no one has seen it in months, and aside from doctors, no one else has ever touched it until today."

"Will you show me?"

She took a deep breath, her body sinking deeper against mine. "I don't know how you do it. I've been hiding with shirts and hoodies," her voice shook, but she grabbed the hem of the shirt, pulling it up and over, only in a bra now, the scar on full display.

"I can't say I understand how you feel, but I understand how cruel people can be," she said. "Even David said nasty things when the bandages came off. He didn't seem to like that he couldn't see boobs without seeing the scar." She gave a small laugh, but I knew the words would sting. "He made me feel so ugly, like I was ruined as a woman for the world because my cleavage would forever be marred. At the time, it was devastating. Now, I'm just disgusted with him."

I stared in disbelief, not knowing how someone could say something so awful to her after what she went through. I couldn't imagine having to wake up and hear how horrible I looked. I did enough of that myself without someone else telling me. I woke up to an entire support team and a beautiful woman trying to convince me that I was still worth a damn, even without my looks.

I pulled her into me, my lips meeting the scar as a flood of emotions hit me. I couldn't believe that anyone would make her feel less than anything than her perfect self because of one cut.

I made it to her breast before going back over the scar again.

For a brief moment, the world melted away, leaving the two of us in a shared understanding of pain.

"You shouldn't think that you're anything but beautiful," I said, the sound of the rain trying to drown my words. "And you shouldn't hide this to make anyone else feel comfortable."

"So you find me beautiful, attractive even, with the scar?"

"Of course. The scar only adds to it. I know how strong you have to be to go through something like this."

"And you don't look at me and think I'm ugly or deformed or anything like that?"

"Fuck, no. How could anyone think that? You're beautiful."

A smile spread across her face. "So do you think it would be easier to understand that, even with your scar, I think you're handsome?"

I looked away, trying to shift my gaze in any direction that would hide my face from her.

"Walked right into that, didn't I? And easier said than done."

She could say that, but she even said it herself. She could hide her scars. I couldn't hide mine.

"Definitely easier said than done."

Her lips met mine again, and I pulled her closer against me.

She was no less demanding when I kissed her, biting and licking at my lips until I deepened the kiss. I'd never cared about kissing someone, not without the thought that it was leading somewhere else fast, but I could do this all day.

The radio buzzed, Jax's voice coming over it.

"Where are you guys? Are you good?"

I didn't answer, not really caring what he had to say when Ash was still half naked on top of me. She grabbed the bottom of my shirt when I realized this actually was about to lead somewhere else and she didn't seem to have any intention of slowing down.

"Fooooooxxxxx," Jax said.

I grabbed for the radio, holding her tight against me so I wouldn't push her into the dash.

I splayed my fingers out on her lower back and she arched into me.

"We're fine," I said into the radio with a smile at her.

"Oh, good. We were getting worried. Meet at the diner?"

"Yeah, sure." I threw the radio back down as Ash pressed a light kiss to my neck.

I groaned. She was making it hard to think of anything else. Pleasure rolled through me as she did it again and I moved my hips, pushing my hard cock against her.

"Yes," she hissed, trying to pull at my shirt again. Her scar came back into view as she leaned back and I paused.

I had slept with plenty of girls without a thought of who they were, where they were from, even what their names were, but this was the first time it gave me pause enough to stop.

I had also never slept with a girl that was so involved in our lives.

I wouldn't be able to do my normal routine of sleeping with her and disappearing. I didn't even know if I would want to do that. Some part of me screamed that I wouldn't.

The scar on her made me feel too close to her now, knowing she was the one person that might start to understand what I was going through. She was also someone that was trying to understand. She was trying so damn hard to help me that I couldn't treat her like anything less than perfect.

I grabbed her wrists to stop their exploration. "We aren't doing that here."

"Why?" Her eyebrows furrowed, and I didn't blame her for the confusion. I was the one that started it this time and now I was the one stopping it, again.

"Because we aren't. Not here. We should go meet up with the crew."

The crew. I had to remember why she was around in the first place. Sleeping with her would be too complicated when she still had to help them, and it did still bother me that I didn't know anything about her.

She groaned, leaning back against the dash. "Decide that the cut grosses you out? Or just easier to hate me?"

"To be honest, hating you is a lot easier," I said, laughing. "Things like this get messy fast, and I realized that I don't know who you are, which apparently bothers me."

"Right. I'm sure that's the *only* problem." She threw her shirt on and opened the door, crawling out and waiting for me to get out after her.

I walked around, silently pulling the car out and heading towards the diner.

"I do not think your scar is gross."

"Whatever."

"I don't even know your name. Ash is a nickname, not a name."

"I said, whatever. Drop it."

It seems that this time it was her icing me out. She was giving me the cold shoulder just like I had done to her plenty of times.

How she didn't run me over with a car all those times was beyond me. The silence was more frustrating than anything I'd ever faced. The other woman in my life talked my ear off when they were pissed and usually Ash did too.

Which made it even worse how quiet she was now.

We made it to the diner that silence, my mind racing in circles on how I could be dumb enough not to agree to have sex with her right then and there.

The one time I let my brain make the decisions had to happen at the same time that I had the perfect woman in my lap.

The crew was already sitting at a big table with three seats open when we walked in. Two were right next to each other, and one was at the opposite end of the table.

I picked that one, needing to be as far away from her as I could be right now.

I didn't miss the way she stared daggers at me throughout the entire meal.

And I didn't blame her, because right at that moment, I was pissed at myself, too.

TWENTY-SIX
FOX

I'D NEVER BEEN this much of an asshole to someone I actually liked being around. I stayed awake all night thinking it through and I came to the same conclusion I had yesterday.

I was the dumbest man alive.

I had spent too much time last night thinking about her on top of me and reminding myself over and over why I had to stop it.

I didn't know who she was. The way she was going out of her way to hide things was bothering me more than anything else, but I knew I shouldn't be treating her like the problem when it was me. After what happened to us last year, I was too cautious to trust a new person coming around. I had been so hard on her about it without coming out and telling her what was happening.

I had been too busy facing my worst fear, apparently.

The worst part was that I never knew how much I used my looks as a crutch. Ransom always gave me shit for being the charming one, but really, it was the confidence that I was hot. I never realized how pathetic I was, walking around like I had the world when all I had was a good-looking face. Even more pathetic was how I didn't even feel like I knew who I was without that good-looking face.

Somehow, though, everything was coming back to me slowly. The full life that I lived with people who cared about me was coming back into focus, and I knew that was because of her.

Because of the girl who scarred me in the first place. The girl I couldn't stop thinking of now.

At this rate, I was going to need therapy for the rest of my life.

I threw another tool down. I was getting sick of fixing this damn car when all I wanted to do was go talk to her.

Our car hauler pulled in, a car on the back that I was all too familiar with now.

My blood boiled as I saw Jax in the driver's seat, Ash next to him in the passenger seat, laughing and smiling like she was having the best damn day of her life.

I stalked out, pulling the driver's door open.

"What's going on?"

Jax gave me a smirk. "Ash decided to bring her car over here today. Needed to put it on our lift and get it finished."

I looked over at her, her smiling face making my chest tighten. "And you called him?"

"Quinn and Ransom were busy. And I don't have Kye's number," she said sweetly.

Damn.

I knew that tone now. It was the one that seemed to come out right before she got vicious.

I was right yesterday when she was so quiet. She was pissed, and I didn't think any half assed apology was going to convince her that I was worth forgiving this time.

"And you had his number?"

"He gave it to me when I agreed to racing with you all."

Jax was still beaming, the smug look on his face taking everything in me not to knock his teeth in.

"Right. And you called him to get the car, even though I offered?"

"Oh," she said, that sweet smile still plastered on her face. "I figured that offer was off the table from you now. I think you've made it obvious I'm in your space and you don't want me there, so I will do better to stay out of it. Jax offered to bring my car over and help me finish it before the big night. Now that you guys know I can race, it seems having a car that can keep up with me is a priority."

"The offer was never off the table. I told you I would help you whenever you needed."

She rolled her eyes and laughed. "Wow, good to know. It was really hard to tell that you still wanted to help me when you were busy pushing me away for the…" She pointed at her fingers, fake counting. "Hundredth time."

"I'm sorry. I was a little too caught up worrying about protecting my friends from someone who seems to be hiding everything about themselves. For all I know, you could be with a rival team. You could be helping to sabotage us."

Jax looked at us and laughed. "If you think for one second that I need protection from her, please leave me at her mercy and don't think twice about it."

She scooted across the bench seat and wrapped her hand around his arm.

"Watch out babe, I bite," she teased.

He tipped his head back and groaned. "Oh no," he said dryly, waving his hands. "Help. I'm in hell."

If I had any doubt that Ash was dangerous before, I didn't now. Every word and movement was laced with venom intended for me, and it was working exactly as she intended.

I knew Jax was joking. I assumed she was too, but something

in me still snapped. It wasn't that long ago that I was that person. Joking, flirting, relaxed and at ease in every situation and all I wanted to do was be that again. Not be so wrapped up in my own mess that I couldn't even think straight.

Not only that, she was mine. I'm the one who touched her and kissed her and saw her scar. Jax could fuck right off if he thought he had a chance now.

I couldn't do this. I was going about this all wrong and needed to stop while I was still ahead.

I stalked back into the garage and grabbed my keys before heading to the car.

"Fox, wait! Where are you going?" Jax asked.

"Out."

"Wait. I was kidding. We both were," Jax yelled, but I slammed the door. I didn't need to hear any more. I needed to drive.

And I did. I didn't stop until I had left town and come back, finding myself parked in front of the diner.

The car idled as I thought about what came next.

I either moved on and let Jax deal with Ash and the races.

Or I sucked it up, apologized again, and changed my attitude.

I leaned back and gripped the steering wheel. I don't know who I thought I was kidding. I had driven the whole way here, already knowing that I was going to apologize. Not only apologize, but try to beg her to forgive me with her favorite food and drink.

I ran in, grabbing the order before heading back to the garage. The sun was going down now, the sunset throwing enough light to bathe everything in gold and the weather perfect enough to roll the windows down as I drove.

The bay doors were open and I could see everyone gathered around her car still, working on something and probably drooling over it. There was no doubt that it was a beautiful car, but I was only looking for Ash.

She finally glanced out at me as I got out of the car and turned away just as fast.

"Ash. Can you come here?"

Her eyes narrowed as they met mine, but she didn't move.

"No."

"Please."

"Why?"

"I need to talk to you."

"No, I don't think you do."

The crew was silent now, looking at the car, and pretending that they weren't listening to every word.

"I do. Please. Only for a second. Come on. I have something for you."

It was enough to pique her curiosity, and she finally came over to me.

"What do you have for me?"

"First, I have an apology."

She crossed her arms. "I don't know if that's worth hearing. You're really bad at apologizing. It really never includes the words 'I'm sorry.'"

I smiled. She looked so cute with her hair up, dirt smears on her arms, and the angry little scowl on her face. I really needed to not find her hot when she was angry, especially when that anger was directed at me.

"I am sorry, and this will be the last time I'm apologizing for being such an ass."

"Ahh, getting sick of apologizing? Just going to ignore it and move on next time it happens?"

"No. I'm not going to let it happen again."

"Doubt it."

"I guess that's smart of you. Could you at least accept my apology?"

"No."

"Ash, please. I really am sorry."

"I don't feel like you are sorry enough. I showed you something about myself and you ran. Words aren't going to suffice this time."

"And what would make you feel like I'm sorry enough?"

She looked back at the crew and then up at me with a smirk. I knew she already had her plan in place and it wasn't going to be good for me.

"Alright then. I recall a while ago, at one of the other points you apologized, you made a good point, something about falling to your knees in surrender. Maybe now would be a good time to demonstrate that, along with telling me exactly why you are sorry."

"You want me to…get on my knees and what? Grovel?"

"You can call it whatever you want. I want to see you on your knees for me baby," she said.

I didn't hide my smile. "You should watch your mouth because if you talk to me like that again, you're going to find yourself on your knees with something between those perfect lips." Her eyes flared, and she was about to bite back, but I continued. "You want me to do this in front of everyone knowing that I won't hear the end of it?"

"Yes, I do," she said, the sunset covering her in a warm glow. It was hazy, calming, and felt like a dream come true. I was quickly running out of reasons to fight against her everyday.

I glanced back at the crew who were all blatantly staring now, but turned away, trying to ignore them. I kept my eyes on her then, trying to find a way to memorize every second of this as I moved down onto my knees.

Her mouth dropped open. "I can't believe you are actually doing it."

"Yeah, me either. Unfortunately, I am quickly learning that I would do just about anything for you."

"Except apologize," she said with a smile.

"I am literally on my knees apologizing."

"Fine, let's hear it," she said, crossing her arms.

"I am sorry for being a jerk after you *finally* shared something about yourself. And please understand that it had nothing to do with you and everything to do with me."

"You were disgusted by my scar when you don't want people judging yours."

I stood back up, wanting to reach out for her, but knowing that wouldn't be well appreciated now. "No. Not at all, Ash. It had nothing to do with that. I spiraled about other things. There is *nothing* wrong with you."

"Your timing is impeccable, then."

"I agree. I have had so much to deal with that I'm not as charming as I once was." That seemed to make her smile more. "At least I am still half as charming?"

"Yeah, I guess that does work in your favor. I'm still mad that you made me feel bad about it when I have never made you feel bad about yours."

I leaned closer, knowing that the crew was straining to hear every word. "Please believe me when I say that it took everything in me not to continue. I stayed awake all night wishing I wouldn't have stopped, but I had to. And if you don't believe me, I will pull off that hoodie and kiss every inch of it again in front of everyone."

Her hands came up against my chest. "Let's not go that far. They haven't even seen it yet. Let alone see you trying to eat me alive."

"Fine? In private then?" I leaned in more, her hands staying against me.

I knew I was falling back into her, everything about her pulling me in, and I had to stop. I needed to keep more focused than this.

She stared at me in silence, looking over my face, but I didn't think she was staring at the cut. I always felt so on display, but the more time I spent with her, the more I realized that she was never staring at it, only at me.

"Why the sudden change of heart? Why all of this?"

"Because I don't like being this person, and if I'm stuck with him, I am at least going to try to fight the urge to be terrible all the time. None of my friends deserve that. You don't deserve that. It's never been a problem with you, Ash, not really. I don't see any flaws in you even with that scar. I'm trying to believe that someone could think the same of me."

"Wow, something got through your big head. Okay then, apology accepted, *friend*," she said, the subtle reminder enough to make me let her go.

"Yes, friends. And that brings me to the second point I had." I reached into the car, grabbing out the takeout bag and iced coffee. "I brought you these."

Her mouth dropped. "That's for me? I'm starving."

I held it back. "Yes, but only if you agree to one thing."

An eyebrow cocked up, and she pulled back. "What?"

I smiled, the word so threatening. "You have to tell me more about you. I need to know, actually we all need to know who you are."

"Why? Is it that important?"

"Not knowing is driving me out of my fucking mind, and of course it's important. How could it not be? Just something, a little more to go on than only Ash."

"Like I said before, I'm sure you've had plenty of friends around that you didn't know everything about."

"That was different. "

A satisfied smirk came over her. "Really? What part is different? I thought you said we are friends, so it should be fine."

She backed me into the corner, knowing I would have to come clean, that there was more to this than only being her friend.

"What a little hellion," I whispered, shaking my head. "Just be a good girl and tell me who you are, then I will give you the coffee."

She huffed. "Tomorrow."

"You'll tell me tomorrow?"

"Yes. If you give me the food and the coffee, while also playing nice, I will tell you."

I handed it over and reached in, grabbing the rest of the bags.

"What's all that?"

"Same thing you learned last time we went to the diner. The number one rule of being with the crew is to never show up with food unless you're feeding everyone."

"Got it. Thank you for this."

"Thanks for forgiving me. Again."

"It won't happen again," she said, still smiling as she sipped her coffee. "Three strikes. You're out."

We walked in and set everything down until I was cornered by Jax and Ransom.

"What do you two want?"

"You got super pissed that I showed up with Ash and her car, stormed out, and now you're back and happy?"

"Yep. It's all worked out. For now."

"What does that mean? You're good with Ash staying, then?"

"I was never mad about Ash staying."

"Right, just mad at anyone but you hanging out with her."

I rolled my eyes. "Yeah, and it pisses me off that she called you instead of me, but only because I had offered to help first."

"Again, *right,* that's the only reason."

"I told Ash to come clean about who she is. If she does, we're good."

"And if she doesn't?"

"I don't know."

"You didn't care that much about who she was when this started. What's changed?" Ransom asked.

"It's because she's all over him and somehow that's bad," Jax said.

"I thought she was only doing that because she felt bad for me."

"Give the girl more credit than that. Fuck, that's rude." Jax shook his head.

I had been so wrapped up caring that she found me repulsive that I didn't realize what I was implying. I was a bigger asshole than I thought.

"You're right, and I apologized to her."

His eyebrows shot up. "What? I'm not sure if I heard correctly. Did you say I was right?"

"Yes." I gritted my teeth. "You're right. And now she has until tomorrow to come clean, and I'll figure out how to handle it if she doesn't."

They shook their heads, but it wasn't their decision.

Ash looked over at me once and I had to look away.

I wasn't going to tell anyone that I was just as scared to know the truth about her as I was not knowing.

TWENTY-SEVEN
ASH

SATURDAY CAME, and I knew it was the deadline for Fox's demands. He wanted to know what was going on, and I didn't blame him. I had already run through a thousand scenarios on how to tell them, but each one ended badly in my head. I couldn't see any possible way this could go right. I knew how serious they all took loyalty and honesty. I didn't know if this was going to feel like a betrayal or if they would understand.

I was relieved to see Ollie's name come up as my phone rang. We texted here and there, but he was so busy lately that actually getting a chance to talk to him was always a nice surprise.

"Hey? What's going on?" I asked, attempting to pick up my apartment while we talked.

"Not a lot today, luckily. What are you up to?"

I gave him the update, telling him about Fox and the crew, along with the fact that I still hadn't told them who I really was.

"Oh, babe. You have to tell them. You know you shouldn't have let it go on this long. Plus, what's wrong with you? Why wouldn't they be happy to know who you are?"

"Yes, but what if they are *too* happy about who I am? What if they want to use me for things?"

"I told you years ago to drop all those snobby friends and only hang out with me. They got in your head even now. Not all friends are going to be like that and if, for some reason, they do act like that, you walk away. No, you run away. Be honest, though, do you really think that's going to happen?"

I thought it over, but it was an easy answer. "No."

"I'm sorry, I didn't hear you."

"I said no."

"Exactly. You need to trust yourself more and do what you know is right. Which, in this case, is telling them the truth. Also, get out of that damn apartment."

"I have been getting out! And it's hard to trust yourself when you spend months on end thinking you've lost your mind."

"Yeah, you haven't been out with me. Nice to know that you'll run around town with them, but don't call," he said. The tone was almost joking, but I know I had been a terrible friend for the last year. "As for losing your mind, that was because of David, not because of you. You are smart. If you think they are good people, they are."

"Thank you for sticking with me even when I didn't call. I really do appreciate you not dropping me as a friend."

"I could never," he said, and I could almost hear the smile. "I know you went through a lot and I know you needed time, but that's over. You need to move on with your life."

"And luckily, I have a smart, wonderful friend to help me do that."

"A friend that you owe dinner. A nice, fancy dinner."

"A nice, fancy dinner in my life right now is burgers at the diner. If that suits you, then yes, my treat."

"Eww," he said with a laugh. "Kidding. Fine, I'm in. Now

run along and tell your friends how awesome you are. Call me if you need."

We hung up, and I grabbed my keys. I needed a drive before I told anyone, anything. I knew the crew was great, and pretty level-headed, but I was still the outsider, and I didn't think I wanted to be anymore.

The sound of a knock at the front door made me jump. My mind immediately thought of David. I was starting to worry each time I heard a noise outside my door that he was there, lurking around and waiting for another chance to 'talk' to me. No one else should be here now, and he was the only one I could think of that would show up unannounced. Now was not the time to face David. I had too much to worry about and talking with him was only going to cause me more panic.

The pounding started again, and I crept to the door, looking out into the hallway and only seeing the top of a head, the red hair giving her away before I could even ask who it was.

I pulled open the door. "Scout? What are you doing here?"

Her face said it all.

Scout looked ready to kill me.

"What am I doing here?" she yelled. "What have *you* been doing here?"

"Whoa. I don't know what that means. Do you want to come in?"

"No, I don't want to come in," she yelled, pushing past me into the apartment.

I shut the door, not needing all my neighbors to hear her yelling at me. Especially when I didn't know what she was yelling about yet.

"What's going on?"

"How could you do this? Do you know what Fox means to me? Do you know what they all mean to me?" she was still yelling, pacing around the living room. "Fox is my best friend. He's my brother in every sense."

"Yes, I've noticed."

She shot me a dirty look but continued. "I go everywhere with him. Growing up, he was always there for me. He's my hero, and he got hurt trying to be yours."

"I know that. Scout, I'm still not sure what's going on right now."

"You lied," she said, finally stopping and turning to me. "You lied to all of us. But worst of all, you lied to him. He has basically given up on his life because of what happened to him. Because of what he did for you."

"I lied?"

"Oh, don't even play that with me. I can tolerate a lot of things, but lying? Admit it right now or you are never going to see any of us again. Especially Fox. I will make damn sure of it." She pulled out her phone, but was watching me, waiting.

I stilled. I wasn't going to insult her any longer and act like I didn't know what she was talking about.

"How did you find out?" I said. My throat was so tight that the words hurt.

She clicked her phone and turned it to me.

It was a picture of me kissing Fox at the baseball game. The caption talking about how Ashton Holt resurfaced at a game on a date. It was a niche social media page, but there were still enough likes to make me panic.

"Has he seen this?"

"No. Not that I know of. At least not yet. He will soon."

"How?"

"Well, either you're coming with me to tell him and show him this now, or I'm going to do it."

I didn't doubt her for a second. It seemed like I was about two wrong sentences from being cut from all of their lives, but I shouldn't have been surprised. I should have known Scout was going to be the most protective of Fox.

"It's all true. That's me. I'm Ashton Holt."

"And you didn't think to tell us? You didn't think we should know that you're a part of Holt Racing? You are an opposing team for the Legends race. Why did you lie?"

"I didn't want to lie. I just kind of kept it to myself. I couldn't bring myself to tell you guys. You treated me so great and I've really never had friends that just liked me for me. It's always about cars, or money, or thinking they will get better status being around my dad. This was the first time in my life I had friends because of me."

"And you really thought we would use you for those things? Have you not come to know us at all?"

"No, I have. I know now. I've known for weeks. But getting the nerve to tell any of you has been almost impossible because it suddenly felt like such a big thing now that I kept it for so long. I swear I was trying to do it today. I was getting the nerve to go over and talk to all of you. And talk to Fox."

Her lips pressed together so hard they were turning white. "You should have told us."

"I know. I know," I said. "Will you forgive me? Will any of you?"

"I know Fox only came to ask you to race because of us. He didn't want our hard work going to waste and didn't want me to miss out on my first competitive race. I hated asking him, but I didn't think there was a way to convince you unless you knew he wasn't terrible."

"I never thought he was terrible."

"He isn't. He did all of this for us, and I know we all let him down. He knew something was off about you hiding things from the beginning and we told him to drop it. That we needed you to race with us, and he did. He dropped it, or at least tried to."

"And I don't want to let any of you down. I want to race with you and I want to win."

"But you can't because you're on another team."

"No, I'm not. I was serious about helping, and I'm going to keep working on racing with you guys. I really think I can do it now, and I haven't been on the Holt racing team for over a year."

It was the truth, but saying it out loud was shocking. Between my wreck and leaving, an entire year had passed since I really raced with Holt racing, since I've raced at all.

She rolled her eyes. The difference in Scout when she was pissed was almost intimidating. She looked ready to kill and I quite honestly thought she could do it if someone hurt her friends.

I was beginning to think any of them would.

"The only way in hell that you are racing with us is if Fox says it's okay. We should have listened to Fox sooner. You're seriously still going to race with us if everyone is okay?"

"Of course. I didn't tell you my full name, but I didn't lie. That's why you were so mad? You thought I was going to back out?"

"Well, why wouldn't I? If I was you and had the choice to race with us or Holt, I know who I would choose, and it wouldn't be our little misfit team."

"I'm choosing the misfit team, I promise. So, what now? You want everyone to know the truth now?"

"Are you going to be the one to tell them?"

"Of course. I'm a lot of things, but I'm not a complete coward."

"Could have fooled me," she snapped.

"Ouch. I'm sorry, Scout. I really am. It was never about you guys. It was about me and what I've been through lately."

"Yeah, well, we went through a lot too, but we still welcomed you in and never lied."

"I know. I'm sorry."

"Fine. Apology kind of accepted, but I'm telling you now. If Fox doesn't accept it, you can't be around us anymore."

"I know."

"Then, let's go."

I grabbed my stuff and followed her out.

"I see why Fox and Jax call you the Vipers. You looked like you wanted to kill me."

"Honestly, when I saw that photo, I was ready to. I can't believe you would do all that to Fox and not tell him the truth. I know you like him and I know he has some sort of feelings for you. I couldn't figure out why you wouldn't tell him, at least."

"He has some sort of feelings for me?"

"Now is not the time to try to get your little crush figured out, *Ashton*."

"I don't have a crush."

"Yeah, right. Where's your car?"

"Over here. Listen, you already said you kind of forgive me. Don't get pissed again."

"No promises, why?"

We turned the corner, my car already parked outside the garage. I had washed it earlier, but was planning to lock it up and get a cab over, worried the car would add too much shock to telling them who I was.

"You're kidding me, right?"

"No. That's mine."

Her mouth fell open. "I've barely touched a car this nice, let alone rode in one."

"What a perfect time for the first ride." We got in and I noticed her face, the pure joy and awe as she looked over every inch. It was the exact feeling I had when I first sat in it.

"Alright, maybe take it around the block once before we go,"

Scout said, running her hands over the interior. "Dammit, this is nice."

I pulled out, taking a right to go the long way to the garage, not that I minded. I needed all the time I could get before facing Fox.

I raced down the road for a second as Scout groaned. "Please let me drive this."

I looked at her over the top of my sunglasses. "You're blackmailing me into telling my secret and now you're asking favors?"

"Yeah, and if Fox approves, then welcome to the family. I assume this isn't the last time we will fight." She wasn't even looking at me. Her eyes honed in on the dash.

I looked back to the road, a car in the rear-view mirror catching my eye.

"Shit," I said.

"What?"

"The car behind us. I think it's David."

"Are you serious?" she asked, turning back to look. It was supposed to be a gold Range Rover, but unfortunately for him, it turned out more mustard brown than gold, which made for a very disgusting car color.

"What's he doing?" I asked, turning down another side road.

"Still following us. Surprisingly, that little maneuver didn't work," she said with a laugh.

"You know, if you all are so good at street racing, stop asking me to drive."

"Ash, he's getting closer."

"I don't know what to do."

"Drive faster!" she yelled.

"Wow, you and Fox should really check that you aren't related, because you sound exactly the same."

"Ashton!"

"I'm going!" I hit the gas, turning down another side road, taking us away from the garage now.

"What are you doing? Turn back, go to the garage."

"No? Why would I lead him there?"

"Because everyone is there and can help? He isn't going to bother us if that crew walks out. Call Fox."

"No, I can lose him," I said as the car started ringing.

"What is that?"

"Apparently, the bluetooth took your request." I hissed as Fox's voice filled the car.

"Hey what's up? Are you heading here?"

"Um, not much, and yeah, I was on my way to see you," I said, calming a little at the sound of his voice.

"Ready to tell me more of your dirty secrets?" he asked with a laugh.

"Can I *only* tell you the dirty ones?"

"I think I would like–"

"Stop. Talking," Scout yelled, her face scrunching up.

"Scout?" Fox asked. "What are you doing there?"

"It's me, and please do not finish this conversation. We have more important things to worry about, anyway."

As she spoke, I hit the gas, the car sputtering and not going any faster. "Well, I think we have another problem now."

"Turn!" Scout yelled, and I listened, veering the car to the right and onto another side street as it slowed.

"Go faster!" Scout yelled, as David rounded the corner behind us.

"I can't! Something is wrong."

"What's going on?" Fox asked.

"You need to teach her how to street race is what's going on," Scout said.

"It's too distracting. It's not like going straight down a road."

"One of you better answer me about what the fuck is going on," Fox said, the deadly edge to his voice catching my attention.

"David is following us and now something is wrong with my car," I said. "It's not going more than thirty miles an hour."

"Where are you?"

"Not far. Five minutes on a good day. Ten at this rate," Scout said.

"Drive here now, Ash. Start heading this way."

"No, I don't want him to follow me there. I don't want to cause any problems."

"You aren't causing the problems. If he hurts either one of you, that's going to cause problems. Him following you is already a problem. Fuck, Ash, get here now or I'm coming after all of you. He is not allowed to stalk you."

"He's serious, Ash, go."

I nodded, a sob bubbling up. I don't know when I got to be such a crier, but it was like every emotion was always one sentence away from the surface now.

"Okay and I'm sorry Fox. I wanted to come tell you about myself. I didn't want it to happen like this."

"I do not care who you are. I care that you are in danger. I care that Scout is in danger. Just take a deep breath and come here now."

"Okay. I'm coming.

I turned onto the main road that the garage was on after four more agonizing minutes. David seemed to back off, idling slowly behind us.

"What is he doing?" Scout asked, watching as David came closer and then backed off.

"Waiting," I said.

Fox was still on the phone, but aside from asking us how much longer every five seconds, he wasn't saying much.

"Waiting for what?"

"Me to pull over and need help. David isn't good at a lot of things, but he is smart and devious. He would have known that he could mess with my car and then try to be the one to save me."

"Maybe it's time to let him know that's my job now," Fox said.

"Are you in the road?" I asked, seeing someone pacing back and forth across the road ahead of us. Luckily, it wasn't a very busy road, mainly quiet businesses lined the street, but it didn't mean no one ever drove down.

"Yes," he said, turning to face us. I could finally make him out, but we were at least another mile away. "What the hell are you driving, Ash? And what is behind you?"

"This is my car, and that is David's Range Rover."

The rest of the crew filtered out on the side of the road, watching as we came closer.

"Is that an Aston Martin?" he asked, the implausibility in his voice hard to miss. "Why do you have that?"

"I told you, it's my car."

"If that is stolen, Ash, you better drop Scout off and keep driving. Why the fuck do you have that? You wouldn't seriously take her to steal a car."

"Of course I wouldn't. I don't even know how to steal a car!" I yelled. Scout screamed something as David's Range Rover came around us, cutting himself across the road so I couldn't go any further and Fox could no longer see us.

"Shit. Stay here," I said.

"Yeah, right." Scout jumped out, staying close to the car.

"What are you doing?" I yelled as David jumped up. He stepped towards me, my car only a few feet from him.

"Your car is having trouble. I thought you might need help," he said, looking me over.

"What did you do to my car, David?"

"Nothing, it's fine. I can help you fix it."

"Pretty sure I can help her fix it, too. Doesn't mean you can stalk people," Scout said, and I wondered how she could be so calm.

He shot her a dirty look. He was never one to like a girl standing up to him, and being around someone like Scout would be his worst nightmare.

"Why are you doing this? Why are you following me?" I asked.

"Because I need you home! I have told you I need you home. My entire life is on thin ice and I need you to come back and help me. I can't do this without you, Ashton, please."

That's when I saw why Scout was unbothered. No one was going to hurt her. She already knew what was coming down that road and I guess I should have, too.

Fox was there, and nothing about him looked sweet or harmless.

He looked every bit of a hulking beast that he had come to think he was, smeared with grease, oil, and a layer of sweat with his backwards hat that wasn't hiding an inch of the scar. Even I took a step back at the angry, lethal look of him.

"You need to leave," he said to David.

"I need to talk to Ashton."

"Ashton doesn't need to talk to you."

David turned back to me. "Ash, I'm sorry. I'm not trying to keep scaring you or hurting you. I don't know what I am supposed to do to get you home."

"Not stalking me, scaring me, and trying to punch me in the face would be a great start."

"You know I don't want to hurt you. I've never hurt you before. That was an accident. No one understands why you left. I don't even understand and I really need you home. You don't understand what is happening. Your dad is getting impatient. He isn't going to let me keep racing."

"Because you can't drive!" I shrieked, angry now. "I can't believe he trusted you with a car in the first place."

David looked away, and I could only shake my head. "He didn't, did he? He didn't even know you took it to the race the other night?"

"I was trying to find you. I thought you would be with them and I ended up being right. He wouldn't mind if he knew why I went. He needs you home. He needs you home just as badly as I do."

David stepped forward like he was going to reach for me. I tried to step back, but I only backed into the car. It didn't matter, Fox was already between us.

"If you touch her, you're going to get a mark on your face to match the one you gave her." Fox pushed him back, giving me more room to move around the car more.

"You can't touch me!" David yelled. "I know the sheriff and you cannot touch me."

"We all know the sheriff," Kye said with a laugh. "Pretty sure we've all spent time with him. That doesn't really impress us."

"Or scare us," Jax said, throwing up his hands in confusion. "What's he going to do? Arrest us for stopping you from stalking her?"

They leaned on the front of the hood of David's car with Ransom and Quinn behind them, his arm slung over her. Aside from Fox, everyone seemed in good spirits.

David tried to step around Fox, reaching for me again. "Ashton, we need to talk about us, about your dad, too. We need to talk about the business and our life together."

"No, I–"

"She will call you if she wants to talk to you," Fox said. "Don't follow her. Don't touch her car. Don't touch her."

David's hands waved wildly, making something fly across the front of the car.

"Ouch," Scout said, whatever it was, hitting her in the stomach.

Fox didn't seem to care to find out what happened. He lifted up the wrench and slammed it into David's driver's side window, shattering it to pieces.

"My watch!" David yelled. "My car! What the hell?"

"Leave," Fox yelled.

David didn't need any more convincing, jumping into his car and taking off as the crew moved back, surrounding my car now.

"Damn," Scout said. "Is this a Rolex?"

"Probably," I said, knowing David would go to great lengths to look as rich as possible. "Whatever it is, it's yours now."

I turned back, all eyes on my car.

"Going to explain your car now? *Ashton*," Fox said.

"Or more about the asshole that has a Range Rover and a Rolex?" Jax asked.

"Yeah, this is my car. The one I drive every day, at least."

"And it is?" Quinn said, truly not knowing.

"An Aston Martin Rapide AMR," I said.

"Well, I don't know much about different cars yet, but I know *that* is a nice car," she said.

"Nice is an understatement," Ransom said. "There were only about two hundred of those made, and they probably go for over two hundred thousand."

Quinn's mouth dropped. "He's kidding, right Ash?"

"No, he's not kidding," Fox said.

"I can explain why I have this."

"I told you if it's stolen, don't even bring it on our property.

We've been down that road before and none of us are dealing with it again."

"I really look like that much of a criminal?"

"Considering the secrecy, it could explain it all. Including the nice RX7 we have here," Fox said. "Which also has to leave if it's stolen."

"We both know I'm not a criminal. Although, I'd love some backstory because it sounds like you might be," I said.

"I don't think that's important right this second. If you aren't a criminal, I think we need to know how the fuck you have this," he said. "And what that guy is talking about?"

"Fine," I said, raising my hands. "Before you come for me, just give me a second. I was planning to tell you guys today, anyway. And thanks to Scout, I had to drive this car, which wasn't part of the plan."

"And here I was pissed, wondering why you didn't drive the Lambo instead," Jax said.

I smiled at him, knowing they weren't ready to know that my dad had two of those currently, and that I had driven them often.

"Don't even get an attitude with me," Scout said, but she was half laughing as she walked around the car to the crew.

"I knew I would have to tell you today, but it's harder than I thought." I took a deep breath, closing my eyes, knowing everything could be about to change. They stood as a united front, and I was on the outside while they waited for my confession.

"Alright," Scout said. "You've had enough time. Get to it."

"I don't know where to start."

"How about the picture?" Scout offered.

I groaned. "That was definitely not where I wanted to start. Thanks," I hissed at her. "Scout came across a photo of you and I together, Fox."

"I don't know what that means. We've never taken a picture together."

"Someone took some pictures of us at the baseball game and posted it online. Scout came across it. One is a picture of us making out."

"Oh, fuck my life. Someone had to take a photo? Do I even want to know what they wrote?"

"No, probably not."

Scout handed the phone to me. "She's going to read it, anyway."

"You know Scout, I think we are going to have a talk later," I said with a groan, taking the phone and looking back at the photo. "It really is a great photo, though. If that helps."

"The caption?" Fox asked, as everyone else gathered closer.

"It says Ashton Holt was seen making out with her mystery date on Thursday. With her exit from racing after the nasty wreck, we wondered if we would ever see her again. Now, we need to learn if she will ever race again."

I met Fox's eyes before I continued.

"I'm Ashton Holt, daughter of Chad Holt," I said, knowing that anyone in racing would know his name. It was nearly impossible not to. The words were like a weight off my chest, letting me take a full breath.

Quinn gave a dissatisfied stare. "Why would we care who your dad is?"

"Because he's one of the best drivers alive," Fox said. "Because he's won Formula 1, multiple times, rally cars, drifting, drag racing. The guys had his hand in nearly every racing ring and him, or his teams, have won in all of them. As far as I know, he's started his own Formula 1 team now." His eyes were hard and unreadable.

"And he owns other winning racing teams too," Ransom said. "His company has to be worth millions."

"Easily," Jax said.

"Well, that explains how you know how to drive so well," Quinn said.

"And explains the Holt turbo you brought me," Fox said.

"And the fucking limited edition Aston Martin." Jax said, like no one else was taking that into account.

"Hey, didn't we watch some of his daughter's drag races at nationals last year? Didn't she win in the top ten or something?" Kye said, like I wasn't right there.

"That was me and yes, I did." I said with a laugh. "I placed seventh in the nationals."

"Oh shit, I raced Chad Holt's daughter," Jax said.

"Yeah and lost," I said, smiling.

"Hell, he's like a king of racing," Ransom said.

"Which makes you a racing princess," Fox said.

I scrunched my nose. "Eww. Let's not call me that. Please."

"Shit," Fox mumbled, his eyes glued to the car as he got lost in thought.

"I'm sorry I haven't said anything sooner. I just — I really liked getting to know you guys as me, not as Chad Holt's daughter. Are you guys mad?" I asked, but everyone seemed to ignore me, as Jax apparently had a more important question.

"Can we sit in it?" he asked. His mouth still hadn't closed, and I didn't blame him. The car was beautiful.

"If you guys help me figure out what's wrong with it, you can all take it for a drive." I said, trusting each one of them to handle it.

I was watching Fox though, seeing if that would make him smile. His lip twitched, but his face stayed hardened.

I was expecting the worst and hoping for the best because after what just happened, all I wanted was Fox arms around me, but I knew I couldn't ask for that or expect it.

"Do you guys hate me for not saying anything?"

They all looked at each other, seeming to make a silent decision, but it was Jax who spoke up next. "Why didn't you want to tell us? I mean, I think we can all agree it's pretty cool."

"I have dealt with a lot of shitty people in the racing world who ignored me until they realized who I was. Then they wanted to be my best friend, try to date me, marry me, sleep with me, anything to get closer to my father and everything that came along with it. The people that I thought were my friends wanted money and had me pay for everything. I got sick of it and then I met you guys and you loved cars and racing. I haven't been home in a while and then it felt like I was home, but I could leave all the drama behind," I sighed. "Well, the money and fancy car drama, apparently drama follows no matter where I go. Then, it just got easier to not say anything. Are you guys mad?"

"I personally am not mad," Quinn said.

"You know, I think I can put the hard feelings aside if I get one drive in that thing." Jax said, with a smile.

"Absolutely. Same," Ransom said, and Kye agreed. They all looked at Fox, waiting for his response, but his face was still a mask of emotion.

"Let's clear a bay out and we can get it fixed," he said, waiting as all of them took the hint and walked back towards the garage.

"Thanks, guys," I yelled, and waited till they were all inside before looking back at him. "Fox?"

His name shook him from a daze. "Yes, Ashton?"

"Do you want me to go?"

"You could barely make it here. How are you making it back?"

"I can figure out how to get it back by myself if you want me to go."

"Of course you could. Your fucking Ashton Holt. I'm sure you can figure out how to get your Aston fucking Martin home."

"I'm sorry."

"Pretty big secret, huh?"

I shrugged. "Better than being a criminal?"

He shook his head with a small laugh as he fidgeted with his hat. "I guess, yeah, better than a criminal. At least I think so," he said.

"Do you understand why I didn't want to say anything?"

"I've never been in that position, but I can imagine why you wouldn't want to go around telling everyone."

"At this point I would keep it a secret forever if I could. I had to leave everyone because I didn't know who to keep around."

"But now you want us to fix this car? Shouldn't you take it to a special, fancy mechanic or something?"

"Right now, there's no one else I would trust it with," I said, meaning it.

"Then let's go get this done."

"Does this mean you're fine with all of this?"

"Fine with who you are? Of course I'm fine with it. I never cared who you were, Ashton. I only wanted to know who that was. As for lying to me, to all of us, no. I'm not fine with it."

"So, what does that mean?"

"It means we will get your car fixed," he said, opening the driver's side door and waving me inside, but I didn't get in, turning to him instead.

"And then?"

"Then you and I can talk in private, not in the middle of a road with our friends waiting around the corner trying to hear every word."

TWENTY-EIGHT
FOX

Ashton fucking Holt.

As though she wasn't already perfect, now I have to add that she is one of the top female racers in the country, rich, and, unfortunately, still as perfect as she was yesterday.

Part of me was hoping that whatever secret she had would mean she wouldn't be staying. That she wouldn't be racing or hanging out with us anymore. Not that I wanted to do that to the crew and their race, but Ash, Ashton, being anywhere near me was a fight against myself every day, and part of me hoped her secret coming out would end that.

I didn't think I was one to get attached easily. I could be friends with anyone, but letting someone so close in my life was different. But she fit perfectly into our lives, into my life.

And now I knew that I wouldn't fit into hers.

Scout grabbed my attention. "Psst."

"What?"

She turned her phone around, the photos of Ash's wreck on the screen. The pieces clicked together, and I remembered hearing about her wreck at the time and remembered everyone expecting to get word she was dead. I'm sure I've seen her picture around, but rarely and I never thought that's who was here with us. At most, I assumed she raced with a group, but nothing as acclaimed as Holt.

But she hadn't died that night. She survived only for everyone in her life to tell her she wasn't strong enough to do it again. For her asshole boyfriend to tell her she was ugly now that she had a scar across her chest.

I woke up to everyone telling me how much they cared and loved me. And it's not like the girls that did look at me like I was disgusting meant anything to me.

Scout scrolled on, going to her racing stats and pausing to read through snippets of interviews and stats on her wins.

She was amazing.

Like she read my mind, she turned back and looked at us.

Scout's guilty smile was too obvious to actually hide anything.

"What are you two doing?"

"Googling you," Scout said.

"Oh no," Ash said. "Please don't."

"Too late," Scout said. "I've already scrolled through pages and pages. You shouldn't feel bad. It's all amazing stuff."

"Well, thanks. Coming from you, that means a lot." Scout didn't look up from her phone, but I could see her lips pull together. She wasn't going to admit it yet, but she already liked Ash before, and I knew she was thrilled to have another girl around and one that liked to race.

"So Ash," Jax said, "what other cars do you have, aside from the RX-7?"

"I had two cars for drag racing and one for rally racing, aside from that they were mostly my dads or we all shared them. The teams tend to beat cars up and so did I while I learned everything, so having cars to test on is the best option."

I walked back over as they talked and I looked over the car. Ransom was underneath and Kye was getting too distracted by the engine to really be looking it over for a problem.

I started my search, looking over anything I could, until I finally came across wires that looked like half had been pulled out or loosened.

"I found it," I said, everyone stopping to look. "I think he messed with the wires. It would be the smart thing to do. Your car would go into limp mode and once you stopped, he would know exactly what to do to magically fix it."

"Ash, I assume this isn't the first time he's messed with you?" Quinn said. She already knew about the mark on her face, but I was glad Quinn was letting Ash tell her story herself.

"No, not the first." she shook her head. "As you can all imagine, my dad's business is worth a lot. David is the son of my dad's best friend. We've known each other all of our lives and somehow every one was convinced that must mean we are destined to be together. I really think my dad's friend has changed, and he hasn't noticed. Just like no one noticed David changing. At first, I thought David was trying to take over the business. It was like he was obsessed with my dad liking him and letting him into the business, but then I realized that wasn't all of it. He didn't just want the business, he wanted to be the star racer of Holt." She sat back, pulling herself up onto a workbench that we had and looked at me.

"He wanted the position you had," I said.

"Yeah, he seemed to. After my wreck, he had so much ammunition to use against me racing. Then my dad, I think out of concern more than anything, bought it all and basically started to ban me from racing. I would try to go to the track and he would find out, and there would be a fight. We've always been close, so I figured we would move on from it, but then David kept interjecting. Telling my dad how bad I was, and that I was too scared to race again. He basically ended my career before I could even try to get it back. David wrecked a lot of his cars and I guess his dad wasn't happy about it, so he clung to me further. Something changed. He was clinging to me like a life force, but putting me down at every turn. He would tell me these horrible things and soon I was believing them."

"What made you leave, then?" Scout asked.

"I went to the track one day. David was there with my team and was in the middle of telling them that I had decided I wasn't racing again. That I decided to settle down and racing wasn't going to be a part of that. I heard it, I heard every word, and then he had the audacity to tell me I misunderstood. That he was only telling them that to prepare in case I couldn't come back, but that wasn't what he said. He was making my decisions for me and I was so exhausted I had stopped pushing back. Overhearing that conversation made me realize I hadn't been losing my mind, though. For months, he made me feel like I'd lost it. I went home and cried when I told my dad, but he didn't know what to do. He said if I was that stressed going to the track, then I couldn't be trusted behind the wheel. It broke me. I still didn't think about leaving, though," she said, shaking her head. "That night, my dad and him sat me down and said David would be taking my spot in a few of the races. That was it for me. The two people I thought had my back, didn't, and they took away the chance to race again. I ran out of reasons to stay."

"But why follow you now? If you left, wouldn't he have what he wants?" I asked.

She shrugged. "Kind of? But I think whatever plan he has is falling apart without me. Something has changed, and he needs me around to get back on track. My dad wants me back around and he somehow thinks David is the person who will talk me into it. Probably because he can. He's a master at manipulating me. Plus, I think there was a trophy factor in keeping me. Not to sound conceited, but he's more popular with me around, has more access to money or cars, people like him more if I'm there. I don't know why exactly, but it seems he's getting a little more obsessed about us staying together."

"Because they like you, not him," I said.

"I guess. He made sure to never let me think that."

"So, how do you get him to stop?" Scout asked.

"Well, I can see now that ignoring him isn't going to work, so at this point, I need everyone to see him for what he is and cut him off, even if it means my dad cutting off David's dad too. Right now, I can't even talk to my dad without the information getting back to David, so I don't. I'm a little stuck on what steps to take next."

I couldn't believe she was dealing with any of this. Not only having to leave your life, but being stalked for it? Every part of it made me more angry. All this time she has been here worrying about me, trying to help me, and dealing with all of this on her own. She had someone stalking her, and she was spending her time and energy dealing with me being an asshole.

I pulled off my hat, pushing my hand into my hair and trying not to rip it out.

I was the problem here. I should have helped her sooner. I've been worried about my face and racing, without paying enough attention to what happened before. I knew he would cause more problems. I knew he would come back around and yet I sent her home every chance I could to deal with this herself. To make her feel like she couldn't say anything more to me or any of us. To make her feel like she had to stay at her apartment, knowing he knew where she was, and had to be there alone.

If I didn't hate myself before, I did now.

Every terrible scenario I could think of came over me. I stepped away, moving to the other side of the car and taking a deep breath.

"Well, since you guys all seem okay with this, I would love to change the subject to something better and see if you guys wanted to go to the beach tonight."

"The beach?"

I spun back. "We can't ignore what just happened. We should be taking care of that, not going out."

She kept her head held high, not worried about my attitude or sudden outburst.

"We can take care of it tomorrow. The problem will still be there. For tonight, I would love to go out and have a good time and maybe forget about my problems, hopefully with the people I can now actually call my friends."

My mouth snapped shut again, and I nodded. She deserved whatever the hell she wanted and if going out was going to help, then fine. I would still be here tomorrow to take care of it.

"Of course we are your friends. The beach sounds fun," Quinn said.

"I am in," Scout added. "We haven't really gone in a while."

"So it's a yes, then? You guys want to go? It's like a party night with bonfires and tons of people out. They have fireworks too," she asked, turning to all of us guys. "There will be lots of hot girls, too. Dancing, partying, bikini-clad hot girls. Ones that I'm sure would love tall, hot, dangerous street racers."

"Well, Ash. You and I are officially best friends. Not that there was much doubt before, but now I know for sure," Jax said, and I laughed.

"So that's two of you. Kye, Fox?"

Kye looked around. "Sounds like trouble and I am in."

"Fox?"

I didn't answer at first, and I didn't know what changed, but she huffed, stalking over to me and grabbing my hand to lead me outside.

"What are you doing?" I asked, laughing as she dragged me farther out to a tree that bordered the parking lot.

"You've barely talked to me and it looked like you were about to say no. I'm trying to figure out what's going on."

I looked back at her car before turning back to her.

"Have you decided?" I asked.

"Decided what?"

"Decided who is driving your car first."

"I'm thinking about it. Jax has been pretty nice to me. Scout too. I mean, I guess everyone has. Other than you."

"Nice to you?" I leaned into her. "I think I've been more than nice. I'm the only one here who is scarred for life for saving you. I'm also the only one here who has given you an orgasm. I think that's pretty nice."

"Are you sure about that?" she said, smiling over at the crew.

My chest shook with a growl, putting my finger under her chin and forcing her eyes back on me.

"Well, no one else here is cut up, so I'm guessing you're insinuating that someone else gave you an orgasm." I leaned in closer. "Good to know. I'll remember that you want someone else's hands on you the next time you're begging to come on me."

Her mouth dropped open. "That's not what I meant. I was joking."

"Hmmm."

"Does this mean you are coming with us?" she asked.

"Maybe."

"What were you thinking about? Why didn't you answer me back there?"

I backed off, not ready to stay that close to her.

"What do you mean? I was thinking about exactly what you were talking about. A dancing, partying, bikini-clad hot girl. One that you think would love tall, hot, dangerous street racers."

"Well, I guess that makes sense," she said, crossing her arms with a scowl.

"Aww, come on, don't look so pissed off," I said, running my fingers down her jaw. "Do you want me to tell you about it?" I said, stepping closer and dropping my voice. "She's tall, and beautiful, and I'm pretty sure her hair hides two little horns because the only conclusion I've come to is that she's a little hellion trying to wreck my world. I've never met someone so determined to get what she wants and apparently I'll give it every fucking time. Somehow, she has taken over every minute of my life. It's the worst type of pain every time she touches me and I only want more. I think I've become a masochist. As much as I want to see her fall to her knees, she asks me to fall to mine in front of the entire fucking world and I do with pleasure. I would every damn time."

Her mouth fell open, before she snapped it closed, biting at her lip and it was all I could look at.

"It must not be me then," she finally said, a winning smile on her face.

"And why's that?" I asked, loving every defiant attitude filled word out of her mouth, knowing it only made it that much sweeter when she did give in to me.

"Because I won't be wearing a bikini. It couldn't possibly be me."

"Why do you say it like that? Do you have one?"

"Of course."

"Do you like it?"

"Yes."

"Then you should wear it."

"No. I couldn't with my chest."

"Wear it. You will look good."

"And if someone gives me nasty comments about my scar?"

"I'll give them a matching one," I said.

She looked me over. "You wouldn't do that."

"I would."

The huff she gave me only made me smile, which, based on the deeper scowl I got next, wasn't the right response.

"Does this mean you are fine with this new information about me?" she asked, not backing away from me. We were close enough to touch, but I couldn't bring myself to do it.

"No. I would have preferred you to be a criminal. At least then I would have known what to do with you."

"We both know that you know what to do with me," she said, a sly, secretive smile spreading over her. Before I could say anything, she turned her back to me, heading into the garage, and leaving me to follow.

"I had another surprise for you all," she said.

"You don't have to do anything for us. Going out for the day is plenty," Quinn said.

"No, really it's ok. Tomorrow I have some of the rally racing team meeting us at our tracks and we will be racing with them."

"When you say your tracks, do you mean the fucking empire that is Holt's racing paradise?" Jax asked.

"Well, that isn't the official name, but yes," she said with a laugh. I could barely process the words. "My dad's track. The Holt track. I checked in and my dad is going to be gone this weekend so I asked some of the racers to come in. If you guys want to, we can go and race with the guys on the national team. They are super nice and happy to show us anything, along with just having fun."

"Seriously?" Ransom said.

"Seriously," she said.

"I think it's safe to say that's a yes from all of us." I said, and she turned, smiling up at me.

"Ashton Holt," Jax said. "I would absolutely like to become

Mr. Ashton Holt if you are looking," he said, a smartass smile across his face.

"Sorry Jax," she said in a huff. "You're only after me for my money and race cars."

"Aww, that's not true, honey. I also want you for your hot body," he said, and I smacked the back of his head. Ash was already laughing so hard, though, I couldn't be mad.

"Still last on the list, babe," she said before the rest of them moved back towards the car

I stayed behind with her. "You do know you don't have to do any of this, right? We don't need you taking us places or paying for anything."

"I know. I want to. You guys were nice to me before you knew, well, some of you," she said with a sharp look, "so sharing it feels fun again. Like I can actually enjoy it with other people."

"Ok. As long as that's it."

"I'm going to go get ready with them at your guy's place. Be ready to go in an hour." She walked off, not giving me any chance to say anything else. Not that there was much to say.

I didn't know what to do now.

Everything was out in the open and it felt like one last chance to prove if I was going to be an asshole forever or actually take a chance. A few hours to decide what I wanted, find the courage to be myself and show her that I might have anything to offer or walk away from whatever was between us.

I had to make a decision, knowing that no matter what the outcome was, my life would once again never be the same because of Ashton.

TWENTY-NINE
ASH

Quinn had driven me to my apartment before heading back to theirs, while leaving the guys with my car. They seemed more than happy to keep it there to make sure nothing else was wrong with it, and I assumed there would have to be a test drive or two before I saw it again.

Not that I cared.

This group had given me more in the short time that I had known them than any friends ever had. I couldn't even begin to figure out how to repay them for helping me.

We all made it up to the upstairs apartment, changing and getting ready before heading back down.

Jax whistled as we walked into the garage.

"Wow, you guys look great. Ready to go?"

Ransom groaned as Quinn came in, telling her how good she looked. My chest tightened at the ease they had with each other. They made each moment look like the best moment of their lives and I had to turn away. Scout got in with Jax and Kye and I waited, not seeing Fox anywhere.

"Is Fox going to back out because he has my keys?" I asked, looking around at each of them.

Quinn shook her head. "No. I doubt he would back out without saying anything."

I rolled my eyes and groaned. "Go ahead, I'll go grab him, or the keys, and meet you all there."

"You sure?"

"Yeah, go ahead. If Fox isn't coming, I'll meet you there by myself."

She nodded as I headed back upstairs. I didn't knock, pushing open the door to Fox's apartment. It was quiet and for a minute I wondered if he was even still there.

"Fox, if you're ditching us, I at least need my keys back," I yelled.

"I'm not ditching you. I didn't know you were ready. I needed a minute," he said, stepping out of his room.

For a moment, we only stared at each other.

He was only in board shorts and a backwards hat but somehow, looked better than ever. There was no doubt that Fox's face was god level hot before the cut, but I never lied about him still looking good now. The healed cut left a line down his face of scarred skin, the mark through his eyebrow, cheek and lips, but it wasn't gross, or monsterish, as he seemed to think. It only showed his true colors, and I hoped that one day he would see it as a mark of bravery, not something that he needed to be ashamed of. The man seemed unmoved by danger if someone needed him, and that was now literally etched across his face. I don't know how he couldn't see how amazing it was.

"You're staring at my face."

"It's a good face," I said with a shrug.

"That's not why you are looking."

"How do you know? Can you suddenly read my mind?"

"No, but it's not hard to figure out."

I rolled my eyes. "I was thinking about how brave that cut made you look, how it showed a level of bravery that a lot of people could only dream of having. I was also thinking how hot you looked, but you're really ruining it."

He came closer, grabbing his stuff to go.

"I really wish I could read your mind. It would make this a lot easier," he said with a small smile.

"It's probably better that you can't. Imagine the dirty thoughts you would be subjected to every time I was around you."

That stopped him, making him turn and look me over. "Didn't I tell you to wear a bikini?"

"Ha. Didn't I tell you not to tell me what to do?"

"You did, but fuck if I don't love the way you listen when I do," he said, stepping closer now, his body inches from me.

He leaned down, running his nose along mine, and I could only hold my breath as he moved over my cheek to my jaw.

"I love what happens when you don't listen too."

I sucked in a breath. "Just so we are clear, I am wearing a bikini. I only wore this dress overtop."

"So you almost listened, but put on a dress that covers you. Completely."

"Unlike you, I don't walk around without a shirt on."

He was silent, and I finally looked up at him, the grin on his face impossible to misunderstand.

"You better not be picturing it!"

"Are you sure we should go?" he asked, leaning back into me. His lips hadn't touched me, but the way he was tracing my face with nose was sending a shiver down my back. He moved to my neck, going down to the top of the dress before running back up to my ear.

"Did you have something else in mind?"

"Yes," he said. I was breathless as he moved closer to my

lips.

Cars honked from downstairs and Fox froze.

"I assume that's our warning to leave," he said, not moving away from me.

"I gave Quinn directions. I told them to go ahead and I would catch up."

He pulled back with a smile. "What exactly were you coming in here to do that was going to run you so behind?"

The horned honked again.

He groaned. "Do *you* want to run away to the Bahamas with me? At this point, I don't think Quinn's ever going to leave her boyfriend. Scout is scared of sharks, and I need a break from these people's horribly perfect timing."

"How many women have you asked to run away to the beach with you, exactly?"

"Including you? Three. But that's only because I met Scout and Quinn before you. If I met you first, we would already be there."

I rolled my eyes. "Wow, third choice. I should have assumed."

He pushed me towards the door, shutting it behind us as he leaned down to my ear. "Don't be jealous baby, the only reason I couldn't ask you first is you were too busy playing with those damn race cars."

"You joke, but the number of times I heard that I won't find a husband if I keep *playing* with those race cars is astronomical."

We made it down to the garage, and he shook his head. "I couldn't imagine telling Scout she better stop racing to find a boyfriend. Find one that can keep up, then it might be worth her time."

"And what about you, Fox? Can you keep up with me?"

"I don't even know," he said, blowing out a hard breath. "Am I really driving?"

"Yes. Do you not want to?" I asked, really hoping he was going to drive.

"Of course I want to. I only assumed you would want to drive your car."

"I like racing, not driving. I'm more than happy over here. Please, be my chauffeur."

"Chauffeur? Is that what you normally have?"

"What? No. You think I live with beautiful cars and pay someone to drive me around?"

He winced with a small smile. "Well, I don't know. You're rich enough too. I still don't know what to think about all this."

"So it is bothering you. Why?" He pulled out, turning onto the main street in front of the garage, but not bothering to catch up to the rest of the crew.

"Because you're Ashton Holt. You are Chad Holt's daughter, and I am having a hard time processing that still. I grew up watching him race. He's an idol. And I've seen your races before. I mean, you've done great keeping your face out of the spotlight. And now what? We're friends?"

"If you want to be. I've said it before though. If you want me to race with you guys, and then leave you alone, I understand."

"See if Scout and Quinn, and apparently Jax, would let you not hang out with us now."

I smiled. I did love them all. "You guys are a tight group. If you don't want me around, I think they would understand."

"It's not that I don't want you around. I don't think it's ever been about that. I know I've been an ass, and most of that is me being stuck in my own head. Now, though, it's that I don't know what to do with you around now."

I could think of at least ten things I wanted him to do with me right now.

"I get it. I wasn't the most pleasant person to be around when I was healing," I said. "Then to have me around as a reminder? I hope you know I felt bad about it. I didn't want you to have to keep reliving that night. I love hanging out with you all, though. And aside from your attitude, I've liked everything we've done together."

"Everything?" he asked with a smirk.

"Yes, *everything*."

"Noted. Having you around hasn't been bad. Not nearly as bad as I made it out to be. And plus, I now get to brag that I helped Ashton Holt race again. That seems like a pretty big deal."

"It probably could be if I ever get to race competitively again."

His face fell as he looked over. "Why wouldn't you?" he asked, eyebrows furrowing as we came to a red light. "Because your dad and David told you that you shouldn't race anymore? Your dad has wrecked plenty of times. How could he really tell you not to race again?"

"He thinks I've lost my mind, or that I'm completely helpless. After the wreck, he started treating me like glass. I understand if he's worried about me, but how he went about it was horrible. All I heard from both of them was how sensitive I was being and that I needed to calm down. I was helpless and fell right into David's plan. It's hard not to believe the people that are supposed to care about you."

"You were helpless because you were injured and they exploited that," Fox said.

"It was David, more than anything. I think he saw an opportunity to take what he wanted and went for it, trying to make me lose my mind until I handed it over. It was hard to wrap my mind around what was happening then. When I left, it took weeks to feel like I didn't actually lose my mind. I thought at first it was because I made the wrong choice. But I'm glad I left. I don't think I would have ever seen the truth if I stayed."

"Left and took this car with you? Good choice."

"No, I didn't take this car. I bought it."

"You bought it or your dad did?" he asked. The words didn't have any bite to them, though.

"I did. I was racing and making good money and didn't have any bills, really. My dad did pay for most of my living, so I was spoiled on that part. After I was placing in national races, I could afford to go out and get this for myself. Luckily, I saved a ton too, because that's what I'm living on until I can sort out some part of my life."

"And you're set to hold out for longer if things don't get fixed?"

"I should be good for a year or so. If it doesn't get fixed after that, I don't know what I could do. I would like to race again," I smiled over at him. "Especially now that I know I *can* race again. But I would need a car that's ready to go and don't want to do much else aside from the racing part. I was working and helping my dad with his business, but obviously that's a niche business. Outside of that, I'm kind of useless."

Fox laughed. "I think those are two good things to be good at. You could work at any car shop. I'm sure other racing teams would take you in a heartbeat. You can work with us if you're ever driven to that level of desperation," he said, flashing me a smile.

"You joke, but I might have to take you up on that. Lucky for you, though, I can help grow your business with my eyes closed after helping at Holt Racing."

"I don't doubt that for a second,"

His hand moved off the shifter, and for a moment I thought he might reach out to me, but he only grabbed a pair of sunglasses.

My body thrummed like a magnet when he was around, like

an unknown force that was pushing me near him, only settling if I touched him.

It was torture.

He turned down a road that I knew didn't lead to the beach.

"Where are you going?" I asked as he turned into the diner. The place was a familiar stop for me, but I didn't know why he would bring us here.

"Grabbing something."

"You're hungry?"

"Wait here," he said, shaking his head as he jumped out.

He hadn't called in an order, but I guess we should have thought to bring food.

A few minutes later, he was already walking back out, two iced coffees in his hand.

"What are those for?"

"Here. This one is yours." He handed it over, remembering what I ordered.

"And you got yourself one?"

"I assumed you weren't sharing."

"Very good assumption. Not that I am complaining, but why did you stop for these?"

"Aside from finding out they are delicious?" he asked with a shrug. "I thought you liked iced coffee and being a spoiled passenger princess that likes her drinks?."

"I do."

"Well then, drink it and enjoy the ride."

He pulled out, letting the back of the car swing and hitting the gas. The smooth motion, not even spilling my coffee.

"Are you fine if I go faster to catch up with the crew?"

"Yeah, of course," I said, sipping my coffee and leaning back to watch him drive.

I took a deep breath, expecting a rush of panic, but instead, I felt a relaxing calm wash over me.

THIRTY
ASH

FOX PULLED into the parking lot, letting the car idle for a minute after we parked.

"Are you sure this is the group you want to hang out with?" he asked.

"What? Where did that come from? Why wouldn't I?"

"I don't know. I showed you where we grew up, I mentioned that we did some not so great things to get where we are. Why would you?"

"Why would I care where you grew up? And we do have to elaborate on this car stealing thing. But does it even matter? I like who you are now. I like who you all are. Do you not like me because I grew up rich?"

"No. I don't really care," he said.

"Exactly. So that's it. Plus, what's the difference? Would anyone guess where you grew up while you're driving this car?"

He gave a hard laugh. "No, no one would. I feel like an imposter."

"I don't know why, because everything I've heard about you made me think you were a cocky, overconfident fuck boy.

Shouldn't you feel right at home in a car like this?" I said, with a sweet smile.

"Excuse me? What did you call me?"

I smiled harder. "You heard."

He pounced, reaching over, as I pushed the door open. The seatbelt stopped him, giving me precious moments to get out and run.

I made it to the sand before turning back.

He was headed our way, the rest of the group already setting up their stuff next to me.

"Uh oh," Scout said. "What did you say to piss him off?"

Fox was close enough now that I took a step back, meeting his eyes and smiling more. "I called him a cocky, over confident fuck boy," I said, listing each word off on my fingers.

They were quiet for a moment before erupting into laughter.

"Looks like she figured you out, Fox," Jax laughed.

Scout and Quinn were almost doubled over.

"Oh damn," Scout said. "That's it exactly."

"Ash, you better run," Quinn said, still laughing.

I looked over at her before looking back at Fox. He was already in motion, heading right toward me.

"No!" I turned, running towards the water. "I was kidding!" I yelled.

I didn't stop until I was knee deep when I turned to him again. He hadn't stopped, though, picking me up and continuing on as the water rushed over my legs.

"Wait, I still have my dress on."

"I don't care. I'm a cocky fuck boy, right? Why would I care about a thing like that?"

"Fox," I demanded, holding onto him as he waded out, the water at his chest now. "Where are you going?"

"Ashton," he said, softly. "I like being able to say your actual name."

He didn't try to hide away when I looked at him this time, letting me look over every part of his face without hesitation.

"If you keep staring at me like that, I'm going to drop you off here in the water and I can barely touch the bottom now, so you'll be swimming for a while."

"You wouldn't."

"Of course, I would."

I couldn't stop looking though, his arms holding me tight against him, the sun beating down, making him look like the hero I knew he was. I didn't want to look anywhere else.

"Stop looking at me."

"No," I whispered, leaning down. "Never."

"You know, you make me feel like it could be okay to look at," he said quietly. "I don't know how I've gone this long without you in my life."

He pulled me in closer until his lips were almost on mine, but I wasn't going to wait. I closed the distance, his lips crashing against mine.

His hand cupped the back of my head, pulling me into him as his tongue slid against mine. My legs tightened and even in the water, I could tell how wet I was. His hand moved from my head down my back, finding its way under my dress.

I broke the kiss, breathing hard as I leaned back into the water while he held me.

"Mmm, what a good fuck boy," I said with a laugh.

"Call me fuck boy all you want," he said, lowering me down until my pussy was tight against his hard cock. "Because that's exactly what I'm going to do. I'm going to fuck you until you can't move. I've had weeks of being teased. Weeks of touching and tasting you without any relief. I can absolutely be your fuck boy, because that's all I'm going to be doing for days to you."

"Fox," I gasped as he slid two fingers into me.

"What, baby?"

Pleasure rolled through me. "Are you sure you can deliver on that?"

His fingers moved slowly, teasing me as he laughed.

"Do you remember what happened last time you taunted me?"

I thought back to the night in his bedroom. "Yes."

His hand slipped around the back of my neck, pulling me back up to his lips.

"And do you remember that in all this time, I haven't had a chance to get off?"

"Yes, not for my lack of trying, though."

"Then believe that I will deliver on fucking you all night. First, I'm going to make you want to come so bad you beg me for more. I'm going to make you feel how I've felt for weeks until you realize my cock is the only thing that's going to soothe you."

He pushed his fingers into me again, making a wave of pleasure roll through me.

"That doesn't seem fair."

"It's the only thing that seems fair. You've made me get on my knees and beg for you. Now I want you to do the same."

"And if I don't?"

His smile brightened again. "That's fine. The punishment will be just as sweet for me and you'll still end up on your knees either way. On your knees, over my lap, bent over every fucking surface I can find."

His fingers moved faster, and I could feel every part of me tightening. I pulled myself closer, wrapping myself up in him until my lips were against his neck.

"Are you going to come for me, hellion?"

"Yes," I breathed. I was close, each push of his fingers ready to push me over the edge.

"Good," he said, pulling his fingers out. The sudden loss of him jarring, my orgasm falling apart when it was so close.

"What are you doing?" I reached for his hand, trying to pull it back to me.

"I already told you what I'm doing."

"Fox, that isn't teasing, that's —" He laughed, cutting me off with a kiss.

"I know what it is and I plan to do it over and over until you feel as wild as I do."

"What if I told you I already feel that way?"

"I wouldn't believe you," he said, biting at my bottom lip.

I groaned. "If you think you are going to do that again, you are wrong. That will not end in orgasms, that will end in murder."

"Mmm. Vicious, that only turns me on more," he said, his hands moving down my sides. "What are you thinking about now?"

"Going to my car and taking care of this problem myself. *Again.*"

"Then, I won't be letting you out of my sight all night."

"Fox," I groaned. "Please."

"Fuck, I love hearing you beg too. You're putting up a terrible argument for me to help you when you are so hot asking nicely for it. Honestly, you're fucked either way because asking nice or threatening me only makes me want to do it again."

"I am very much not fucked right now. That's the problem."

He laughed against me, trailing his hand down my spine as he kissed me. "I take it back. You're not a fuck boy. One of them would already be giving me the best orgasm of my life."

"You've got a filthy mouth," he whispered against my lips.

"Alright, then. Let's put it to work."

His chest rumbled. "I'm getting you out of this water and off of my body before I fuck you in front of everyone."

My pussy tensed at his words. I'm glad he had some sliver of control because right now I would absolutely let him.

I looked back. We were far enough out that I doubted they could see anything, but I knew we couldn't exactly go at it out here.

"Can't we just leave?"

"Oh no, you invited everyone out here. Now we have to hang out for now," he said, walking me out of the water.

"I made a mistake."

"With inviting everyone or letting me touch you?"

"I was going to say going out today, but you're right, letting you touch me was a mistake because I need more and you are holding out on me."

"Come on, hellion, back to hang out and try not to pass out over me again."

"Again? You only wished for it to happen the first time. It didn't actually happen," I said, dropping from him when the water was below his waist.

He huffed and wrapped his arms around me from behind, almost carrying me out of the water.

"Don't worry. At some point, my winning attitude and charming smile is going to make you swoon."

I spun in his arms to face him, but he kept walking, carrying me along with him.

"Right, right, that winning attitude is *really* going to get me to swoon. Are you going to admit that we are more than friends yet?"

He laughed, kissing my head. "We are something, baby. We sure are something."

***

We had gone back to the rest of the crew, Fox sitting down next to me and both of us somehow carrying on like nothing had happened. The rest of the day was left to hang out, swim, play games, and try to forget about everything else in life. The beach had filled up more, clusters of friends gathered around each other like we were.

Night fell and soon everyone was starting fires, sitting around relaxing.

It was so familiar to me, the beach, the group of friends, having fun, but this time it was with a different type of group. A group that somehow made me feel like I had known them my entire life.

"Hey, Ash," Scout said, beckoning me over. I got up, passing Fox and not missing the way he looked me over.

"Hey, what's up?"

"I just — I'm sorry for earlier. How I treated you? Forcing you to tell everyone. I should have handled that better."

"It's okay. I understand why you did it."

"You do?"

I nodded. "I didn't like lying to you guys. It was so nice having friends that had no expectation of me based on my name."

"And I didn't like learning that you were lying." She hung her head further. "We had a friend betray us pretty badly lately and I guess it made me act out. It's not like yours was necessarily a bad secret, but it was still a secret. And I've seen how Fox acts towards you. I didn't want him to get hurt at all, you know?"

I grabbed her hand. "I do know. I want to make sure you're fine with me sticking around. Actually fine, not just fine for everyone else's sake."

Her eyes went wide. "Of course. No, please don't feel like I don't. I love having you around. Like I said, I acted on impulse and high emotions and I shouldn't have. I'm trying to get better when I do get a temper, but I have not perfected that."

"You don't have to explain that part to me. My own temper tends to get the best of me. So, we're good then?"

"Yes, very good. Which leads me to my next question," she said.

"Okay. What is it?"

"You would say that you're a confident person, right?"

"I like to think so."

"And I'm assuming that means you've approached guys and, I don't know, hit on them."

The pure happiness that spread through me was unmatched.

"Yes, I would say I have done that a time or two."

"Great. Do you think you could help me do that now?"

"Scout, are you asking me to be your wing woman because the answer is a resounding yes? I will absolutely help you hit on guys."

"And you don't think that would be an issue tonight with…" She nodded in Fox's direction. "Him."

"No, it's fine. It's for you. Come on. Let's do this. Who do you have your eyes on?"

She pointed to a nearby group of guys spread out around one of the fires. They were all good-looking guys, and there didn't seem to be any girls with them.

"Great choice, let's go."

"Wait, shouldn't we tell everyone what we are doing?" she asked.

"And give them a chance to stop us? No." I shrugged. "I'm sure they will see what we are doing, anyway. Plus, Quinn isn't going to come with us and I would hate for her to feel even more left out."

"Even more left out of what?" she asked, walking up behind us.

"Oh, sorry. Scout and I are going over there to talk to those guys. I figured you wouldn't be coming with us."

She snorted. "Not only would I be drug back here by a caveman," she said, jerking her thumb at Ransom. "I don't feel like hitting on any guys right now. I'm good."

"I don't blame you for that. We'll be back soon."

I caught Fox's eye as I looked back and smiled. He quickly looked back at the fire, but I could see his lip twitch, trying to hide his smile.

Since the moment I told him who I was, there still seemed to be something a little off. He was all over me more now, but still wasn't making it clear if this was going any further. I know he needed me to help with their race, and I was starting to wonder if that was stopping him now.

I had pushed and pushed for him and I thought we were on a new path based on what happened out in the water, but then he closed himself off again, sitting away from me and losing himself in his own head, finding one more excuse to keep his distance.

Scout and I had walked up to the group of guys, and I was pleased to find they were even better looking up close. Scout smiled, but it was my turn to speak up.

"Hey guys," I said, giving a smile. "We saw you over here and wanted to introduce ourselves. I'm Ash, this is Scout."

They all smiled back, then went around telling us their names. I forgot every single one the moment it came out, but kept smiling.

"So, what do you guys do?"

"Lifeguards here during the day."

"Oh, interesting," I said. "That explains the abs and perfect tans."

"And you girls? Work or just beautiful for a living?" One of them asked, his Australian accent making both of us smile.

"Well, beautiful, of course, but we also race cars."

Eyebrows shot up. In seconds, Scout was sat down next to

the guy she had wanted to talk with and he was flirting as hard as he could to keep her attention.

That was the extent of my job here, so I stayed back, trying to politely talk to all of them, as my eyes kept wandering back to Fox.

He looked so good with his hat pulled backwards and shirt still off, of course. He looked relaxed, too. He was still leaned back by the fire and all I wanted to do was go cuddle up next to him.

I was debating on leaving Scout to talk while I went back over to him until one of the guys stepped closer.

"You seem to be sticking to the outskirts. Don't like being the center of attention?"

"Not usually. Does anyone?"

"I can't say I mind it."

I laughed. "Well, by all means, don't let me stop you." I motioned to the center of the group.

"I have all the attention I need with you talking to me."

"Mmm, how sweet," I said, dryly. "A little cheesy too." It didn't take me long to assess guys like this anymore. He was in a phase of life where everything had to be a 'good time' and tonight was no different for him.

I realized then that it was different for me now.

I thought that I would get back to that point when I started going out again, but ever since I met the crew, and Fox, I wasn't worried about trying to find a fun time when I went out.

Not only was I always having fun with them, but the thought of movie nights and hanging around the garage sounded more fun than parties and clubs.

"But it made you smile. That's all I was going for," the guys said, recapturing my attention.

I wasn't going to explain that I wasn't smiling for him. I was smiling about the annoying beast of a man behind us who couldn't seem to stick to one decision.

If only he would be the caveman, or the beast, and sweep me away from this boring conversation.

The guy talked for a few more minutes until someone turned on the music.

"Come on. Dance with me a second."

"No thanks. I should head back."

He didn't listen, pulling me closer and swinging me around. It was at that inconvenient time that I realized he had been drinking. A lot based on his sloppy movements.

Strangely enough, it brought me right back to the night at the club. I had danced with so many people that night, but the only time my heart made any notion that it was still going was when I walked out and saw Fox leaning against his car.

I heard a laugh go through the crew's fire and noticed that Fox wasn't with them anymore. I went to look around for him, but a hand wrapped around my arm, tugging me backwards out of the guy's grip.

Fox.

"Here," he said, handing me a hoodie and leaning down to my ear. "You better not be thinking about getting your satisfaction from this guy."

I turned. "You're the one that got me all hot and bothered and then let me loose on a beach of half-naked men. Maybe you should rethink your strategies."

He stalked away, handing a hoodie to Scout too, who looked less surprised at his kindness.

She smiled up at him and continued her conversation, seemingly at ease with this guy now.

I pulled on the hoodie, trying not to overthink what he had done, but it was hard to believe he had only done it out of the kindness of his heart. Was any guy that sweet?

As soon as it came down over my head, the guy was pulling me back to him. I turned back to Fox, but he was already gone.

"Whose that?" the guy asked, nodding to Fox, who was already sitting back down with the crew. He had leaned back against a log, staring into the flames, and I wondered why he even thought to bring me a hoodie.

"Oh, one of my…friends."

"You don't sound too sure of that. Just a friend?"

"Um, yeah, a friend." I didn't exactly think of Fox as just a friend, but I didn't know if he would want to be called anything different.

He tried to move me again, but I protested this time, sick of entertaining him.

The guy's hand snaked around my waist, grabbing my hips as he pulled me away from the fire even more, getting us closer to the water now. I pushed my hands against his chest, trying to slow him down.

"Wait, no, sorry," I said. "I think you're getting the wrong idea. I was just hanging out with Scout over here."

"No, come on. We can talk more over here."

I pulled my hand away, slipping it out of his grasp.

"Thanks, but no thanks." I stepped back, ready to turn, when he grabbed my arm, yanking me back towards him.

"Why? What's wrong with talking?"

"Nothing, but, like I said, I think you're getting the wrong idea."

"No. I'm not. Really, it's fine."

I turned back, crashing into a hard chest.

"Ashton," Fox said, steadying me and stepping to my side.

The guy stepped back a few feet, surprised at Fox's sudden appearance.

"Yes?"

"What's going on over here?"

"Oh, I was telling him that I needed to get back and he was politely telling me goodbye."

"Really? It didn't look polite."

I gave a small shake of my head as Fox moved a little closer, making sure he was angled between me and the guy.

My shield against the world that seemed to be there any time I might need him.

"It was fine. He wasn't going to stop me, were you?"

"No, I mean I was going to persuade you, but not —"

"I'm taking her now," Fox said, cutting him off.

He put his hands up. "Fine. I'm not trying to stop you then."

Without a word, Fox leaned down and threw me over his shoulder.

"What are you doing?" I yelled. "Put me down!"

"No."

We made it to the crew, but he kept going, heading to the parking lot.

"Fox!" I yelled. "Where are you going?"

"The car."

I shut my mouth and yelled, the frustrating cry making him laugh.

"You think this is funny?" I asked.

He didn't answer as I tried to shimmy my body back down over him.

His hand came down over my ass, spanking me before he dropped me to the ground. My feet touched before I was lifted back up. His hands forced my legs around his waist as he started moving again.

"So what? This was your plan? Ignore me all night until you're ready to kidnap me?"

"No, but when you ran off to flirt with every other guy on the beach. I got upset and had to make a new plan."

I rolled my eyes. "I didn't go right to him. I was helping

Scout talk to a guy she thought was cute. I owed her anyway and you accusing me of flirting with all the guys is pretty rude, Fox"
"

"Fine, maybe you weren't, but it felt that way. That wasn't only you helping Scout. You seemed happy to talk to them, so before we make it to the car, tell me, who do you want? Me, him, another guy, who?"

"What are you talking about? I don't want him."

"Maybe, but he sure as fuck wants you, but yet a few hours ago, you were getting off on me."

I gave a tight laugh, trying to control the anger that was bubbling up. "Wow, that's a lot coming from you when I have basically thrown myself at you multiple times, and you push me away over and over. Now it matters what I do with someone else?"

"I pushed you away because you were lying to me. I didn't even know your actual name until this morning, so I think I should get some leniency."

"Maybe a little. I'm sorry for that."

"No, you're not, or you wouldn't have been down on that beach with some other guy."

"I was trying to go back and see you, or have you come see me? I was waiting for something, anything, from you, but apparently you were too busy getting a pissy attitude. You're being a beast in all the wrong ways. And what? Is kidnapping me supposed to be you making a move now? I thought you would be so much better at this," I said.

He shook his head. "Damn, I really got myself a mean one," he said. "I'm never going to get away with anything."

"No, you aren't."

The overhead lights of the parking lot cast a sinister look over his scarred face that I couldn't read, but then he smiled.

He pulled me in hard and fast, his lips crashing against mine as my back hit the car. It wasn't gentle, the bruising force was full of irritation. He deepened the kiss, tangling his tongue with mine, and held me tighter. His fingers dug into my thighs and I thought there would have to be marks from each one tomorrow. I didn't care. I couldn't care.

My body was on fire and I needed everything. All night I had been waiting for him to drag me away for this, and it was everything I had hoped it would be.

We both pulled back, neither of us seeming to want to but needing a breath. Fox didn't wait, though.

"Tell me what you want. Who you want. Tell me and I'll believe it, but I need a clear answer."

He set me down, following me as I leaned back against the car. His hands caged me in, and his jaw tightened.

"You, Fox. Of course, my answer is you."

"Are you sure? Because the moment you get into this car with me means no one else. It means I get you. I get to kiss you, fuck you, have every inch of you to myself tonight. It's your choice to make, but you have to make it."

I thought it over.

Go back down to the crew, sit at the fire, enjoy the night, maybe even talk with the lifeguards again.

Or get in with him and, from the sounds of it, have his hands on me all night.

I've never gotten into a car as fast as I did then.

THIRTY-ONE
ASH

He walked around and got in, turning the car on and pulling out without a word.

I could barely stand it, the quiet making me lose my mind.

"At least I know you weren't hesitating with your decision," he said.

"I haven't been the one hesitating."

"No, you've just been the one teasing me. Did you do that on purpose? You were trying to make it look like you were flirting with him?"

"Maybe a little. And who are you to talk? You withheld my orgasm on purpose."

He groaned and reached over, catching my hand and kissing it before setting it down on the shifter. Then he moved to my thigh, his fingers lingering there for a moment before moving up, taking my dress with it.

"Thank you for the reminder. Such a tease. You knew exactly what you were doing, though, didn't you?"

"Yes," I breathed, trying to hide my whimper as he slowly moved up my leg.

"Are you ready to shift?" he asked.

"You want me too?"

"Yes," he said, wanting me to control the gears as his hand continued its agonizingly slow ascent up my thigh. "Now. Shift."

I moved the shifter into the next gear.

"I can't do that again, not while you're doing this."

"I think you can handle it for a few more seconds."

His fingers worked quick at the ties on my bottoms until he moved them out of the way. Then he moved up, his fingers dipping into me and circling my clit.

"Fox," I gasped. My hand fell off the shifter and my head fell back, closing my eyes to enjoy every second, but he apparently wasn't going to let me.

"Eyes open, Baby. Ready to shift again?"

"I can't do both," I said as his fingers pushed against my entrance again, making my hips push up. He was teasing me, getting so close, but stopping right before he made it.

"Ok then, I'll need my hand back."

I groaned, shifting a gear when he said it again.

"Look at that. All that driving experience is really coming into use."

He moved his fingers back, pushing into me now. My body picked up right where we left off, already being pushed to the edge of my orgasm.

I moaned, but he stopped, pulling back and setting his hands on the steering wheel.

"No, please, don't stop," I cried. "*Please*, don't do this to me again."

"I like hearing those sounds you make when you get all frustrated. I like watching you get so close. Maybe stop looking so hot when you beg for it."

He reached back over, running his hand back through my wetness, pushing into me once before pulling away again.

“This isn’t going to end well for you. You think you’re so in control?” I asked, raising a brow at him.

He didn’t say anything, just smiled and kept his eyes on the road.

I wasn’t going to let him tease me over and over without repercussions. I pulled at the string on his board shorts and reached in. He hissed as my hand wrapped around his hard cock.

My mouth fell open at his size.

I mean, I felt it through his pants. I thought I’d seen and felt enough of it to get the picture, but it wasn’t quite the same as wrapping my hand around it.

“Excuse me? You’ve been walking around complaining that you can’t get laid and this is what you’re working with?”

“I haven’t been complaining that I can’t get laid.”

I looked up at him. “Basically.”

“Don’t look at me like that when you’re holding my dick.”

I moved up his length once before he grabbed my wrist, stopping me.

“You’re greedy. No one told you that you could do that.”

“No one told me that I couldn’t do that.”

“Unless you want me to pull over right now and take care of this, you better get your hands off of me.”

I smiled. “You’re threatening me with the wrong things,” I said, licking the tip of him.

“Ashton,” he growled.

“You’re right. It is fun hearing you get all frustrated.”

“I’m driving.”

“And doing a great job.”

I licked again, his hand wrapping into my hair and giving me a light pull.

I looked up, moving back towards my seat as he pulled my hair. “Yes? Is there a problem?” I asked.

"Yes, a big one."

I laughed as he adjusted his shorts, trying to slide his cock back in. "I really don't think it's going to fit," I asked.

"In the shorts or in you?" he asked, flashing a wicked smile.

Thankfully, I was sitting down because every part of me went weak at the words.

"Can you please drive faster?"

"Can you stay in your seat?"

"Yes."

"Then, yes."

The car jumped forward as he raced down the streets. He seemed to have no trouble pushing the car to its limits, and the world went by in a blur.

It took twenty more minutes before he finally pulled into the apartment garage.

By the time he parked and turned the car off, I was ready to rip my clothes off myself.

He looked over at me once before getting out and coming around to my side.

"If I can recall right, you liked when I did this."

He grabbed my wrists, pinning them to my back and walking me to the front of the car. "Let's find out what else you like. Put your hands on the hood."

He pulled at my dress, the straps breaking as I bent over the hood.

His hands moved down my sides, putting me more at ease as I pressed my face against the warm hood of the car.

"Fuck, you're perfect," he said as he pinned my arms at my back, using them to pull me up against his hard chest.

"So are you."

"I'm not."

"You are," I said as he bent his head to my neck. His teeth

grazed over my skin and I tipped my head back, giving him more access. "I like your strength. I like when you use it on me."

With my words, he bit down, his teeth bringing a pleasure and pain that made me moan, warmth flooding between my legs.

His fingers moved along me again, but I pushed back. "No, no way are you teasing me again. Let me turn around," I said, trying to spin.

"No."

"Fox," I demanded.

"I want you like this," he said. "And I want you now."

Without another word, he slid on a condom and positioned his cock at my entrance. His hand came around my throat as the other one grabbed my hip. "There's still time to change your mind."

I could barely hear his words, my body setting on fire at every touch. I had never let anyone touch me so roughly, and now I craved every powerful touch.

"What?" I gave a stifled laugh, realizing he wasn't moving, waiting for my answer. "If you stop, after all the teasing you have done, I'm tying you to your bed and still doing this."

He gave a deep laugh and pushed into me. My body stretched around him and I yelled out with the sudden fullness. "Yes," I hissed, "more."

He pulled out of me. "Would you like that? To have me tied up so you can have your way with me, or would you rather be tied up, letting me worship every part of your body until you can't move?" He slammed into me again and I couldn't stop as I yelled his name. "Fuck, you feel good," he said, the words making my body clench and taking me further to the edge.

"Fox." I yelled out. I have had orgasms before. It wasn't a new sensation, but this wasn't like the others. Each thrust made me lose my mind more. This was different. This was Fox. Every part of me tightened. He had brought me so close to having an orgasm twice now that it was already there, building and coiling inside me.

His hand wrapped around my waist, touching light against my clit as I came undone. My body tightened around him and I couldn't hide the yells of my pleasure. My vision exploded and I could feel my eyes roll back as I fell against the car, panting as he thrust into me once more. He groaned and slowed, before starting to run his hands up and down me again.

"Yes." I said, turning over as he left me and I laid back on the hood, letting the cool metal calm my shaking body.

"Are you okay?"

"Better than okay."

I stayed laying across the hood as he stood, a smile spreading across his lips and I couldn't help but smile back. "Problem?"

"You're laid out naked on the car," he said.

"I noticed."

"If there's one thing I could stare at for the rest of my life, it would be this. You satisfied and naked right here on the hood." His cocky smile radiated such genuine happiness that it made my heart almost hurt with joy.

A shiver ran over me, my body shaking as the cold of the metal and cool air of the garage came across my bare skin.

"Come on," he said, picking up our clothes and then me. "Let's get you upstairs before anyone shows up."

My legs wrapped around him and I held on as I kissed along his jaw, kissing his lips and then kissing the scar across his face. It was healing more and more. The angry red cut had turned into a white line, the jagged edges never going to go away.

I leaned into him, his touch soothing now that I was satisfied. Being in his arms made me feel safe and at ease, like I had never felt before.

I sighed when he set me down on the bed and threw the covers over me.

"Was that a bad sigh? What's wrong?" he asked as he sat next to me, running his hands through my hair.

"Nothing's wrong. Aside from you doing that is somehow making me want you all over again. Maybe this time I can ride you," I said.

He groaned, running a thumb over my bottom lip. "You have a dirty mouth. Drives me fucking crazy when you say all those things you want." I flicked my tongue out, hitting his thumb and scraping my teeth along it. "I lied," he added. "Everything you do drives me crazy."

"Are you going to lie down with me?"

"You're staying?" His voice holding a little too much surprise for my liking.

"Oh," I said, sitting up. "Oh, I mean no, I can go. Of course, I'll go." I threw off the blankets, getting two steps before his arm came around me and he tackled me back to the bed. Pinning me underneath him.

"No. I meant it as a good question. Like, you want to stay?"

"Of course I want to stay."

I leaned up, grabbing his lips and pulling him back down until I was wrapped up in his arms.

"Does this mean that if I go shower, you're not running away?" he asked, and I couldn't hide my laugh.

"If you think I'm running away from you naked in the shower instead of joining you, I think we have a lot more work to do in convincing you exactly how much I like your body."

He nuzzled closer, kissing down my jaw, neck, and chest. "I don't know what I did to deserve you in my life, but I'm glad. You're a fucking dream come true."

"A dream, right? Not a nightmare?"

"There may have been a few of those mixed in. Come on, let's get you cleaned up and into bed."

I nodded. "And maybe something to eat?"

He laughed, picking me up, and walking us into the bathroom. "Yes, hellion, we can get absolutely you something to eat."

THIRTY-TWO
ASH

I WOKE up and reached out for Fox, but the bed was empty.

"Fox?" I yelled into the quiet apartment, but there was no reply. "I swear Fox, if you left, I'm going to kill you," I yelled, staring up at the ceiling, wondering if he would really sneak out of his own apartment.

He appeared at the door, leaning against it and looking me over. "I didn't leave, but I've thought about it about ten times already."

I looked at him, shirtless, in a pair of sweatpants, his hair still messy from sleep and coffee in his hand. How could one guy look so good? I groaned, surprised that I was already ready for him again.

"Why have you thought about it that many times already? Was last night that terrible for you?"

"What? No," he said. "I am very, *very* pleased with what happened last night. But I didn't know how you would feel this morning waking up to my face and didn't know if me being gone would help."

"Help? You actually thought that sneaking out of your own

apartment after sleeping with me would help the situation?"

He closed his eyes and rubbed his jaw. "Listen, I didn't think it was a great plan, so I stayed, but I'm not exactly sure what to do now. I don't know what else to do other than try to force myself to leave you alone."

"I don't want you to leave me alone. I would prefer you be obsessed with me right now, like, can't stand to be away and want to touch me every second. I would prefer you next to me."

He smiled, the shy smile so unlike him that it made my heart tighten. "Don't do that. Don't look so cute on top of all your hotness. You can't be both," I said, flopping back onto the pillows.

"You're absolutely amazing," he said, kissing my jaw and neck before reaching for my lips again.

"I know you won't believe me," I said, turning to face him. "But your scar is hot. You have this rugged and dangerous look now and it adds to the whole bad boy, racer thing you were working on. It looks like you would fight someone in the streets and then fuck me on the hood of a car." I smiled. "Oh, wait."

"There's that dirty mouth again."

I laughed. "I can't help it. There are too many dirty thoughts up here when you're around. I have to get some of them out."

"You know, it was a blow to me for this to happen to my face. I feel like I've been relying so much on my looks to feed my ego, but it wasn't doing much else. I wasn't happy, not on anything more than a superficial level. I thought about it like crazy when I met you. Wondering how I could be anything to you when I was suddenly not good looking. It was like I didn't have anything else to offer. Between that and dealing with the pain, I didn't go about any of this the right way. I've been so far in my head about it, I didn't know how to get out. I'm sorry." His eyes were closed. "For all of it, and thank you for continually telling me to knock it the fuck off."

"Wow. That's not what I was expecting. You're actually very good at apologizing when you mean it," I said, wrapping my arms around him. "And you're welcome. What made you change your mind last night?"

He laughed and kissed my head. "You. Everything you said, knowing you could have anyone you wanted. You're everything anyone would dream of. Last night, seeing everyone looking at you. I thought, fuck it. Even if I only had you for a night, it would be better than never having you."

"And if you had me for more than one night?"

"Any day or night after the first one would just be pure fucking luck that I could convince you to stay."

I rolled on top of him. "And what about you?" I asked.

"What about me?"

"What about you wanting women? Plural. Are you hoping I leave so you can go back to all those girls again? Now that you think you're all hot again." I said, teasing him now.

"No. I don't want to. None of them make me feel so much like myself, but a better version of him." My eyebrows jumped. "Okay, *sometimes*, a better version," he added with a laugh.

"And you're not worried about the perks of being around me? The cars, the track, my dad?"

"Worried isn't the right word. I don't want you for any of those things, if that's what you're asking. Just the other perks, like getting to race with you, sex with you, movie night with you, maybe even going on a date sometime," he said with a laugh. "But now that you mention the perks, I do have a question. What if you do want to go back? And does your dad really not think you could take over the business?"

I groaned and flopped back onto the bed. "I don't know. He hasn't come out and said those exact words, but he keeps pushing and pushing that I really should be running it with David. As though David knows more about the business or cars than I do. Do you know I had to whisper in his ear what was going on when we were at the races and what the cars were for so long? Like even last year, I was telling him what cars were on the track. How is that the guy that would help me run a business like Holt Racing? Shouldn't he at least know about the cars?" I shook my head, realizing how much I was ranting, and sat up. "I just realized I haven't had anyone to talk to about this. Not someone who cared to listen and not side with them immediately."

"I could imagine most people aren't going to disagree with someone like your dad."

"No, they don't. That's the other thing. David isn't making his own decisions about big things. It's his dad or mine that makes his choices and when he does make a choice, it's wrecking beautiful cars and doing drugs. I don't know what to do. I want to be a part of the business. I want it more than anything. It's what I've worked towards my whole life, but not if it means running it with David. I would rather start over on my own. I did start over on my own."

"You still could. You can create your own team and race. And you are still a Holt, so it's not like you would lose the association completely."

"But I wouldn't even touch where I was at before."

"Maybe not. But I think no matter what you do, you will be better than before. Would you want to run Holt alone or with someone? Someone other than that guy, obviously."

"I don't know. I guess I always grew up thinking I would run it with my dad, but I know that couldn't last forever. I would rather someone be there. It's more fun when you have someone else to do it with. I think the past year feeling so alone proved that I like having someone to talk to and bounce ideas off of and Holt racing is huge, but it can't be someone random. It needs to be someone who cares about the business, the cars, the charities, the teams, all of it. They have to care and know what they are talking about."

I looked at Fox, not adding the words that were so close to slipping out.

It would have to be someone like him.

"I think those are fair job requirements." He laughed. "And I think you could find that person, but David needs gone first."

"Yeah, he does, and I don't know how."

"Didn't you say you're worried he's up to something? Is there a way to find out what he's doing and prove it to your dad?"

"Maybe. I think this freak out is money related, which means he might have got himself into some deep money trouble. Going to the track today might help give me something to go on. They all know him there."

"That's right," he said, a smile growing on his face. "I'm going to race rally cars with you today."

"Does that mean you are excited?"

"Yes, but there's one thing I need to do first."

"What's that?"

He moved fast, covering my body with his. "You," he said as he kissed me, his lips trailing over my face and neck and chest.

The world faded around us as he watched me, fucked me, made my body clench around him, and then carried me into the shower to clean me up.

"Does that usually get better and better?" I asked as he ran a towel over me.

"I don't know if I can guarantee that, but I am willing to continue seeing if we can make the orgasms better each time."

A knock echoed through the apartment, and we both froze.

"I know we don't knock, but I didn't want to walk into any naked asses." Quinn yelled.

I grabbed for one of Fox's shirts as he pulled on a pair of

shorts before we walked out into the living room.

"How does one pair of shorts make me want to go get you naked again?" I mumbled.

"I can absolutely kick her out if you need more," he said, flashing a smile.

Quinn was in the kitchen. "First of all, I needed to come see when we were leaving because the rest of the crew hasn't stopped asking. I finally made them go down the street to the garage to leave me alone for a minute. And second, I ran out of coffee creamer, and Jax only had those gross energy drinks in his fridge."

Fox sat down on the stool at the counter and pulled me against him, not shying away from reaching for me in front of her.

"We are leaving in an hour if that's good with everyone and I will also need to borrow some more of your clothes," I said.

Quinn shut the fridge and turned to me, a smile growing on her face as she tried to hide it. "Oh yeah, not wanting to wear the same dress as last night?" She started laughing and Fox did, too.

"That wouldn't be possible," he said.

"You two are the worst." I said, slapping Fox's arm. "Do I get clothes or do I have to try to go home like this?"

"I'll be right back with some," she said, shutting the door behind her.

Fox started kissing my neck. "I'm going to go get my own clothes on."

"You sure you don't want to only wear that?"

He laughed. "Not unless you're wearing this." He tugged at the shirt.

"Not a chance."

"Then I'm going to cover up," he said, kissing my forehead. "And we are going to head out to the track. Maybe today is the day I'll beat you in a race."

THIRTY-THREE
ASH

HIS PHONE RANG before he could get far.

"Who is it?" He stopped at the bathroom door.

"Ransom," I said, already handing the phone over.

He grabbed it, his other hand snaking around my back and pulling me into him with a kiss on my forehead. The simple, comfortable gesture making me melt into him further.

"Hey," he said, connecting the call. "What's up?"

I jumped when I heard Ransom's voice as Fox hit the speakerphone. "Hey, you need to get down to the garage."

"What? Right now?"

"Ransom, we all need to get ready to go," I said.

"Then you guys need to get down here quick," he said. "We have a problem."

"Is everyone ok?" Fox said.

"Everyone's fine. Just get down here. Now."

He clicked the phone off and I was already grabbing my clothes to put on. I was still wearing borrowed clothes and with where the day was headed, I would need to borrow more.

Fox was ready and waiting as I pulled on a pair of shoes and grabbed the keys. "What do you think it is?"

"I don't know. There's been some break in problems in the past, so I'm hoping no one is messing with our shit again."

The drive felt like seconds as I flew down the road and pulled in.

"I will never get over how good of a driver you are," He said, grabbing my hand and kissing it.

I smiled. "I'm glad it doesn't scare you off."

"Never. It turns me on too much to scare me off," he said with a cocky smile. "Plus, how could I feel like any less than a king around you when you scream my name so loud during sex?"

"Well, I'm glad to see your ego is back." I said as he leaned over, kissing me and pulling out the key.

"It is, but in case my ego suddenly becomes fragile, I think I'll drive back." He said, but I knew it was only because he loved the car.

We hopped out. Everything looked fine at first, the building like we had left it last night until I turned and saw Fox's car.

Or at least what used to be Fox's car.

"What the fuck?" He said, his long strides getting to it before me.

Ransom and Jax were already standing around it, staring in silence.

Every single piece had been hit. The windows broke out, body parts smashed to pieces and a line of spray paint over the crumbled hood. I'm sure there was more, but I didn't want to look further. My heart raced, panic filling me as I looked over the car.

"What happened?" I asked, daring to look down the side of it once.

"Looks like someone came at Fox's car with a vengeance."

"Do you know who would do this?" I asked, did they really have enemies that would come after their stuff like this? I know Fox said he had problems in the past, but what could they be into now?

Fox ripped open the hood. The metal had been beaten and bent, making it snap and pop as he pulled it up.

"Oh, no," I said, my stomach dropping.

"The turbo is gone," Jax said. The bright red turbo that should have sat in full view had been ripped off, the rest of the engine looking like someone had hit every inch repeatedly. Every piece that could be broken or dented was, and the entire thing was ruined.

David.

The turbo being the only thing gone had to be him. I looked around, wondering if we would even spot him and his ugly car, but if he was watching, I didn't see him.

"Fox, I'm so sorry."

"Sorry? Why would you be sorry?"

"The turbo is gone. The only piece stamped with Holt. It had to have been David" I sucked in a deep breath. "I haven't seen him in days, but I'm sure he's still following me." Tears pricked my eyes. I knew how hard Fox would have worked to build this car, and it was all taken away because of me.

Ransom picked up a funnel that had fallen to the side of the engine compartment and we all noticed the missing oil cap.

"Shit, he put something in the engine?" Jax asked.

"Probably. It would make sure we couldn't use it again," Ransom said, still digging around.

Fox exploded, hitting the hood and making me step back. He let out a string of curse words as he walked around the side of the car and hit it again.

"Fox," I said, taking a slow step towards him. "I'm so sorry. We can fix this. I swear —"

"My car can't be fixed, Ash, and you fucking know it."

He turned to me and I took a step back. His face had fallen, the happy smile gone, replaced with the same hollow look he had when I first came to the garage to talk to him.

It felt like we were right back at where we started, and the loss hit me with an intensity I've never felt before. I hadn't felt this way when David and I broke up. It had been a relief that went over me when we finally ended it. Now it was turmoil, anger and disgust cutting into every corner of my chest.

David kept taking and taking from me.

I couldn't go back to Fox hating me.

And I couldn't let David take him from me, too.

Fox wouldn't want me here if David was lurking around, breaking his things. What would be next? The garage? His apartment? The rest of the crew. I knew that would be the last straw for Fox.

I couldn't sit back and let David keep getting away with it.

I stepped into Fox and he stepped back, but I was reaching for the keys that were still in his hand. I ripped them away and turned back, going to the car.

"Ashton. Stop," Fox called. "What are you doing?"

"Going to run an ugly ass Range Rover off the road with David in it," I said, reaching the car as an arm snaked around my waist.

"No you're not." Fox said, pulling me back to stop me.

"*Yes*, I am. That asshole has taken so much from me. My life! He ruined me until he took my entire life away. Do you know I wouldn't have even run out of that club if it wasn't for him? You wouldn't have had to protect me if he hadn't shown up unwanted. Then he's stalking me, attacking me, now this? Now you're going to hate me all over again? No, I can't. I can't lose you now just because of him."

"No, you're not. I do not hate you."

I jerked away, but he dragged me back in. "Before you go all warrior princess on the world, can you calm down and give me a minute? My car was ruined. I need a minute, Ashton."

"I thought that would be easier if I weren't here," I said, quieting down.

"No. That will not make it easier. Then I will be here worrying where you are and if he got to you again. For all we know, he could be waiting for you to show up and try to kick his ass."

"I can't have you hate me all over again." I said, realizing I was shaking.

"And I don't."

"But you're mad at me."

He took a deep breath. I knew I wasn't helping the entire situation, but I couldn't help it. I saw the way his face changed. "I'm not mad at you. I'm mad that my car, the one I have been working on for years, is ruined."

"Yeah, and that's my fault, too. You were right before. I keep making great strides in trying to ruin your life."

"Did you sneak out here last night and come wreck my car?"

I crossed my arms with an exasperated sigh. "Of course not, but the only reason it's ruined is because I forced myself into your life.

"I'm upset about my car, but I don't blame you. It's not your fault that guy's a fucking prick. Come on, please stay with me while I have to look it over more."

"You're sure?"

"Yes," he said, grabbing my hand. "And I could use your angry warrior princess vibes while I have to stare at my car in ruins. At least then I might not start crying," he said, smiling down at me. I pulled him down, kissing him once.

"I'm sorry about your car," I said, quiet, as we walked back over.

Ransom was looking at something underneath and jumped up.

"Is anything still in one piece?" Fox asked.

"I'd say there's going to be close to nothing usable on this. He brought tools and knew what to cut, what to hit, what to dump in it. I'd say the only reason he didn't light it on fire is so you had to look at it like this."

Fox groaned, looking inside the car. "That asshole even stole my steering wheel."

"Here," I said, pushing my keys at him. "Have my car."

"Are you offering him your Aston Martin?" Ransom said, peeking out from the other side.

"Yes. It's in my name. It's one hundred percent mine. Have it. You can have it," I said, shoving the keys at him again.

"Baby, I don't want your car."

"Pretty sure you can take that one if someone offers it," Ransom said, but I ignored him.

"Well then, take it until I get you a new car," I said. I could hear the panic boiling up again. I know he said he wasn't mad, but it kept getting worse. There was nothing left of it, and I couldn't figure out how he couldn't blame me. I shook as I pushed the keys into his hand, forcing him to take them.

"Just calm down. For my sake, *please* calm down," Fox said, pulling me into his arms. "You don't need to get me a new car or give me yours."

"I absolutely do."

"You don't. We will figure it out."

"You're at least using my car in the meantime."

"Fine. It's not like I wasn't planning to try to use it whenever I could, or spend every minute with you, anyway."

"Good," I said into his chest, realizing we were supposed to be leaving for the track. "Would going to race cars make you feel better? Maybe there's one of my cars there we can bring back with us."

He pulled back and looked down. "The going out to race would actually make me feel better, but no, I don't need to steal any of your dad's car. Can we cover this thing up so I don't have to see it right now?" Ransom and Jax ran inside, grabbing a car cover and throwing it over the top without a word.

"Come on. We'll run to the apartment to grab Quinn and Scout, and then we can all head out," I said. "And now my ego is the fragile one, so you are going to drive my car and you're going to like it." I demanded as we walked over.

He leaned down behind me, kissing my neck and grabbing my hips hard. "Yes, ma'am."

THIRTY-FOUR
FOX

WE WENT BACK to the apartments, waiting in the car as everyone else got into theirs. After only seconds in the silence, I leaned over, deciding to spend the time making out with Ash instead of sitting there thinking about my car.

It felt like I was almost back, scar or not, I felt like myself again. A better version that wasn't running myself into the ground as hard as I had been.

Kye pulled up, revving next to us with Scout and Jax in his car. I groaned, annoyed at being interrupted, and rolled down the window to talk to them until Ransom and Quinn pulled up behind us.

"Looks like make out time is over then," she said as I rolled it back up, sealing us in the quiet, the hum of the engine the only noise.

I pulled out, the others following behind us.

"Do you want to put on some music?"

"Always," she said, pulling out her phone. "Do you need sad and dramatic for today or something to get ready to race? Maybe a bit of both to soften the blow when I win?" A sly smile spread across her face as she connected her phone.

"You choose." I looked at the screen, watching as my name flashed across. "What was that?" I asked, looking back to see it was already gone.

"Nothing."

"Yeah, it was. That one had my name on it."

"What? No, no, you misread something."

"Ashton, I know damn well that was my name," I said, not able to hide my smile. The realization that I liked her was just as much of a punch to the gut as realizing how much she liked me back. "Did you make a playlist for me?"

"No," she almost yelled the words. "I didn't make a playlist *for* you. I made a playlist *about* you. Those are two different things." She looked down, scrolling, and trying to ignore me.

"They are. That sounds even more intriguing. Put it on. I want to hear what goes through that head when you think of me."

"No, no, I'm not doing that. Do you know how embarrassing that would be?"

"I wasn't going to play this card, but my car was just ruined and hearing your playlist about me would really help ease the pain." I put a hand to my chest and grimaced, trying to find sympathy.

"I know you're being a smartass," she huffed. "But it's working. Fine, one song, you get one."

"How many are on it?"

"A few."

"Then I want to hear three of them."

"Three?"

"Yep, give me your top three."

She groaned, scrolling through whatever list she had. "If you make fun of me, Fox, I will not hesitate to kick you out of this car."

"I would never, baby. Now come on. Help cheer me up."

"I'm taking you to an insane race track. It's like a playground for racers. Won't that cheer you up?"

"Maybe a little, but not more than hearing your thoughts about me. Unless they are all about eating my heart or kicking my ass. I heard some of those songs you played before so it wouldn't be that much of a surprise, I guess."

"I'd rather you hear those than my actual feelings," she said.

"Good to know we are both super healthy when it comes to talking about our feelings."

"Hey, I don't mind talking about them, but letting you listen to the songs that make me think of you is different."

"Come on. Play it."

She hit play on the first one. "Oh no, Taylor Swift? I've never heard this one, but I know she has some ruthless ones."

I listened to the words, all about masterminding being together, and I couldn't stop laughing.

I smiled over at her and my eyes went back to the road as I listened.

"You masterminded this whole thing then, huh?"

"I had too." She said with a smile, "You would have kicked me out and never seen me again if we had left it up to you." I grabbed her hand, bringing it to my lips and kissing it.

"Then thank you for masterminding this whole thing."

"You're welcome." She said, this time pulling my hand up and kissing it back before dropping them both back on the shifter.

The next song started to play, and she yelled. "Nope! Not that one."

She grabbed for her phone and hit pause.

"Why not? Let me hear it. I liked the first one."

"No. No, that's a bit intense. Let's try a different one."

"Ash, I already saw the name. I can look it up later."

"Then you can do that. Far, far from me, so I don't burn up in embarrassment."

"Fine another, then."

She clicked through more, finally hitting one. One that I was expecting about being a villain and pushing my buttons, which seemed fitting. The last was called Black Widow, the angry girl screams coming through as I laughed.

"Is this about my tattoo?"

"Something like that."

"What does that mean?"

"You'll see, soon."

I shook my head as we pulled down the private road.

"What do you listen to during your races?"

"Mostly things like this."

The crew was way behind us, so I stopped and pulled off her seatbelt.

"What are you doing?"

"They are going to be a minute, so I'm going to enjoy the entire minute." I grabbed her hips and drug her over the console until she straddled me.

"Mmm, much better." I pulled her against me, catching her lips with mine. My fingers pulled at the top of her leggings. "Pull these off. Let me taste you."

"While we have time to make out. We do not have time for that."

"I'm going to make time."

She looked behind us, but I already heard their cars coming up behind us. "We need to move."

"Taking you home sounds better now."

"Better than racing?"

"So much better."

"I'm going to take that as a high compliment and now force you to move the car. Now go on. Everyone is waiting behind us," she said, both of us glancing back to see everyone had caught up.

She tried to move back into her seat, but I grabbed her hips.

"You stay put."

"You have to drive."

"Up a driveway and through a gate. Not exactly racing down a road."

I put the car in gear, the car creeping forward up the driveway, as I held onto the steering wheel with one hand, leaving me free to roam with the other.

I grabbed onto the back of her neck and urged her down.

"I would love to fuck you like this right now."

"While driving?"

"I think I can manage. I just want to watch you ride me like this. Please, please, let me take you back home."

"Not a chance. We're going to have fun and you're going to have to suck it up and race some cars."

"I promise going home with you would be plenty of fun."

I pulled through the gates as Ash waved to the security guard. A big smile came over his face as he waved back and yelled a hello.

I parked and grabbed her, kissing her once. "Just a heads up since you don't want to go home yet. I'm absolutely going to be making time to fuck you before we do get home."

"And just a heads up to you. That's not happening. We are here with other people."

"I can still figure out a way. How can I make it happen?"

Her smile grew. "According to your rules, you have to get on your knees and beg for it."

"Done," I said, as she pushed open the door and nearly fell out.

Jax had parked next to me and scrunched his face as he saw us.

"Pretty sure that's not how you're supposed to drive. I don't know much about those fancy cars, but I think they still have passenger seats."

"Passenger seat? What a concept. I'll have to remember that for next time," Ash said, laughing.

"No, you definitely don't have to remember that. Where you were at was fine."

I got out and tried to figure out what to look at first. "This place is insane."

There were two giant garages in the middle, with tracks on both sides. Based on the stadium style lights, there were more tracks behind the garages, too. Every surface you could want to race on all on one giant racing empire.

She pointed to where we needed to go, a few cars already lined up next to a circle dirt track.

Everyone was getting out, awe reflecting on each of their faces. It was something the crew had talked about since we started; private tracks, faster cars, being professional drivers. We had wanted it all, *still* wanted it all, and now we were getting to drive at one of the best private tracks in the country.

Ash waved us along as she ran over, jumping onto one of the guy's backs that stood looking out over the track. Jealousy tore through me as the guy looked over his shoulder, his face lighting up with recognition.

"Ash! You actually came."

"Of course I came. Why wouldn't I?"

"Because you haven't been around in months. We got so used to you being here, it's been a bit quiet without you."

I couldn't help but take a step closer to her. I wish my mind wouldn't be running through every terrible option of what was going on, but it was.

Had she slept with him? Did he want to? Had he tried?

She was barely mine, and I was ready to act like that beast to keep her. I tried to calm myself instead of blurting out every jealous thought, knowing she wouldn't be a fan if I did.

"I'm sure your wife is keeping the place loud enough. Is Tara here?" Ash asked, looking around.

The knot in my chest unraveled, making me hate myself a little more.

"She's coming later with the kids."

Ash turned, introducing all of us to the three guys. "These guys have all been great about teaching me about racing in general. My dad taught me about drag racing and on different tracks, but these guys really helped when I learned on the dirt."

"We didn't have a choice. This girl's a damn bulldozer, came in here after the place was built and demanded we help," another guy said, walking up and knocking into her shoulder. He was a lot closer to our age than the other guy, and I knew the possibility was there. She gave him a tight but genuine smile.

"Not that we minded," he added with a wink, and I knew right then that he did have a thing for her. At least at one point.

"Guys, this is Raf. Raf, these are my friends." She turned, telling him who everyone was.

I didn't know if it was the destruction of my ego lately or Ash, but I had never been this close to dragging a woman away like a beast.

"And this is Fox," she said, smiling up at me as her hand wrapped around my arm. At least she made it obvious that we were a little more than friends.

"That from racing?" Raf said, motioning at the scar on my face. Ash didn't give me a chance to answer, though.

"Actually, no, Fox saved my life. I was out one night, and a guy came after me. Fox stopped him."

"Oh shit dude, that's crazy."

"It's been a pretty crazy few months," I said, looking over at her, but her smile never wavered.

"Don't doubt it with her around."

"Thanks, Raf," she said, flipping him off. "We're going to grab cars."

"You guys race, right?" Raf said.

"Yeah, but not this type of racing," I said.

"Well," Cole said. "We're about to have fun, then."

Ash shook her head, waving at everyone to come with her. "It's not that bad. A little weird on the dirt, but after a few laps, I think you guys will love it."

"You're just excited to kick my ass again," Jax said, knocking into her arm.

My chest rumbled. I grabbed her, pulling her into my side and wrapping my arm around her.

"You okay?"

"Aside from feeling ridiculous at how pissed I am that everyone is touching you, I'm fine."

"But none of them are touching me like you do," she said with a wink.

My chest swelled, and I moved, pulling her off her feet and wrapping her legs around me. "You know all the right things to say, don't you?"

"Yes, yes I do. Now get this door open so we can see what cars we get today."

THIRTY-FIVE
ASH

THEY PULLED THE DOORS OPEN. All of it felt so familiar that I was surprised at how comforted I was at the sight.

"My dad built this entire place, so he had somewhere he could test cars and drivers. It started out a lot smaller, of course, and he built it up over the years. There's two drag strips, a smaller dirt course, a bigger dirt course, and then a round track right behind this. He keeps all the test cars here and I've kept mine here since I would come to race so much. It didn't make sense to haul them. I know this is a lot to take in."

Cars lined the walls. We housed about forty cars in there that were all in various forms, from beat up to brand new.

"These are all test cars, so there won't be anything too fancy."

"Not too fancy? There are hundreds of thousands of dollars of cars in here," Ransom said.

"Yeah, and you can drive any of them that you want, but for today, we will want the cars back here."

I walked towards the back left where the cars we were going to use were lined up. There were five total.

"Sorry, I thought we had more of these," I said, looking around. "One might have been wrecked too badly to bring back in."

"I don't need my own. I'll watch," Quinn said, smiling at Ransom.

"Perfect. Fox, you're sharing my car with me." I grabbed keys and handed them out as they picked their cars. Mine was last in the line and Fox walked over.

"Is your car painted to look like a Black Widow spider?"

Mine wasn't in the greatest shape, but it was all black, a red hourglass painted on top.

"It is. All my cars have a red and black color. I liked the look of them and then my car started to get the name black widow. I really didn't mind it, considering the females are the dangerous ones."

"So that's why you were so interested in my tattoo."

"It's not the most rare thing in the world to get, but I thought it was interesting. I wondered why you chose it."

"I never knew why I got it. It seemed right at the time." He ran a hand down my jaw. "Although, now it's become my favorite."

The crew caught our attention, and I leaned over the back of my car, waiting as everyone bickered about who got which one. Fox came up behind me, immediately grabbing my ass.

"Right now? There are still people here."

His hand trailed over my ass, giving it a light smack before moving further down.

"Fox," I hissed. "What are you doing?"

"Taming my little hellion that can't seem to stop making me so jealous, I lose my mind. I would hate to let you forget whose hands you like on you the most."

His hand moved over my leggings, giving me just enough to want more.

The hanger filled with the sounds of engines as the others pulled out and went for the track.

They rounded the corner and Fox didn't hesitate. His hand pushed onto my back, holding me in place against the car.

"Don't move."

I stilled, waiting as he pulled down my leggings before looking over my shoulder, surprised to see him getting on his knees.

"What are you doing?"

"You told me I would have to get on my knees and beg. That's exactly what I'm doing."

"We shouldn't—" My words were cut off as he leaned in, burying his tongue into me.

I moaned. The door to the hanger was open, but the cars alone would drown out any sound. That was as long as no one walked back over here.

His tongue moved from my pussy to my ass before going back to my clit. His mouth came down over me, sucking until I was nearly crawling up onto the car.

"Where do you think you're going?" he asked, standing up and turning me around. He lifted me onto the car, pulling a condom out of his pocket and sliding it on before dragging me to the edge.

"I told you I would get on my knees and beg, and I did. Now, you're going to let me fuck you till you scream." He positioned himself at my pussy, sliding himself through my wetness, but didn't move forward.

"I am?" I said, smiling.

"I damn well hope so."

His hand wrapped around my throat, his fingers tightening until he was sliding me across the car to him.

"Let me hear you, baby. Do you want it to be me fucking you right now?"

"Yes," I breathed.

"This is mine. All mine. I don't want anyone's hands on you. Just watching you having to touch them is driving me out of my fucking mind."

I moaned, trying to clamp my mouth shut as my body tightened and coiled, each thrust building.

I opened my eyes, seeing Fox watching me.

"Come for me, baby. Now."

And I did. My world exploded as I fell back onto the car, his hips not slowing as I was pushed over the edge.

BY THE TIME we made it back out, everyone was already lined up on the track talking, and not seeming to mind that we disappeared.

"I'm going to go race now," he said, leaning down to kiss me.

"Great, I'm going to go watch you race now." He smiled and got into my beat-up car, ready to go race. As he drove over to line up with the rest of the crew, I went to the deck that overlooked the track. Quinn was already there, but wasn't taking her smiling face off Ransom.

In minutes, they took off, racing around with their headsets on, but only using them to yell at each other. Cole walked over, watching as they made it around and went again.

"They are good."

"I wasn't worried about that."

"So, is this why you haven't been around? I was worried it was something worse. Your dad said you were throwing a fit."

"Throwing a fit? What a rude way to say I called him out for his attitude and dumb ideas. I was throwing a fit for a good reason. David and I broke up and things got nasty. Dad sided with him and I couldn't deal with that."

He groaned with a shake of his head. "David has been a pain in the ass lately."

"Why?"

"He keeps coming in here and taking cars without telling anyone. We show up to test and practice and cars are gone. The newer ones, of course. I've tried to tell the other guys higher up what's going on, but they are assuming these cars are getting wrecked. Then they're on our asses to stop wrecking them."

"What cars?"

"Two rally cars now, two of the nice drag cars, and one Ferrari that was being stored here for someone. According to David, it was his dads, but we both know he wouldn't leave a car that nice here."

"And my dad doesn't care? Who do you think bought the Ferrari?"

"As far as I've been told, no, your dad doesn't care. And I would bet my own money that it was bought with your dad's money somehow," Cole said with a shrug.

I shook my head. "And that's why I needed a break. He's a mess, and now he isn't leaving me alone."

"Well, if you can't get through to your dad, I doubt any of us have a chance. So what happened? Took a break from the racing world and went out to find yourself some racers?"

"I guess so. It was pure coincidence."

"Looks like it worked out in your favor."

Raf hopped up the steps to the viewing platform with us. "Shit, Ash, your boyfriend knows how to drive."

"He's not — I mean, I don't think he's my boyfriend."

The cars roared around again and I could see Ransom and Fox were comfortable with the dirt now as they tried to get past each other.

"You racing today?" Cole asked, saving me from any more boyfriend questions from Raf.

"I was going to do a few laps. I just wanted to watch them for a while."

We sat in silence as the crew went around, each of them getting better each time.

"Come on," Cole said. "Wave them in Raf. It's time for me and Ash to race."

Raf did, and the crew came in, each one jumping out with smiles on their faces. Fox got out, sweat beading on his forehead as he wiped it away. It had been less than an hour and I was already stuck on how hot he was, ready to take him up on his offer to go back home now.

"That was amazing," he said, leaning down to kiss my cheek. "Thank you for the present."

"Anytime."

"Are you driving?" he asked.

"Oh yeah," Cole yelled. "I taught her how to do this track, and I need to make sure I can still beat her. Four laps, Ash," he said, pulling his door shut. I walked to my car and Fox followed.

"I like the guy, but you better go kick his ass now."

I laughed. "Oh, I'm planning on it." I slid a headphone in and he surprised me by leaning down and kissing me. It wasn't that he hadn't done it before, he just hadn't done that in front of anyone but the crew. "What are you listening to for today's race? My playlist?"

"Too sappy," I said, scrunching my nose. "I'm going angry girl rock."

He smiled and gave me another kiss before running up to the rest of the crew on the deck. I got in and we lined up.

Four laps weren't much on this small of a track and I knew the minutes would fly by.

We took off, making a clean first lap. Cole beat me around a corner and I was working to catch up. Racing around this track had been a part of my life for years. Cole and his wife and the rest of his team had been a part of my life for years.

And I missed all of it.

I made it around the next three laps without falling into endless panic or sadness, but by the time I parked the car and got out, the heavy realization of how much I missed these parts of my life had sunk in.

Fox came over, wrapping his arms around me and picking me up. "You just get better and better. Good job," he said, kissing my cheek.

"Thanks."

He gave me a strange look, but the crew was already gathering around.

Another hour went by as I stood there with Fox. The rest of the crew taking turns going around the track with some of the race team, learning more and having fun. Fox seemed content next to me, not racing again and not saying a word as we watched.

Finally, they all came to a stop again, parking the cars and sitting around.

"I think it's time to go," Fox said.

The rest of the crew nodded their agreements and pulling the cars back to the hanger.

"Hey, Cole," I said, catching his attention. "If David comes back around for these things, can you text me?"

"Yeah, of course. Why? What's going on?"

"With how he's following me, I think I should keep some sort of tabs on him."

"Good idea. Yeah, I'll keep you updated with anything we know."

"Thanks guys." I said as we walked away. "Today was amazing. Hopefully, we can come back again one day."

"It's still your home, Ash. You should come by whenever you want."

I forced a smile. "I think those days are over, but I guess I can hope. I'll talk to you later."

"Come on. Let's get home," Fox said, pulling me close and steering me back towards the parking lot, the crew right behind us.

"How about we stop for food instead?" I asked, my stomach growling.

Jax ran up. "I second stopping to find something to eat."

Everyone else chimed in, all in agreement.

"There's a place around here I want to try," Quinn said. "Let's go."

I leaned into Fox, agreeing.

"Are you sure you don't want to go home?"

"I need sustenance if I'm going home with you."

"Great point. We aren't staying late."

I looked around, everyone walking out together as I tried to tell myself that I was building a new life. A life I really did like with people I was coming to love, but letting go of everything still hurt. Stepping back into my life for a day wasn't enough.

I missed my dad, the teams, the beautiful parts of my life that were impossible to replicate.

I still wanted the life I was building with the crew and Fox. I still couldn't help but miss the life I grew up in, the one I knew so well. I missed talking to my dad and the good moments we had together. I missed when he cared about me and my racing, the endless nights he would spend helping me get better, or working with the team to get cars ready.

I couldn't know for sure what David was telling him behind my back, but at the end of the day, my dad believed him over me.

And that betrayal had hurt more than anything.

I looked at Fox, feeling horrible for missing that when he

was offering me any life that I wanted to go after, but I couldn't help it. I wanted the best of both worlds now.

He helped me into the car, making sure I was tucked inside before going around and sliding into the driver's seat.

And as soon as his door shut, I burst into tears.

THIRTY-SIX
ASH

"Ash, what's wrong? What happened?" he asked, reaching over and wrapping his arms around me.

"Nothing. Nothing. I'm fine."

"I don't think you can pretend you're fine when you're bawling your eyes out. Come on, Ash, what is it? The driving? Did you have a panic attack?"

I pulled away, trying to calm myself down.

"No, no, that wasn't it. I just…"

"What? Tell me?"

"I don't want you to be upset."

"Okay?" he leaned back in his seat, angling himself to me with his lips pressing tight together. "I can't promise that if the next words out of your mouth have anything to do with that Raf guy."

I gave a sharp laugh that came out with a sob. "No, that's not even close. I—I miss my life, Fox. And it's not that I don't want you, or the crew in it. I think that made me miss it more today, though. I want you all with me to share all of this. I never had friends come here with me like this and it was so great. It was everything I ever dreamed of having in my life. And I know I sound like a brat, but I want it all. I want real friends who care about me along with this big, fancy life. I want both."

"Of course you want both. Who wouldn't? I mean fuck, I never even had these things and I want both. Do you think the rest of the crew doesn't dream of having something like this? Do you think we got where we were by thinking small about our lives? We all want more, Ash. It has never meant we wanted more without each other. Why would I be mad about you wanting that?"

"I don't know. Because I didn't want you to think it was one or the other. David would always tell me how spoiled I was to think I deserved this lavish life along with real friends. I'm realizing now he never wanted me to want more than what I had in every aspect of life."

"Probably because he knew you wanting more would mean leaving him behind," he said with a grin. "I wish you could forget every single thing he ever told you because it's all bullshit."

"I know, and I wish I could too, but unfortunately, the shitty things he said stuck really well. So, you think it's okay that I still want my old life back?"

"Of course. And I think you deserve to get it back. I also think that part of it is out of your hands, though, and depends on if you can convince your dad to drop David."

"Yeah," I said, taking a deep breath. "I guess it does. I don't like feeling this out of control with my own life."

"I know. I meant it before, though. We can get you racing again. We can set up your life how you want it. I know it wouldn't be the same, but it would be closer."

I smiled, turning back in my seat as he did. "You're amazing when you actually like me."

"Whoa, don't get ahead of yourself, hellion. No one said that

I like you now," he said, the words dripping sarcasm as he pulled out to catch up with the crew.

"Really? The rampant jealousy and trying to have sex with me every second really threw me off then."

"Wait, that's what liking someone is? Damn, it's miserable. I can't think about anything but you. Then again, even when I was mad at you, all I could think about was you." He laughed harder now, grabbing my hand to hold it. "Aside from all that, did you have a good day?" he asked.

"Yes, I loved every second otherwise," I said, settling back into the seat.

"Me too. Almost one of the best days of my life. Are you sure you're okay?"

"I am. I'm not going to look great here soon though, with all that crying."

"I promise that you still look beautiful," he said, pulling my hand up and kissing it. "And we will figure out how to get you everything you want."

"Thank you for somehow being there every single time I need you."

"Thank you for the same thing. Are you sure you want to go in? I can still take you home."

"I'm starving, Fox, and I'm tired. If one of those doesn't get fixed, I'm going to get really bitchy."

"Food it is, then. Come on."

Everything felt heavy, but we walked in, trying to ignore it. I didn't want David to ruin anything else for me. Not a day or night or anything else. I didn't want him to have that control anymore and Fox was right. I would figure out how to get the things I wanted still.

"Tell me what else you need me to do," Fox said, putting his arm around my shoulders and pulling me closer.

"What?"

"I know I'm supposed to be there for you, but I don't actually know how to be a boyfriend. I can be a great friend any day, but that's it. Tell me what I'm supposed to do. What will help you?"

My breath hitched. "A boyfriend?"

"Did you think I was only hanging around to try to sleep with you?"

"I didn't know what to think. I haven't really thought about it. It's been made pretty clear that you've been quite the player, and that you haven't been a fan of me for a while. We slept together and now you think you want to date me?"

"Yes," he said without hesitation.

"I just —" My words were drowned out as the crew sat down with us. "We can talk about this later."

"There's nothing to talk about. You're mine, baby. I can show you again instead, if you want."

"That might be hard right now," I said, hiding the shiver that ran through me.

"I could figure it out if you need," he said, pressing a kiss behind my ear and turning back to the table.

I tried to ignore his hand that was tracing circles on my leg as we ordered and started eating, the bad parts of the day fading away. By the time we were nearly done, I was about to take Fox up on his offer of showing me again until someone stepped up to the table next to me.

Someone I recognized immediately.

"David, what are you doing here?"

Fox leaned back, throwing an arm over the back of my chair.

"Hello, David?" he asked, not hiding the shock in his voice.

"Alright, you really need to back off," David said. "Get off of her."

Fox laughed, reaching down and grabbing my chair to slide it against his. "No."

"She belongs to me," David said.

"Damn, you deserve to be hit for saying that," Jax said.

"This is what, Ash? Your rebound?"

"Please go away. And stop stalking me. I know it was you who wrecked Fox's car. I'm going to talk to my dad. I'm finding out what you're doing and I'm telling him what's happening. I want you gone from my life" "

"He won't believe you. I've made sure of it."

"Listen, David, I'm about this close to taking you outside. You already deserve it for wrecking my car and now you're ruining our night, so why don't you get the fuck out of here," Fox said.

"Wait, did you follow us here?" I said, realizing he wouldn't be here at the same time as us by pure chance.

"You haven't really given me much choice. I thought the car would be enough of a message for you to get home and then I get a call that you were at the tracks so I went only to find I wasn't allowed inside and you were there with this guy. What the fuck, Ash? I thought you were taking some time and then coming back to fix this. I need you to come home. I need this fixed. My family needs this fixed, Ashton.

I gave a strangled laugh. "I really love that you're threatening me about talking to my dad one minute and begging me to talk to him the next. You're a mess."

"Ashton!" he yelled, slamming his hands down onto the table.

"David, I'm really trying to stay calm, but it's not working," Fox said, his words still nothing more than casual conversation as David came to a boiling point in front of us. "I'm taking her home tonight. You're not following us, you're not bothering us, and if you so much as take a wrong step in her direction, your face will end up in a lot worse shape than mine."

David stepped towards the table, but Fox didn't move. His arm still relaxed around me.

"Can we go?" I said.

"Absolutely," he said, getting up and stepping around me until he was between us.

The crew got up, throwing money down and grabbing stuff to go. Apparently, David didn't get the hint, not that he ever did, and followed us out.

We walked out and David ran up to my side

"Ashton, wait," he yelled, the streets echoing the sounds as his fingers wrapped around my arm, digging in and ripping me to the side.

Fox didn't wait, pulling me behind him as he swung, hitting David once.

David screamed, falling to the ground. "He hit me. He hit me, Ash. What the fuck? Are you okay with this violence now?"

"You're just lucky I didn't tell him to keep going. Leave me alone, David." I looked up, expecting to look at the crew, but a bright yellow car caught my eye.

"What the hell is that?" I asked, pointing at it. "Is that the Ferrari you stole?"

"I didn't steal it."

"You bought it with money that you stole from my dad."

"You can't prove that."

I reached into Fox's jeans pocket, pulling out the car keys.

"No? Maybe you're right, but I'm sure as hell going to let him know."

I walked around them, heading right for the driver's side door.

"Ash, no. What are you doing? No!" David yelled. I already knew Fox wouldn't let him come near me again.

I dug the key in, sliding it across the perfect paint. After I carved the door, I walked around, hitting every single panel I could with a deep line.

"Damn, keying Ferrari's and punching people?" Kye said. "This night honestly is only getting better and better."

"There you go, David. Maybe the word thief and liar on the car might make him ask some questions."

"How could you do this? You know how expensive it will be to fix? You know I can't wreck any more cars!"

"Then you shouldn't have wrecked Fox's. I swear if you touch any more of their cars, I will come for every single one of yours."

I was shaking. I was so mad. There was no way that he bought it himself, which meant he either stole it or stole the money. "Have you really sunk that low that you're stealing from him now?"

"I didn't steal the car from him!"

"You're not going to get to me right now. I know you're dancing around the truth. I don't care either way. Stay away from me."

David finally got up.

"Come on. Just ride back with me. We can talk to him about it together."

"No, tell me what you want, what you apparently need from me, right now."

"I'm not going to talk about our business in front of these people."

"Then we have no business. Goodbye."

He rolled his eyes. "Whatever, Ash. You're obviously at a bad time of the month. Maybe we can talk when you aren't out of your fucking mind."

My mouth dropped, too stunned to know how to even respond.

I didn't have to, though.

Just like before, Fox was already in motion. His punch landed square on his nose this time, making David scream again.

"Fuck you guys. Your dad is not going to be happy you took it. I'll tell him what happened here."

"Good. Tell him. And make sure you don't leave any part out. Including you stalking me and wrecking the car."

"He asked me to find you! What was I supposed to do?"

"Not stalk me!" I yelled. "It's done. Don't follow me again."

"We need to talk, Ash. Alone."

Fox walked past him to me. "If I have anything to do with it, I can guarantee that is never going to happen."

He led me away, walking to the car.

"Are you okay?" he asked.

"Yeah, I'm okay. Are you? Your hand?"

"My hand is fine, but you are not. Come on. I'm getting you home now without tears, without anymore ex-boyfriends, and without any other incident. Hopefully."

I THOUGHT I WAS OKAY, but Fox was right, every part of me a mess.

The worst part was that all I could feel was anger. The heavy weight of it I spent months trying to get better and one day ruined it. I was right back to where I started months ago.

"Ashton," he said, obviously not for the first time. "Are you sitting in here all night?" Fox said, reaching over to me.

"Oh, we're here."

He jumped out and came around the car to me. "Come on, hellion. Let's get you upstairs. We need to get you showered and in bed."

"Mmm," I said. The thought of a warm shower and Fox's huge bed making me feel better already.

He walked me up and by the time the door shut, we were already halfway to the shower. He pulled off his shirt and pants, giving me time to admire him as he started to undress me. His hands moved lightly as he peeled everything off.

"Are we showering or having sex? Because this could go either way?"

"Showering first. Let's clean you up." I turned into the shower and he swore. "He already made marks on your arm. Fuck. I'm sorry, Ash. Are you okay?"

I looked down at five red marks already forming on my arm, one for every finger.

"It's ok, just sore. What about your hand?" I asked.

"I'm not worried about me right this second."

"Well, I am. You punched him twice. Hard." I grabbed for it, seeing the split skin at his knuckles. "I'm sorry. I'm sorry you had to do this." Tears were forming now and there was nothing I could do to stop them. "You keep wrecking your body to keep me safe."

He pulled me against him, his naked body warm against mine.

"It's ok. It's not that bad. Trust me, I've had worse. I would do it again and again for you."

He turned on the water, letting it run over us as dust and dirt were washed away.

The next ten minutes were a blur of his hands running over every inch of me. His hands massaging my head as he washed my hair and his kiss as he wrapped a towel around me.

Every touch was more gentle than the last.

It was breaking me, reminding me of how alone I had been. How no one had touched me like this…ever. At least, not that I could remember.

By the time he was done, I was already missing his hands on me.

"Could I have more of that?" I pointed to the shower. "I think that could fix all my problems."

"I'm pretty sure I cleaned your body thoroughly. Actually, I know I did because I was enjoying it so much I did everything twice."

I laughed. "Not the shower. I just want your hands on me more."

"Anything you want."

I pulled him to the bed, getting under the covers as his hands and fingertips began their slow, torturous exploration of my body.

"Fox," I breathed, his hands on me as the minutes ticked by and my body was only wanting him more.

His hands ran up my back before turning to fingertips trailing down my spine. My back ached at the loving touch.

"I need you."

"I need you too, baby."

I turned to face him when he didn't move. "No, I need you closer. I need you."

He rolled on top of me, wrapping his arms under my head until he was propped up on his elbows. "I can give you whatever you want. I want to give you everything."

He kissed down my neck, the light touch too much and not enough at the same time.

"Fox, I don't want to wait." An uncomfortable need clawed at me. He wasn't moving fast enough, not biting down on me like he had before. Every touch was a sweet, light caress. I reached down, positioning him at my entrance.

"Shh. Relax."

"No. Hurry up."

"Wow, is that your dirty talk?" he asked with a laugh as his lips trailed down my neck. "You want to hurry up and get it over with?"

"No, I meant I want you to do what you did earlier. Pick up the pace, hands on my neck, that type of thing."

I could hear him laugh again as he propped himself up and kissed my nose. "No."

"No?"

"No," he said again. "Now you messed me up. I have to start all over." His hands trailed back over me, his lips following everywhere that his lips touched. He stopped at my scar, going over it twice before moving on.

I groaned. It was bliss and agony.

Finally, he found my lips, giving me a deep kiss as he reached to the bedside and rolled on a condom before pushing into me. My body stretched, taking every part of him he was giving, the movement so slow, making me feel every inch of him.

"Fox," I begged, needing him to pick up the pace. "I need faster. Harder."

"No, I want to feel every agonizing second. I can still give you everything you want without that."

I growled. "No, you can't."

"Are you worried about what it will feel like without losing your mind to me slamming into you?" He nuzzled my neck. "Because I am."

"You are?"

"Yes."

He pulled back until he was almost out of me before pushing forward again. I moaned at the sensation.

"Your body still seems to be enjoying it," he said when my hips moved up, taking more of him. "I can give you everything you want, everything you need."

His lips kissed my chest, going back up my neck and then down to my shoulders as he kept his agonizing pace. "I can keep you safe. I would get my knuckles bloody every day for you. A beast if you need it. I'll rip my body apart to make you happy."

Tears gathered in my eyes, the words and loving touch overwhelming as my body still hummed in pleasure from him

"You can have every piece of me, hellion. It's all yours. All for you."

The tears spilled over, running down my cheeks as I bit my lip. I knew he meant every word. My heart constricted under the weight of his words as I came to the edge of falling apart.

"When you saved me, I didn't even know if I was worth saving."

"Of course you are. Never think that. I don't regret it at all."

"Thank you for saving me again and again."

"Hellion," he whispered as he kissed and licked at my tears, moving into me again.

I gasped his name as pleasure rolled over me, the world shattering as my body clenched around him. I gripped his back as he thrust into me again, finding his own release seconds after I did.

We dragged in ragged breaths, but he didn't move from on top of me.

"You're crying. Are you okay?" he asked against my neck, and I nodded, moving to wipe more tears away. "I wasn't trying to upset you. I just didn't think you needed me being a beast tonight," he said with a light laugh.

"That was just…That was very intimate." I said, not knowing what other word could describe that.

"Yes." He rolled to the side, taking me with him. "I meant every word."

"I know," I said into his chest. "That's what made me cry."

He gave a soft laugh. "I thought you needed to know." I nuzzled into him, closing my eyes and taking a deep breath.

He pulled away, cleaning us both up and climbing in next to me again.

"Get some rest."

With a nod, I settled into the bed and into his arms as my world faded away.

THIRTY-SEVEN
ASH

I WATCHED as Fox grabbed another part and added it to the engine. His focus was on what he was doing, but I knew that he saw me watching.

"Are you going to stare at me all day?"

"Yes. You're the one I said I should come by after my class."

"Because I wanted to show you the progress on your car. I didn't think about the fact that I would be ogled all day."

I laughed. "Is this a problem? Do you want me to leave?"

"Not a chance. Here," he said, handing me a wrench, "you know how to use this."

I grabbed the wrench and finished putting the part on.

"Alright," Fox said, sitting against the car, watching me now. "I see why you like this so much. I think it's my turn to stare while you work."

Ransom walked in with Quinn. "Good thinking, Fox. Have her build the engines now. Maybe she'll share some family secrets."

"No secrets, just being put to work. Although, I recall being told that my car would be done for me since I'm racing for you," I said, pointing to Fox.

He rolled his eyes. "Wasn't that promise made *before* we knew how bad of state your car was left in?"

I scrunched my nose. "I don't know. I feel like your promise didn't make any specifications."

Fox's smile grew. "Your car will be done soon."

"Really though," Ransom said. "Any family secrets you're willing to share, we will take all the help we can get."

"I don't have many family secrets, just access to good parts. But if I ever get on good terms with my dad again, I will give you all the help I can with him."

"Really?" Ransom asked.

"Of course. I'm sure I can help you guys somehow. You already have good products." I looked around the garage, the array of cars proving that they had a lot of well paying customers already. "Did you think I wouldn't?"

Jax and Kye walked over. "I think it's more the shock that Chad fucking Holt could know who we are."

"Yes. That," Ransom said with a nod.

I shook my head, and it was Quinn who spoke up. "Speaking of, after what happened the other day, have you thought about going to talk to him? About David I mean."

"I have."

Fox's head whipped over. "You didn't tell me that."

"I decided today. He should be at a party for his charity tomorrow. I figured it would be a good, neutral time to talk with him, but everyone will be there, so it will be a good time to ask around about David. I have to figure out some way to get him to stop and our dads are buddy-buddy with the sheriff, so calling him in isn't going to help."

"What are you going to be asking about him?" Kye asked.

"Apparently, he's taking cars out of the garage at the track." Their eyebrows shot up. "Cole told me the other day while we were there. Different cars. I've been wondering if he's selling them. I think that's how he got the Ferrari."

"But why? Isn't his family from money too?"

"I don't know. It wouldn't be the first time that some rich kid tried to make money when they didn't need it."

"And you think your dad would let him go if he knew this?"

"I would think so. At least, I would hope. I can't imagine this would be the only thing David is taking. My dad was giving him access to a lot of the business, including money related things. If he's this comfortable taking cars, he could already be taking more. Going to this party could help. I know there are girls there that David would show off too and I know they would talk all about him to me."

They all nodded, thinking it over.

"And then what?" Quinn asked. "Like, if this is all confirmed, what are you going to do?"

"Hope that I can show my dad some proof and he will help put a stop to it. There's no way David is going to get caught with how things are right now. Both our dads would turn a blind eye apparently, and without them, the sheriff would never do a thing."

"What time do we have to be there?" Fox asked.

"We?"

"Yes, we. Did you not want me to go with you?"

"I mean, yes, I did. I do. I didn't think you would want to go."

"Pretty sure I want to go everywhere with you, but especially when you have to go talk to your dad about your possible criminal ex-boyfriend that he thinks the world of and who will also be there." He laughed. "Don't think for one fucking second I won't be there for that."

"David's dad will be there too. They are best friends."

"Well, explaining why I broke his son's face will make for great dinner conversation."

"I want you to go, of course, but this isn't a sit around with a beer and grill out party. This is a suit and tie, cocktail dresses, rich people gossiping, dancing type of party. My dad hates them, but has to go after he started his own charity. They aren't really fun."

Fox groaned. "Well, that doesn't matter. I'm still going." They all looked at each other as Fox ran a hand over his face. "But I refuse to wear a tie."

"That's fine, a nice suit, then. Do you have one?"

Fox looked down at his dirty jeans, t-shirt, and scuffed shoes before giving me a look. "Do any of us look like people who have nice suits hanging in their closets?"

Jax knocked my arm. "Not quite one of those fancy boys with suits and Jaguars, huh Ash?"

I shook my head. "Not even a little, and that's the way I like it."

Fox grabbed my waist, pulling me to him with a kiss.

Jax groaned and rolled his eyes. "Oh good. Another happy couple to walk around here." He looked at Ransom and Quinn. "We were running low on those."

He turned, walking back to the car he was working on. Ransom and Quinn followed, prodding him about finding a girlfriend.

Fox leaned in, kissing me again. "If you're going somewhere, so am I."

"We never did talk about that being a couple thing, did we?" I asked.

We had spent the entire week together, but he hadn't brought up the boyfriend thing again and I definitely wasn't going to be the one to bring it up again.

"No, I figured since it scared you off the first time I would wait to say anything again."

"So, how long were you going to wait to bring it up again?" I asked with a laugh.

His face broke into a smile. "Forever? I figured at some point you would just catch on. It's not that I want to avoid talking about it. It's the avoiding being let down part that I was avoiding."

"You think I would turn you down?"

"Maybe you're coming to your senses," he said, kissing my neck.

"Maybe I'm waiting for you to say it."

He turned his hat backwards as he shook his head. "If it's only up to me, then yes, you're mine. Partly because you don't seem to hate my face, partly because I love yours, partly because everything about you is amazing and partly because the thought of seeing anyone else getting to touch you the way I do makes me want to claw my own eyes out."

"Such a flair for the dramatics, Fox. You could have stopped at yes."

"What fun would that be?" he asked with a bright smile.

"Ok then, boyfriend, it is."

He grabbed my face, pulling me against him with a kiss.

"Stop that right now," I said as he trailed his fingers down my spine.

"What? Kissing you?

"No, trying to seduce me into dirty thoughts when we need to go shopping."

"What? I hate shopping. Let's go back to bed."

"Too bad. I like shopping and we need clothes for tomorrow."

He groaned, getting up and beckoning to the crew to wrap it up. "Then let's go get this over with."

I HAD SPENT the last two hours getting ready, so nervous I could throw up. I could hear everyone in the living room, all showing up to give us the support that only your friends could.

My friends.

I took a deep breath. I had decided on a black maxi dress. The top was sleeveless, the front coming to a Deep V and covering my back completely in a mesh fabric. It had two slits up the front of my legs, letting them come out each time I took a step. It was a lot, and it showed a lot. Including most of the scar on my chest.

Fox had seen it plenty of times now, but the rest of the crew had only seen it once or twice. I was putting myself on display, but I couldn't hide it any longer.

Not when I was telling Fox that he shouldn't hide his.

I slipped on the strappy black heels and looked in the mirror again. I couldn't remember the last time I felt this nervous about one of these events.

I stepped out, letting out a shaking breath as I walked into the living room. A round of appreciated compliments coming from the crew, but I was only looking at Fox. He had picked out a fitted black suit and white shirt underneath, the top unbuttoned just enough to look relaxed. He looked powerful and dangerous. The suit was a harsh difference from his scarred face and calloused hands.

"Wow," he said, coming over to me. "You look amazing."

"I was going to say the same about you."

He looked so hot I couldn't stop looking. I looked back up, noticing how stiff he was as his jaw tightened and flexed. His face twisted in the same way it had been before we went to the beach.

“Are you nervous?” I said, noticing the way he couldn’t stop moving around, his eyebrows furrowed.

“No,” he said, like I had accused him of something terrible. “I mean, maybe that’s what that was, but I’m fine.”

I reached up as I pulled his head down to me, kissing his cheek.

“I don’t know if I want to lock you in the bedroom or go show you off,” Fox said.

“I think we can do both, just not in that order.”

He grabbed my hand with a groan. “Then let’s get this over with.”

“Try not to fist fight anybody, Fox,” Quinn said with a laugh as we headed out the door.

“And send us a video if you do.” Jax added as the door shut.

“No fights,” I said, and let out a yell when Fox grabbed me, picking me up and wrapping my legs around his waist as he pushed me up against the wall to kiss me.

“Well,” I said, “now I don’t want to go.”

“Does that mean we can stay?”

“No, but it means we’re not staying a second longer than we have to.”

“Fine,” he growled, carrying me down the steps. “You shouldn’t look so good when we have to leave the house.”

“What was I supposed to wear? Sweatpants?”

“No, that would make me want to stay home too,” he said, only setting me down when we got to the car.

He drove, following my directions as I tried to keep my breath steady. My nerves were getting the best of me, reminding me of all the reasons I left in the first place, and not wanting another crying episode like I had after the track.

We parked, and he got out, pulling me out into the shadows with the nearby cars.

"Wait," he said, his lips tightening. "I got you something."

"A present? Really?"

"I saw it and thought of you. I think it's something you'll like, but if you don't, that's ok."

"I'm sure I'll love it."

He pulled a box out of his pocket and opened it, turning it so I could see a necklace sitting inside.

I sucked in a breath as my mouth dropped open. A silver spider sat in the box, a red jewel on its back and another hanging off two of its legs. "It's a black widow."

"I thought with everything, you might like it."

I smiled, "I love it. It's perfect." I said, pulling it out. He helped me put it on and I looked down. The spider sat low enough on my chest to be a main feature, with my scar in the background. "I think this is the nicest thing anybody has given me."

He grabbed my arm, walking me in. "I'm sure that's not even close to the truth. I know people have given you more expensive gifts."

"I didn't say it was the most expensive. It's the most thoughtful, nicest gift I've ever been given. Getting a gift because someone thought of you is more meaningful than any expensive gift." I stopped at the top of the stairs, turning to kiss him. "Thank you."

"You're welcome."

"Wow, hot and gets me pretty things. I'm dreading going in there and having to fight other girls off you when you look like this."

"You're worried about that? Look at you. I already know of one guy in there that's trying hard to get you. I'm sure there are others."

"Only one I want, though." I said, kissing him again, "We

better go in. I've thought about dragging you back to the car about ten times since we got out."

"If we both have the same idea, I don't understand why it's a bad idea?" he asked with a laugh, pulling the door open as we walked in.

THIRTY-EIGHT
ASH

THE SOUND of music and chattering voices filled the air, and I could already feel the excitement and dread of guests. Some hated this type of party, some lived for it. I had always been somewhere in the middle, but didn't seem to have the energy to care about anything but getting this over with and going home.

"Are you ready for this?" I asked, pulling him through the crowd.

"No."

"Perfect." I smiled back at him. "Me either."

I found my dad in his usual post at a party, near the drinks table. I was surprised at the eagerness that came over me to see him again, even after everything that had happened. It's what made me drop Fox's hand and tap on my dad's shoulder, interrupting whatever conversation he was engrossed in.

He turned, and shock transformed into joy as he pulled me into a hug. "Ash? What are you doing here?"

Tears welled in my eyes as I realized how much I had missed him. He had always been my best friend, taking me to every race and event, teaching me how to race and drive for hours. We spent so much time together. The last few months without him had been strange.

"I came to check in. See how you're doing," I said, finally letting him go and stepping back in front of Fox.

"Missing you. Could this mean you're coming home?"

"I'd consider coming around more if you're ready to talk about —."

He cut me off, raising a hand.

"Let's talk about this later, honey. They will be serving dinner, and we need to get you a seat with me."

"Alright, fine. I'm here with someone, so we'll need two places."

"Did David come with you?" he asked, almost excited.

I rolled my eyes, wishing I knew what his obsession was with David.

"Definitely not." I looked back at Fox before grabbing his hand and pulling him next to me.

"This is Fox. Fox, this is my dad, Chad Holt."

My dad did the polite thing by shaking Fox's hand, but I could see he wasn't happy.

"Nice to meet a friend of Ash's."

"Not a friend, boyfriend," I said before Fox could reply.

He took a deep breath in. My dad had never met a guy I was dating because the only guy he ever knew that I dated was David, and he was thrilled when he found out we made it official. With his current obsession with David, meeting Fox wasn't going to be a happy surprise.

"Did you do this to make a scene, Ashton?"

"Excuse me? Do what to make a scene?"

"You know David will be here tonight. Did you bring this guy to cause a problem? David has been waiting to see you. There's no need to make him jealous."

"I brought Fox because I am dating him and wanted him here. If you have a problem, I can leave now before I 'cause a scene'."

My dad waited, "No, no. I want you to stay. You too, Fox. If you two could keep the dating thing to yourself for the night, that would help."

My mouth dropped open, but I stomped forward, following him to our seats.

The table was arranged, making room for us both as speeches and dinner started. The table filled, and I cringed as David and his dad sat across from us.

"Well, here we go," I said to Fox. He grabbed my hand under the table, squeezing it once and setting our entangled hands on my leg. His fingers moved, rubbing a thumb back and forth on my bare skin.

"David," my dad said, sitting next to me. "What happened to you?" His face was bruised, the yellow and purple marks still healing.

His eyes flew to Fox, who smiled over, his face so innocent it hurt.

"Accident on the track."

I gave a small laugh, making my dad look over at me.

"Ashton," he hissed. "While I love that you're here, I assume you didn't lose your manners?"

"Have any of you had a chance to meet Ash's friend Fox?"

David and his dad shook their heads, but it was David that answered. "No, I don't believe we have."

"Really?" I said. "I thought you two had met already. My mistake. This is Fox."

"So nice to meet you," David's dad said.

"Truly," David said.

"Great to meet you two. I love getting to meet some of Ash's friends," Fox said. His voice was excited and light. I couldn't get over how well he played the role. The giddiness running through me that David had to keep his mouth shut for once.

"Well, these two have been more than friends for a while now." David's dad said, "Isn't that right, David?"

"Yeah. Nearly two years together."

My eyebrows furrowed, but Fox answered. "Really? I'm surprised Ash hasn't told me more about you. We met months ago now, and she hasn't mentioned a boyfriend named David."

I hid my smile. His calm demeanor worked well in a room where every word was passive aggressive and underhanded.

"That's enough," my dad hissed at us before turning back to the table. "So Fox, what do you do? Going to school?"

Fox looked at me and I knew what he meant. I gave him a small nod. I didn't think there was any reason to lie.

"I'm part owner of Hollows Garage."

"Wow," David said. "I think I just drove past that place. Wasn't there a wrecked car out front?"

Fox's hand squeezed mine harder, but his face didn't change. "There was. Track accident. You know how other people can ruin something for everyone."

I moved my hand out of his, resting it on his thigh. I loved his calm confidence, the way he handled things without raising his voice or needing to lash out. It was something I couldn't always do, my body snapping to fight whenever I felt cornered. He wasn't like that, though. His hand grabbed mine, stopping it, but I wiggled it out again. Sliding it over the pants that fit him so well.

Tanner's dad laughed. "Been there, haven't we Chad?"

My dad looked up, "Plenty of times. Hollows Garage? Do I know that name?"

"One of their cars was brought to the track one time by one of your friends." I said. "It did really well."

"That's right," my dad said, unable to hide how impressed he was. "I remember that now. It was a nice car. Well good for you Fox. I know that is no easy feat." My dad looked over at me, ready to ignore Fox now.

The rest of the table spoke more as another plate was delivered. My hand stayed on Fox's leg, feeling his pants swell as we sat there. I gave him a small smile and took my hand away, wondering if it would bother him enough to do something about it.

Another course came and went before I was over it. David stood, excusing themselves, and I did the same only a second after watching them go.

"I think we're going to take a walk around."

My Dad nodded. "Fine, but please don't run away before we get a minute to talk."

"I won't." I gave him a small hug and got up, taking Fox's hand even with my dad's glare.

We made it halfway to the door before Fox said anything. "This is a first for me meeting a girlfriend's parents and all, but I think I'm doing great."

I laughed. "I'd say so with the circumstances."

I stopped, stepping outside. "Want to take a walk before the next part? I'm worried the rest of the night isn't going to go as well."

He wrapped his arms around me from behind, kissing my neck. "Yeah, let's go. And you're here to gather your information and then we can leave. You don't have to worry about anything else tonight."

"Yes, then I get to go home with you."

"And I will get you there faster than you can blink. I can't wait to rip this dress off you."

I groaned, falling back against him. "You touching me like that makes this part even harder."

"Why?" he asked, stroking my hip.

"I need you to hang back for a minute while I talk to Celina. I'm assuming she's the ring leader here now and is the most likely to be hooking up with David."

"Why does that mean I have to hang back?"

"Because if she sees you with me, she will know I'm not actually interested in learning more about David. She'll also be hanging on you like a fucking dog with a bone, and I might kill her if I have to see that."

"I think you're forgetting the scar. I'll wait in the corner for you. Just yell and I'll come to you."

"Fox," I said, turning in his arms. "I think that you're forgetting that these are girls starved for a mysterious bad boy, and orgasms. You're definitely going to be a bone in a room full of starved dogs. The scar is only adding to the dangerous mystery, and hope that you can bring them to places these other guys aren't."

He ran a hand down my jaw. "And what about you? You don't think the guys are going to be all over you, hanging on every word out of that filthy mouth? Dreaming of it being their cock you're teasing under the table?"

My legs clenched. I knew what I was doing, what I had been doing at the table, what I was getting us into the moment the next words left my lips, but Fox had been so gentle with me the past few days, I needed to know he wouldn't be forever, that he didn't see me as weak now.

"And what if they do? What if they dream of me on my knees in front of them? What if they think about getting me off? If they are thinking they can make me come better than you do?"

He looked around once before spinning me, my back against him as his hand wrapped high around my throat, his fingers tightening as he led me into the woods.

"I don't think anyone's going to make you come like I do

because I know your secret," he said as he pushed me up against a tree, my hands bracing myself.

"What's my secret?"

"You like to be fucked hard. You like to be bent over and used until you can't move. You get pleasure from my hands around your throat. Provoking me with your filthy mouth so it can scream my name," he whispered the words to me as his hand wrapped into my hair. "Isn't that right, baby?" He jerked my head back, pulling my hair and making me moan as his hard cock pushed against me.

"Mmm, I know what that mouth does, and I know it can answer. Tell me, have you ever let anyone else know? Have you ever shared your dirty fantasies with anyone else?"

"No. No one else knows." I said, my words begging for what I hoped was next.

His hand left my hair as he crouched down, ripping my underwear down and moving my dress to the side.

His tongue found my wetness. Sucking my core and dragging his tongue to my ass. I gasped, gripping the tree to stay standing.

"Fox now. I need you now."

He stood again, positioning himself at my entrance. One hand came around my neck and the other covered my mouth.

"Try not to scream my name too loud or everyone is going to know how rough you really like it." He pulled out a condom, rolling it on before slamming his cock into me, not slowing or stopping as he pulled it out and slammed it into me again. I screamed, his hand muffling the sound, "Or would you like them all to know that you're mine?" His hand dropped from my mouth. "Do you want them to see how good of a girl you are at taking my cock?"

His hand tangled in my hair and tightened, my eyes rolling back as every part of me burned. It was a filthy dream come true.

I came apart around him. Coming so hard, I almost fell over as my legs shook. His hand dropped from my hair and wrapped around my waist, holding me up as he thrust into me once before pulling out.

"Fox," I breathed. Trying to gain any other thought in my head. He leaned over, kissing along my shoulder and neck.

"Such a good girl when I get my hands on you, a rabid little hellion every other moment, though," he said, laughing into my ear. "And I promise that I love every second of it."

I stood leaning against the tree, my chest heaving as he fixed his pants and reached down to fix my dress.

"I don't think these are usable," he said, tucking my underwear into his pocket. "But I'll be sure to give them back later."

He took a step, wrapping his arms around me and dragging me from the tree into his arms. "You okay?"

"I don't know that I've ever been better, but then again, I could say that every time you fuck me like that."

"Mmm," he nuzzled into my neck. "Just to keep track, you like to be fucked in the woods, on cars, in garages. I'm so excited to see where I get you next. And I'm glad I'm the one that gets to have you in each place."

He kissed me, deepening the kiss as I spread my fingers across his chest.

"I can barely walk."

"Good, hopefully you don't walk in there and change your mind about me then."

"I would never."

"I hope not. I might lose my mind completely."

I melted into him. "I'm not choosing anyone else."

"I'm not either," he said, kissing my head. "Do you think you can make it through the rest of the night, or should I just carry you around?"

"I want to say carry me, but I don't think that will make any of this easier."

"Probably not." He ran his thumb over my bottom lip. "Let's go inside and get this over with so I can get you home."

THIRTY-NINE
ASH

THE ROOM WAS NEARLY OVERFLOWING, the bodies not so much forced against each other as they were grinding on each other.

Fox squeezed my hand once before retreating to the corner of the room. Eyes followed him as he went and I tried not to get jealous, everyone looking to see the mystery man that was taking up space.

I turned, pulling my attention from Fox to look for Celina.

She was near the center of the crowd, the room gravitating around her. That's where I had been at one point, the room revolving around me and I hadn't even known it.

"Ashton!" she yelled, pulling me into her arms. "I didn't expect to see you here."

"At my dad's party?"

She laughed, the sound so fake I almost gagged. "I meant out! We haven't seen you in months. Again. You keep disappearing."

"Well, I decided it might be time to come back and see about fixing a few things."

"Really?" she said, her perfect eyebrow curving up.

"Yeah."

"With your dad or with David?"

I shrugged, "Both maybe?"

"Wow, Ash. I hate to be the one to tell you, but I think David moved on."

"What? Really?"

"I mean, I have been kind of seeing him now. You know, you can't leave a man like that and expect him to wait forever."

I tried to look stunned. "But is it serious? Has he actually told you that?"

She crossed her arms. "Of course it's serious."

"Okay, so he has let you know what he's doing, right?"

"If you mean working with your dad to race, then, yeah, he's obviously told me."

"What does that mean? He's racing for Holt?"

She rolled her eyes. "Don't even act like it's a surprise, Ash. You left. Someone obviously needs to take over."

I already knew it was coming, but the blow of it still hurt.

"Yeah, of course. I meant, has he told you about the money, the cars?"

She was getting pissed now. "Is that really any of your business anymore? Are you jealous that he gets the cars and money now and you don't?"

"No, I still have plenty of that on my own, actually. Is David really going to be racing, though?"

"I don't know, Ash, and I really don't care. As soon as you left, things only got better for him. Racing, working, money. I mean, he just bought a Ferarri, Ash. And he got me this," she said, sticking her wrist out with a diamond tennis bracelet attached. "I think his friend is the one driving anyway, so does it matter? David really cares for me, Ash, and we are happy together. I'm sorry things didn't work out for you two, but I think you coming around like this is a little pathetic."

I stifled my laugh, looking to see a glimpse of Fox through the crowd. "Wow, so it is serious between you two."

"It is and I would prefer not to have a problem between us, Ash, so I hope you can finally let him go now," she said with a satisfied smirk. "I think he's happier now, anyway."

"Of course he is. Just be careful. He's got a way of twisting things when he talks. It makes everything sound better than it is. I won't be causing you two any issues."

"Thanks for saying that. Really. I know how hard it must be to see him gone and happier now." She was only trying to rub it in my face, but she didn't realize how little she had that I wanted.

"Yeah, so hard. I'll see you later." I said, pushing away from her and into the crowd. I circled around, making my way back to Fox.

He came into view, smiling down at the girl hanging on his arm. I could feel the anger before it even fully arrived.

"What's up, you two?"

"Oh, wow! Ashton, you're here."

"Yep. Dad's party and all. Figured I should show up. What about you two? What are you doing looking so cozy over here?" My eyes flashed to Fox and the smirk he was giving me was infuriating.

"Oh, we were very cozy," Jenny said, bumping against Fox's arm. "I was telling Fox all about everyone here. He's new around here and didn't know anyone," she laughed, touching his arm again. It took everything in me not to rip it off. "Oh wow, sorry. Where are my manners? Fox, this is Ashton Holt, Ashton, this is Fox," she said his name in a purr, looking up at him with a smile I knew all too well. She thought she already had him in her perfectly manicured claws.

"Ashton was it? I assume Chad Holt is your father?"

"He is."

"And aren't you one of the best racers around? If I recall you placed in the top ten in nationals, correct?" His smile was so bright I realized he wasn't flirting with her, he was flirting with me.

"That was me. I've actually been getting pretty good at street racing, too," I said, wondering if this would have been our conversation had we met in a different way.

"Really? Wow, I love a girl who knows how to handle a car." He looked down at Jenny and back at me. "Although one could argue that those girls are always a bit of a handful."

"I have been called that, among other nicknames. Does that mean you know how to drive?"

"I do, mainly street and drag racing, but I've recently tried out rally and think I'm ready to get into that."

"Wow, a man who's skilled in all areas. I'm impressed."

"You two seem to have a lot in common." Jenny said, annoyed.

"It seems we do. What about taking a walk with me, Ashton?"

"And where are we walking to?"

"I was recently on a nice little path in the woods. We could go there. Or I could show you my car. I'm super rich, so I have a really nice car."

I held out my hand. "Perfect. Lead the way."

"My pleasure."

We moved through the room, his arm going around me as he moved us out of the cramped space and back into the fresh air.

Fox wrapped around me, pulling me aside and kissing me till I couldn't breathe. "Fox." I whispered.

"I told you that was going to be torture. I think I saw five different guys looking at your ass."

"Me? You were worried about me when I find you cozy in a corner flirting with another girl?"

"I wasn't flirting."

"You absolutely were."

"If I was, it was only because she was spilling secrets left and right. I could only smile and agree as she gossiped over what everyone's fucking secrets were. No wonder you had no one to trust around here. I said hi, and she started spilling her guts to me."

I rolled my eyes. He wasn't lying, she was a gossip. "Did you find anything out about David?" I asked as we stepped outside the tent.

"Ash?" I heard a voice say and immediately smiled.

"Ollie? I didn't know you were coming!" I threw my arms around him as he picked me up.

"Maybe because you haven't called me in days. Again," he said, but he was smiling. "That's okay, though, when you look so happy."

"I am happy," I said, meaning it. Even if I did miss parts of my old life, I was quickly realizing that I could live the rest of my life in the new one I had created and be happy.

"Good, because I was sick of your moping. We had to come out tonight. Steven is trying to see if your dad will have him join his F1 team. He's got it in his head that F1 is his new dream, which is fine because who doesn't want a boyfriend that is a Formula 1 driver."

"I would offer to talk to my dad for him, but that might not help the situation right now."

"Don't even. He doesn't need your help. If he wants to be a driver, he's doing the work himself." He scrunched his nose. "Ok actually, I take that back. I have to be a good boyfriend and say that if you are ever back on good terms. I won't be mad if you say a few good things."

"No problem, but no promises. Oh, Fox, sorry. You remember Ollie?"

"Yeah, I do. Nice to actually meet you."

"Mmm, and nice to meet you. I always knew Ash could get someone better looking than David, but wow. You're something else entirely." Ollie smiled. "A better personality too, I hear."

"Damn. I hope so," Fox said.

Ollie smiled. "I am glad I ran into you, though. We need to talk. I was going to have to call you tomorrow, but this might be better."

"Why, what's going on?"

He looked around, grabbing my arm and pulling me further to the side. Fox was like glue, stepping with me with a furrowed brow.

"I've heard a lot more about David. There's been talk at the track more and even Steven is hearing a lot of it. He's got worse, Ash. He's threatening people left and right with the most ridiculous things. There's word going around that he's in some deep issues with money that he can't tell his dad."

"I assume that's why he's taking his cars then. His dad was already at the end of his rope with him messing up cars and getting into trouble. I think he was one wrecked car away from being kicked out."

"Well, you might have sealed the deal with the Ferrari, then," Fox said with a laugh.

Ollie's eyebrows shot up. "Did you mess up that man's Ferrari?

"Only because he stole it, somehow, and he wrecked Fox's."

"Oh, babe, I was about to congratulate you. I don't need any reasoning. But seriously," he said, looking around again, his face etched with worry. "I don't know what's going on, but I am getting a bad feeling from him. So was Steven. He's giving us the creeps. And he was just looking for you. Have you talked to him?"

"Only at the table with our dads there," I said.

"Well, keep an eye out. I think he's on his warpath tonight, and from the sounds of it, you're the main target."

Fox squeezed my hand. "I think I'm okay tonight, but thanks. Do you know anymore about him with these cars? Is he reselling them or is it like a chop shop type of thing?"

"I'm not sure. I know that he asked Steven if he would like to help them move some cars around for some extra cash, but Steven declined when David wouldn't tell him what he was driving and why. There are enough rumors about them that he isn't going to risk his career helping them do whatever illegal shit they are doing."

"So he's stealing cars and trying to get my dad's own drivers to help?"

"It sounds like it."

"But he has to be doing this all from somewhere. Even if he's just selling the cars, he would have to store them. Would he be doing it out of your dad's garages?" Fox asked.

"I doubt it. He would have too many random people coming and going. Aside from David, apparently, my dad takes security seriously. He would have to be doing it somewhere my dad wouldn't find."

"So we need to find a second garage or storage place that he's using," Fox said.

"It looks that way."

I shrugged as Fox grabbed my hand. "I guess that means it's time to go get tonight over with. Thanks Ollie. We'll go see what we can find out."

"Like I said, be careful and please get rid of him, because I want you back around. We miss you."

"I miss you too." I turned to Fox. "Ready to go talk to my dad again?"

"Ready as I'll ever be."

We walked back in, the crowd mingling around tables as

music played. My dad still sat at his table, talking with his friends. He always claimed he had to walk and talk with the room but would end up sitting with the same group of guys that he always did.

"Hey, dad." I said, "Do you have some time now? I'd like to get going soon."

He nodded. "Of course, honey. David is in the office already. Let's go up there."

"David? Why would he need to be there?"

"We have some things that we all need to talk over. I think that's the only way this is going to be fixed."

"Fine," I said through gritted teeth, my heart beat roaring in my ears. Fox's hand rested on the small of my back as we walked, and I leaned into him further.

"Give me a second. I'll be right in," I said as we reached the doors.

"Alright, please don't run out. It's just us, honey. We need to work it out."

"Yeah, of course." I said, waiting as he went in before turning to Fox. "I don't think I can do this."

"Of course you can."

"No. With David in there? No. He's going to change up all my words to use them against me."

"And now you know it's coming and can be prepared for it."

"But even if I'm ready now, when I walk in there, it will all fall apart. I start off strong, but halfway through the conversation I end up apologizing to him, even if he's being the asshole."

"I think it's safe to say he's always being the asshole. I'll be right here. Do you want me to come in with you?"

I shook my head. "No, no, you're right. I know better now. I need to try to do this myself. I just don't know if I can."

"Of course you can. You can do anything you want to do. You need to see that. Do you think I'm strong?"

"Obviously."

"Do you think I do whatever other people tell me or let them boss me around all the time?"

"Aside from your friends? Not at all. Even then, it's iffy," I said with a smile.

"Then you should also believe that I will not give in to people just because. I would never get on my knees and do whatever I'm told to do for anyone. Anyone but you. Please see how powerful you are, how amazing you are. If you think I am stronger or better than David in any way, and yet I will bow to your every want and need, then please see that you hold all the power in the room. Do not let them tell you otherwise because, you're right, he is going to try, but you don't have to listen."

He was looking down at me, his hands wrapped around my waist, and I knew I could do this with him. "I feel like I'm going to war."

"Close enough."

"You are stronger than me, Ashton. You are kind, smart, brave, very determined, and they should be in there begging for your forgiveness. Not the other way around. They need you, not the other way around."

"You're right. Thank you," I said, reaching up to kiss him. "I'm still calling you in there if I need you."

"And I will be waiting right here." He squeezed my hand once before dropping it, and I knew there was no more waiting.

I walked into one of the offices and I closed the door, leaving it cracked in case I needed Fox.

"I'm glad you came out tonight. I've missed you," my dad said as he sat down. David was already sitting in one of the chairs at the desk, barely looking my way.

"I've missed you too. Is there any reason David has to be here? Can I not even talk to you without him around now?"

"He's here because he is involved in this. Obviously, you two had a big fight, but that doesn't mean you can run away from your life."

"We didn't have any fight," I said. "I left because of how you both were acting."

"We never had a fight. You and David broke up," he said, holding up his hand before David could protest. "And then you ran out of your life. I know breakups can be hard, but this isn't the way to deal with them. Then bringing that guy around tonight? For what, Ashton? To make this harder? From everything I have heard, there is nothing here that can't be worked out."

"Well, you've heard a lot of lies then because there is no repairing any type of relationship between us. Not only did he help in ruining my life, but he's stalking me now."

"And I've heard that you keyed one of his cars."

"Because he wrecked Fox's car!"

"And it comes back to that guy again. What a surprise. I can't tell you how to run your life, but I can promise you that giving all of this up for a guy like that isn't worth it."

"And giving it up for David would be? I met Fox months after I left. How is this suddenly his fault?"

"Because I'm sure he's telling you anything you want to hear so that you don't come back here."

"You're delusional."

"No, I'm right. I know exactly what type of guy Fox is and I don't like it. I'm sure he's into the fast cars, and girls, and whatever other trouble he can find. I see the tattoos, and that scar? What kind of fights is he getting himself into to get something like that?"

I could feel my entire body run cold before flooding with anger. "A fight where someone was attacking me. A fight that he didn't have to get involved in, but put himself at risk of being killed so that I was ok. Someone robbed me and even after I gave them everything they came after me. Fox stopped him from getting to me, and the guy apparently had a knife. Do you know what he could have done to me? I was alone." I was yelling now, remembering that night and how scared I had been. "That guy you're judging is the reason I am here and in one piece right now. So I hope you are proud of your assumption now. Didn't you always tell me not to judge people? And his tattoos are nothing compared to how many you have. You have one on your neck!. Do you think people should judge you for that?"

"They do judge me for that."

"And you like it so much you want to do it to others?"

He shook his head but wasn't saying anything.

"That's what I thought. I came tonight to talk to you about him," I said, pointing to David. "He's stalking me and I want it to end. He's following me, threatening me and now messing with my friends. Also, Fox's car wasn't wrecked on a track. It was wrecked when David and his friends came and beat the shit out of it."

"I did not!" David finally said, standing up and coming over. "You're going to accuse me of things like that in front of your dad? You can't even prove it. Based on what I've seen and what your dad is saying, it sounds like he is making his own enemies and trying to make it your problem."

"No, you're the only problem here. And I know you are stealing cars. I don't know what for, or where you're bringing them yet, but I know you're taking cars from the track." I turned to my dad. "Did you know that? Did you know that everyone else sees him taking them and I'm assuming selling them to take the money?"

"I think someone would have told me if that was happening."

"You know what, Ash? I'm worried about you," David said. "You went through so much with your wreck and then learning you couldn't race anymore. I'm worried this guy isn't helping you move on from that." He turned to my dad, the fake worry on his face making me sick. "What if this guy is just trying to get close to her before she comes back and has all this stuff? He knows what the value would be to him if he runs that garage."

I gave a sharp laugh. "You think Fox wants any of this? What about you, David? Why have you been coming to me crying that things are so bad and that you need me here? What money trouble do you have that you need my dad to help bail you out?"

"I'm perfectly fine with money. I don't need your dad's money for anything. I'm here to help now that you've bailed."

My mouth dropped. In one sentence, he changed everything. From running away to bailing on them. It didn't matter what I said, David could make this all my fault.

"He's right, Ash. I asked for more of his help after you left. I thought you would be staying to help run the business, but instead, you ran when things got tough."

My stomach churned and I could feel my chest tightening.

There was no winning.

There was no changing his mind when David was better at this game.

"I want you safe, taken care of," my dad continues. "I want your future safe and taken care of. I want you with someone who will help you to succeed, even further than I have done. I was trying to hand that to you and you ran out on us."

"And what? I can't consider anyone else? David is the idiot you choose for me. What about what I choose? What if I would rather Fox's help? What if I want all of those things, but with someone else?"

David laughed. "The guy runs a stupid shop that no one knows. How could he ever run something like Holt Racing? How could you even think he would be a better fit when I've been working years to learn this business? That's so disrespectful, Ash. Not only to me, but to your father, who has worked to build this company from the ground up.

My dad nodded in agreement. "Ash—" He started, but I was the one to hold my hand up this time, the pain in my chest twisting like a knife. David's eyes were trained on me, the satisfied smirk so suffocating that, for a second, I thought I wasn't going to breathe again.

Somehow I never put it together that he made my panic attacks worse. Each day away from him had made them better, and since being around Fox, they had almost disappeared completely.

My stomach churned harder. The impossible feeling that I don't know my own mind making me feel like he was right.

"Fox." My voice was hoarse, but he still walked in, coming to my side in seconds. "I'm having a panic attack," I whispered to him.

"Alright, I'm here," he said, wrapping an arm around me and leaning down to whisper in my ear. "You're fine. I've got you. This isn't your reality, baby. We are going to leave tonight and go home to watch one of your favorite movies together, and I'll be with you all night and all weekend. This isn't the life you live. Remember what I said, you hold all the power in here. You're the Queen and he only wants the power you already have."

I took a deep breath, turning to face David and my dad again.

"I'm leaving. I won't be coming back until he is gone."

"Ashton, you know I can't—"

I put up a hand. "That's a lie. You can. This entire place would only run better without him gone. I hope you know that anything you thought he did before was only because of me and my hard work. And really, I don't care. I can't even be near him without a panic attack now. There is no way I would come back willingly. At this point, he's trying to ruin my life to have more money and power. I wouldn't be surprised if he's the reason I wrecked. So yes dad, I am absolutely telling you that you need to choose between him and me. I wasn't clear before because my head was such a mess, but I will be clear now. I don't have proof right now that he is stealing from you, stealing cars and trying to get your own drivers to help, but I have been told by people I trust and believe them. Unlike you. I have a lot to do so we can talk about this in a week or two when I've calmed down and you can let me know what you decide, but David will never be a part of my life again. And if you don't trust me, if you value David's opinion over mine, then I'm not a good fit to run the company one day, anyway."

I looked at him, the world falling apart as I said the words. Not realizing how hard they were to say, to even think about.

I leaned into Fox, needing him to hold me up. "Let's go."

He pulled me in close, leading me out as I tried not to cry, the last sliver of hope that things could be repaired dying away.

FORTY
FOX

I WALKED her back into the main room, the amount of people alone making it suffocating. I couldn't believe another night had been ruined for her because of David. She hadn't been lying. He was invading every second of her life that he could. Now she couldn't even talk to her own parent by herself.

"Wait here," she said. "I need to go clean up." She smiled up at me like a king before running back into the crowd.

I waited, groaning, the moment I saw her dad come across the room to me. Anger rolled through me at the sight of him. I couldn't understand how he could treat her like this and not see what a loser David was.

"I see she hasn't run out yet."

"Not yet."

"And she's been doing okay?"

"Aside from her father agreeing with her abusive, stalker ex-boyfriend that she's lost her mind, yeah, she's been great. And is racing again, if that's any concern to you."

"She shouldn't be."

"I don't know who you *think* she is, but you're wrong. You

may think some pretty shitty things about me, but at least I'm not stupid enough to underestimate someone like her."

He looked at me and sighed. "It's not that I have anything against you, but we all know your type, Fox. All I've wanted is the best for my daughter."

"I can understand why. She's amazing."

"Well then, you can understand why I feel like someone else is more suited for her."

"Yeah, I can understand it."

"If we can agree that you understand me, I hope you think about leaving her alone and having her come back home."

"I don't know if I can do that, and honestly, I'm not the one standing in the way of her wanting a relationship with you," I said. "You know, I used to look up to you. It was life changing to know that someone could work their way up to what you have. It gave me and my friends some hope when we started our garage. Funny how a view of someone can change so easily."

"Well, if you suddenly find a way to do that and have her reconcile this fit she's having with me, let me know. I have a world of resources for your business. I can make sure you and anyone else on your team is set for life."

"You're offering to help my business if I don't talk to her, and encourage her back to you and David?"

"I am. I worked hard for what I have and apparently you're trying to do the same. You can see that I want my daughter to have the best life possible. We know she'll get over this phase of life and come around, anyway. Who could turn down this life? This way I get her home faster and you don't leave empty-handed. I have to go, but stop by the house alone if you make the right decision."

My hands flexed and fisted. I couldn't believe what he offered me.

Helping our business in exchange for never being with

Ashton again. I knew damn well what help from him would mean. I knew it would change our business forever.

And at this point, I knew what leaving Ash would do to me.

Our business brought enough money that I didn't need his help. We had done fine so far and would keep doing that.

There wasn't anything Chad Holt could offer me that would change my mind.

I knew there had to be someone better for her, someone not so scarred up, but I was going to do whatever I could to be better.

I walked over to the little space where the DJ sat, playing soft songs for people to dance to, and requested one myself as she walked back out into the crowd.

The melody started playing and her eyes jumped to mine, making my smile grow.

She didn't know that I saw this song playing that night. Even though she tried to skip it, I saw it.

I wouldn't choose anything else over her. I would try to shove aside the doubt I had in myself. I had to try to show her that I did care.

She walked over, letting me pull her against me.

"Did you play this?"

"I did."

Her lips pursed together and cheeks reddened. "So, you did see it that night."

"Yes. You aren't that fast. You thought of me when you heard it?"

"Yes," she said, the words shaky. I couldn't believe she was the nervous one here.

"When?"

"When what?"

"When did you hear it and think of me?"

"The day we were out racing. Well, I was trying to race. The only reason I could do it that day was because you were there. I felt safe. I knew that if I only got down the road, you would be there to help me. Literally, since the moment I met you, you have given me everything and all I've wanted to do is give back a fourth of what you've given me. It felt fitting. Ever since I found you guys, I haven't missed my life here as bad. It felt like home, even when you were a jerk."

"I would give you everything I have and don't expect anything in return. And you tried to hide this from me?"

"Of course I did. Who wants to admit to feelings like that?"

We moved, dancing as the song played.

"You're home is with us," I finally said, trying to not let my voice break. I didn't know when I got so damn emotional, but it seemed to be coming in waves tonight that I couldn't stop. My chest was in a vice that kept tightening and there was nothing I could do to relieve the pressure other than tell her everything I could. "This isn't your only option in life. Starting right now, we are building a racing team, and you're leading it. This will never have to be your only choice."

She looked away, but I saw her eyes fill with tears.

"I never thought of another path in life."

"Different path, same destination," I said. "You keep racing as much as you want just with a different team. I'm sure you've learned enough to help us in a lot of ways and we will help you with everything we can do."

My eyebrows jumped when she started laughing.

"What's so funny?"

"I've been sitting around my apartment for months, wondering what the hell I was going to do with the rest of my life. Come to find out that the answer to all my problems was about twenty minutes down the road."

"I'm here for anything you need."

"Anything?"

"I think I already proved that once tonight, but if you need it again, we can absolutely figure that out. The balcony looks pretty empty right now."

"How dirty," she said.

"As far as I can tell, you like it dirty." I kissed her cheek. "I'm serious, though. We will get everything sorted out."

It sounded like a promise and I knew as soon as I said the words, it was a promise I didn't know how to keep.

FORTY-ONE
ASH

I ROLLED, expecting to see Fox next to me like he had been every morning since the night after the beach, but he wasn't there.

"Fox," I yelled, but didn't get a response.

"Fox?" I yelled again, the apartment seemingly empty. I got up and grabbed my bag, relenting that I would need clothes after my third night in a row being here. The thought of going back to my apartment to stay, though, sounded too cold and lonely. I liked it here. There was Fox, of course, but the rest of the crew was all here. Loud, nosy, and comforting.

He had made coffee, but it was already growing cold, which only made me worry.

The garage was closed today, and he didn't say anything about going out this morning.

I walked over to Quinn and Ransom's, knocking and hoping I wasn't waking them up. Hoping that he was here with them.

"Hey, what's up?" Quinn said, pulling open the door.

"I was just seeing if Fox was here."

Ransom was sprawled out on the couch. "No, haven't seen him today. Why?"

I shrugged. "He was gone when I got up. I figured he was over here."

"Hold on. I'll text him."

"I tried that. He didn't respond," I said as his phone pinged almost immediately. "Did he seriously just text you back?"

"Yeah, I told him I needed help on the car. He says he's at the garage."

My eyes widened. "So he texts you back, but not me, and he snuck out of his own apartment?"

"Maybe he had something to do today?" Quinn offered, but based on Ransom's face, I didn't think that was the case.

I turned with a groan.

"What are you doing?" Quinn said as she followed me into Fox's apartment.

"Going down there," I said, grabbing my bag.

"Call me if you need anything, and try to give him a minute or two to explain himself."

"Thanks," I said before heading out. Even more annoyed when I realized that Fox has my car still, so I had to walk.

The garage was dark when I walked in, all the lights off with only one bay door open and I could see Fox bent over a car, cursing at something he was working on.

I made it about halfway to him before he noticed me. The groan let me know just how unhappy he was to see me.

"What the hell?" I said, putting my hands on my hips.

"What are you doing here?" he asked, the words more of a threat than a question. It felt like the first time I walked in here, the scowl, the anger, more importantly, the *annoyance* that I dared to come here.

"I was going to ask you the same thing. Did you really sneak out of your own apartment? Didn't we already agree that wasn't a great thing to do?"

"Yes. I needed to work on this."

“Alright, fine, let’s say you had to. Then what’s with the attitude, and ignoring my texts?”

“I needed a minute to think.”

“Think about what?”

“I just —” He turned, setting down a wrench. “I needed to figure out how to deal with this.”

“Deal with what, Fox? Can you tell me what’s going on?”

“I went to sleep and everything was fine and then this morning everything was different.”

“What does that mean?”

“It means last night I was still trying to wrap my head around you being in my life. Going to that party was a lot. I saw what your life was, what it could be. I woke up realizing that the whole place is your life. After your dad talked to me, I still thought I was okay, but then it all sank in and what he said started to make sense.”

“My dad talked to you? When?”

“When you went off to the bathroom. He grabbed me to talk.”

“And what did he say?”

“Nothing, both of us already didn’t know.”

“What did he say, Fox?” I asked, nearly yelling. Panic gripped me at what horrible things my dad could have told him.

“He told me what kind of guy you need and how wrong I was. The usual, I guess, but he was right. You go to those parties and want to be a part of that world. You want to run that huge business and want someone who can help you do that one day. I can’t do that. I don’t have a fancy business degree or rich parents that showed me how to do that. I can’t help you with that, and I can’t be some guy that has suits and goes to fancy charity dinners. I mean, even my face rules me out for that. There are plenty of guys there that could be that for you, but it’s not me. I’m a mechanic, Ash. I help run a small business and even that part is new to me. I build cars, I race cars. I don't involve myself with giant corporations with cars, and you need someone who can. Someone who can shower you with money and time and run a business with you. Someone who can sit at those functions and talk to those people."

"You could have fooled me. I thought you did better than me last night."

"Last night, all I could think about was how amazing you are. I wasn't thinking of the long-term consequences that would come with us being together."

"Are you seriously trying to get rid of me right now? And not only get rid of me, but tell me it's because of who I am? Because you wanted it when it was fun cars and racing, but now that I have this whole other side that isn't as fun to deal with, you're backing out of any future with me? I don't remember even hinting that, even if I did fix things with my dad, you should help me run Holt Racing. I may never go back there."

"But you might. You want to. And I overheard what you told your dad. That I would be someone you choose to help you, be with you, and run the business. You didn't say it to me, but you're obviously going to want that, even if I fully believe you can handle it yourself. You want a guy who can be there with you to help."

I couldn't stop myself. I started laughing.

"I'm glad you find this funny."

"It is. You're worried about things that aren't even happening. You're worried about not being good enough for a business that I currently have nothing to do with and may never have anything to do with. Right now, I'm one step away from selling my car because I'm broke and have no idea what job I'm qualified for. I would have to ask *you* for a job. Then, on top of it, you're worried about not being good enough for parties I don't want to go to. I have tried over and over to tell you that I want you and this is what I get when things are hard?"

"It doesn't matter. It's still something to worry about."

"Fine, you can stay and worry about it all day. All night too, for all I care." I grabbed my keys off the tool box and turned. "Have fun worrying without me, though. I'm not doing this. I'm not going to beg you not to hate me anymore, and I'm sure as hell not going to beg you to love me."

"What are you doing? Where are you going?"

"I'm leaving," I said, grabbing my bag off the ground. "And I'm going home. To *my* home. If you're too much of a coward to face me when you're upset, then you are finally right, you don't deserve me."

I got to the car and sat idling, wishing he would stop me, wishing for him to stop worrying about everything and understand that he couldn't fix everything overnight. Even I was still dealing with the effects of my wreck and life almost a year later.

I had been chasing after Fox for weeks, but this time I wanted him to chase after me.

FORTY-TWO
FOX

I WATCHED as she stalked to the car, popping the trunk to throw her bag in.

The office door opened, and I jumped.

"Fuck, Jax. How long have you been there?"

"Long enough to know that you better run to that car before she leaves."

"What?"

"You're being ridiculous. A guy would literally kill for someone like her and now you're just going to let her go because you are scared about what could happen. Don't be stupid and go stop her. She has given you every opportunity to be with her and now you're throwing it away again. You are never going to find someone so perfect for you again, Fox. So you better run, and you better offer her your fucking life to forgive you. Some of us aren't so lucky to find love even if we want it. I don't even know if I could forgive you for pushing her away like this."

"Damn, Jax."

"Yeah, yeah. I'm awesome. She's fast and her angry music just started, so you better run."

And I did, making it around the front of the car as she moved into gear.

The window went down. "Move or I'm going to run you over."

"I expect nothing less, but I'm not moving."

"Why? We just had this discussion. I'm leaving."

"And I can't let you. I fucked up."

"There's no way that you figured that out that fast. Move."

"I did. I swear I did because the moment I realized I might never see you again, I knew that I fucked up. Then Jax really drove the point home. Please, can you wait?"

I needed her.

I needed every second with her.

"I'm sorry. I freaked out this morning and let everything get out of hand. I don't want you to go, though."

"And I don't want to stay."

"You have every right to go and every reason to want to go, but please don't."

"Why?"

I pulled at my hat, flipping it back and resisting the urge to continue messing with it. My body was buzzing with a pent up energy. I didn't know where to place.

"Fox?"

"What?"

"Why should I stay?"

I bent over the hood, my heart beating so hard I could only think the worst. "This has to be a heart attack," I said, my own voice unfamiliar.

"Look at me, Fox," she said, but I couldn't move my head.

"Look up, take a deep breath, and walk over here. Staying frozen is only going to make it worse."

I groaned and pushed up off the car. When I looked at her, a leg still in the running car, my breath quickened again.

"Can you not leave until I talk?"

She nodded, reaching in to turn the car off and shutting the door. "I won't. Unfortunately, the panic attack isn't getting you off the hook completely, though, so I will need you to actually talk at some point."

"I wouldn't expect it to be. I don't know what to do. How do I keep apologizing? How is it even going to matter? What if I agree to get on my knees and beg for your forgiveness anytime I fuck up?"

She let out a hard laugh. "At this point, that's a reward for you, not a punishment."

I couldn't stop my cocky smile. "Okay, you got me there."

"So, then, if you don't want me to drive away right now, I'm going to need something better."

I looked up, taking another deep breath as my body relaxed more. "If I told you that, tomorrow was the biggest race of your life. If the rest of your racing career hinged on winning one race tomorrow. Not just winning, but winning flawlessly. If I said you would never race again if you failed at this. What would happen?"

She put her hands on her hips and the annoyed scowl on her face only reminded me that I better make this make sense.

"I would probably have a panic attack and throw up. Repeatedly."

"Because you care about it. Because it's everything you have ever wanted and one shot at it does not seem fair because what if it's a bad day? What if you can't fight the panic attack off? That's what you are to me, what you do to me."

"I make you have panic attacks?" she asked, horrified.

"No. Well, kind of. I mean, you are everything I could ever want and the thought of being good enough for you is overwhelming. I know I can be the person for you. I know it's in me because you are everything I want and need, but when it's time to step up, I panic. I second guess everything. Just like you know damn well you could win that race, but you pull up to the starting line and dread sinks in. I couldn't breathe when I woke up, and saw you there because how could I ever imagine being what you need? I wake up every morning and worry about this. What if I fuck up that day and lose the person that I need? I sound so ridiculous, but you are that race to me, Ashton. If I don't win you, keep you, every day, then I know I'm done. I know that I'm never finding another person that I feel this way about."

"Wow, that's not what I was expecting. But how does pushing me away help that?"

"I never said I was a smart man," I said, with a laugh. "And I think some part of me wants to push you away before you wake up and realize this for yourself."

"But I'm not going to? If you think I'm so great for you, why is it hard to believe that I think the same thing about you? You literally freaked out because I think you're so great for me. And you might not like this, but I wasn't lying. In a completely hypothetical situation, if I had to take over Holt Racing right this second, there would be no one else I would ask for help from," she said, her eyes not leaving me. "Okay, that's a lie. I would ask for help from you and the entire crew. But I understand why that could be a scary statement. When I said it, I meant it, but I wasn't thinking how intimidating that thought could be. I grew up in this life. I need someone who can be confident about this. Someone who isn't going to run every day. Someone who can stand by me. You are allowed to have bad days, but you are not allowed to run from me."

"I wasn't trying to. I came to the garage. I did not run away to the Bahamas."

"Fine, I guess that's true. But next time wake me up instead of leaving me there alone."

"So that means I do get a next time because I am sorry for leaving this morning and having a meltdown."

"Of course there's a next time. Healing is a hard journey. It's not a one-way path, and I had plenty of setbacks. It's like you pushing me little by little to race. I can't force you to let go of all the doubt or pain all at once. As for worrying about who I am, you need to realize I'm more than my last name."

"I did the exact thing you were worried about me doing. This is why you didn't tell me before," I said, struggling to not grab her now.

"Yes, you judged me by my father. Not for who I am."

"You're right and I shouldn't have. Thank you for stopping my panic attack. I was spiraling out of control." He reached over, grabbing my hand. "Thank you. Ashton, I don't think you understand how much you saved me. Not the other way around. You have saved my life a thousand times since we met," I said, taking a deep breath. "And I love you. I'm so damn in love with you that I can't even stand the thought of losing you. I promise that no matter what is happening in my fucked up head, there is never a doubt that I love you. I love you so much that I can't figure out how I would live my life without you in it."

"Well, every time that thought comes up, you have to stop it to remember that I love you too and I want to be in your life."

"You do?"

"I very much do."

The weight of losing her lifted. Hearing the words out loud soothing every anxious part of me.

I moved fast, picking her up and carrying her around the car.

"I'm taking you home now and taking you to bed to do every single thing I should have done this morning."

FORTY-THREE
ASH

THIS TIME, I woke up before Fox, too nervous about the races to stay asleep.

It was my first race back in a competition and I could already feel the panic looming. It was all around me, threatening to take over.

After an hour of pacing, Fox walked out.

"I see what you mean. Waking up and not seeing you next to me *is* terrible," he said with a smile, leaning down to kiss me. "How tall are you?" he asked, pulling back and standing up straight, apparently assessing our heights.

"I don't know? 5'10ish. Why?"

"Because you are not short."

"Wow, well, thank you for pointing that out. No one has ever made me feel bad about that before." I said with a roll of my eyes.

"I meant it as a compliment. Or maybe it's a turn on? Actually, it's both. Look," he leaned down, kissing me. "I'm not even breaking my back to kiss you. And this," he said as he jumped up, sitting on the counter, and pulling me into him, kissing me again, “still great. Oh, one more,” he jumped off, sliding behind me and pulling my ass into him before bending me over the counter. “Fuck baby, look at you, the perfect height.” His hand wound into my hair and he pulled me back. “Everything about you is perfect.”

Sometimes it was frustrating how well he already knew my body because he made one move and I was ready to go. He must have noticed. His other hand coming down over my ass until he bent to kiss me, pulling my head back as far as he needed.

A knock came at the door and he let me go as the crew filtered in.

“Do you guys ever go away?” he said with a groan as he wrapped his arms around me.

“Do you guys ever stop trying to go at it?” Jax asked, opening the fridge. “And in the kitchen? Really? I eat in here.”

“It’s my apartment,” Fox said with a laugh.

“And?”

“Eat at your own place.”

“Wait,” I asked. “Where’s Kye?”

“That's why we’re here,” Ransom said. “We have to go pick him up, and I figured you should ride with me so everyone else can get ready to race.”

“Where is he?”

“A police station two towns over. Apparently, he was caught racing and was already on thin ice with shit. We have to go pick him up or he’s not racing tonight.”

“Is he racing tonight even if you do pick him up?” I asked.

“Then Quinn is going to get a crash course in racing. I don’t care if you push the car down the track. We aren’t giving it up now,” Jax said.

“Crash course and racing shouldn’t go together,” Quinn said. “Please hurry up and go get him so that I don’t have to,” she said.

"Come on," I said. "Let's hurry up. If we go now, we can get back in time to help everyone set up."

He was already grabbing his things and coming back over to kiss me.

"Please be back in time. I don't know if I can do this without you."

"Of course you can," he said. "But you won't have to. I'll be there. And here, these are for you." He pushed something into my hand.

"These are my keys," I said.

"Yes they are. Your car is downstairs and waiting. We finished it last week, and it's been tested too. I was hoping for a better surprise than this, but hopefully you're not too disappointed.

"Seriously? How could I be disappointed?" I threw my arms around him. "Thank you. Thank you so much for giving me this part of my life back."

"You deserve every part of it. I love you. I will be back soon, and I am taking this away," he said, taking my cup of coffee.

"What? No, why? You can't do that."

"You are already shaking, and caffeine is not going to help."

I groaned. "You suck for being right. Love you. Be careful and get back in time."

"I will," he said, groaning as he kissed me. "I do not want to leave you."

"Go now or you're going to miss the races."

He groaned again, but followed Ransom as they left.

Jax was staring at me.

"What's up?"

"Nothing. I'm glad you two have figured it out and you're here to stay now."

I smiled. "Me too. Thanks for all your help in this."

"Now you owe me. Let me know if you have any hot, single friends that you haven't told me about."

"My hot, single friends consist of Scout now, and even if I did, I think you can figure out your one-night stands on your own."

"Don't you dare bring me into this conversation," Scout said with a scrunch of her nose. "I'll be downstairs with my car whenever you all are ready to go."

"Lucky for both of us, I don't need to. Contrary to what everyone tells me I do, I no longer do one-night stands, and haven't for a while. Not really my cup of tea."

"You're serious?"

"Dead serious."

"Aww you poor little romantic. We'll find you a girl. For now, we have to go win a race."

"Yeah, yeah, let's go."

IT TOOK two more hours to load up the cars and get them to the track. By the time we unloaded, I was starting to get more anxious.

"I'm so nervous," Scout said, echoing my own thoughts. "I've raced so many times, but this feels so much more important. If I lose, we could all lose."

"You're not going to lose. You're an amazing driver. Don't even let yourself think about losing," I said.

"How did you do it? How do you race with a team of people counting on you night after night?"

"It gets a little easier each time. It's different for you, though. This is your family behind you. They only want you to do your best and be safe. When you win, that will just be a bonus."

She looked up at me, lips pursed. "But I still want to win."

"And you will. Scout, I have raced with a lot of people. I've seen everyone on your crew here drive and watched most of them race. They are all great drivers, but you're one of the best here because of your focus. I can see the focus you put into your races and training for them. It's a professional level of focus you have. Don't let anyone get in your head and know that you are going to win. Just because I was given a better opportunity in life for racing does not mean I am better at racing. You can go out there and win for your team. And no one is going to be mad either way."

Her face hardened, and she nodded. "You're right. I know you're right. I can do this with my eyes closed."

"Exactly, but you're not going to."

She laughed. "No, not going too. Thanks. I love all the guys, but racing can be different for me and I don't always think they understand why. It's wild to have you here and be able to talk to someone who has experienced this." She pulled me into a hug. "Now, it's time for both of us to go win."

She slid into the car and I went to mine. I nearly cried, sliding behind the wheel.

The fact that they all came together to actually finish this was one of the nicest things any friends had ever done for me.

I'd been given gifts, vacations, parties, but nothing as thoughtful and time-consuming as this. I knew it was the a deal we made, but I had made a similar deal with my dad and David for this exact car and it still ended up being in pieces, and apparently left with a blown engine.

Now it was nearly perfect.

"We'll start being up soon. Until then, we hang out a bit."

"Have you talked to Fox or Ransom? Are they headed back yet?"

"Haven't heard a word. I can't imagine they will be much longer."

I couldn't take it anymore. I texted Fox again, the panic in my chest growing like a bubble that I knew would burst.

Where are you? Are you okay?

Finally, the little dots appeared.

I'm fine. We are about to head back.

Good.

Is everything okay?

All fine. Races start soon. I miss you.

I don't think I've ever been sent an I miss you text

Never?

Who's there to miss me? I'm around the crew every single day.

Past girlfriends?

I don't think there was ever an 'I miss you' type of relationship

Well, I can assure that you are missed and might be in a lot of trouble because of how much I miss you and need you here. Not only me, I think Scout is going to kick your ass if you three miss her race.

I'm sorry. I had to go help Kye.

I know. I'm not mad about that. Just get here. All of you.

He sent a string of emojis back that went from racing cars to eggplants and water.

I rolled my eyes and smiled.

"I'm guessing Fox got back to you?" Jax asked.

"Yes, he did, and they will hopefully be back in an hour or so."

"Great, because our races are coming up. I moved up to be the first of us, then Scout, you, Ransom, and Kye.

"Well, then," I said. "Let's get all the cars ready and get to racing."

ANOTHER HALF HOUR WENT BY, and we already had a win for Hollows Garage with Jax's race going as smooth as anyone could hope for and winning without any room for dispute.

"You did amazing," I said, hugging him after Scout and Quinn had jumped all over him. "Good job."

"Wow, complimented on my race by a great Holt. My racing career is complete."

"Is that what your goals are? A racing career?"

He shrugged. "I don't know what my goals are. For today, though, my goal is winning."

"Well, you got us off to a great start."

My hands grabbed his arm, fingers digging in as I saw the cars.

"Jax," I hissed. "That's David."

The bright blue car was stamped with Holt along the side and was surrounded by three other nearly identical cars, each in a different color.

"Those are the standard show cars we would take to side races. They aren't the fastest we have, though."

"We?" Jax asked. "You're with us now." He threw a supportive arm around me. "All of our cars can kick their ass. Come on, don't even look at him."

I did, walking past without turning my head, but there was nothing I could do when he stepped out in front of us.

"Ashton, what are you doing here?"

"You didn't hear?" Quinn said. "She decided to go out and find a winning team."

David crossed his arms. "Like your sad team could win against us."

"I think you mean against my dad's team, you can barely race."

"Well, I've been practicing. Are you racing, Ash?"

"Good thing," Jax said. "I heard you couldn't race to save your damn life."

I smiled. "Yeah, I'm racing."

"Seriously?"

"Seriously."

"You know your dad isn't going to be happy about this."

"Oh no. What will I do now?" I said, and Jax gave me a squeeze, his arm still around me.

"I thought you were with the other guy. The tall one with the fucked up face."

"I am," I said.

"I'm standing in until he gets here," Jax said. "Is there a problem?"

"No, I don't want any problems." He lifted up his hands. "I'll just wish you good luck in your race. Good luck to *all* of you."

"What's that supposed to mean?" I asked, my back going rigid.

"Exactly what I said. Good luck to all of you."

He was too calm, too polite to make me comfortable.

He smiled wider before waving. "I'm sure we will talk later, Ashton. Bye."

I ripped away from Jax's grasp as David turned to walk away.

I was going to kill him. It was a threat, and all I could think about was pushing my nails into his eyes. I could too. I could jump on him and do it.

He was up to something and I knew it wouldn't be good for us.

Arms wrapped around me, picking me up and walking me the opposite way from David.

"Hello, my little hellion, trying to rip another man to pieces?"

"Fox," I breathed in relief as he kept carrying me, heading towards our cars. "You're back."

"Just in time too, apparently. Poor Jax wasn't prepared for you to attack. I'm going to have to put you on a leash."

I gave a snorting laugh. "I'm sure *that's* the only reason you want me on a leash."

His chest rumbled as he set me down next to my car. "It's like you can read my mind."

"It's not that hard when all you're thinking about is sex and cars."

"You are very close. It's usually sex with you on, and in, cars. David piss you off?"

"Yes, he threatened us. I was about to claw his eyes out."

He ran a hand through my hair and down my jaw. "What did he say?"

"He said *good luck* to all of us."

Fox smiled. "He wished us luck?"

I pushed away from him, knowing he couldn't believe me. "Yes, and he meant it as a threat. I don't care if I sound irrational. I know how he meant it."

"Shh, Ash, I believe you. I think you are completely right," Fox said, pulling me back in. "Do you know what he would be doing?"

"I have no idea, but now I'm even more on edge. We should

have gone before to look for the cars he's stealing. We shouldn't have waited."

"There's no use thinking about it now. We need to race and we all need to do it safely. Come on, let's check over Scout's car for her before her race, and then get you ready. I will keep an eye out for David and anything he could be up to. You have a race to win, hellion, and that's all you need to worry about."

FORTY-FOUR
FOX

We stood around Scout's car as she got ready. Her race was in minutes with Ash right after her. Kye was going over the engine with me when Ash walked back over.

"What did you get in trouble for?" she asked, leaning against me.

Kye let out a long, hard breath. "Well, first, my car was taken. I technically lost it in a race two weeks ago, but never handed it over because of the race today. Then, I was arrested for fighting because they literally jumped me to take the car. And don't worry, they didn't get into any trouble because they were able to flee in my car," Kye said, shaking his head. "And before I get some annoying lecture from you too, yes, I do realize it was stupid, but I thought I had a deal worked out with them to not take my car. Apparently, no one honors verbal agreements anymore."

"You know better than to bet your car on a race. That's the stupidest thing you could do," I said.

"Well, I'm full of stupid ideas. Obviously, this can move to the top of the list."

Ash looked at me and then at Kye before walking around the car and wrapping her arms around him. I shouldn't be shocked at anything she did anymore, but this had me. We all loved Kye, but he always wanted to keep to himself and get in trouble. None of us blamed him. We all went through it and we were happy to wait around until he was over it. With this, though, I wouldn't have been surprised if he pulled away, but he didn't. He only hugged her back.

Even more surprising, he smiled as she whispered something to him.

"Alright, Kye is using my car. It should be good to go by then anyway," she said with a grin.

Scout came back around to the cars. "Time to go!" she yelled, getting into the car.

The minutes went by fast as I got her to the line, set her up and watched her go down the track without a hitch.

That made two wins for us, and only brought us closer to the finals. Not only would it put our name out there more, but there was a pretty large check for the top spot, too.

Twenty minutes later, I was at the line with Ash, making sure she was actually ready to go.

"Are you okay?" I asked, crouching down next to her.

"No. I can't do this. You drive for me."

"I can't, you know that. You can do this. You have done this a hundred times, you can do it one more. You don't even have to win."

The car next to her on the starting line backed up, getting off the line and back onto the line. It was hard not to recognize it with the giant Holt sticker across the side.

"Shit," I mumbled, trying to block the car from her view, but she had leaned forward, seeing it as clearly as I had.

"What's he doing?" she asked. "Why did they change who I'm racing? This had to be what he was up to."

"Look at me. It doesn't matter who you are racing. You are an amazing driver, no matter who is next to you. Just worry about the road, not him," I said, blocking her view more.

"Why are they making me race him?"

"I will go ask if you promise to ignore him. Don't worry about him anymore tonight. If this was his plan all along, then he's doing it to mess with you. It's not worth letting him get in your head. Just pretend it's any one of us next to you."

I waved Jax over.

"What's up?" he asked.

"Think about Jax. Pretend you're racing him. The smartass who you've already beat once. You know you can do this again."

Jax smiled. "You barely beat me. I was only being nice."

"Nice?" she asked. "You were not. I beat you fair and square."

"Not at all. You were freaking out, and I knew you needed to win."

"You're lying."

"I am not. I'll prove it. Let's race again and I'll win this time."

"You're an ass."

"I have to go. Keep that in your head. Don't think of anything else, and remember that I am right here. All of us are. Are you okay?"

She nodded harder, almost bouncing in her seat as I checked the harness. "Okay, go win hellion." I pulled at the door, making sure it was closed tight before stepping back with the crew.

Before the race start I went over to the stand and asked about the changes. It was exactly what we both thought. David requested the race, probably paid whoever he needed to pay, and they let him change. It's not like it was the most complicated plan. He knew it would shake Ash up even more, and from the sound of it, he had already got under her skin tonight.

Jax came up next to me.

"Is she good?"

"She's going to do fine."

"Good, because we are close to winning. Scout kicked ass for her race and won. And of course, I won too, so don't worry."

"I heard you almost lost," I said.

"Almost doesn't matter. I still won."

I laughed. "I guess that's always true. Two rounds won. Now it'sAsh, Ransom, and Kye to go."

"She's got it. You think this was David's plan? Just mess up her race?"

"Looks like it. I was expecting something more from him honestly, but I'll take it. She's still going to win."

The lights finally changed, and she took off.

It was perfect, her take off nearly flawless as she got out ahead of David.

"Who would have thought the girl we begged to be on our team would be better than all of us?" Jax asked.

I couldn't respond, watching her move down the track. She was about to win.

I've watched hundreds of races and never been so on edge.

Watching your entire heart go down a road as fast as they possibly can without wrecking was my new idea of hell.

She kicked it faster at the last second, passing the finish line at least a car's length before David. The fact that he even stayed that close was a shock to me.

The crew erupted into cheers and Scout jumped onto me. I lifted her the rest of the way.

"She did it!" Scout yelled. I smiled back at her but froze as my eyes saw the brake lights were still on.

David's car stopped sideways in front of Ash's, blocking her path to turn around and come back down.

"Fuck. What's he doing?" I asked, realizing too late that he had got out of the car and was by Ash's driver's side door.

"Go get down there," I yelled, setting Scout down and running towards Jax's car that was closest. He got in the driver's seat and took off, moving around people that were crowding around to see what was happening at the other end.

He finally made it through, going down the track, but David's car was gone.

"Fuck," I yelled, hitting the dash. "Fuck."

We pulled up to her car, but I already knew it was empty.

I couldn't see any tail lights in the distance now and knew Jax was waiting for me to make a move.

"Go. Now." I said, sliding behind the wheel of her car. "Go get her."

FORTY-FIVE
ASH

I GROANED, the side of my head ringing from the hit.

Before I opened my eyes, I thought I had wrecked, but now I realized I was still moving.

Bile rose in my throat as I saw the speedometer. We were going way too fast for David's skill level. We would crash any second now.

My head rolled as I looked over. Everything suddenly got even worse.

It wasn't David in the driver's seat, like I assumed.

"Liam? What are you doing? Did you seriously kidnap me?"

"I didn't kidnap you."

"Pretty sure knocking someone out, ripping them from their car, and then driving off with them would be considered kidnapping."

"Whatever. Call it what you want. It was David's idea. I'm only here to drive you."

"You know David? Why would you help him?"

"Because helping him only helps me get what I want. It's a win-win for both of us."

"And what is it you want?"

He snapped a picture.

"Oh, come on, was that necessary?" I asked, knowing I looked terrible and probably had a knot forming on the side of my head.

"It was. Fox will want to know what's going on."

"Wait, what? You sent that to him? From *your own* phone? That was a terrible idea." I said, quickly realizing my hands were tied behind my back. I kicked my feet, realizing they were tied together too.

"That guy stole my girlfriend. The love of my life. He took her without a fucking thought, so this will at least give me a taste of his own medicine."

"Please tell me that you don't mean that he stole me."

"No, but way to be the narcissistic bitch I assumed you would be. I barely know you. No, he took my girlfriend from me last fall. I was ready to marry the girl and Fox came in and swept her off her feet and then she was gone. She never wanted to fix things with me again."

"Do you think that could have just been because you were a dick?"

He laughed. "You think I'm a dick? Do you even know Fox? He's an asshole. The only people that like him are those other assholes he hangs around. All they fucking do is piss people off."

"Fine, whatever you say. Can you please slow down?" The kidnapping wasn't bothering me as bad as watching the speedometer rising and rising, each click higher making the panic grow.

"So your friends can catch up to us? Not a chance."

"No, it's because I'm scared to be going this fast," I said, hoping he had any empathy.

"Yeah, right. You just beat me in a fucking race. I'm not going to buy that either."

I could see other cars behind us, but I couldn't tell if any of them were actually Fox and the crew, but none of them seemed to be keeping pace with us.

Even if they did come after me, we were already minutes ahead which was too much when he was going this fast.

"I can't handle going this fast. Please, pull over."

"We are almost there. David will take over soon."

"What does that mean?"

"Just shut up or I will knock you out again."

The world flew by and the only reason I listened to him was so that I could concentrate on not throwing up or passing out.

Although puking in his car might prompt him to pull over faster.

Just when I thought he was about to, he pulled over, turning us into the parking lot of an abandoned warehouse.

"Wait, is this it? Is this David's warehouse?"

He ignored me, getting out and walking around to pull me out. "Stop. Talking. Fucking walk."

He pushed me forward, not realizing how tight my legs were tied together. I fell, my face breaking the fall as it hit the gravel.

I laid there, taking in the world around me, making note of every single thing I could.

One of the warehouse doors was open, the small amount of light letting me see inside. I wish it wasn't a shock, but it was. At least ten of my dad's cars were lined up inside, some muddy, others with obvious body damage. Cars that could be worth hundreds of thousands of dollars looked wrecked and beat beyond repair.

"What did you do?" I yelled out, trying to set myself upright, but it was Liam who pulled me to my feet. "I thought you were selling them? They are ruined," I cried.

"Shut up or you're going to fall again."

He moved me right inside the door as David appeared.

"Good, you made it on time. I'm grabbing the last of my things and then we are leaving."

"I'm assuming we includes me? Where are you going? What are you using these cars for?" I asked.

"To your dad's cabin up North. You and I will stay there for a few days and finally get a chance to talk."

I let out a harsh laugh. "And then what? Go home together like nothing ever happened?"

"I obviously know it will be messier than that. I've dealt with you before. I'm not stupid. But if you don't, then your friends and boyfriend are going to have more problems."

"David, stop. You don't really think this is going to work, do you?"

"No, I know it's going to work. It has to work."

I shook my head, not knowing how to fight with someone who was obviously not thinking straight.

"Is this just where you keep the cars you're stealing?"

"So you do know? I was hoping Celina was lying when she said that she told you."

"No. I already suspected it. She just confirmed, but you can't be selling these. You can't be in this condition."

"Selling them? Fuck, that girl is dense. I told her what was happening. I'm not selling them, Ash. They needed fast cars to move drugs. I make more in a week doing that than I would selling them."

"But why? Why would you have to risk this all to make money?"

"I've been trying to tell you, Ashton. I've been trying to talk to you for weeks. Everything spiraled out of control after you left, and I had to find a way out of it all. It just keeps getting worse. I had to find a way out."

"Out of what, David?"

"Out of the mess I made. The mess *you* made."

"*I* didn't make a mess. I was in a wreck. That wasn't my fault."

"No, but then, instead of letting me take your place on the team, you wanted to convince your dad that you would be back to racing in no time. Then, after I shut that down, you decide to leave and both of our dads somehow make it my fault."

"Because it was your fault. If I had any doubt before, I don't now. You were trying to get my dad to not let me race anymore. You were the one that told him over and over that I wasn't ready and now you admit it. You didn't want me to race again, because you wanted my place on the team."

"I did. Of course I fucking did. Everyone was so proud of you and thought you were so great, but then they would look at me and think I was a loser. That I didn't amount to anything, because you were so great. Then you broke up with me and that view of me seemed to only get worse. They blamed me for breaking us up and you running off. I tried to tell them it wasn't my fault, that I loved you, but they didn't believe me. Then my dad fucked all of us and lost pretty much everything. That turned into my fault, too."

"Lost everything?"

"He ruined his business. They are looking at him for money laundering and we're broke. I had to step up. I had to be the man of the house and when your dad wasn't giving me my rightful place on the team, I had to find other ways."

"So you became a drug dealer? And stole cars to run drugs?" My head spun, and I didn't know if it was from being hit and falling or finding out that my ex-boyfriend was suddenly a drug dealer.

"I'm not the drug dealer."

"A drug runner is not much different, David. You're still going to jail."

"No, I'm not. You won't say a thing once you understand."

"Understand that you passed up every opportunity to make your life better without doing anything illegal? But you chose something different. You had every chance to race that I did, but you never wanted to work for it. Now this? How did it even start? And why do you even need me around?"

"Because your dad is fucking everything up. He knows that our family business isn't doing so well, but apparently doesn't care. Your dad felt bad for me at first, but after you were gone, he was less and less enthusiastic about me working there without you."

"Because I'm his daughter. You have no right to that business."

"I deserve it because I worked for it when you didn't," he said, and I could only roll my eyes. "Then that same week you left, I wrecked my dad's car again. He told me I needed to grow up and make enough money to fix my car myself to prove I was worth anything. I decided to take one from your dad and sell it. It worked. It was so easy, but there still wasn't enough money. Then I found this. It's been so easy and dad's finally proud of me for making money."

"But does he know *how* you're making money?"

"No, why would I tell him that?"

I only shook my head, watching as he threw another bag into the car.

"I know I fucked up, Ash. That's why I need you. I need your help. We both know you're the one who can organize all this stuff for me. I didn't mean to, but I had to. The money was so good and my dad finally didn't hate me. But now I need more cars. I still owe some money and they need it now." His head fell. "We started using the money we made when the drugs sold. I didn't mean to. It was like a cash advance, but I didn't realize how much I spent until last week."

"What do you mean?" I asked. "You owe who money? Now what, you need to pay them for the drugs?"

"A bit, yea."

"How much is a bit?"

"Like half a million."

My mouth fell open. "Oh, that's all?"

"Come on, you know damn well that's nothing for your dad to pay. And part of it's your fault. You fucked up my car."

"I love how you keep putting blame on me. I can't believe this ever worked. Fox was right, and you have no power with me anymore. You want my dad to pay?"

"Don't you dare even talk about the guy you've been cheating on me with," he said, coming closer, trying to look threatening, but all I could think about was how pathetic he looked. "And of course I do," he continued. "My dad isn't going to give me a dime now that he thinks I'm making money with your dad, your dad isn't going to give me a dime until you come home, and they aren't going to pay me anymore from the drug running until I fix my debts. So I came up with a new plan. A temporary plan to a temporary problem."

"Wait, are you doing this whole kidnapping thing because you love me or because you need money? And what is this plan you have?"

"It's simple. I already called your dad that you were taken by Fox and his friends, who all have a rap sheet, by the way. I've been telling your dad how bad their business is doing and the trouble he and his friends get into. I told them he's demanding money for your return. It won't be a far jump in logic to think that he will let you go in exchange for money. Now we are going to go up to the cabin and wait for them to arrange the money. I'll tell him I will be the one to deliver it because I know Fox and then go pay off the people I owe. It's simple and I wind up the hero of it all."

"Are you forgetting that I can tell my dad what really happened?"

"No, I'm not. That's why you have that nasty mark on your head. I'll tell your dad you hit your head bad and are confused. Along with that, if you do, I will be sending the guys I work with to Hollows Garage. I will let them know that they are criminal street racers and my drivers. Again, easy for them to make the jump that they took the money, not me."

"Wow, David. If it wasn't so disgusting, I would almost be impressed."

"You should be impressed either way. I'm saving your life from that trash."

I don't know what I thought before, but I realized it now. "You really think I belong to you, don't you?"

"Of course you do. You have since we were kids. You're mine, Ash and I will do whatever I need to keep us together."

"Even when I don't want to be? Even if it means hurting me?"

"Even then. I know what's right for us and I will take care of it no matter what breakdown you are having at the moment."

It was exactly what I thought. David would never see me as an equal, only a woman that he could, and should, control.

"Damn," he said. "I've missed you so much. Come here."

He grabbed my head and pulled me forward, nearly knocking me over as he kissed me. His lips were wet and forceful, the feel of him like a wet fish wiggling under my own lips. I gagged, trying to push him away, but with my hands and feet bound, I only fell over again.

I rolled to my side, not able to believe anything that was happening. There were two people that I had known my entire life. Two of them that I was taught to trust and rely on. Even if my dad wasn't directly involved, those two people were why I was rolling around, tied up on a dirty warehouse floor with a broken face, and being used in a new way to get money.

Hours ago, I was having one of the best days of my life. I was safe and living my dreams again with the people I had only known for months.

"You need to give me my money so I can go," Liam said.

I laughed. "I thought you were just here to piss off Fox?"

"For the hundredth time, shut the fuck up. I can't stand the sound of your voice anymore," he said, kicking me over further.

I groaned and rolled, trying to get myself sitting again.

I wasn't scared of David. I knew him too well to feel scared, but something about Liam was setting me on edge. The longer this went on, the more on edge he was getting.

Then I heard it. The distinct sound of the new exhaust on my car. The one that Fox had just finished and given me that night was now flying across the parking lot, coming straight for us.

FORTY-SIX
FOX

I COULD ALREADY SEE the open warehouse door and car as I turned the corner.

"That's definitely the one that was racing," Jax said over the radio. I installed one in Ash's car for her, hoping that meant she would be driving and racing with us for a long time.

Then the first night she drives it, David takes her. Kidnaps her right in front of me.

Overwhelming anger coursed through me as the outline of someone standing in the garage door came into view. The figure leaned down to pull another person up off the ground, and I could only guess that was Ash. I was already pissed, but then I saw him lean down and kiss her. I was livid. Every part of me was so angry that it burned.

I sped the car up, headed right towards them until I was close enough to see them bathed in my headlights. The car kept moving, the tires screeching and kicking up loose rock as the tires locked up on the half paved parking lot.

I got out, glad that Jax was right behind me, his car rolling to a stop next to mine.

David's face was full of anger, but one look at Ash tied up and sitting on the ground had me seeing red. I grabbed David's neck, dragging him across the ground as my other hand smashed into his face. He screamed as bone crushed under my knuckles.

Another guy stepped out from the warehouse, the headlights shining over him.

"Liam?" I asked, not understanding how he could be here. Or why he would even know to be here? I set David back down and stepped towards Ash.

"Hey, Fox! You finally made it," Liam said cheerfully.

"What are you doing here?"

"What do you mean? Didn't you see my text?"

I pulled out my phone, looking at a dead, blank screen. "My phone died hours ago. You sent a text?"

His face turned red, and I almost laughed at how cartoon-like he looked. "Are you fucking kidding me?"

Laughter from behind me caught my attention. "Ash? Are you okay? Are you hurt?"

"I'm okay. Just a headache," she said through a quiet laugh. "Liam's mad you stole his girlfriend."

My mouth dropped. "What? What are you talking about? Didn't you steal my girlfriend, Liam?"

"Yeah, as payback. You took my girlfriend. Last fall, you hit on her and took her home. She never talked to me again!"

"Wow, dude. That's tough, but I'm assuming a girl who leaves you at the drop of the hat probably didn't like you too much to begin with," Jax said.

His eyes went wide, and he pulled out a gun.

"Great, Jax," I mumbled, stepping back.

"Listen, he was already unstable before I said anything."

"Liam, I didn't take your girlfriend. I don't even know who you are talking about."

"Are you fucking kidding me? You can't even remember her

name? You ruined my life for a girl you can't even remember? You're horrible. You deserve every fucking second," he yelled, pointing the gun in Ash's direction.

"Damn," Jax mumbled. "Brought a knife to a gun fight again."

I wanted to yell, but it was David who started screaming.

"No! No, she can't be hurt or I'm not going to get my money."

"What money?" I looked from her to David to Liam.

"The money he is getting by telling my dad that you kidnapped me and are holding me until he pays. Also, just in case, he supposedly wants to take me to my dad's cabin."

Jax laughed and pulled out his phone. "This is wild."

If a gun wasn't pointed in Ash's direction, I would probably be as calm as he was because he was absolutely right.

"Stop. Everyone stop. Nobody move," David said. "Liam, you better point that gun at them and let us get out of here."

"Or what? I don't know why you think I'm suddenly your lackey in this situation, but you've got it wrong. I don't give a shit if you get out of here or not. All I need is for Fox to feel the pain of what I felt."

David grabbed Ash, lifting her up to her feet. "Come on, we are getting out of here," he said, kicking at her feet and pulling her along. "Move. Faster. Come on, Ash." David was almost begging now. "Come back to your life. Come back to your dad and Holt Racing and me. Please. Just get moving."

Her eyes found mine, and she smiled. "I miss parts of it, David, but not you. Please, let me go home."

"I'm trying to take you home!" he screamed.

"I want to go to my new home! The one I like being at. The one where people do not try to hurt me or use me for money," Ash yelled, pulling away from him.

"No, you need to come home with me. Not them."

His arm snaked around her waist and he picked her up. She tried to slam back, and it was enough for me.

"Stop. You do not get her back that easily! I never got my girl back," Liam yelled, lifting the gun again, as I went at David, who was already turning her, making her his personal shield.

This time, though, he pulled the trigger.

My world fell to pieces as screaming broke out.

I didn't know who was screaming, though.

Every part of the last few months, with her halting to a stop. Every part of my life falling apart with one small movement from Liam.

Liam moved, spinning to run, but I wasn't going to let him. I grabbed his shirt, ripping him backwards and swinging my fist around, hitting him in the jaw.

He yelled as I held onto the shirt and drove my knee up into his back. I wanted to kill him, and I was about to until he pulled out of his shirt, slipping out of my grip.

Jax was already hitting at my arm. "Ash," he said, and I looked over. "I'll make sure he's gone. Get her in the car."

I ran over, kicking David out of the way, and falling to the ground next to her.

"Ash. Are you hurt?" I grabbed her face, trying to focus her eyes on me.

Since the gun went off, I knew. Every part of me knew that she was hurt, and when she didn't answer, every fear was confirmed.

"It's okay. Ash, look at me." She did, her eyes wide with fear. "You'll be okay. We're getting out of here, and you don't have to worry about them. I will deal with them. We need to get you to the car. Can you move? Move your fingers, your toes, move your legs. Please, be okay," I pleaded quietly as I tried to move her into the light, but froze when she yelled.

"Don't do that," she screamed. "My leg. It's my leg."

I looked down to see blood pooling around her leg.

Jax had come up behind me. “I’ve been on the phone with Ollie. He’s already called your dad and the police. They should be here any minute.”

“Ollie?” she asked, her voice high pitched and confused. “How did you even call Ollie?”

“I have your phone,” he said, crouching down with a smile. “Don’t worry. I already made myself your background.”

I cursed, pulling off my shirt and trying to tie it around her leg.

A strangled laugh came from her. “Always trying to take your shirt off,” she said before laughing more, the movement making her entire body shake.

“Hold still, hellion. I’m trying to stop the bleeding.”

She only laughed harder as I pulled her into me.

“I think I’m going to have another scar.”

“Trying to outdo me?”

“Always,” she said, quieter now.

“Just hold on. We’ll get you help soon.”

“Thank you. Thank you for coming and thank you for saving me all the time.”

My hands came down around her head, pulling her face up to mine and kissing her as gently as I could.

“Always. Love you.”

She was silent as the sirens came closer. Everything in my life reduced to the girl in my arms, knowing she was in pain, and wanting to do anything to stop it, but only being able to sit here.

She was quiet, closing her eyes and taking deep breaths as I watched every rise and fall of her chest.

Finally, lights surrounded us and seconds blurred by until they were loading her inside of the ambulance, the chaos finally coming to an end as I got in with her.

"Hey Fox," she said, her head rolling to look at me. "Love you, too."

FORTY-SEVEN
ASH

AFTER TWO DAYS at the hospital, I was glad to be out finally, even though the pain in my leg was still there.

Fox carried me up the steps to his apartment, insisting that I stay there while I heal, even though I told him that could easily be a month or two.

He set me down on the couch and I hissed as I settled in.

"Shit, did I hurt you?"

"No, *you* didn't. Any movement hurts right now."

He sat down on the floor next to the couch, careful not to move me as his fingers started tracing lazy circles back and forth over my good leg.

"Looks like you really are going to have one more scar," he said. My leg was bandaged, and they said I would luckily have no long-term damage, but there would be a scar and it would take some time to heal and drive again.

"At this rate, we are going to be covered head to toe in them."

He shrugged. "Hopefully, this is it for us with horrible injuries and scars."

“The injuries are horrible, not the scars,” I said, looking over his scar. It had healed completely now. The small blotches of red turning to white where the skin would never be the same.

“I know. I think I’ve come to terms with it. I know how I acted was superficial, but it’s hard going from hot to monster.”

“You went from hot to hotter.”

“I think you might be the only person who thinks so,” he said, leaning over and kissing me. “But that’s all that matters.”

His words made my throat tighten, seeing that he had really come to terms with his appearance. He had told me before that he had no regrets about what he had done for me, but seeing him embrace his scar finally let me let go of the last bit of my own grief and guilt.

“I can’t tell you how happy that makes me,” I said, fighting back tears.

“I can’t tell you how happy you make me,” he said.

I couldn’t help it any longer. The tears fell as the door burst open.

“You guys are back,” Scout said, rolling over the back of the couch on the opposite side of me. Jax rolled over with her, landing on top of her.

“Get off of me!” she yelled from underneath him.

He kept rolling until he landed on the floor, laughing the entire way down. My tears were replaced with laughter, happy to see everyone as Ransom, Quinn, and Kye piled onto the couch surrounding me as Fox yelled to not shake the couch or get any closer to me.

“It’s okay, Fox. I’m fine.”

“No, you’re not. They can’t be messing around and have you hurt more.”

I grabbed his hand, squeezing it tight as I looked around at each of them.

"I've been half knocked out for two days. Is anyone going to tell me about the races yet?"

Lips pursed and faces scrunched.

"So we didn't win?"

"No, we didn't," Ransom said. "They did decide that due to the poor conduct of David's team, though, they were kicked from the races and you were counted as the winner of your race."

"Really?" I took a deep breath. "Well, I'm glad something good came of that night then. I finally did it. I raced again and won. And now I won't be doing it again for a while," I said, laughing. "So it was decided that David was the one driving?"

"Good job for kicking his ass. He didn't have a chance to win against you," Fox said, still trying to slowly move closer to me.

"Wait, why didn't we win, then?"

"Because then I lost," Kye said. He looked so upset that I was surprised he sounded so calm.

"Well, that's fine. You can't control every race."

"I could have. I jumped before the light and they immediately counted it as a loss."

"Kye, it's okay," Scout said. "Nobody is upset at one loss." She looked at me. "What everyone is leaving out is that we still came in second overall, so we *barely* lost. I'm still counting it as a win because we are already invited back for next year."

"That's amazing!" I yelled. "Kye, you shouldn't be upset at all. We are going back!"

"*We* are going back?" Scout asked. "Does that mean you are officially going to race with us again next year?"

"I hope I can officially race with you again as soon as my leg is healed up."

Her smile grew, and she nodded. "Damn, we're going to be amazing next year."

"Does that mean you aren't making up with your dad? You're not going back to Holt racing?" Jax asked.

I shrugged. "I'm going to talk to him at some point, but as of right now, no, I won't be going back to race with him. I'll see what else happens after I talk to him. Honestly, I'm hoping I can help you guys build your team more?" I asked.

"Obviously," Jax said. "If you're not going back to Holt, we aren't letting you go anywhere else."

Everyone seemed to agree, letting me settle in more. Fox leaned over until his lips were at my ear.

"I wasn't going to let you go anywhere any way."

"Oh no?"

"Nope. Are you sure you're going to want to race again once you're healed up?"

"Of course I'm sure. Please don't tell me that you don't want me to race anymore. I can't take another person telling me that after an injury."

"I wouldn't dream of it. You'll be racing in no time, and I'll be right there with you every single time."

"Perfect because I already know what my first race back will be."

"What race is that?"

"You. I have to win another race against you."

His smile grew. "You think you're going to win against me a second time?"

"I know I am," I said.

"Not a chance."

"Well, I guess we'll have to settle this on the track, then. May the best driver win, and by 'best driver' I mean me, obviously."

He laughed, kissing my cheek and settling in next to me as the crew picked a movie.

"I have a feeling the rest of my life is going to be me trying to keep up with you."

"It very well might be," I said with a quiet laugh.

"I wouldn't want it any other way," he said, finally moving

next to me on the couch and wrapping his arms around me with a kiss.

It was that moment that made everything worth it, the highs and lows, the wins and losses - it all led up to this. In his arms, I knew I had found my real home.

EPILOGUE

ASH

One Month Later

We walked into the office building at the track, my crutches slowing me down.

"I will carry you," Fox said. "You don't have to walk."

"You're treating me like I can't walk at all."

"That's because you can't. I literally watched you fall over trying to make tacos last night."

"And that's because you gave me four margaritas and no food while I'm on crutches! Anyone would slip a time or two trying to put them together."

"You're so cute when you're drunk. All you talk about is how hot I am and what you want to eat."

"Because you are hot when I'm drunk. And you have asked to carry me every single time I have stood up. At some point, I am going to have to walk."

"Not true. I can carry you everywhere."

I rolled my eyes, pushing the door open to my dad's office. It was the first time I had agreed to talk to him since I left the hospital, but I knew we needed to.

He was already there, staring out over one of the tracks.

"Damn," Fox mumbled. "This is nicer than I expected."

We sat back in the chairs, and he looked us over.

"You both look good. No more injuries?"

"No, not any more since the last time you saw us."

"Good," he said, the room falling silent.

"I really want to get this over with and go home," I said. "How about you tell me what happened?"

He started on his story. I expected a sob story, begging for forgiveness, but his story shocked me.

"You're sick?"

"Yes. At first, I thought it was just years of beating my body up, but then they told me it was more serious. It can be managed, not treated. It's not an excuse, Ash, but a reason. I was getting sicker, and I knew how hard the business has been to run on my own. For so long, I had it stuck in my head that I would drop dead at any second. Although, I've learned that I can manage it with medication and treatment for a lot longer than I thought. This business, though, it's too much for one person." He shook his head, trying not to look at me. "Then David and his father kept telling me how much he could help, how much he already knew about it and could help lessen the load for you. It got into my head too much until they made me doubt even further if you should do it. I didn't want your health to suffer like mine. Then they told me I needed to worry about the family name, putting these stupid things into every conversation that you wouldn't even want the business. That you were telling David that you didn't want any of it, even our last name. That you wanted no connection to it, to me. I was so wrapped up in my own problems that I listened. I was worried you were being honest with David, but not wanting to hurt my feelings with the truth."

"You should have talked to me."

"I know. I know how horrible it all is now. I've messed so much up."

"You did," I said, holding Fox's hand tighter. "At this point, though, I can't say I've hated the outcome. I do hate that you sacrificed our relationship for David."

"I know. I do too. Once I finally listened to my doctors and stopped feeling sorry for myself. I realized how I blew it all out of proportion. I'll be around for a lot longer and even if I wasn't, I should have never forced a business partner on you."

"You were forcing a husband on me!" I yelled. "I'm not letting you sit there and think you were just handling business. You were trying to handle my entire life. You wanted me to stop racing."

"Only because I was facing my own mortality and couldn't face yours, too. Again, a reason, not an excuse for my behavior. I wanted someone next to you that would carry the load and not be afraid to become a Holt. David was more than eager to change his last name and now I realize I was ridiculous for thinking that was because he loved you. It was so important to me for you to stay a Holt. You're my only child. What's left of this place if I'm gone?"

"I will always be a Holt. I never planned to change my last name," I said, quietly.

"You didn't?" my dad asked.

"No, I've always been proud of you and your legacy. It was never an option for me to get married and change it. Before all of this, it was never going to be an option for me to leave Holt racing at all. You're the one who chose that."

Fox laughed beside me. "Anyone who meets Ash and understands your business would understand her choice. Not only for your hard work, but for hers too."

My dad's eyebrows jumped. "Really?"

"Of course. Ash is strong-willed and wants to run this business. Who would be surprised at that choice?"

"I don't know. I guess I had the idea that most men would be upset at the woman not taking his name."

"I'm not an expert on the subject, but I don't know that those types of men would last a day with your daughter."

"I'm sitting right here, you two," I said.

Fox squeezed my hand again.

"I'm glad you finally told me the truth," I said. "And I'm glad you finally believed me about David."

He shook his head. "I can't believe I didn't before. I never thought I would be one of those fathers. David and Liam will be in jail for some time now. I'm going after every cent taken and every minute of them hurting you. Both of you. Along with damages done." He opened his desk drawer. "Including you Fox. From my understanding, one of your cars was damaged due to David?"

"As far as we know, but we have no proof that it was him. It could have been Liam."

He raised a hand to stop him. "I think we can all agree it could have been both of them, which means it could be my fault. Here is a replacement."

He handed him a set of keys. "I assume a new Supra will do? I've already had a few things updated, but feel free to grab any parts you want to make further upgrades. It should be delivered to your garage before you guys make it back."

Fox held the keys out, reading the small tag attached with the make and model written on it. "This is brand new. It's way nicer than my last car. I couldn't take it. I personally don't want to feel in debt to you."

"No, no debts. No IOUs. You've had your world torn apart to keep Ashton safe when I ignored her. I don't think you need handouts and I'm sure you could build a car yourself. This is a replacement for damage I did, and a thank you."

"This isn't fixing it all," I demanded. "One car doesn't undo everything that happened."

"I wouldn't dream that it did, but I hope it can show that I would like to start again. With both of you."

"We can try. I don't want anything to do with the business for now. I'll be helping Fox at their garage while I figure things out and start racing more again at some point."

"Of course. Would you agree to come and see me sometimes? Or I can come to see you?"

"We can work on that."

"That's all I will ask for, then. I would love to meet all your friends, though. I watched all of your races at the Legends race, and to say I was impressed would be an understatement."

"They are going to flip out hearing that you watched," I said. "Aside from all this drama, they love your racing."

He smiled. "Then I'm going to push my luck and offer the tracks whenever you all want to use them."

"Thank you. We might take you up on that."

We talked for a few more minutes before I knew it was time to go.

I walked around, giving him a hug, which seemed to surprise him.

"I'm glad you're okay. I'm glad to see you," he said, squeezing me tight.

"And I'm glad to know what is actually going on with you. I'll see you soon?"

He nodded and his words stopped me at the door. "I hope to see both of you soon."

"I think that would be great," Fox said before we stepped into the hallway.

This time, Fox did carry me back down to the car.

"I'm too exhausted. Mentally and emotionally."

"Aww, you poor little hellion." He set me in the passenger seat. "Running around raising hell really can wear a person out. Let's get you home to rest," he said as he shut the door.

"Rest?"

"Rest. After we get you physically exhausted, of course."

WE MADE it back to the apartment when Fox laid me out on the couch, taking his time to undress me as he licked and kissed every part of me.

It didn't take long before he followed through and made sure I was physically exhausted.

He laid out next to me on the couch, pushing a pillow under his head.

"So you moved all your stuff into our apartment?"

"Our apartment, huh? You really like saying that, don't you?"

"Of course I do."

"We have about ten of these blankets on the couch now that I brought mine over. Should we get rid of some?"

"You women and your blankets everywhere." He moved closer, pulling all of them around him.

"Does that mean you do want me to get rid of some?"

"Are you kidding? These things are my favorite. Not a chance. I think we need to buy more."

"Good to know that you aren't re-thinking this moving in thing. It was a little fast."

He reached out for my hand. "Not fast enough. I still have to convince you to drop Reed as my last name and make me Fox Holt before Jax swoops in.

"That's true. He has been bringing me coffee and you know that really is my love language."

"What an ass," he said, climbing over top of me. "You're all mine, and I'm all yours. He doesn't stand a chance."

"That's true. Fine, I'll let him down easy," I said with a laugh.

He leaned over, kissing my head. "Thank you for saving me. Thank you for giving me this life."

"I could say the exact same thing to you. I love you."

"I love you too, hellion."

ALSO BY KATE CREW

Thank you so much for reading Fox and Ashton's story!

If you enjoyed Wrecked Love, please consider leaving a review! Support from readers like you means so much to me and helps other readers find books.

If you loved the crew, make sure to reach Ransom and Quinn's story in **Heart Wrenched.**

Ready for more of the Hollows Garage series? Follow the crew next in…

Racing Hearts

Made in the USA
Coppell, TX
02 November 2024

39519003R00226